THE TRUTH:
SALVATORE'S REVENGE

By

Ta`Mara Hanscom

REATA
PUBLISHING

Sioux City, Iowa

The Truth: Salvatore's Revenge

Edited by Kimberly J. Cotter, Editor in Chief

Cover design and concept by Jordan Thomas Gibson
Cover art by Heidi Hutchinson
Back Cover concept by Ta`Mara Hanscom
Back Cover design by Jordan Thomas Gibson Gibson
© 2012 Gibson Photography™

Photography by Laura Veronica Gibson

Models: Jim Hanscom and A.J. Hanscom

Printed in the United States of America
ISBN 978-0-9844514-4-9

You may contact the author with comments at
TaMara@TaMaraHanscom.com

CAST OF CHARACTERS

Joshua Hansen   Married to Mona (Spencer) Hansen

Noah Hansen   Brother of Joshua Hansen,
                           married to Carrie (Miller) Hansen. *(Dec. March 1981)*
                           Currently married to Tillie (Caselli-Martin) Hansen.
                           Ty Hansen – Carrie's son, raised by Noah Hansen
                           Jake Hansen – Noah's son with wife, Carrie
                           Alex James Martin IV – son of Alex & Tillie Martin
                           Laura Rose Martin – daughter of Alex & Tillie Martin
                           Annie Laurie Hansen – daughter of Noah and Tillie

Guiseppi Caselli   Married to Rosa (Rosa Matilde Rochelle) Caselli

Petrice Caselli   Eldest Caselli son, married to Ellie (Elaine Netherton)
                           Michael Petrice Caselli – son of Petrice & Ellie
                           Gabriella Elaine Caselli – daughter of Petrice & Ellie

Vincenzo Caselli   Second Caselli son, married to Kate (Katlin Martin)
                           Alyssa Katlin Caselli – daughter of Vincenzo & Kate
                           Angelo James Caselli – son of Vincenzo & Kate

Marquette Caselli   Youngest Caselli son, married to Tara (D`Annenci)

Sam Martin   Eldest Martin son, married to Becky-Lynn (Tucker)

Burt Engleson   Married to Diane Engleson

Andy Engleson   Son of Burt & Diane Engleson
                           Pastor at Christ the King Church

Ginger Maxwell   Daughter of Burt & Diane Engleson and life-long friend
                           of Tillie (Caselli Martin) Hansen. She is married to
                           Bobby Maxwell and they live in Las Vegas, Nevada.

Mario Ponerello* a/k/a **Jack Nelson** – married to Della (Miller) Nelson

*Mario is the arch nemesis of Marquette Caselli. Marquette has sought after Mario since The Great Palermo Diamond Heist of 1968

Antonio Ponerello a/k/a **Ben Simmons** – eldest son of Mario Ponerello

Charise Nelson   Daughter of Mario Ponerello & Della Nelson

Salvatore Ponerello*   Brother of Mario Ponerello.
                                          *Presumed dead.

Dr. Schneider Rauwolf a/k/a **Roy Schneider** – biological father of Ty Hansen

Detective Joe Patterson   Married to Jacqueline Holliday Patterson
                                          Jason Henry Holliday Patterson, son of Joe &
Jacqueline Patterson

Reata   Ranch near Centerville, SD – Vincenzo Caselli inherited Reata from Uncle Angelo, the brother of his father, Guiseppi. Vincenzo and Kate live there, and there are many events throughout the year that take place on Reata. Also, Uncle Angelo and his beloved wife, Penny, rest there.

For my amazing family,

Jim, Heidi, Charles, Charlie, A.J., Sarahi, Laura and Jordan:

Thank you for everything. You brought the Caselli Family to life right before my very eyes — as if it all really happened. Because of your obedience and conviction, others will be blessed by the message the Caselli Family has shared with us since 1996, even up until this moment. Reata Publishing could not have done this without you.

I thank our gracious God for you every day, and it is right for me to feel this way about all of you, since I have you in my heart.

You are my treasure and I adore you.

Ma`ma

And now these three remain:
Faith, hope and love.
But the greatest of these is love.

I Corinthians 13:13, NIV

Prologue

Ucciardone Prison, Palermo, Sicilia
August, 1968

Salvatore Ponerello, Sr. dropped to his knees on the concrete floor of his small prison cell, weeping. "My son is gone?" he cried. "My loyal, perfect son?"

The guard nodded.

"I must see Marquette Caselli!" Salvatore wailed, his tears unrestrained. "Bring me Marquette Caselli and I will tell you anything you wish!"

The guard nodded and hurried to report the request to the prison's warden.

Sicilian authorities were encouraged. They asked Marquette to visit Ponerello, giving him full authority to offer Salvatore a lesser sentence if he would provide the location of fifty missing diamonds.

Salvatore Ponerello was tall and lean with piercing, dark eyes. His grieved expression narrowed as he took a seat on the other side of the glass where Marquette waited. His face was more aged than Marquette had expected, but his body was not stooped at all. His shoulders were straight, broad, and strong.

Salvatore sneered as he looked at the younger man. "How could you work against one of your own?" he asked. "Have you no honor?"

Marquette was taken aback. "You are not *my own*," he said. "You are *Mafioso*."

"You prejudiced dog. Do you not understand what we work for?"

"Why did you ask for this meeting?" Marquette interrupted brusquely. "Was it just to bash me, or did you actually have something of worth to tell me?"

Salvatore laughed. "I shall escape this place you have confined me to, Marquette Caselli!" he declared. "I swear it upon my god, Daedalus! He will come on the wings of eagles and deliver me from this place!"

Marquette rolled his eyes, standing from his seat as he said, "You must be truly insane if you think for a moment *that* will happen."

"I swear to you I will take a revenge upon you and your family that you will feel in decades to come!" Salvatore ranted.

"You do not have such power over me, for my God is the God over all, and He will protect me from whatever witchcraft you possess," Marquette retorted.

Salvatore laughed again. "I *will* have my revenge," he promised. "And because of the death you forced upon my son, I will make you hurt in years to come."

"Save your breath, for you will need it to fight off the prisoners who so want you dead," Marquette replied.

Salvatore got to his feet, putting his hands upon the glass dividing them. He gritted his teeth together and yelled, "I shall pray every day for Daedalus to curse the very ground you walk upon!"

"Pray all you want," Marquette scoffed. "Jesus Christ is the Lord of Lords, and He will not allow a hair upon my head harmed. And if I were you, Salvatore Ponerello, I would ask Jesus to forgive my countless sins so that when you do leave this place, you may join Him in the Kingdom of Heaven."

"What if I choose not to bow in silly submission to your faceless God?" Salvatore asked with an evil grin.

"Then you shall burn in hell for all eternity."

Salvatore Ponerello's maniacal laughter rang off the walls of the prison.

Marquette swallowed away his nausea, hurrying for the door....

Shortly before suppertime in South Dakota, Marquette placed an overseas phone call to his mother. It was nearly midnight in *Sicilia*, but Marquette always called his family when he was finished with a big case.

"Oh, my Marquette!" Rosa exclaimed. "You were in the *Argus Leader* today! And we saw that smart car they put you into! Your little sister has passed out papers to all of the neighbors. We are *so* proud of you!"

"The front page?" Marquette asked, surprised. "How did I look?"

"Like a star!" Rosa answered, laughing. "Papa says you need to get rid of your ponytail, now that you are so famous, but I thought it looked just fine."

Marquette chuckled, but he was tired and troubled, and Rosa heard it in the tone of his voice.

"What is wrong, my son?" she asked.

"John and I are traveling to *Roma* tomorrow," he began, sighing heavily. Marquette heard his mother catch her breath on the other end.

"But why, Marquette?" she whispered.

"I want to see the memorial," he answered. "And who knows when I will be this close to *Italia* again."

"But, Marquette —"

"Ma`ma," he interrupted gently, "it has been twelve years. Do you not feel I have had to go through enough? I need to lay her memory to rest once and for all, and if I can just read her name upon the granite plaque, then I can come home and be at peace."

Rosa shook her head, but said nothing to her son. In her heart she knew that it would take more than just a granite plaque to bring Marquette peace.

*****

"Ever been to Rome?" John Peters asked with a crooked smile as they bumped along in the tour bus. He took off his round-rimmed spectacles and cleaned them with the handkerchief from the breast pocket of his dark suit.

Marquette shook his head. "And it is pronounced *Roma*," he corrected.

John nodded as he put on his spectacles. "You mean to tell me that you lived in Italy and never visited *Roma?*" he asked, being sure to pronounce it correctly.

Marquette smiled faintly with a shake of his head. "When I lived in *Italia*, we were very poor. There was not time or money to travel to *Roma.*"

John nodded, looking out the window of the old bus. "Well I have," he replied. "I knew a guy here — great informant — but he up and became a priest. We still write letters every now and then. He's one of the pastors over at Santa Susanna — that's an American parish here in *Roma.*"

The bus came to a stop, and the tour guide at the front began to speak Italian.

"She says," Marquette interpreted, "that we are being left off at the Great Crash of 1956 and that we will be picked up in one hour. We are encouraged to shop the merchants along the way as long as we are back here in one hour."

John and Marquette followed the rest of the passengers off the bus and into the street. A great granite wall stood near unused and broken tracks, and Marquette strolled in that direction.

"Where are you going, Marq?" John asked, noticing the sudden despair in Marquette's eyes.

"I knew a family involved in that crash," Marquette answered quietly. "I would like to see their names."

"I'm sorry," John replied, taking a closer look at the carved stone. "Who were they?"

"The D'Annenci family," Marquette answered. "And their mother, Sophia Pasquelucci." He took a breath as his finger traced the names. "Here they are…Sergio, Zina, Conrad…" He swallowed hard, his eyes suddenly filling with tears.

John saw the overwhelming emotion in Marquette's eyes and put a friendly hand on his shoulder. "I'm sorry, Marquette."

Marquette shook his head. "But her name is not here," he whispered. He took a deep breath and looked at John. "Why is her name not here?"

"Whose name?"

"My Tara!" Marquette exclaimed in a whisper, his eyes going back to the wall, searching frantically. "Her name is not here and neither is the name of her grandmother, Sophia!"

"Who's Tara?" John asked with a frown... *Marq's never mentioned a Tara...what on earth is he talking about?*

"She was the love of my life," Marquette replied with a suddenly elated smile. "She must still be alive!"

"Now, Marq," John said, attempting to calm his friend, "this could just be a mistake —"

"No," Marquette interrupted with a shake of his head. "This is no mistake. I have never been able to let go of her memory, even when I heard of her death. I could never bring myself to believe that she had left this world. *My Tara lives!*"

John watched Marquette search the names on the wall again. *The poor guy has finally lost it*, he thought. *This is some kind of stress-related battle fatigue left over from Vietnam, or Ponerello's curse has already kicked in.* "Marquette," he said in a stern tone. "This is a mistake. Don't get worked up this way."

Marquette turned to look at John, smiling as he said, "This will be an easy mystery for us, John. Let us find whoever compiled the list of fatalities. That person will know for sure."

"It's been twelve years since this crash," John reminded him. "Whoever compiled the list will never remember who lived and who did not."

"I *must* find out for myself," Marquette insisted. "Please help me, John."

John sighed heavily as he looked back into Marquette's hopeful expression. "I don't know, Marq..." he began.

"Please, John."

John swallowed hard and slowly nodded.

The closest church to the crash site, St. Vincent's, was within walking distance of the memorial. They noticed that the cornerstone was dated 1903, and once they'd made contact in the church office, were delighted to learn that it was indeed the church that had compiled the list of fatalities — as well as survivors.

"I am quite certain that the memorial wall is accurate," the secretary assured Marquette politely.

John didn't know a word of Italian, so he whispered to Marquette, "What did she say?"

"She believes the memorial wall to be accurate," Marquette answered. He looked at the secretary, speaking Italian, "Please, *Signorina,* it is imperative that I see the actual lists. I believe that a missing loved one could be on your survivors' list. If she is, I will attempt to find her."

The secretary took a deep breath and began to nod. "Give me a moment," she said. "Wait here, and I will see what I can find." With that she turned, her high heels clicking down the long hallway.

"Where did she go?" John asked.

"To find the list," Marquette answered. He gave his head a nervous scratch and began to pace.

John's stomach felt as if he were going over hills. *I find it hard to believe he ever had a girl*, he thought. *He's so serious, so dedicated to our work — I never saw any sort of a sign that something was missing in his life.* He watched Marquette pace, noting the strained expression in his frown and the set of his jaw...*he's like a different person...I've never seen this part of Marquette. The love of his life? How was he able to hide this from me?* "Why didn't you ever mention Tara before?" he asked.

Marquette shrugged, answering as he paced, "I did not want you to misunderstand me..." He stopped pacing and looked at John, confessing, "I even keep a journal every day. *I write to her.* I was afraid that I was just a little crazy and hiding it very well."

John looked at Marquette, thinking, *you write to a dead girl every day? You're not just a little crazy. My partner's nuts...where was my detective prowess on that one?* He sat down on a nearby bench, rubbing his temples with his fingertips, staring down at the floor. "Should we call your family, Marq?" he suggested.

Marquette shook his head. "They would never understand."

John glanced above his spectacles, studying Marquette as he said, "This isn't like you at all. Why *can't* we call your family?"

Marquette looked at John, narrowing his eyes as he studied his friend's expression. "Why does that frighten you?"

"I don't know," John snapped. "It just does. You call your family before you change your socks in the morning. I can't imagine why you wouldn't call them now."

Marquette laughed out loud, alarming John even more.

"Listen to me, my friend," Marquette said with a smile. "I cannot explain what I am feeling, just that I am certain we will get information on my Tara and I will be with her once again!"

John wanted to argue with him, but couldn't find the words to even begin. High heeled shoes clicked in the hall, and they turned to see the secretary with a tattered folder in her hand.

"Both lists are in here," she said, handing the folder to Marquette. "The survivors, and there were only a handful, are listed at the top of the first page. You cannot take this file with you, you must read it here."

Marquette took a breath as he opened the file, explaining to John, "She says we must read it here." He suddenly closed the file and handed it to John. "Will you look for me? See if her name is not on that list — the list at the top of the first page is for the survivors."

John stood from his seat, taking the file from Marquette, quickly opening it, certain that the names Marquette sought would *not* be there. *Hopefully this will straighten him out and we can get back to work...but he's going to the vet's hospital when we get home.* He scanned the short list of survivors, taking a sharp breath when he saw Tara's name.

"What is it, my friend?" Marquette asked. "Is she *not* there after all?"

"She's here," John whispered, amazed, his eyes glued to the list. "And so is Sophia Pasquelucci." He handed Marquette the list. "Good news, especially for me. You're not crazy after all."

Marquette stared at the names on the list, feeling his legs go weak. He slumped into the bench. Glancing up at the secretary he asked, "Who compiled this list?"

"Father Stefano Gabanelli," she answered, looking at Marquette with concern. "Are you all right, sir?"

Marquette nodded and asked, "Where can I find Father Gabanelli?"

"I do not know," she answered. "He was gone from this parish when I began my employ here ten years ago."

"Is there a record of transfer?" Marquette asked.

The secretary shook her head. "There was a fire here shortly after the crash and very few records were saved. All of our transfer records were completely destroyed, as were our birth records. That file is all that remains of our death records prior to the crash — and it was delivered here by a secret messenger in 1964."

Marquette raised an eyebrow...*secret messenger?*

"What's happening, Marq?" John asked quietly.

"She says that Father Gabanelli compiled this list, however, she does not know his whereabouts because of a fire that destroyed pertinent records," Marquette answered, frowning. "And the only reason for this particular record's existence is that it was delivered by a *secret messenger* in 1964."

"Wow," John replied dryly. "Church intrigue." He smiled with confidence and said, "Well, I bet I know somebody who can help us, *secrets and all*. Get up, Marquette, and tell this woman thank you, so that we can be on our way."

Marquette smiled faintly, rising from his seat. He closed the file, handing it to the secretary as he said, "*Grazie*," and he and John hurried out the door.

*****

Frank Bailey came home from World War II to his family's business in 1945, just as he promised them he would. His beautiful Italian bride came along shortly thereafter.

Frank was now forty-eight years old and senior comptroller for Bailey Industries. All of his siblings worked there, and he also put his niece to work there after she finished college. She had an incredible propensity for mathematics, and Frank knew exactly where he could use her. She audited the vast set of books for Bailey Industries, tracking down thieves within the company from coast to coast.

Frank's blond hair was thin on top now, his pale blue eyes lined by frequent smiles. He was tall and slender, and he wore black suits every day, giving most the appearance that he was a very serious person. However, it was his secretary that was serious enough for both of them.

Mrs. Charles was stern. Nothing escaped Frank Bailey's very professional assistant. She kept her silver hair tightly drawn back at the base of her neck, tiny bifocals rested on her sharp nose. She always wore dark suits and sensible black shoes.

Mrs. Charles unfolded the World section of *The Chicago Times*, laying it out on her desk. She poured herself a cup of coffee, settling comfortably into her chair. Frank would arrive at the office soon and she wanted to have a chance at the paper before it became part of the mess on his desk.

She read through the various articles, finding nothing of particular interest, until she turned the page, spying the photo of a man with a ponytail stepping into the back of a limousine. The caption read: "South Dakota Man Orchestrates Sicilian Capture." She glanced at the article below, carefully sipping her coffee as she read. She nearly choked when she saw the name Marquette Caselli. At that moment, the door to the office opened and in walked Frank.

"Good morning, Mrs. Charles," he said with a smile, removing his black hat, hanging it on the rack by the door.

Mrs. Charles' eyes were big and round as she stared at her boss, trying to make words come out of her hanging-open mouth. *I've found him!* was all that she could think, yet couldn't form a single syllable. The boy that Frank and his niece had searched for was right there in the paper.

Frank laughed at the expression in his seemingly astonished secretary's eyes, teasing, "Whatsamatter? Cat got your tongue?"

She shook her head slowly, closing her mouth, putting a shaky finger on Marquette's photo. "Frank, look at this," she whispered.

Frank smiled as he walked to Mrs. Charles' desk. He glanced down at the photo she pointed at, frowning as he began to read the article. "Marquette Caselli..." he whispered, staring in astonishment...*Marquette Caselli, it can't be!* Poor Tara could only say that name with tears and regret. They'd searched for the young man for eleven years, finally making the decision only last year to stop, hoping to end Tara's agony, so she could begin a new life without him.

"John was with him," Mrs. Charles said quietly, continuing to skim through the article.

"He lives in D.C.," Frank murmured. "Wonder if his mother's still alive."

"Says here his parents live in Sioux Falls, South Dakota," Mrs. Charles replied.

Frank continued reading aloud, "'After immigrating from Italy in 1956, where they have remained. Marquette's father, Guiseppi Caselli, was prompted to make the move by his brother, Angelo Caselli, who served with General Miller in the Apennines...'" Frank's voice trailed off as he finished scanning the article.

"We were looking in the wrong place," Mrs. Charles said.

"I see that...but all of the information I received said that General Miller was from Colorado."

"Says here he owned land in Centerville, South Dakota, at the time he sponsored Angelo," Mrs. Charles added, reading from the article. "'Which he bequeathed to Angelo Caselli when he died. Vincenzo Caselli, Angelo's nephew, and his wife, Kate Martin Caselli, were left the land when Angelo passed away in 1964.'" She looked up at Frank. "Do you think we should call them?"

A thoughtful frown spread across Frank's brow as he answered, "I don't know. Why didn't Marquette look for Tara? Surely he must have found out by now that she survived the crash."

"Oh, poo!" Mrs. Charles admonished. "That deceitful bunch back in Italy probably never told him!"

"Oh, Mrs. Charles," Frank argued politely, "they lived and died for one another. I can't imagine that the Andreottis wouldn't tell Marquette that his beloved Tara was still alive."

"Well they sure didn't tell *us* where Marquette was, now did they?" she retorted. "They left us to flounder around Colorado and the surrounding areas —"

"It's been twelve years," Frank interrupted. "Perhaps he's no longer interested. They were very young and a young man's heart can be fickle."

Mrs. Charles tapped the article with her index finger as she replied, "Says here that Mr. Caselli is unmarried."

Frank took a thoughtful breath and nodded. "Give John Peters' liaison a call. Maybe she can get a hold of him and have him call us."

Mrs. Charles reached for her Rolodex, quickly thumbing through it as she murmured, "I know I saved John's card the last time he was in — "

"And remember?" Frank interrupted. "He was talking about his partner — "

"Marq," Mrs. Charles finished. "Oh my goodness, Frank, he's known Marquette the *entire* time. Why didn't we ever call him for help?"

"Because he was always busy," Frank reminded.

Mrs. Charles nodded, finding the card. She quickly picked up her telephone and dialed the number. Within a matter of minutes, the connection was made. Mrs. Charles swallowed away her nerves as she blurted, "Hello, Phyllis. I need the name of that boy — I mean *that man* — you know the one?"

Phyllis laughed and asked, "What man?"

Mrs. Charles cleared her throat, speaking more professionally she said, "The man who works with Mr. Peters. I need to contact him."

"Marquette Caselli," Phyllis answered, and Mrs. Charles heard some papers rustle in the background. "They're currently in Rome."

"Mr. Bailey needs his number in Rome," Mrs. Charles stated.

"Alrighty then," Phyllis answered. "You guys must have a big one."

"Oh we do," Mrs. Charles replied. "Biggest one ever."

Phyllis located the number and gave it to Mrs. Charles, who wrote it down on her steno pad.

"Thanks, Phyllis, you're a lifesaver," Mrs. Charles said, hanging up the phone. She tore the number from her pad and handed it Frank.

Frank held the number in his hand, looking down at it for a very long time.

"What's wrong, Frank?" she questioned.

Frank shook his head. "I can't believe it. We looked for so long and now here it is, right in my hands."

*****

John contacted his old friend at Santa Susanna, who knew a clerk in the central registrar's office of transfers. Through the clerk, John and Marquette learned that Father Gabanelli had been promoted to bishop in 1956, shortly after the train crash, and then to archbishop in 1960. In 1964, Pope Paul VI appointed him cardinal, and he transferred into Vatican City.

Through John's friend, Marquette and John were allowed into the Vatican, but only as far as a waiting chamber. A young guard stayed behind to watch them, while another went to ask Cardinal Gabanelli if he would have visitors. Soon, the other guard reappeared.

"The cardinal will see Mr. Caselli and Mr. Peters," he said. "Please follow me."

The young guard led them to the cardinal's chamber, where they were presented to an old man, heavily draped in crimson robes, and securely bound in a wheelchair. He could not rise to greet his guests, but offered them a feeble wave and faint smile.

Marquette shook his head in dismay. The man before them was extremely aged, and he wondered what, if anything, the cardinal would remember about the crash survivors. The bit of hair showing on the sides of his head was white against his red cap. His face was deeply furrowed with wrinkles, and his black eyes were shadowed with bushy, white brows. His sunken mouth and jaw made obvious his lack of teeth.

"Cardinal Gabanelli," John said, kneeling on his left knee, kissing his ring. He stood up, moving aside for Marquette.

Marquette frowned at John's greeting, but submitted and did the same.

"I'm John Peters," he introduced. "This is my associate, Marquette Caselli."

The old cardinal nodded, studying the two of them in silence. When he finally spoke, his voice was weak, his English heavily accented as he said, "I *almost* did not see you this day…" he hesitated, looking at Marquette. "You are *Italiano*, and of some reputation I understand."

Marquette nodded, producing a photograph of Tara, handing it to the cardinal. "Cardinal Gabanelli," he began. "I am here to ask you some questions about the train crash in *Roma*."

"1956," the cardinal murmured, taking the photograph into his shaky hands.

"Yes," Marquette replied. "We understand that you compiled the list of survivors. I am looking for two ladies —"

"We pulled only five from the crash that day," the cardinal blurted, looking intently into the photograph. He slowly nodded his head as he said,

"There was an old woman with her. She asked me not to tell anyone that they had survived." Marquette gasped, and the cardinal looked into his hopeful eyes.

"Why?" John questioned, his heart beating in his throat.

The cardinal looked back at the photo, explaining, "She told me that a man and his son would come looking for them and I was to tell them I did not recall ever seeing them."

"Did the man and his son come?" Marquette asked.

The cardinal swallowed hard, answering, "They came..." he hesitated as he looked at Marquette. "Dear son, I prayed for wisdom. I did not want to lie to them, but I hid the list of survivors and told them that I did not recall ever seeing an old woman and a girl. They visited me several times, determined to find the truth, but the last time they came, I called the police to take them away. The boy cried bitterly and my heart broke for him."

Marquette's emotions surged within him. "Where did they go after the crash?" he asked.

Cardinal Gabanelli shook his head, answering, "I helped the woman make several calls to the United States. She would not tell me where she was calling or whom she had reached. I hid her and the girl in my apartment for two weeks, and when the time came, I took them to *Napoli*, where the woman said that she had made arrangements to board a ship owned by a wealthy businessman in the United States who had agreed to pay their way."

"The man and his son," John questioned. "Do you know their name?"

"Andreotti," the cardinal answered.

Marquette's eyes were wide with surprise, obviously overwhelmed with the information that he had just received.

The cardinal reached for Marquette's hand and said, "She was very beautiful." Marquette looked down at the cardinal, watching tears suddenly well in his eyes as he continued, "She did not belong with that boy, and somehow I knew it...what will you do with this information?"

"I will try to find her," Marquette answered. "There are no other choices for me but to find my Tara."

The cardinal nodded, took a deep breath and closed his eyes. He turned his face upward, whispering his prayers in Latin. When he finished, he looked intently at Marquette and said, "Go. Find her as quickly as you can."

"I will, Cardinal Gabanelli," Marquette replied, stooping to kiss the cardinal's cheeks as he often kissed his own father and siblings. "Thank you so much. You cannot possibly imagine what this means to me."

The cardinal smiled tiredly as he said, "To be without the love of your life would be a life of emptiness. For me it would mean being without God. I will pray that He guides your footsteps to her."

Before John and Marquette went back to their hotel, Marquette insisted that they stop at a church to spend some time in prayer. John had never been a "religious" person, but Marquette was so distressed, and had had several troubling days in a row. It all seemed to begin with Ponerello's great curse, and now the thing with Tara.

John waited patiently in the pew while Marquette went to the front of the sanctuary, where he knelt for an hour, praying in Italian, weeping until his shoulders shook. John was uncomfortable, to say the least, as he'd never seen a man behave in such a way.

After that, they returned to their hotel and ordered dinner to be served in their room. John was nearly finished with his steak before he worked up the courage to speak.

"So they went to America," he said. "Who do they know in America?"

Marquette had wolfed down his food and was working on the *caffè* John didn't want to finish. He set down his cup answering, "Tara has an aunt there — but I have never known the city…never cared until now. I am certain that is where they went."

"Hmm…so how old were the two of you when you were separated?" John asked.

"We were both fifteen years."

"Kinda young, weren't ya?" John remarked

Marquette shrugged. "Marriages at that time could take place at the age of consent, which was sixteen. We had only a few months left to wait." He got to his feet and walked to the balcony, gazing down into the city below them. "I promised her I would keep a journal of every day of my life until we were together again, and I could never bring myself to stop writing to her."

John raised his eyebrows in surprise, murmuring, "I really can't believe you never mentioned any of this, Marq. And now you're both twenty-seven years old. What if she's changed her mind about you?"

Marquette shrugged again, turning from the window. He smiled faintly as he said, "All things work together for good to them that love God, to them who are the called according to *His* purpose."

John stared back at Marquette. He was always slipping in Bible verses here and there, consistently sharing what he called the "Good News." For the most part, John had grown accustomed to his partner's subtle preaching, but tonight was very different. There was something in Marquette's tone and demeanor that made John ask, "How do you know that there's a God in heaven, Marquette?"

"Because He put it inside of me to know," Marquette answered, placing his hand over his heart. "And I know He dwells within me because I asked Him to."

"Because you believed yourself a sinner and asked Jesus for forgiveness?" John asked, repeating the message Marquette had given for the past eight years that they'd worked together.

Marquette nodded with a small smile. "Certainly you know the message by now, my friend. My Jesus died for you as well as he died for me so that all of us who believe could live forever."

John nodded in understanding.

"You must make a decision, my friend," Marquette reminded, as he had several times in the past. "I wish nothing more than for you to share eternity with me."

John nodded again, promising, "I'll make a decision here one of these days." He grinned at Marquette, adding, "But right now we gotta put our heads together and find your Tara — how 'bout this Andreotti character? Do you think he knows where she is?"

Marquette frowned. "Recall, John, that you met Luigi Andreotti while we were in Chicago eight years ago — "

"Our layover after we solved the Markelle case," John blurted. He raised a brow, adding, "He couldn't get away from us fast enough — do you suppose he had Tara there with him?"

"Yes, I *do* suppose," Marquette replied, his eyes wide with realization.

"But why wouldn't he tell you that he had her there?" John questioned. "In fact, why the big deception about whether she lived or died in that crash?"

"Well…" Marquette sighed heavily, putting his hands into his pants pockets, clinking the change. "There is one little matter I have left out of the details." He paused, looking at John with a sly smile.

"And that would be…" John coaxed.

Marquette took a deep breath, explaining, "My Tara was promised to Luigi."

John's eyes were huge with surprise. "You mean an arranged marriage? People really do that?"

Marquette nodded. "Yes, my friend, people really do that. And since Tara was not at the age of consent, which is sixteen, tradition was that she had to marry Luigi upon the death of her father."

"Whoa," John muttered, shaking his head in disbelief.

"It is how we took care of one another in the valley," Marquette continued. "A nonsensical rule of tradition that I want to make perfectly clear I would *never* consent or submit to."

"But Luigi would?" John questioned.

Marquette nodded. "For he loved Tara nearly as much as I."

"Wow, she must really be somethin'."

Marquette chuckled. "Oh, yes, she is really something, John. I cannot wait for you to meet her."

John got up from his chair, collected his billfold from the dresser and eased it into his pocket.

"Where are you going, my friend?" Marquette asked.

"To visit with the concierge," John answered. "I'm gonna see if he can help us get a couple of tickets to O'Hare tonight. You get your stuff packed up and I'll be back as soon as I can."

"But Chicago is a very big place," Marquette pointed out. "It will be difficult to locate her there. Where will we even begin?"

"We'll start with the phonebook."

*****

John got them seats on a tiny, private jet that took them from *Roma* to *Milano*. They would then take a commercial jet from *Milano* to Amsterdam, finally connecting with a flight that would take them directly to Chicago.

Though it was nearly two a.m. when they boarded their flight in *Milano*, and they were exhausted, neither could sleep because of the turbulence over the Alps.

"So," John began with a yawn, "why would Tara's grandmother want to hide her away and why didn't they call you when they had reached America?"

Marquette stretched his long legs comfortably out in front of him, answering, "I would like to believe that Sophia tried to hide Tara from Luigi. And as far as not contacting me when they reached America, that is because the crash took place before any of my letters reached Tara. We were moving to America and were in the middle of the Atlantic Ocean when the train crashed in Roma. When I arrived in Sioux Falls, I began to write to Tara immediately with my new address — but she was already gone."

"But Luigi must have found her," John reminded. "How would he know where to look?"

"My number one guess is Pietro," Marquette answered. "He runs the local supply store and mail office near *Castellina* there in *Chianti*, where we all lived at one time — and where the Andreottis have resided for many generations. If Tara's aunt, who came to America shortly after World War II, mailed her any letters *before* the crash, Pietro would have intercepted them and taken the return address directly to the Andreottis."

John frowned. "Why would he be so loyal to *that* family, rather than yours?"

"He is married to Luigi's sister, Marsala," Marquette answered. "And I am told that when he was young, he wanted Tara's aunt, Claretta, for his bride, but an American soldier came along during the war, swept her off her feet, and took her to America."

John's heart stumbled as the familiarity of the story rang in his ears. "*Where* in America?" he asked.

"I told you...I do not know, and never cared until this moment," Marquette answered, yawning and rubbing his forehead.

"What was the name of the soldier?" John asked.

"We called him Frankie," Marquette answered, smiling at his memories. "I was very small when Frankie came to us, but I remember his kindness. Apparently he was hurt in battle while our fathers were away and he stayed with us until he was well again."

John chuckled and shook his head. "Marq, you're never gonna believe this, but I have this friend named Frank, and he's always talking about his service in Italy, and that he was shot up over there and his wife's family patched him back together. His wife's name is Claretta."

Marquette's mouth fell open in surprise. "John..." he whispered, unable to say anything else.

John nodded. "Frank lives in Chicago, Marquette. We'll go see him first thing."

*****

When Frank called Rome, he learned that John and Marquette had already departed the hotel. It was too late to contact their liaison in D.C., so Frank was forced to wait until the next day before he could gather any further information. He was waiting in the chair at Mrs. Charles' desk when she came in the next morning.

"You gotta call that woman in D.C.," he said quickly, getting to his feet, rushing to close the door behind Mrs. Charles.

"What on earth for?" she asked, untying her scarf.

"I can't make heads or tails of that Rolodex of yours," he explained. "And Marquette and John left the hotel in Rome last night." He took Mrs. Charles by the elbow, escorting her to her desk. "Now, just call that woman, or give me her number."

Mrs. Charles flipped quickly through the Rolodex, reaching for the phone at the same time. It wasn't long before the connection was made and Frank listened to the other end of the conversation.

"I'm sorry," Phyllis said. "They didn't notify me that they were leaving the hotel already…and sometimes they're like that. They just pick up and follow a clue without telling anyone. I guess I could call John's wife. Perhaps she might know where they went."

"Yes, please do that," Mrs. Charles replied. "Call me back as soon as you can." They hung up and she saw Frank's disappointed expression. "She'll call us back," she said, finishing the removal of her scarf.

"I shouldn't have hesitated," Frank lamented. "I was just so unsure." His shoulders slumped as he sighed, making his way to his office.

"At least we know how to reach him now," Mrs. Charles encouraged.

Frank nodded his head as he went into his office, closing the door.

John and Marquette hurried a cab driver through the busy streets of Chicago, heading for the Bailey Industries Building on LaSalle Street.

"I hope I do not become sick," Marquette murmured as the taxi jostled along. "I am so nervous. Never before have I felt like this. Perhaps I will faint."

John laughed, but it wasn't his normal hardy expression of humor — it sounded more distressed than anything. "Don't faint, Marq," he said.

The cab came to an abrupt stop and John handed the driver a fistful of cash as he and Marquette scrambled from the car. "Keep the change!" he yelled over his shoulder as they rushed for the building.

Once inside Bailey Industries Building, they spied a directory between two elevators, and hurried over.

"Let's see…" John muttered, his finger going over several lines on the directory, looking for Frank's name. "There!" he exclaimed. "Seventh floor.

The elevator opened at that moment and the two of them stepped inside. The young lady operator asked, "What floor, please?"

"Seven," Marquette answered with a smile.

She nodded, closed the heavy doors, and turned the crank.

As they felt the elevator moving beneath them, Marquette suddenly grabbed John's arm, whispering, "I think I am fainting after all."

John rolled his eyes. "Okay, let's just forget about this then. Let's just go."

Marquette shook his head. "Let us continue…but I am afraid."

"I'm terrified," John replied. "But we're goin' in there and we're gonna find Tara."

The elevator stopped and the operator opened the door. Marquette and John paused in the doorway, looking into the magnificent lobby. John gave Marquette a soft shove out the door, stepping out behind him.

In the center of the lobby was a circular desk, occupied by one woman with a headset.

"The receptionist," John said, starting in her direction.

"May I help you?" she asked.

"Frank Bailey, please," John requested.

"Do you have an appointment?" she asked, looking the two of them over. By now they'd journeyed several thousand miles in less than twenty-four hours. Their shirts and slacks were crumpled and their faces unshaven.

"Yes," Marquette lied, flashing a most charming smile, laying down one of his business cards. "John Peters and Marquette Caselli at your service, *Signorina*."

John followed Marquette's cue and laid down one of his cards as well, following with a hopeful smile.

The receptionist narrowed her eyes, looking suspicious as she said, "One moment, please." She dialed a number on her switchboard.

Mrs. Charles picked up the phone on the first ring, praying that it was finally Phyllis returning her call.

"Mrs. Charles," the receptionist began. "I have two gentlemen here that claim to have an appointment with Mr. Bailey." She paused. "Marquette Caselli and John Peters?"

Mrs. Charles felt her mouth go dry as speechlessness grabbed a tight hold of her throat.

"Mrs. Charles," the receptionist said. "Are you still there?"

Mrs. Charles nodded, attempting to clear her throat. "Send them in," she blurted, hanging up the phone. She lurched out of her chair, barging into Frank's office, leaving his door hanging wide open.

Frank was sitting on the window ledge behind his desk, eyes closed, obviously deep in prayer. When he heard the commotion in his office, he opened his eyes and looked at Mrs. Charles. "Yes?" he said.

"He…he's here," she whispered, clearing her throat again.

"Pardon?" Frank said.

"Marquette and John are here," she said, aloud this time.

At that moment, the door to the outer office opened and the two disheveled travelers walked in. Frank squinted, recognizing John immediately, and then his eyes looked upon Marquette.

"Oh my dear Lord," Frank whispered, sliding off the ledge to greet them.

"Frank," John smiled, extending his hand in greeting. "I know this is unexpected."

Frank took John's hand in a fairly weak shake as he replied, "You have no idea." He swallowed hard, but his voice began to tremble as he continued, "I've been looking for the two of you since yesterday."

John raised an eyebrow and looked at Marquette, who only smiled and shrugged.

"Yesterday's paper," Mrs. Charles said, unable to take her eyes off of the handsome Italian. She smiled and nodded with approval. "My goodness, Frank, what will she think of that ponytail?"

Marquette extended his hand to Mrs. Charles. "How do you do?"

Mrs. Charles took his hand, but was pleasantly surprised when Marquette lifted it gently to his lips and gave it a soft kiss. "Rebecca Charles," she murmured through a grin. "And you must be Marquette."

"We're actually here about your niece," John interjected, looking at Frank, noticing his surprised expression. "You see, Frank, Marq and I were talking on our flight from Milan —"

"*Milano*," Marquette politely corrected, smiling.

"Yes, *Milano*," John began again. "And the funniest thing happened along the way —"

"I tried to reach you," Frank interrupted. "I called the hotel in *Roma* yesterday, but you had already left."

"Why?" Marquette asked.

Frank had to swallow away his emotions before he could speak. "Tara has an office just down the hall from me," he said, his voice trembling. "I'd like you to see her."

Marquette's feet suddenly felt like lead, seemingly frozen to the spot where he stood. *Go see her? Now?* Marquette stared at Frank, thinking perhaps he'd be sick. "Does she know about me?" he asked.

Frank shook his head and answered, "I wasn't sure how to handle this, Mr. Caselli. I wasn't sure how you'd react or what you'd say." He paused to clear his throat, continuing, "I want you to know that we've looked for you for many years."

"She wanted to find me?" Marquette questioned.

"You're all she's talked about since she was a kid," Frank replied. "She would never date, and the best have tried, but she held out for you."

Marquette felt sudden tears dropping from his eyes, and he quickly wiped them away, laughing nervously. "I *will* faint now, John," he said, staggering backwards to lean against the wall where John stood. John put a strong hand on Marquette's shoulder, steadying him.

"How long have you known about Marq?" John asked.

"Just yesterday," Mrs. Charles blurted. "We saw your picture in the paper yesterday."

Marquette nodded. He suddenly threw his arms around John, holding him tightly. "What shall I do?" he whispered, taking a deep breath. He let go of John and fished a handkerchief from his pocket. "I cannot see her like *this*," he murmured, laughing nervously again as he wiped his eyes.

"Well, you've looked better," John commented wryly, and Mrs. Charles laughed nervously.

"Her office is right this way," Frank said, heading for the hall.

Marquette watched Frank leave through the open door, hesitating as he looked at John.

"Come on," John said, giving Marquette a shove. "This is why we're here."

Marquette took a deep breath and forced himself to follow Frank. John fell in behind them.

"Incidentally, she does the same thing that you do, only on a smaller scale," Frank said as they walked down the hall, stopping to knock on a door. He waited only a second before walking in.

An elderly woman was sitting at a desk and she smiled at Frank. "Good morning, Mr. Bailey," she said, glancing at Marquette and John. "What can we do for you today?"

"Is Tara in her office?" he asked as he strode toward the closed office door, resting his hand on the knob.

"She's on a very important call," she replied.

"Thanks," Frank acknowledged, opening the door. He reached for Marquette, pushing him into the office ahead of him. He and John followed.

Near the windows overlooking the city stood a woman on the phone. Her back was to them, but she turned slowly to see what had caused the commotion in her office. She gasped, nearly dropping the phone when she saw them. "I will call you right back," she whispered, dropping the phone into its cradle. Her petite body was dressed in a straight white skirt with a matching jacket, a pale blue scarf tied at her neck. Her wavy, black hair fell gently on her shoulders, and her soft, dark eyes began to shine with tears.

"Oh, my," Marquette whispered, unable to take his eyes off of her. "It really *is* you." His voice trembled with emotion as he said, "I have thought of you every day since we parted." He walked across the small office, reaching for her hand.

She took his hand into her own, looking into his handsome eyes. "Marquette?" she breathed.

He nodded, folding her into his arms, holding her as tightly as he could. "I have loved you every moment," he whispered into her hair. "Would you please marry me?"

"I will marry you, Marquette," she answered, beginning to cry.

"Now hold on you two," Frank said, stepping into the room. "You've been reacquainted for nearly thirty seconds. We have to get blessings. Nonna

Pasquelucci has authority here, and Mr. Caselli needs to call his parents.

Marquette and Tara laughed through their tears. "You are right," Marquette agreed. "I will call my parents immediately, and then we will ask Nonna Pasquelucci for Tara's hand."

"I can't imagine there's gonna be a problem," Frank said, getting out his handkerchief to dry his tears. "You can call your family from here and then we'll go over and see Nonna and Claretta." He paused to look at the two of them for a moment, feeling his tears begin again. "I'm so happy for you."

"Thank you, Uncle Frank," Tara said, putting her arms around her uncle. "My life will be so wonderful now."

John watched the dramatic scene with a lump in his throat. He took off his spectacles and dried his tears with his handkerchief. *Thank you, Jesus,* he thought. *Please forgive me for not believing and forgive me for my other sins. Please dwell in my heart so that I'll see You...and Marquette, in eternity....*

THIRTY YEARS LATER...

Chapter 1

Anchor Marina Dock, Lake Ontario
Cape Vincent, New York

May 1998

Jason Holliday Patterson had nothing to worry about. It was well known that Senator Caselli didn't keep personal security while away from D.C. Using the cover of a small gaggle of reporters on the dock, he slipped through the late evening shadows onto the glamorous yacht.

He pressed his tall, slender frame into the wall, listening to the waves splash against the yacht. A bead of sweat rolled down the side of his face and his heart pounded in his ears. *Just go in*, he told himself. *Isn't this why you're here?* Clutching his gun against his chest he crept around the corner, peering into the lighted room below. Dozens of formally dressed people mingled and danced, while waiters and waitresses bustled through with trays of food and drinks. An orchestra was playing somewhere in the background. Jason rolled his eyes with disgust. *Humph. Rich folks. Hope they're havin' a good time.*

He inched past the lighted room and arrived at the doorway of what he presumed to be Senator Caselli's office. He tried the knob and groaned. *Locked.* He tucked his gun into his waistband and reached for the metal pick in his pocket. With his left hand he held the knob steady. His right hand worked the tumblers. At the sound of several clicks, the knob released and the door creaked open. He quickly slipped into the dark room, and closed the door behind him.

Jason fumbled in his jacket pocket for his penlight. He switched it on, and shined it around the small office. He caught a glint of something white under the corner of a chair, and Jason focused the small beam on it. A paper matchbook. He picked it up and looked at the cover. *Circle Q Bar & Grill.* Frowning, he tucked the matchbook into his pants pocket.

Something cold and hard suddenly pushed against the back of Jason's neck, and he jumped with surprise. He reached instinctively for the gun tucked into his waistband.

"Don't even try it," demanded a deep, female voice from behind him. "Just put your hands on the back of your head and turn around. *Slowly.*"

Jason put his hands on the back of his head, and turned around. A light came on and he was face to face with a tall woman in her mid-twenties. Her black eyes were frowning at him through the soft, black, whispy bangs covering her brows. The rest of her hair was very short, showing off the diamond earrings dangling from her feminine lobes. She was dressed in a clingy, exquisite white, sequined gown that fit her six-foot figure to a "T." She was stunning, to say the least, except for the .38 Special she held at Jason's head.

She raised one sultry eyebrow. "Whatcha doin' in here, pretty boy?" she asked.

Jason swallowed hard, searching his mind for an answer. *Who is she? Does she work for Andreotti or is she one of the Casellis? She looks like a Casélli...except for how tall she is...wonder if she knows how to handle that piece.*

"Answer me," she prompted with a frown.

Jason cleared his throat, and tossed his sandy, blond hair out of his eyes. He smiled shyly, attempting to flirt. "I was looking for the bathroom and just got lost," he answered.

She nodded at the gun in his waistband. "Try again."

Jason looked down at his gun and back at hers. As usual, he was in over his head, out of his jurisdiction, and without a warrant. "I work for Andreotti," he blurted.

"And what do you do for him?"

"Security. I'm his body guard." Jason, impressed with his quick and clever lie, smiled with confidence.

She sighed. "Slowly, take your weapon and drop it to the floor."

"Listen, Miss, just let me go about my business and I'll be off this boat in no time."

Her face was stern, and her eyes bored into his. "Drop the gun, pal," she demanded.

He thought about refusing, but she appeared to be so...*authoritative.* He let out a soft breath, reached for the gun, and dropped it to the floor.

She stepped closer to him, the muzzle of her gun pressing into his temple. Beads of sweat ran down the sides of his face as she reached inside his jacket. Her hand brushed past his badge, and she pulled it out. She opened the leather wallet and saw his detective's shield. She shook her head and made a soft 'tsk' noise as she murmured, "Good grief, you're a cop." She let out a disgusted breath. "Rapid City, South Dakota?"

Jason swallowed and nodded.

She sighed heavily, tucked the wallet back into his pocket, and took a step backward. She raised her black eyebrow again demanding, "Now, you'd better tell me what you're up to, because Rapid's an awfully long way away. Obviously, you wouldn't have a warrant."

"I followed...I'm doing some investigative work," he explained. "I

2

thought I might be able to find some information here."

She seemed satisfied with his response. She lowered her gun and stepped back a few more feet. She gestured at his weapon on the floor and said, "Go ahead and pick it up, but holster it."

Jason stooped to pick up his gun, and tucked it into the safe holster beneath his arm. "Can I go?" he asked.

"Not yet," she answered abruptly, as she lifted the material of her dress to her mid-thigh, to place her weapon into its secret holster. She smoothed her beautiful dress and looked him in the eye. "I've got a couple of questions for you first —"

"Who *are* you?" he asked.

"United States Deputy Marshal Alyssa Caselli."

Jason took a deep breath. *So, she's a Caselli.*

"Now, tell me what's going on with Andreotti, and I *might* let you go," she ordered with a frown.

"I really can't say," he answered. His confidence had returned now that she'd holstered her gun.

"Oh, bull," she retorted. "I'll arrest you for a terrorist attempt on the Senator and his family, and I'll make sure it's a very long time before the Public Defender comes over to see you. The jail here is really a dive. How much time are you willing to spend in it?"

Jason gulped at her determined threat as the back of his shirt began to soak with perspiration. "Okay, I *followed* Andreotti," he admitted. "He met with the Senator yesterday and I saw them come into this room."

"Where did you follow him from?"

"All the way from Rapid City," Jason answered.

"Does he know you're here?"

Jason shook his head.

"How long have you been following him and why?"

"About six months. I think he's selling tainted drugs."

Alyssa's eyebrows knit themselves together. "Drugs? You followed someone thirteen hundred miles across the country, out of your jurisdiction no less, for drugs?" She shook her head. "Come on. What else?"

Jason swallowed and rolled his eyes. "He *may* have been involved in a murder."

She raised her eyebrows with surprise. "And you haven't involved the Feds *why?*"

Jason sighed heavily as he answered, "Look, I didn't want the little creep to get away and I needed a break. *Please*, just let me off this boat and I promise not to bother your family again."

Alyssa stared hard at him, considering his request. "I can find you in an instant," she murmured.

"I know."

Alyssa nodded, taking a deep breath. "Get off my uncle's boat," she said. "And if I see you again, I'll call the local police and have you arrested, and I'm sure you'll be in a lot of trouble."

Jason smiled with relief. "Thanks."

Alyssa turned toward the door of the small office, hesitating to look back at Jason. "Luigi's no big deal," she said. "I'm sure you've confused him with someone else."

"Maybe," Jason pretended to agree with a nod of his head.

With that, Alyssa turned and left the room. Jason turned off the light, and left the boat the same way he'd gotten on.

Guiseppi Caselli was eighty-one years old. His head was bald and shiny but his black eyes still sparkled with life. He moved a little slower these days, but Rosa didn't mind. She held tightly to his arm as he led her through the crowded yacht. They had both dressed for this event: Vincenzo's fifty-eighth birthday. Guiseppi wore a sharp, black tuxedo, as had all of the men. Pretty Rosa was dressed in an elegant, black gown that reached to the floor. It had long sleeves and a high neck, and a row of shimmering sequins at her middle. Her silver hair was up in a twist, and at seventy-eight years of age, Guiseppi thought her dazzling.

"The Senator has a fine boat," he said with a smile, giving Rosa's hand a soft pat.

"Yes he does," she agreed.

Guiseppi's eyes lit up with sudden surprise, and Rosa followed his gaze to the very tall, red-headed man approaching them. "Well if it is not that dear young, Ty Hansen," he smiled. He and Rosa reached for the young man's hands.

Ty bent over to hold the two of them at the same time. He put his arms around Tillie's little parents, giving them each a kiss on the face.

Guiseppi put his hands on Ty's cheeks, giving them each a kiss. "How is my favorite baseball player?" he asked.

"I'm great. How are you guys?" Ty asked with a smile.

"We are well!" Rosa answered, reaching for Ty the same way her husband had, kissing him. "Are your cousins with you?"

Ty nodded, glancing around. "They're here somewhere. Uncle Patty and Aunt Ellie left Washington early, so Gabby and Michael and I had to take a commercial flight over."

"How is my Gabriella?" Rosa asked, her eyes showing tender concern for her granddaughter.

Ty faked a grimace as he answered, "Oh, you know, she's glad the year is almost over with, and she's threatening not to go back. *Again*."

Guiseppi shook his head. "Why does she continue to make these threats?"

"She *hates* Washington," Ty answered.

"You and Michael seem to enjoy it so much," Rosa pointed out.

Ty raised his eyebrows and laughed. "What's *not* to love?"

Tillie straightened the bow tie on Noah's black tuxedo, smiling into his handsome eyes. His sandy-colored hair was mixed with gray strands now, and it had started to thin on top — just a touch. "You look *great*," she whispered.

"This cumber...thing is too tight," he complained. He reached around his back, tugging on the fabric. He hadn't been in a tux since their wedding day nearly four years ago. He wondered *again* how he'd allowed himself to be roped into putting on another one.

"Don't touch it," Tillie said with a giggle, reaching under his coat for his hands. "You look *so* nice."

"I look like a waiter," Noah grumbled, making Tillie laugh again.

"Shhh." She gently touched his lips with her index finger. "My family *loves* to dress up and this is fun for them."

Noah softened then, giving her one of the lopsided smiles she loved. He looked into his pretty wife's black eyes, unable to resist just one soft kiss. She was dressed in a pale pink, floor-length sequined gown that fit her slender figure perfectly, and her dark curls were up.

"Okay," he whispered, slipping his hands around her waist, nuzzling her earlobe. He caught the softest scent of Chanel No. 5. "I'll try to behave myself, but you know how hard it is for me."

Tillie chuckled, but as she glanced downward she noticed his *cowboy boots!* "Noah!" she gasped in amazement. Her black eyes flew open with surprise. She looked into her husband's expression and frowned.

Noah deliberately looked away and groaned, "Those shiny shoes just didn't look right, Angel."

Tillie gently touched his chin, drawing his eyes back to her own. "You didn't even try them on, did you?" she said.

"They were *stupid*," Noah excused with a faint smile.

Tillie couldn't help but laugh. "Cowboy boots and a tux?" she questioned.

Noah's blue eyes danced with dreadful mischief. "Come on, how was I gonna dance with those little plastic slippers stuck to my feet?"

Tillie laughed again and shook her head. "Whatever, Noah."

"And besides," he said, pretending to leer at her, "you're pretty enough for the both of us. I could have come in rags and no one would have *even noticed* me."

"There is my ageless sister!" Came an excited voice from behind them. Tillie and Noah turned to see Petrice and Elaine coming toward them.

"Hey, Patty," Noah said with a smile, extending his hand.

"Noah," Petrice greeted, taking Noah's hand, then reaching for his sister. "And my Angel. You look lovely this evening." He planted a soft kiss on her cheek.

"Thanks Patty," Tillie said, smiling at her older brother, then reaching for Elaine. "Hi, Ellie. You look great as *always*."

Elaine's pale cheeks showed the faintest blush. She was nearly six feet tall, towering over her slightly built Italian husband. "Thanks, Angel," she said.

"And how do you like the boat?" Petrice asked with a curious sparkle in his black eyes. He and Elaine had purchased the new yacht and put it in Lake Ontario, just a short distance from their home on Cape Vincent.

Tillie smiled at her brother and said, "It's more like a ship, but I *love* it. I haven't gotten sick at all."

"That is good," Petrice acknowledged. Something caught his eye and he suddenly waved.

Noah and Tillie turned to see that Marquette and Tara had finally arrived and were heading toward them. When they were close enough, their typical greetings of hand shakes, embraces and kisses commenced.

"Where is little Annie this night?" Marquette asked curiously.

"Elaine got us a sitter," Tillie answered.

"And we know her very well," Elaine added. "She used to babysit for us when the kids were little."

Vincenzo and Kate came toward them, and more greetings were passed out as everyone wished him a happy birthday.

"How old are you this day, Vincenzo?" Marquette pretended in a curious tone.

"You know that, my brother," Vincenzo answered with a sly expression. "For you are barely a year behind me."

Marquette grinned. "But do you not think I have aged remarkably well?"

"No," Vincenzo answered with a coy smile.

"Now stop," Petrice chuckled. He took a deep breath, continuing, "I have something to tell you all."

Tillie noticed Elaine stiffen at Petrice's words. She looked to her brother for an explanation. "What's going on Patty?" she asked.

Petrice smiled and put his hand on Marquette's shoulder. "An old friend of ours, from *Italia*, happened upon me the other day. And I do not want you to get upset Marquette, because that has been too many years ago and forgiveness is in order."

Marquette looked at Petrice with suspicion and asked, "Who, pray tell, *happened upon you* the other day, dear brother?"

"Luigi Andreotti," Petrice answered.

Marquette gulped and Tara gasped.

Petrice squeezed Marquette's shoulder and began again, "Now, Marquette —"

Marquette moved away from Petrice's grip, scolding, "What on earth did *that* devil want?"

Tara scowled, adding, "Petrice Caselli, have you forgotten the twelve years he *stole* from us?"

"Twelve years the two of them will *never* get back!" Kate gasped with a frown.

Petrice raised his hands, attempting to smile at his siblings as he said, "Yes, yes I know."

Tillie could only stare with an open mouth as Petrice's explanation unfolded.

"He has lost his entire family," he continued. "He is alone in the world. I could not very well turn him away."

"It is a hell of his own making," Marquette said with a frown.

"He is *very* sorry," Petrice insisted. "He has attempted to contact you many times over the years, but, as you very well know my brother, you are extremely difficult to catch up to."

Vincenzo took a deep breath, and shook his head. "Well, what did the old blackguard have to say for himself?" he asked.

"Just that he has regretted what he and his father did for many years," Petrice answered. "He has prayed every day to the Lord for forgiveness."

Marquette shook his head with a frown, but said nothing.

Elaine looked like she was about ready to burst, and her voice finally gave way to a quiet announcement, "Petrice has invited him to your party, Vincenzo."

Vincenzo raised both of his eyebrows and pointed at himself, saying, "You invited him to *my* party?"

"I felt sorry for him," Petrice defended.

Tillie gasped and whispered, "Wow, Patty!"

"In fact," Elaine narrowed her eyes, pointing discreetly in Luigi's direction, whispering, "the old blackguard is just over there."

Marquette's eyes opened wide as his gaze followed Elaine's pointed index finger into the crowd near the punch bowl.

"This could really get hot in a couple of minutes," Noah whispered into Tillie's ear, and she nodded in agreement.

"Can we not finally put the past to rest and forgive him?" Petrice said with a smile. "After all, he was only acting upon the wishes of his father and that should count for something."

Vincenzo and Tillie looked at Marquette, and shrugged at the same time.

"It's your call, Marq," Tillie said with a doubtful look in her eyes. "Whatever you wanna do, I'll back you."

Vincenzo added, "Whatever you wish, Marquette."

Marquette looked at his wife and asked, "Can you forgive him, my love?"

Tara rolled her eyes. "He has been completely forgiven for many years, as everything has worked itself out for good. However, I cannot promise that we will become best friends."

"Very well, then." Petrice said with a sigh and a relieved smile. He waved a tall, slender gentleman to come over.

"This oughta be good," Noah whispered into Tillie's ear, and she couldn't help but smile. If this had happened ten years ago, Vincenzo and Marquette would have threatened to thrash Petrice on the spot. But now that they all hovered near the sixty-year-old mark, they didn't seem as willing to spend their energies on threats.

"Luigi," Petrice greeted with a gracious smile and handshake.

"Petrice," Luigi said, returning the Senator's handshake. His eyes immediately fell upon Elaine and he reached for her hand. "And beautiful Elaine. You look *splendid* this evening."

"Thank you, Luigi," Elaine replied politely, but Tillie saw her sister-in-law shudder at Luigi's touch.

"And Tara," Luigi greeted, reaching *not* for Tara's hand, but for Kate. "The years have been so good to you."

"Excuse me," Kate said with a polite smile. "I'm Kate Caselli."

"Oh, pardon me," Luigi said with an embarrassed smile, the whole while hanging onto Kate's hand, gazing into her eyes.

"She is *my* wife," Vincenzo said, raising his eyebrows, extending his hand to Luigi.

"Vincenzo," Luigi acknowledged, dropping Kate's hand and reaching for her husband's. "Happy birthday."

"Thank you, Luigi," Vincenzo replied. "It is good to see you again."

Luigi reached for Marquette's hand. He looked him the eye and said, "Please forgive me, Marquette."

"All is forgotten," Marquette said with a smile. "And we are sorry to hear about your family."

"Thank you," Luigi said with a nod. He reached for Tara's hand, smiling into her eyes. "And lovely Tara. How long has it been?"

Not long enough, Tara thought as she allowed Luigi to grasp her hand. She hadn't seen him since that horrible day in 1964 — the day she'd refused the last of his marriage proposals.

"This is our baby sister," Petrice continued the introductions.

Luigi reached for Tillie's hand, lifting it to his lips, placing a soft kiss upon it.

Tillie was horrified. Certainly she'd received the same type of greeting from other European men, but *this* felt different. She wanted to bolt for the door.

Noah wanted to flick the man's face from his wife's hand. *You're nothing more than a common lecher,* he thought, *and I find it hard to believe that you were acquainted with the Caselli's.*

"The beautiful Angel," Luigi breathed through a charming smile. "And I must remark on how much you look like your father."

"Thank you," Tillie acknowledged, forcing a gracious smile, wriggling her hand free of his lengthy grasp.

"Noah Hansen," Noah said, abruptly grabbing a hold of Luigi's hand, giving it a firm shake, holding it longer than appropriate. He made eye contact with Luigi, frowning as he held a stare.

"The husband of my sister," Petrice graciously introduced, noticing that introductions had suddenly become awkward.

"How do you do?" Luigi greeted.

Noah looked into Luigi's dark and aged eyes, catching an instant of familiarity in the Italian's expression, though he couldn't remember from where. "Where do I know you from?" he asked brusquely.

"Luigi lives in Rapid City," Petrice offered.

"Really," Noah said, allowing the man's hand to drop. He put his arm around Tillie, taking a step backward.

Luigi nodded, continuing to lock eyes with Noah as he said, "Perhaps we have seen one another around town."

Noah stared hard into Luigi's expression, and asked, "So, what brings you all the way to New York?"

"A convention," Luigi answered.

"A convention of what?" Noah gruffly prodded, and Tillie almost laughed. She bit her lower lip in an effort to hide her smile, wondering what thoughts were rolling around in her suspicious husband's head.

"Psychology," Luigi answered. "I am a counselor."

"Oh," Noah said with a nod, letting out a deep breath. He took a firm grasp of Tillie's hand, backing away. "Hey, I promised Angel a dance. I'll catch you guys later." With that, Noah turned and led Tillie away.

Petrice laughed nervously as he watched them go. "They are newlyweds," he explained.

Marquette looked at Luigi with a curious expression and asked, "Psychology? Last we heard you had graduated with a pharmaceuticals degree."

Luigi smiled and admitted, "Yes. However, I did return to the university and obtained a master's degree in social work."

"How did you come to be located in Rapid City, South Dakota?" Vincenzo asked.

"There is a high concentration of troubled youth in the area and that is my specialty," Luigi replied. "I counsel young men who wish to leave the gang life and rehabilitate themselves."

Petrice smiled with approval. "A noble cause," he said with a nod.

Tara watched Luigi's eyes and his mouth as he prattled on about his *noble cause*. He had *no* Andreotti family resemblance, and his diction was way off. His accent was more *Siciliano* than *Tuscano*. And though she hadn't seen him in nearly thirty-four years, she found it hard to believe that this was the man Luigi Andreotti had become.

At a table that seated just the three of them, A.J. and Laura attempted to give Jake another lesson in knightly obligations. While Jake behaved like the perfect knight *most* of the time, there were still a few things about him that could be polished up a bit.

A.J.'s dark eyes shined as he smiled at his stepbrother. "You see, Jake," he began, "Uncle Marq says chivalry is an art and that is the most important thing a man can learn, second only to the acceptance of Jesus as our Savior and Lord."

Jake frowned and shook his head. "I don't think women like that stuff anymore," he muttered. His blue eyes danced with delight when he saw Laura frown at his response. His lopsided smile was exactly like his father's, as he grew more to look like Noah with every passing day.

"Oh yes they do," Laura quipped. "Noah does it for Mom, and you need to submit to this for Heidi."

"Why?" Jake questioned.

A.J. sighed with a smile. "Uncle Marq says that the preciousness of women has been diminished and it's very important that the few knights that are left in the world, *like us*, perform our chivalrous actions in public so others will learn by our example."

Jake relaxed his frown. "Okay," he relented. "What do you want me to do now?"

A.J. scratched his chin. He rose from his seat, and Jake was again amazed at the height A.J. had reached over the last few years. The kid was a good five inches over the six-foot mark, and his shoulders were very broad. He looked just like his late father in his black tuxedo, especially when the light caught his wavy, blue-black hair.

"Come here, Laura," A.J. said with a smile. She stood from her chair beside her brother. Laura was only five feet tall and built like her grandmother. It was comical to see her tiny shape next to her brother's larger one.

A.J. looked at Jake and said, "Now, pretend that you are about to sit down with a girl." He slid a chair out from the table. "Wait for her to stand in front of it...like this..." A.J. politely waited for Laura to take her place in front of the chair, and he continued, "Then you slide it under her like this." He slid the chair with grace under Laura and she took her seat. A.J. slid out his own chair and took a seat beside her.

Jake frowned skeptically. "And that makes girls happy?" he asked.

"Oh, yes," Laura answered with a smile. "Mom *loves* it and so does Heidi."

"Now," A.J. continued, "Laura, pretend that you have to use the ladies' room."

Laura nodded and stood from her chair. A.J. stood immediately from his seated position. "You always stand when a lady stands," he instructed.

Jake stood from his chair with a curious expression. "Why?" he questioned.

"Because it's polite," A.J. explained. "And also, if we were sitting at this table and Laura walked up to us, we would need to stand to acknowledge her presence."

Jake frowned. "What for?"

"Because," A.J. answered, "as men we need to show her that we appreciate her."

"And girls *really like* this?" Jake questioned.

"Yes," A.J. and Laura answered at once.

"Well," Jake began, his expression becoming mischievous. "What if she's a *feminist*? They're *totally* against stuff like this."

"You still stand," A.J. affirmed with a serious expression. "She's still a lady, whether or not she knows it, and it's our responsibility as knights to emphasize her preciousness."

*****

Captain Angelo Caselli saw his sister at the punch bowl, surprised that she was already there. She hadn't expected to leave Denver until late in the afternoon, and had even called him to say that she wouldn't arrive until well after the party had started.

"What are you doing here so early, Deputy?" He asked, putting his hand on her shoulder, giving her a soft kiss on her cheek.

"Hey, Angelo," she greeted, returning his kiss. "I just got here."

"Have you talked to Papa and Ma`ma?"

Alyssa nodded, gesturing toward their parents and uncles, who were still visiting with Luigi a short distance away. "Have you had a chance to talk to *that* character yet?"

"Yep," Angelo answered with a faint smile. "He's a *creep*. I can't believe they used to be friends."

"Well, he's probably changed a lot," Alyssa suggested.

"I think it's amazing that Uncle Marq and Aunt Tara would even speak to him."

"I think it's weird that he just *happened* by," Alyssa mused. "I got a bad feeling about that."

Angelo raised one of his brows. "So, are ya gonna check him out?"

Alyssa narrowed her eyes in Luigi's direction. "As soon as I get back," she murmured.

Angelo laughed, leaning close to his sister's ear. "By the way," he whispered, "how do you carry your piece and your badge when you're dressed like *that*?"

"I manage."

"Ty tells me you are threatening to leave school again," Guiseppi said as he waltzed his pretty granddaughter around the small floor. She was just a hair taller than her grandfather, and a good six inches shorter than her mother. She had Petrice's soft, wavy hair and Elaine's almond-shaped blue eyes.

Gabriella groaned. "Grandpa, I may have said something in an exasperated moment, but I *didn't* mean it. I only have a year left. I'll stick it out."

"A child must be educated," Guiseppi persisted.

"I know, Grandpa."

"Will you scare your Papa this fall when it comes time to return?" Guiseppi asked with a frown.

"No," Gabriella promised, smiling into her grandfather's old, black eyes. "I promise to be the sacrificial lamb and go without a fight."

Guiseppi laughed. "That is my girl. Now, what do you have planned for your future?"

Gabriella shrugged and admitted, "Don't know. I know I'm supposed to write, and Ma`ma wants me to write, but the only thing I've been able to get published are a few articles in the *Post*. And that's just because

Ma`ma writes for them and Papa is that mean old Senator from New York." She sighed and her blue eyes suddenly sparkled with delight. "You know, Grandpa, I'd rather get married and live on a farm in Iowa than stay in this God-forsaken part of the country."

Guiseppi smiled. "And how about that nice, young congressman from Iowa? Have you seen him at all?"

"No. Papa manages to keep me steered clear of him. I wasn't even invited to his last fundraiser. Can you imagine that Grandpa? Senator Caselli's daughter wasn't even *invited* to a fundraiser that he *personally* hosted. Do you know how *stupid* that looks?"

Guiseppi chuckled. "Would you like me to speak with the Senator about this?"

"Yes. And then you can tell him that I'm old enough to date now. Good grief, I turn twenty-one this month and I haven't been out with anyone but my brother and Ty Hansen."

"Well, has anyone asked?" Guiseppi questioned.

Gabriella sighed heavily. "Are you kidding? Everybody's terrified of my father. I guess they're all afraid they'll wind up in the middle of a congressional subcommittee investigation if they so much as *look* at me."

Guiseppi laughed and said, "Gabby, dearest, you are even more comical than my own Angel. With your wit and charm, I cannot imagine the Lord will make you wait much longer."

Tillie nestled in Noah's arms as they waltzed around the dance floor with a few other couples. Occasionally, they'd glance back at the awkward group her brothers were still in just a short distance from them.

"He's *really weird*," Noah whispered.

"He gives me the creeps," Tillie whispered. "Did you see him with Alyssa?"

"I thought Vincenzo was gonna smack him or something," Noah replied with a faint smile. "What *is* it with that guy?"

The song ended and the couples on the floor stopped dancing to applaud. Luigi bid Tillie's brothers good-bye and started making his way across the small room, heading directly toward Noah and Tillie.

"Oh, brother, here he comes," Noah said, attempting to speak without moving his lips.

Tillie whispered, "If he asks me to dance, I'm gonna pretend to faint. Okay? Drag me out by my feet and make it look good."

Noah laughed and nodded.

"Mr. and Mrs. Hansen," Luigi said with a charming smile. "I am leaving and thought I should say good-bye."

Noah smiled politely, extending his hand to Luigi, who took it and gave it a shake. "Have a nice convention," he said.

"Thank you," Luigi replied. He seemed to leer at Tillie when he reached for her hand, saying, "Mrs. Hansen, how lovely you are. Perhaps the three of us could get together sometime."

Tillie, trying not to gulp, covered her appalled impression of the man with a gracious smile. "Perhaps," she said, working her hand out of his long grasp, taking a step backward.

"I shall give you a call," Luigi promised. "It was nice meeting both of you."

"You too," Noah said, trying not to frown.

Luigi turned, and left them. Tillie let out the breath she didn't realize she'd been holding.

"We'll get together with *him* when hell freezes over," Noah muttered.

Chapter 2

Laura peered from behind the small, wooden bar in the ballroom of Uncle Patty's yacht. *I hope he doesn't see me,* she thought. *What's he doing over there? Does Uncle Patty know about this?* She held her breath as she watched Mr. Andreotti going through a box of papers. He took them out, one at a time, and read them over and over. *What's he looking for?* She wondered. She felt a fly on her face, and as she reached to shoo it away, her hand knocked a glass out of the bar, smashing it on the floor. Mr. Andreotti looked up in surprise, dropped his handful of papers, and charged at her. Laura screamed at the top of her lungs....

"Laura, wake up!" Gabriella's gentle voice was attempting to calm her screaming cousin. She reached for Laura's shoulder, giving it a soft shake. "Wake up, Laura. You're having a bad dream."

Laura's black eyes flew open and she sat straight up in the bed. She was breathing heavily, her face and neck drenched in perspiration.

"Hey, kiddo," Gabriella said, taking a seat on the edge of the bed. "You okay?"

Laura shook her head, answering between breaths, "I had the *worst* dream — that creepy old man at the party last night."

Gabriella grimaced. "Yuck. What did you dream about *him*?"

"I caught him looking through some of Uncle Patty's papers," Laura began. "Then he saw me and I think he was gonna *kill* me." She shuddered. "There's something *weird* about that guy."

"Definitely something creepy. Now, come on. Ma`ma made all of us breakfast and Grandpa wants to go fishing. Wanna get up?"

Laura nodded. Aunt Ellie's pancakes would be the perfect thing to get rid of her nightmare memory.

West on Tibbett's Point Road, toward the old light house, Petrice and Elaine Caselli had made their home for twenty-two years. Originally built in 1854, the three story brick home had been in desperate need of repair and restoration. Under the masterful direction of Elaine, the contractors had created a work of art.

Available to Petrice and their children was a considerable amount of private beach, and from their deck they watched ships from all over the world pass through the blue waters of the St. Lawrence River and Lake Ontario. When the Senate went on summer break, they made tracks for Cape Vincent, with their fishing gear and spent hours off the shore at the east end of their small village. Their favorite catch was walleye, and if they properly cleaned and filleted the fish, Elaine fried them up for dinner.

All of Petrice's family stayed the night. The adults, as well as Annie, were in the third floor guest rooms, and cousins bunked together in the bedrooms on the second floor. Elaine was up early, along with her sisters-in-law, cooking sausages and pancakes for their hungry family. The children were all fed first, even the older ones, and the adults waited until last. Guiseppi and Rosa ate with their grandchildren, and reminded them to put on their warmest clothes so they could go out and do some fishing.

Annie was an early riser, like her mother, and she patiently watched the frantic breakfast preparations from Noah's lap. She ate the pancakes he chopped into small pieces, and occasionally offered him a slimy bite. He always accepted her offers, and she'd smile into his eyes. Even though everyone said she had his eyes, Noah saw the reflection of her mother in Annie's expression. *This is the best part of being a father*, Noah thought as she slipped him another piece of pancake.

The hot topic of conversation that morning was none other than "*that lecherous Luigi Andreotti.*"

"Somebody needed to get him a fresh bucket," Elaine said, seating herself with the last stack of pancakes.

"For what?" Petrice asked, looking up from his breakfast with a curious expression.

Tillie elbowed his side and dryly replied, "To catch the drool."

Noah couldn't help himself and he laughed out loud. Annie didn't know what her father was laughing about, but she clapped her pudgy little hands together and laughed as well.

Noah gave his little baby a squeeze and a soft kiss on the top of her curly head. "That was funny. Isn't your ma`ma funny?" he chortled.

Annie giggled, "Ma`ma's funny."

Petrice looked across the table, allowing them a small smile as he replied, "As a matter of fact, I saw no drool. I saw our old friend trying to be cordial with our wives."

"You'd better never get *that cordial* with someone else's wife," Elaine pretended to admonish with a frown.

"I am afraid to admit it, my dear brother," Vincenzo said politely, "but I believe that our old friend, Luigi, has developed some lecherous tendencies."

Marquette's eyes opened with surprise. "*Some?*"

"He *totally* grossed me out," Tillie said, and her sisters-in-law laughed. Tillie rolled her eyes. "Sorry...I've got teenagers in the house and sometimes I sound like one."

"Poor old Luigi," Petrice lamented with a wistful expression. "He used to be such a nice, young man. He lived only to please his father."

"He lied right to our faces," Marquette frowned. "He lied to me in 1960, and he lied again to you in 1962. Both times, he knew of Tara's location, and yet he did not reveal it to either of us —"

"But his father," Petrice interrupted kindly. "You know that Lorenzo and Sergio were very close."

"He certainly looks different than I remembered," Tara remarked. "I do not remember that dreadful scar he now carries on his left cheek. And the years have not been very good to him. He has a hard and bitter look about him that was not typical of the Andreottis. How long has his family been gone?"

"Fifteen years," Petrice answered. "And he can barely bring himself to speak of it."

"What happened to them?" Noah asked, accepting another bite of pancake from his daughter.

"There was a dreadful fire at the winery and all were lost," Petrice answered. "All except for Luigi and the workers. Lorenzo made sure to get the workers out first."

"That was noble," Vincenzo commented.

Marquette nodded. "We did hear of a fire at the winery some years ago, but I do not recall ever hearing of Lorenzo's passing."

"But everyone in *Chianti* knows of the falling out between the Casellis and the Andreottis, and many have chosen sides," Vincenzo reminded. "Most would certainly not bring Lorenzo's death to your attention. By your own admission, Marquette, there is still anger and resentment towards you for marrying Tara D'Annenci. She was promised to Luigi, and her father passed before the age of consent."

Marquette rolled his eyes. "A thirty-year grudge match is not of God."

"But it is real," Vincenzo continued. "And it has kept you at odds with many in *Chianti*."

"He seems taller," Tara mused.

"So, who manages the vineyards now?" Noah asked.

"He told us that he has workers who take care of it," Vincenzo answered.

"Is he a citizen now, or what?" Tillie asked.

Marquette nodded. "He received dual citizenship a few years ago. He lives between the two countries much the same as Tara and I do."

"By the way," Vincenzo said, "and not to change this most interesting subject, but are we all planning to attend the reunion at Angel and Noah's place?" He heard a murmur of yeses all around the table in response, and Vincenzo continued, "Angelo has taken leave, and Alyssa is also planning to attend."

"Our kids will be there," Elaine added. She looked at her husband curiously. "Did you say something about your secretary getting us rooms at the Rushmore Plaza?"

"Yes I did," Petrice answered. "We will have rooms on the same floor, next door to one another."

"Hey, I sent Sam and Becky-Lynn an invitation," Tillie said, smiling in Kate's direction. "But I haven't heard from them yet."

Kate's smile faded as she replied, "I'll give him a call and see what's up."

*****

Guiseppi was delighted to see that his sons and Noah had ventured to the beach where all of the grandchildren were fishing together. He smiled at Petrice, reaching for one of his hands. "Patty, my boy," he said, "We must talk. Can we take a short walk?"

"Of course, Papa."

"We will go this way," Guiseppi said, hooking his arm into his son's, leading him away from the others. As he shuffled along, he turned his face into the sun and took a deep breath of the cold air blowing across Lake Ontario. "Such a beautiful place. You must certainly love it here."

"We do."

"I will be eighty-two come this October," Guiseppi continued.

"Eighty-two?"

Guiseppi gave Petrice's arm a soft pat. "Goodness but the time flies!" he exclaimed. "Sometimes it feels as if it was only last week we came to America and your sister was but a babe."

"And look at her now. Some of her babes are nearly grown adults," Petrice commented.

Guiseppi's eyes sparkled with delight...*he is playing into my hands this time!* "Yes, yes they are," he admitted. "But they are not nearly as grown adults as your beautiful babes." He pretended to frown as if to be thoughtful. "Now, let me think, Patty...are your babes the eldest of my grandchildren?"

Petrice laughed and shook his head. "No, Papa. Vincenzo's babes are older."

"Oh, yes. I forget, I guess, because Gabriella seems to be so mature."

Petrice groaned. "What has she put you up to?"

Guiseppi pretended to be aghast. "Nothing! Why would you say such a thing?"

Petrice stopped walking, facing his father as he said, "I do *not* want her with a politician —"

"But she seems to care for the young man a great deal."

"She *does not care* for the young man," Petrice protested with a frown. "She is *infatuated* with him, and on top of several other problems I can see developing in their relationship, he is *Jewish*."

"Do you not believe that the Jews need the Lord as well as the rest of us?" Guiseppi asked with a smile. "Perhaps your beautiful Gabriella is just what Mr. Goldstein needs to lead him to the Lord.

Petrice rolled his eyes. "My Gabby has been carrying on about young Mr. Goldstein since she was seventeen. She has allowed herself to be caught up in some fantasy about an older man. Good grief, I must have been a *terrible father* or she would not want such an older man."

"You know, Patty, our Angel was seventeen when she met Noah —"

"Oh, Papa, that was *completely* different. You and Ma`ma prayed for Noah for fifteen years before they even laid eyes upon one another."

Guiseppi shrugged his old shoulders as he said, "Does it really matter, son?"

"Of course it matters!" Petrice retorted. "I do not want my daughter with a politician. Especially not right now. We are practically in the middle of an impeachment and Mr. Goldstein does not have the time to court a young lady, much less figure out a way to get himself saved. I am certain that God does not want this particular man for my Gabriella."

Guiseppi took a deep breath, offering with a smile, "Let us consider Mr. Goldstein for just a moment. He is very well respected and he never speaks out of line, especially when he is with his elders. He has manners like I have only observed in my own sons. He has been compliant with whatever restrictions you place upon your daughter, when we both know good and well he *is* interested in her."

"No, Papa. She is *too young*. And what if Mr. Goldstein is a blackguard in disguise? Have you already forgotten what we went through with Alex Martin? What he put our Angel through? Do you want that for my Gabriella?"

"Of course not, Patty. But you know, Alex never fooled Marquette. It was the rest of us who would not listen."

Petrice sighed. "And what if I allow the two of them to become involved? Say, for instance, we all see through his blackguardly disguise, but my Gabby does not. Then what will I do?"

Guiseppi chuckled. "I do not believe that Gabby will choose a blackguard."

"Angel did."

Guiseppi shook his head in adamant disagreement. "Angel did not *choose* Alex. She chose Noah, and I *gave* her Alex." He took a breath, frowning into Petrice's eyes. "You pray about what I have said, Petrice. I am nearly eighty-two years old and I know something of what I am talking about."

"So did ya tell Angelo that Harry called ya?" Michael asked, elbowing Ty, who was reeling in yet another fish. Ty had caught more fish during his visits to New York than Michael and Gabriella combined in their entire lives.

"You mean that guy from the Baltimore Orioles?" Angelo asked, giving his reel a tug, finding nothing there.

Ty chuckled. "Guys, he actually came to see me in person. Pulled me out of a lecture day before yesterday."

"They must want you *bad*," Michael said with a grin. "What did you tell him?"

"I told him that I have to talk to my dad first," Ty answered.

Angelo smiled and shook his head. "That's awesome, Ty. Are they gonna put you on a farm team?"

"Nope." Ty looked at his companions and smiled. "They're gonna put me on the *pitcher's* mound."

Michael laughed and slapped his thigh. "Oh come on! Are you serious?"

"Serious as a heart attack," Ty replied.

"Did you tell your dad yet?" Angelo asked.

"Haven't had the chance," Ty answered. "We flew commercial yesterday and barely made it to the party."

Angelo laughed and shook his head. "Ty Hansen, you're one cool kid."

Ty chuckled. "Yes I am."

Angelo and Michael laughed.

"Hey, here he comes," Michael said, smiling and waving at Noah as he walked toward them. "He's gonna be so happy for you, Ty."

"Hey what's up over here?" Noah asked with a smile, giving Ty a pat on the shoulder. "I haven't had a chance to talk to you since you got here."

"And you're just the man he wants to see," Michael said, his blue eyes sparkling with amusement. Noah was struck with how much he looked like Petrice. Michael had his mother's blue eyes, but his personality was pure Italian.

Ty handed Angelo his pole and asked, "Would you watch this for me?"

"You bet," Angelo answered as he took the pole. "Maybe I'll catch something for once."

Ty and Noah walked a little way down the beach. They found themselves some rocks to sit on where they could watch the rest of the grandchildren with their poles. Alyssa had stopped fishing quite a while before, and she and Kate appeared to be having quite a discussion off by themselves.

"They look like they're into it," Ty said, slyly pointing his thumb in Kate and Alyssa's direction.

Noah took a breath and whispered, "Kate thinks that Alyssa is working too much and she wants her to take some time off this summer."

"Hm," Ty quietly mused. He turned his focus back to Noah, smiling into his father's eyes. "Dad, I've got some really strange news."

"*Strange* news?"

"Well," Ty began, taking a deep breath. "You know, we never even talked about this, and now all of a sudden it's happened..." He hesitated again. "A scout came and talked to me this past week."

Noah felt his heart fall. "No kidding?" he whispered. *I know what that means.* "Well, what about school? You've still got a year left."

"I know," Ty replied with a nod, and Noah saw the delighted expression in his son's gray eyes. "They wanna put me directly on the team, Dad. No farm team stuff."

"Well…" Noah tried to get back some of the wind that had been knocked out of him from Ty's announcement. "What are you going to do?" Ty was nearly finished with school…*and almost home.*

"Well, I'm talking to you about it. I guess I was thinking you might tell me what to do."

"I can't tell you what to do, Ty," Noah answered with a soft smile. "Except that you must know I can hardly stand being so far away from you. I was really looking forward to you coming back to Rapid and working with me."

"I know, but this is something neither one of us ever dreamed would happen."

Noah swallowed. "Well, what team are we talking about?"

"Baltimore Orioles. So my home base would be only about forty miles away from D.C. I could still get together with Michael and Gabby." He laughed and rolled his eyes. "At least until she leaves town next year, but Michael won't graduate until 2001."

As Noah looked at his oldest son, memories flashed back to the time Ty fell in love with baseball. He was three years old and went to the circus. Someone was selling inflatable bats and balls and Ty wanted a set. They played ball for hours that summer. He remembered Ty's Auntie Mona sewing his nickname to the back of his jerseys…*Tiger….*

When his father remained so quiet and thoughtful, Ty said, "Dad."

Noah took a deep breath, offering Ty a faint smile as he said, "You're amazing, Tiger —" Noah's voice caught, but he quickly smiled and nodded. He reached for his son, putting his arms around him. "Do it, Tiger. Tell the man that you wanna do it."

"Are you sure, Dad?"

Noah sighed, "I'm sure. But you're gonna have to come and see me and Angel, and the kids as often as you can."

"I will."

"Okay." Noah held his son as tightly as he could. *This is the worst part of being a father.*

Michael left Angelo fishing alone and went to ask Gabriella what she'd set their grandfather up to — as Guiseppi and Petrice were having an animated argument just a few yards down the shoreline. When Vincenzo saw that Angelo was alone, he joined him on the shore.

"I can only imagine it has something to do with Congressman Goldstein," Vincenzo remarked.

"I imagine," Angelo agreed, reeling in yet another empty line. He sighed, set the pole aside and looked at his father.

"So, tell me when is your time with the Air Force finished?" Vincenzo asked.

"April, '99," Angelo answered, taking a deep breath. "But I'm up for promotion, Papa. In all likelihood, my next assignment will be the Pentagon."

Vincenzo looked confused. "How long will you stay there?" he asked.

"Probably four years," Angelo answered, and his dark eyes shined with an expression that was unfamiliar to his father. "And you know, Papa, Michael's gonna move heaven and earth to be stationed at the Pentagon when he graduates in '01."

Vincenzo felt as if someone had knocked the wind out of him. He whispered, "What has changed your mind?"

"Papa, I can't explain it, but I feel compelled to go —"

"You feel *compelled* to go?" Vincenzo retorted with a frown. "You and I have made plans, Angelo. You promised me that you would return to Reata and start a family."

"And I'll still do that, Papa." Angelo said, reaching for his father's hand. "Please, don't be angry. I'll be done with my tour at the Pentagon in '03, and *then* I'll return to Reata —"

Vincenzo jerked his hand out of Angelo's and barked, "No! You will never come home and our lineage will die with me —"

"Papa, please listen to me. This is the last tour, I promise —"

"You do not even *date*, Angelo!" Vincenzo scolded with a shake of his index finger. "You have *no intention* of finding a bride and making a life! You care only for the things of this world, and how *important* you can become!"

"Papa, that's not true," Angelo angrily defended. "I have prayed and prayed about this decision, and I feel compelled to go."

"And I suppose you will tell me that it is the Lord who *compels* you to renege on a deal you made with your father!" Vincenzo shouted. "I cannot believe this day. It is the *worst* of my life!" With that, Vincenzo turned around and stomped away from his son.

*****

Angelo left without explanation that afternoon, and his relatives wondered what had happened. Vincenzo was quiet, keeping to himself for the rest of the day. He didn't even try to talk to Kate, who was also quiet after her talk with Alyssa. Alyssa left shortly after her brother, and a sullen cloud settled over the Casellis' weekend.

Michael did his best to patch together information, relaying it back to his cousins when they went to Antonelli's for a pizza. Rosa suggested they "*get out of Dodge*" for just the afternoon as she and Guiseppi wanted to speak with their children.

While Rosa listened to the wives of her sons, and her own daughter, weeping with anguish at the choices of their children, Guiseppi listened to his sons, and the husband of his daughter.

The men were seated in low chairs in the sand on the beach. They were dressed in jeans and warm jackets, protecting them somewhat from the cool wind blowing across the lake. The sky clouded over and the temperature dropped. Guiseppi was more than just a little disgruntled about the situation. He wanted to have their discussion *inside*, over a delicious pot of hot afternoon tea. *But no*. The other men insisted upon being men and toughing it out at the beach.

Vincenzo puffed at his pipe with agitation, staring into the clouded horizon. "Angelo has traded my legacy for his career," he lamented. "And his sister is no more interested in settling than he is." He snorted, twitching his head in a strange way, mocking himself, "Happy birthday to me."

Petrice shook his head and moaned, "Gabby wants to run off with a man of a different faith. Where did I go wrong?" He sighed heavily. "At least I still have my Michael."

Noah took a breath and softly said, "Ty was supposed to come home and work for me." He shrugged and looked at his brothers-in-law. "I guess I can wait until this ball thing is out of his system."

Petrice and Vincenzo scowled at their brother-in-law, but Marquette laughed. They turned and looked at their brother questioningly.

"How foolish you seem to me," he said with a smile and a wink. "Try not to feel *too* sorry for yourselves." His smile faded. "My Tara and I would give anything for your struggles. My legacy died the summer I shared the mumps with our dearest Angel. You, my brothers, have at least had your *very trivial* struggles."

Guiseppi smiled at his sons and Noah, and agreed, "Marquette is right. These difficult times with your children are only for a brief season. Mark my words, gentlemen, they will all come home to you, and God will bless. You have raised your sons and daughters in the way of the Lord, and that is something they never outgrow."

Chapter 3
Rapid City, South Dakota

Jason Patterson sat at his messy desk, staring down at the matchbook he'd taken from Senator Caselli's yacht. "Circle Q Bar & Grill," he mumbled aloud. He'd never heard of the place, or least there wasn't a place by that name in Rapid City or the surrounding area. If there was, he'd know about it. City or state were absent on the matchbook, and that struck him as unusual. Directory assistance didn't list anything either. *It's probably some little hick bar between Rapid City and New York,* he thought, *but exactly who's there and who left the matchbook behind on Senator Caselli's yacht? Is this a missing link of some sort? Or am I headed down another dead end?*

He sighed and rolled his eyes. *Of all things I just had to run myself into a U.S. Marshal. Good grief. She'll probably turn me in the moment she returns to work. But, then again, maybe not. Maybe she, along with her uncle, the famous Senator Caselli, is in on whatever Andreotti's up to. They might just let everything go in order to keep the attention off themselves. They must know that I'll talk if they attempt to have me removed.*

"Hi, son," Joe Patterson's friendly voice interrupted Jason's thoughts. He looked up to see his father standing in the doorway of his office.

Joe Patterson had retired from the United States Air Force and joined the Rapid City Police Force in 1968. Originally from Valdosta, Georgia, he'd joined the Air Force as a young man, and was promoted to the rank of major before deciding to retire after twenty years of service to his country. His last assignment had been Ellsworth Air Force Base. When he retired from the military, he and his wife remained in the area with their eight-year old son, Jason. Joe was promoted to detective in 1972 by the Rapid City Police Force, and it was a position he'd held proudly for the last twenty-six years.

"Hi, Dad," Jason greeted with a smile, as Joe took a seat in the old chair in front of his desk. He noticed that Joe's blond hair had grayed remarkably in the past year. He wondered how many more years his father would put in on the force. After all, Joe was nearly sixty-five years old.

"Where were you this weekend?" Joe asked. "Your mom's been lookin' all over for you."

Jason looked away, answering, "I had a few days off."

"Oh, come on, Jason," Joe prodded with a frown. "Where were you?"

Jason sighed heavily and looked at his father with a wry expression. "I followed Andreotti to New York," he answered.

Joe's mouth dropped open in surprise. Jason rose quickly from his chair, closing his office door. He took a seat on the corner of his desk and looked at his astounded father.

Joe slumped in his chair. "Son, you shouldn't have done that," he moaned.

"I know it, Dad, but you'll never guess who Andreotti met with."

Joe rolled his eyes. "Jason, you can't be doing stuff like that. Did you call anyone —"

"Senator Caselli," Jason blurted. "Andreotti met with —"

"Petrice Caselli?" Joe sat up in his chair.

Jason nodded. "And his niece says she's a U.S. Marshall. I've gotta check it out, but I got the feeling she's telling the truth. I'm willing to bet there's something really bad goin' down and it involves the Senator. He's covering it up or he's got people covering up for Andreotti."

Joe was flabbergasted. "Caselli's been around for at least twenty years. I can hardly believe he'd be mixed up in anything with Andreotti."

Jason raised one eyebrow, adding, "Caselli's *sister* lives here in Rapid City."

"That doesn't mean anything," Joe scoffed with a frown. "She's lived here for years. Your mother has even worked for the woman."

"I think it's a connection," Jason said, handing his father the matchbook.

"What's this?"

"Don't know," Jason answered. "Somebody left it behind on Caselli's yacht and I think it was Andreotti. Caselli doesn't smoke, but I've seen Luigi with cigars." He took a deep breath and slowly exhaled. "Caselli's brother smokes a pipe. If I can find the Circle Q, I think I can find somebody that knows something. This could be the link I need to put it all together."

*****

Sal paced his elegant office with poise and confidence, pausing at the window behind his desk, gazing over the city. He sipped at his snifter of brandy and took a thoughtful draw from his cigar. He turned to look at the younger man seated in front of his desk, giving him a charming, but deceptive, smile. "Your information proved to be very useful," he cackled. "I have made a deposit into your account."

The young man hid his grimace beneath his dark expression by looking at his folded hands lying in his lap. This meeting was the last thing he wanted. On the other hand, he didn't have any other choices. *This* was the reason he'd put himself into position all those years ago. *Just in case.*

Sal cunningly raised one eyebrow. "Brandy?"

"No thanks," the younger man answered. *Isn't nine o'clock in the morning just a little early to start your drinking?* He straightened his black tie, getting to his feet. "I really need to be going."

Sal took a sip of his drink and sighed as he said, "Hansen *did* seem to recognize me, though the idiot could not remember from where. Apparently I have not outgrown the resemblance of my dear brother — though Marquette and Tara did not have a clue." He let go with a wicked cackle. When he caught his breath, he continued, "But they were so filled with blinding, Christian forgiveness they could not see past the noses on their faces." He laughed again.

"I must leave," the younger man said, turning toward the door.

Sal laughed again. "Do not rush off, Antonio, for I will be needing your services in just a few other matters...and I will pay you well."

*****

From her office in Denver, Colorado, Alyssa placed a call to Shondra Payne, who was still the managing partner of Martin, Martin & Dale, A.P.C.L., in Rapid City, South Dakota. Shondra had worked for the Martins since 1968. She was a young lawyer back then, and only managed staff and files. Now she was sixty-one years old and the managing partner, a position she inherited when Alex Martin III, died in a plane crash five years ago.

"Well hello, Alyssa." Shondra said with a smile. "Gads, I haven't heard from you in months. Whatcha got going on?"

Alyssa chuckled. "Oh, you know, same ole, same ole. Shootin' the bad guys, askin' questions later."

Shondra laughed. "Well what could you possibly want with little old me?" In the background she could hear Alyssa clicking away at her computer keyboard.

"I need to know if you know anything, right off the top of your head, about a Rapid City detective named Jason Patterson."

"Sure do," Shondra answered. "His mother is the city's mayor right now. Jacqueline Holliday Patterson."

"No kidding?" Alyssa coolly replied. "I don't have that...well...." She hesitated as she clicked a few more keys. "Maybe I can get it in a second."

"Jason's quite a character," Shondra went on. "He's in the paper at least once a week."

"For what?"

"Well, last week his mother announced her intention to run for reelection, and on the same page, Jason had cracked a *huge* murder case. I can't imagine Rapid City won't vote her back in. Having a kid like that on the police force sure hasn't hurt her career.

"Hm. Pretty smart guy?"

"I'd say so," Shondra answered. "We've worked with him a few times on different matters that we've had up here, and I was always impressed." She took a breath. "By the way, are you coming to the Casellis' reunion?"

"Sure am."

"Robert and I were invited," Shondra said.

"Are you coming?"

"Yes," Shondra answered. "Have you heard from your Uncle Sam? Do you know if they're coming?"

Alyssa swallowed and took a soft breath. "Actually, Shondra, I don't know. I'm flying over to Sioux Falls tomorrow afternoon on some business and I thought I'd stop by and see how he's doing."

"It would sure be great to see him again."

"Hey, I'll call you when I get to town," Alyssa said abruptly.

"Sounds great," Shondra said with a grin. She could tell that Alyssa was already on to the next thing and couldn't afford to waste time on small talk.

"Say hi to Roger," Alyssa added quickly. "Love ya."

"Love you, too." And the line went dead. Shondra smiled as she hung up the receiver. Sometimes Alyssa reminded her of Alex.

Alyssa read the information on Detective Jason Patterson displayed on her computer terminal. He graduated from Rapid City Central High School in 1988, served four years in the United States Army, then went to work for the Rapid City Police Force in 1992. Jason was promoted to detective in 1995. His father was also a detective on the same force, and his mother was listed as the current mayor of Rapid City, South Dakota. It was also interestingly noted that Jacqueline Holliday Patterson claimed to be a direct descendant of the infamous Doc Holliday. Alyssa smiled and shook her head when she read that.

"Doc Holliday," she muttered under her breath. She sighed, punched a key to clear her screen, and began a new search. "Now, let's see what we can find out on Mr. Andreotti."

*****

For the past three and a half years, Jacqueline Holliday Patterson served as the first woman mayor of Rapid City, South Dakota. The voters were in love with her *and* her sharp detective son. She was a tall woman with sandy blonde hair, emerald green eyes, and a convincing personality.

Before winning the mayoral election, Jacqueline was a successful family law attorney. She hadn't lost a case in her entire career, though she came close once. It was the *worst* experience of her life, and she nearly stopped practicing law over it. Alex Martin III, South Dakota's best attorney general, sued his wife for divorce. He served the papers to her while she lay immobile in a hospital bed after being hit by a car. Through the entire, traumatizing ordeal, Mrs. Martin remained steadfast in her beliefs against divorce, refusing to engage in a legal battle with the attorney general. She even offered to settle a separate lawsuit Mr. Martin brought against both his wife and Noah Hansen. In the end, however, Mr. Martin dismissed both the divorce action and the additional lawsuit, and Mrs. Martin allowed him to move back home. Jacqueline was horrified at the turn of events, remaining bitter toward Mr. Martin until the day he died.

She quickly fanned through the pink slips on her desk, looking for a message from her son Jason.

"Mrs. Patterson."

Jacqueline looked up from her desk to see her elderly secretary, Veronica, coming through the door with several more of the pink slips.

"Your son tried to reach you while you were out," Veronica said, laying the messages on Jacqueline's desk.

"Thanks, Veronica," Jacqueline acknowledged, taking the messages, squinting for a better look. "By the way, did he say where he was this weekend?"

Veronica tittered in her old, sweet voice, "He doesn't tell me anything he doesn't want *you* to know, Mrs. Patterson."

Jacqueline half smiled.

The intercom on Jacqueline's desk buzzed and they heard the switchboard operator's voice announce, "Mrs. Patterson, Detective Patterson is on line two. Can you take the call?"

"Of course," Jacqueline answered, picking up the line. Veronica smiled and left Mrs. Patterson's office. "All right, where's my infamous son been?" Jacqueline asked.

"Hi, Mom. Dad said you've been trying to get a hold of me?"

"I have. Great Grandpa Holliday is having his one-hundredth birthday and I'd like to have a big family reunion in Valdosta in October. I figured if I let you know early enough, maybe you could squeak some time out of your schedule."

"I'm sure I can work something out."

"Can you come for dinner tonight?" Jacqueline asked.

"Maybe."

"Can you bring that nice girl, Kathy?"

Jason sighed. "I think she's got a boyfriend now."

"Hm." Jacqueline was perplexed. "That's not what I heard. Are ya sure?"

"Pretty sure, Mom — what time do you want me over at your place?"

Jacqueline sighed. "Six o'clock."

"Okay. Bye, Mom."

Jason hung up the phone before his mother could reply. He leaned back in his chair, glancing at the fax he'd gotten from a friend in the U.S. Marshall's Office. Alyssa's photo was in the top, left-hand corner and the information regarding her status was printed neatly along the side and bottom. *She really is a U.S. Marshall,* he thought with a heavy sigh. *Now, are the Casellis involved in whatever Andreotti's up to, or am I barking up the wrong tree?*

*****

"Good morning, Tessa," Tillie said as she stopped by the young girl's desk. Tessa Chambers was the receptionist at Hansen Development, LLC. She had blond hair, green eyes and a smile that could sweeten even the foulest of moods.

"Good morning, Tillie," Tessa greeted. "I bet you're looking for someone small."

Tillie nodded.

"They're in his office."

"Thanks." Tillie limped toward Noah's office. She knocked on the door and let herself in.

Annie was sitting in the middle of Noah's desk, wearing the cute little hard hat he'd picked up for her at a builders convention. She chased computer paper around the desk with a magic marker, while Noah talked on the phone, and attempted to steer the child clear of important documents at the same time. He looked up when he heard the door open, smiling with relief at his wife.

"Hey, I'll call ya right back," he said, hanging up. "Boy, am I glad to see you."

"Ma`ma!" Annie exclaimed, dropped her marker, and reached for Tillie. Tillie lifted the baby off Noah's desk and snuggled her close to give her a kiss.

"Have you been good for Papa?" Tillie asked, looking into the baby's eyes.

"Good as gold," Noah replied, coming around his desk to place a delicate kiss upon Tillie's lips. He smiled and looked at their baby daughter. "But I don't know how you get a thing done."

"Sometimes I don't!" Tillie said with a laugh.

Noah put his arm around Tillie and asked, "What did Burke have to say about the knee?" Tillie had sprained her knee on their way back from New York.

"Oh," Tillie groaned, rolling her eyes. "He doesn't know. Thinks it might be some arthritis or something. He wrapped it up tighter than a drum. Good grief, I can hardly walk. But, he gave me some pain pills and if the swelling doesn't go down, he says he wants to take a look."

"Surgery?" Noah raised both of his eyebrows.

Tillie nodded. "But, he can forget it until Annie gets a little bigger. I can't be off my feet like that. Besides, it's only a sprain. I'll go home and try to ice it for awhile."

Noah grinned. "*That's* never gonna work. What'll you do with little Miss Muffit?"

Tillie shrugged. "I don't know." She kissed the baby's cheek and looked at Noah. "But we'd better get out of your hair —"

"Tell you what, I *have* to go to this meeting because it's for your brothers' and your father's development, but I can come home right after that." He took one of Annie's tiny hands into his own, smiling into the baby's eyes. "And I can chase the baby while Ma`ma fixes her knee."

Annie smiled at her father and then gave his hand a tender kiss.

The loving glance father and daughter shared at that moment took Tillie's breath away. The miracle of Annie never failed to amaze her.

*****

"Here ya go," United States Deputy Marshal Jon Danielson said, laying a small file of papers on Alyssa's desk. He pulled out a chair and slid his tall, lanky body into it.

Alyssa first met Jon at Harvard and they'd served their internship together in Washington D.C. Both of them were surprised when they realized they were working together at the same office in Denver, Colorado. Jon was the quickest thinker Alyssa had ever met, and her best friend. When the mystery of Luigi Andreotti presented itself, other than her senior commander, Jon was the first person she called.

Alyssa reached for the file. "Anything interesting in here?" she asked.

Jon's dark eyes smiled as he answered, "Oh, I'd definitely follow him for a while." He scratched his chin and frowned. "He's an interesting character. His history begins with his college visa, that you already knew about, and then he left the country shortly after his graduation in 1964."

"When did he get his master's in social work?" Alyssa asked, slowly flipping through the pages in the file.

"It looks like he went back to Chicago on another VISA in 1975, and he stayed in the United States until he finished his master's, which was in 1979. From there, he went back to Italy, and it appears that he was there until 1985 because his address is consistently listed as Andreotti Vineyards & Cellars at *Castellina*, in *Chianti*, which is in the province of Tuscany. INS issued him a new visa in 1985, and his address of record became Jacksonville, Florida. He stayed there until he became a naturalized citizen in 1990. Shortly after that, his address changed to Washington, D.C. I learned that from his articulate tax record. He files like clockwork."

"D.C.?"

Jon nodded. "It appears that he lived there until July of 1994. His address changed to Rapid City, South Dakota at that time. He does have a license as an MSW, but I couldn't find a *residence* address on him in the Rapid City telephone directory, only a business. But you know, lots of professionals have unlisted phone numbers, and I have somebody looking into that."

"When was he approved for a dual citizenship?"

"I couldn't find that," Jon answered. "I don't think he has dual citizenship."

Alyssa frowned. "Then why did he tell us he did?"

*****

Noah's meeting ran longer than planned. Before he could go home to help Tillie, he rushed back into the office to pick up an estimate he knew Guiseppi would be calling about that evening. He noticed his office was unusually busy that afternoon, and everyone seemed to be on the telephone, including his assistant, Ben. *Good*, he thought, *I can just slip in, grab Guiseppi's estimate, and head for home.*

Unfortunately, Tessa saw him trying to escape and she caught him in the doorway of his office. "You've got a caller on line six," she said, shoving a stack of letters into his hands. She wrinkled her nose, explaining, "He's tried to call about a bzillion times and I can't get rid of him. Would you *please* take the call?"

Noah sighed, stepping back into his office. "I s'pose I'll have to. But nobody else. I gotta get home to help Angel."

"No problem," Tessa agreed, backing out of his office and returning to her desk.

Noah picked up the phone on his desk and punched line six. "Noah Hansen," he said, fanning out the letters Tessa had handed him, wondering why she always thought it was so important that he see the mail.

"Hello, Noah," came a familiar voice on the other end. "This is Luigi Andreotti."

Noah dropped the stack of letters onto his desk and frowned. "Hi, Luigi," he greeted curtly, but politely. "What can I do for you?" What he wanted to say was *why are you calling me, and what on earth could we possibly have in common?*

Luigi laughed pleasantly into the phone, and asked, "How was your trip home?"

"Fine." *Why's this guy calling me at work? Does he think we're gonna be buddies now because of some long lost friendship that he had with the Casellis?*

"I was wondering," Luigi began in his smooth voice, and Noah could just imagine him smiling like the Cheshire Cat. "Would you and your lovely wife like to join me for dinner sometime? We really should become acquainted. As you know, the Casellis and I go back a number of years."

Noah scowled. His first inclination was to not answer Luigi and slam down the phone. *No way* would he be taking Tillie around that lecherous old man. Mustering every bit of the politeness he possessed, he swallowed hard and answered, "I'll have to talk to my wife first, but thanks for the invite." And with that, Noah hung up the phone and glanced out his office door at Tessa, who was watching him intently.

Noah pointed down at the phone, frowning as he instructed, "If he calls back again, you can tell him that I'm *unavailable* and that I'll be *unavailable* for..." Noah hesitated and took a breath. "*Forever*."

Tessa giggled. "Yes, sir."

*****

He saw her as he drove along Highway 44, east of Rapid City. She appeared to be riding her favorite stallion today: the old black one with the temper. She had the cantankerous old thing under control and that made him smile. Her tiny figure was dressed in blue jeans and a work shirt and her dark hair was flying in the wind behind her.

As he neared the entrance of Rapid Valley Quarter Horse Ranch, she caught sight of his car, and galloped to where he always parked. When the horse came to a stop, she got off, quickly tied the reins to the fence post and ran over to see him.

"What are you doing here?" she asked with a surprised smile, putting her arms around him, giving his cheek a soft kiss. "I thought you were going out of town today?"

He returned her embrace, looking into the dark eyes that reminded him so much of their father. "I have the money we need for your mother's care."

She gasped, backing out of his arms. "But how —"

"Please, do not ask where it came from. Just know that it belongs to you, Charise."

"Oh, no!" she breathed, taking another step back. "It came from Sal, didn't it?"

He stood very still, looking at her, searching his soul for the words he might say to comfort her.

"Answer me, Antonio," she demanded, her eyes filling with horror and regret.

He slowly began to nod, whispering, "Yes. It came from Sal."

She gasped. "What have you agreed to do for him?"

He shook his head. "That is not important. What matters is that your mother will have the care she requires and we will not have to move her."

She shook her head disgustedly, turning away. "Oh, Antonio, Papa told us to stay away from Sal," she said.

"I know that," he said, putting his hand on her shoulder. "But I do not have any other choices in this matter. We all knew that someday he might find us, and I must make it appear that I want to help him. We need the money for your mother anyway, and Sal is willing to pay."

"Does he know about Ma'ma?" she fearfully questioned.

"No," Antonio answered. "He believes she died when she fell."

Charise turned around to face her brother again. "I'm afraid for us, Antonio."

He took her into his arms and gave her a soft kiss on the top of her head. "Do not worry, Charise. I will be very careful."

*****

Noah was holding Tillie in his arms on the porch swing. Tillie's knee was packed in ice, and the swelling had subsided quite a bit. After an energetic day, their baby had settled down for a nap and they were alone. The early spring day in the Black Hills drew out the scent of the pines all around them, and a light wind carried the song of birds as it softly whistled through the trees. Noah told Tillie about Luigi's phone call, and she laughed at her husband's comical portrayal.

"And then he says..." Noah cleared his throat and mimicked Luigi's accent as he continued, "*We should really become acquainted. As you know, the Casellis have completely forgiven me for being such a blackguard —*"

Tillie laughed. "He didn't say *that*!"

Noah nodded, continuing with a mischievous smile, "And then he said, *perhaps your wife would be interested in a date with me —*"

Tillie guffawed. "You're so funny."

Noah even laughed at his untruths. "Yeah, I'm pretty funny."

The sound of a car in the parking area just in front of them, made them both look up and they saw their children were home from school. The old, four door Chevy Impala they took turns driving came to a stop and the three teenagers got out.

"Hi, guys!" Jake shouted from the car.

"Shhh!" Noah frantically whispered with a smile. "The baby's sleeping!"

Jake smiled and nodded his head. Nobody wanted to wake Annie if she was taking one of her rare naps.

Very quietly, they came up the steps. Tillie noticed that A.J.'s black eyes were shining with something devilish as he too casually asked, "How's the knee, Mom?"

"It's better," Tillie answered, wondering what kind of a secret lurked behind her son's expression.

Jake burst into quiet giggles. Laura frowned and slapped his shoulder.

Noah and Tillie smiled curiously at their children.

"Have you guys been up to something?" Tillie asked.

"Laura's got a date," Jake blurted through a grin.

While Tillie and Noah both wore expressions of surprise, Laura's was one of horror. She made a 'humph' noise, frowning at her stepbrother.

"I don't have a date," she said with a scowl. She looked at Jake and A.J. "Go away so I can talk to them."

A.J. and Jake both smiled and made their way into the house. Laura sighed and took a seat in the wicker furniture just across from the porch swing. She was obviously mortified at what Jake had said, and Tillie wondered if she could get past the embarrassment long enough to explain what was going on.

"They are *so* weird," Laura moaned.

"You have a date?" Tillie asked with a curious smile.

"Well, sort of," Laura admitted, her dark frown relaxing.

Noah raised a serious brow. "Sort of ?"

Laura took a breath and explained, "Well, I met this guy a few months ago down at Gospel Gardens —"

"A few months ago?" Tillie clarified.

Laura nodded. "I really didn't think he was interested, because he's a little bit older than me."

"How much older?" Noah asked with a frown.

"Umm," Laura hesitated as she looked at her mother and Noah. "Well, he works for Piper Jaffray."

"Piper Jaffray?" Noah said as his heart fell to the bottom of his stomach. "Is he a stockbroker?"

"Well…yes," Laura answered, and then quickly rambled, "But he's only been at it for less than a year and he says that he graduated from Black Hills State like a year ago, so I think he's like twenty-two or twenty-three. And he's a *Christian*."

"And he wants a date with a high school girl?" Noah asked, his frown deepening dramatically.

Tillie put a gentle hand on Noah's forearm, trying to smile at Laura as she said, "We have to meet him first."

"I told him that," Laura said. "And I told him that I'd have to ask you guys about it." She cleared her throat. "You know, I'll be a senior next year."

Tillie smiled at her daughter, but *inside* her heart was pounding and she was certain she was experiencing slight chest pain. She felt Noah trying to control his own breath as he held her, wondering what he was thinking. A man of twenty-three years of age wanted to date her daughter of only seventeen. *Wow.*

"Why don't you invite him over for dinner, Laura," Tillie said calmly. "We can meet him and visit with him. You know, kinda see what sort of a fella he is."

"Okay," Laura agreed, with a smile of relief, and got to her feet. "Thanks you guys." She skipped into the house.

Noah shook his head. "Twenty-three? *Is he nuts?* Did I sprout gray hair during that episode?"

Tillie chuckled as she reminded him, "You were twenty-three when I met you."

Noah grinned. "And that's *exactly* what I'm worried about. Do you remember anything at all about me back then?"

"Yes, I remember. And this young man is a Christian —"

"So was I."

Tillie gave Noah's cheek a soft touch with her index finger as she said, "He's probably a really nice guy…*just like you*."

Noah's blue eyes danced as he looked at his wife. "I *wasn't* a nice guy, and *that's* what attracted you in the first place."

"Noah!" Tillie giggled. "Let's just have the young man over for dinner. We owe it to Laura to at least give him a chance."

"He's probably some kind of a stalker," Noah mumbled.

"Laura's a smart girl and I think we can trust her judgment."

Noah moaned and rolled his eyes. "Oh, brother."

Chapter 4

Alyssa flew into Sioux Falls, South Dakota, rented a comfortable sedan and drove over to her Uncle Sam's law office. As she walked the hallway to the office at the end, she paused to look at the new portrait her cousin, Laura, had recently given to their Uncle Sam. It was a replica of one of her father's favorite paintings, a portrait of Arturo Martinez.

Arturo Martinez opened Martin Law Office in downtown Sioux Falls in the early 1900's. He had come from Spain as a young boy. Early in his twenties, Arturo changed his name to Alex Martin, and became the first in a long line of Martins to attend Harvard.

Arturo moved his family from the east coast of the United States, deep into the heart of midwestern America when South Dakota became a state in 1889. He vowed to work until the Lord called him Home, practicing law until he was one hundred years of age.

Arturo married Mable James Mulligan and they had seven sons, three of whom died while still infants from a disease that passed through the area. When they were young men, two of their sons went to Tombstone, Arizona, to mine silver. They were later killed by stray gunfire. Another of Arturo's and Mable's sons built a homemade airplane and attempted to fly it across the Gulf of Mexico. He died when the contraption crashed and sank just off the Texan shore. That left only one son, Alex James Martin. Young Alex was sent off to Harvard, and became the family's second graduate.

Alex James Martin married Daphne Banks and they had three sons and a daughter. Two of their sons, William and Matthew, were lost in World War I. The third, Alex James Martin, Jr., whom they called "James," was sent to Harvard as well and became the third-generation Martin to graduate from the prestigious school. Their beloved daughter, Ruth, married Luke Morgan. He was a minister and they moved to West Virginia in the 1950s, where they raised a family of three children.

James married Frances Dale and they had three children. Sam was their oldest, Kate was in the middle, and Alex James Martin, III, was the youngest. In the 1950s, their law practice boomed and the Martins added a partner, MacKenzie Dale, Frances' older brother. MacKenzie opened a branch office at Rapid City, South Dakota.

Sam went to Harvard and graduated twelve years before his younger brother, Alex. He married Becky-Lynn Tucker, but they did not have any children.

Kate married Vincenzo Caselli, and they had two children, Alyssa and Angelo, who both went to Harvard.

Alex married Tillie Caselli and they had a set of twins, Alex James Martin, IV, whom they'd called "A.J." from the time of his birth, and Laura Rose.

James passed away in 1987, and Sam blamed Alex's political ambitions for breaking their father's heart. Their mother passed away shortly thereafter, leaving the adult Martin children without either parent. In 1993, Alex died in a tragic plane crash. That left Sam and Kate as the last surviving members of what had been an amazing legacy.

Kate had the Casellis to hold her up, and so did Sam. But while Kate indulged herself in the love and encouragement the Casellis offered, Sam seemed to retreat from them, especially when Tillie remarried and Annie Laurie was born. All of the Casellis, including Tillie, tried very hard to include Sam and keep some kind of contact going with him. But as the years passed, Sam became more and more distant, even to his own sister. He still operated the family business in the same offices he'd once shared with his grandfather, his father and his brother. He didn't call anyone, not even his nieces and nephews, nor did he send letters or cards. Sam simply practiced law with his precious Becky-Lynn, as if it was all he wanted now.

Alyssa smiled faintly as she continued down the familiar, long hallway until she reached the office at the end. He'd always left his door open, and she quietly watched him for a moment. His silvered head was bent over his desk, obviously absorbed in his work. She saw bifocals resting on his nose. *Those are new*, she thought. *Sam didn't have bifocals the last time I visited.*

She leaned her slender, six-foot frame against the doorway, loudly clearing her throat.

Sam looked up, smiling at his niece. "Good gravy, it's my favorite character!" he exclaimed with a smile. She was decked out in faded blue jeans, black boots, a white t-shirt and a black leather jacket. On the inside of her jacket Sam saw the handle of her holstered pistol. It wasn't *exactly* the attire that fit Alyssa's strikingly beautiful looks. She should have been clothed by Armani and sent down a runway somewhere. He laughed as he got to his feet, and walked toward her. "I hope you're not here on business!"

"Nope." Alyssa smiled as she put her arms around her tall, handsome uncle. It amazed Alyssa that even at the age of sixty, Sam's impressive frame had not stooped at all. He was a good six inches taller than even she, and his shoulders were still broad.

"Well, what the heck *are* you doing here?" he asked with a smile, motioning for her to take a seat. Alyssa seated herself before her uncle's desk and Sam perched himself on the corner.

"I'm on my way out west. I thought I'd stop by and see you and then I'm driving out to Reata to see the folks."

Sam laughed. "You're *headed* out west? Don't you *live* west of here?"

She chuckled. "Well, I'm traveling west by sort of an easterly route. It's a long story."

Sam suspiciously raised a brow. "Well, what are you up to?"

"Same thing, different day. But, I have come across a little bit of a mystery that's got my interest."

"Really?" Sam raised both of his eyebrows curiously. "Can you talk about it?"

Alyssa playfully frowned at her uncle. "I really shouldn't say anything at this juncture."

Sam pretended to grimace. "Is he *bad?*"

Alyssa shrugged. "I don't know yet, but something tells me it's gonna be a big can of worms."

"Well, I'm sure you'll catch 'em. You always do."

"So far, so good." She took a deep breath. "But that's not why I'm here. Now, about this big, Caselli reunion." Sam seemed to cringe at her words and she couldn't help but smile. "What's *that* all about?"

Sam pretended to frown with confusion as he said, "I *may* have heard there was something in the works."

"And it's rumored that you haven't answered Auntie's invitation. That true?" she questioned.

Sam slowly raised himself from his perch on the corner of his desk and meandered around to his comfortable chair. He took a seat, sighed, and sadly smiled at Alyssa.

"What's wrong, Uncle Sam?"

"Nothin'. Just gettin' old I s'pose."

"Bah!" Alyssa softly scolded. She could just about guess what was bothering her uncle and why he'd stayed away for so many years. "You and Aunt Becky should go with Papa in his new conversion van. You guys haven't seen Tillie and the kids in how many years? Have you even seen little Annie yet?"

"Tillie sent me some pictures, but they don't *really* want me out there."

"Why do you think *that?*"

Sam sighed as he answered, "I'm *not* a Caselli."

"That doesn't matter and you know it," Alyssa scoffed. "How long have you known them, anyway?"

"Forty-two years this Thanksgiving," Sam answered. "But it's so awkward now. *You know...*" his voice faded off and he rolled his eyes.

Alyssa shook her head and her dark brows knit with confusion. "No, I *don't* know," she said. "I really don't understand why you stay away. Can't you at least talk to Aunt Becky and see what she says? You guys would have so much fun and it would sure mean a lot to Ma`ma if you would come around a little more often."

"I put in an appearance on Reata at least twice a year," he defended with a smile.

"Okay, Uncle Sam. But at least think about it and talk to Aunt Becky."

"I will," he promised with a smile. "Now, not to change the subject or anything, but your mother tells me that you're working way too much."

Alyssa sighed and said, "I'm on my way out there next. Me and Angelo are kinda on the outs with the folks."

"Everybody still on speaking terms?"

Alyssa slowly nodded. "But barely. You know, Uncle Sam, I just don't get it. They put me through seven years at Harvard and now it's as if they don't want me to work."

Sam gave her a coy smile as he asked, "Don't you get it Alyssa? They love being married and having children so much that *that's* what they want for their kids. They just love you guys and they've loved their life with you. It's not that they don't want you to work, they just want you to be married and have children *more*."

Alyssa rolled her eyes. "Well, I don't even have a boyfriend. No one has so much as asked me out on a date, so it's a moot point anyway."

Sam gave her another coy smile. "Well, maybe if you'd leave the Glock somewhere, like under the bed, it would be easier to get a date. If I was a young man, I'd be fairly intimidated by that thing."

Alyssa chuckled as she replied, "Listen, Uncle Sam, have you seen what's out there for men these days? They're all a bunch of blackguards and crack-heads. I'm not going anywhere without my little buddy." She gave her pistol a loving pat.

Sam laughed. "I guess he'll have to be a special man if he's gonna snag you, Deputy."

Alyssa stayed with her Uncle Sam until noon. He promised again that he'd speak with Becky-Lynn about the reunion, but Alyssa was skeptical.

"I just don't understand it," she grumbled to her parents as they sat beneath the fresh blossoms in Reata's apple orchard. The three of them had taken a single-horse drawn buggy and a picnic lunch out to their favorite place, *just like the good ole days*.

"There's really nothing to understand," Kate said in a disgruntled tone. "He started this after your Uncle Alex died and none of us can do anything with him, not even your grandfather."

"Your brother is a man of deep feeling," Vincenzo said thoughtfully, reaching for Kate's hand. "Do not be so hard on him. I imagine that he is dealing with things the best he can."

Alyssa raised an eyebrow as she listened to her father make yet another excuse for Uncle Sam. She sighed heavily to get their attention, "And speaking of men *with deep feeling...*" she said, pausing to look into her father's eyes. "Have you called Angelo?"

Vincenzo smiled slightly as he answered, "I called him last evening."

"And what's the status on that?" Alyssa quizzed with a professional tone.

Vincenzo and Kate softly frowned at the same time, but it was Vincenzo who replied, "We are trying very hard to understand our children's driving ambitions."

"Thanks. I think," Alyssa murmured.

"Alyssa we know that it's hard for you to understand, but please try," Kate pleaded. "We only have you two children and we'd love to have grandchildren someday. You and Angelo are in your mid-twenties now and neither of you have ever dated. It reminds us so much of —" Kate stopped herself.

"Uncle Alex?" Alyssa asked with a frown.

Vincenzo swallowed and answered, "He lived a tortured life, Alyssa. He had the world by the tail, and he did not even know it."

"I'm not like him," Alyssa stubbornly defended herself.

Kate tried to smile as she added, "There's a lot you don't know about your Uncle Alex. He ran full speed ahead until the day he died, and he missed out on the best part of life."

Alyssa looked at her parents as they sat there together. *They* were her most favorite memories. No one else in the world looked at Ma`ma the way Papa did. His dark eyes always made her smile, which she did a lot of when they were together. And even though they'd been married nearly thirty-six years, he insisted upon calling her "Kate Martin" or simply, "Lovely Kate," every chance he got. The ring of Papa's soft accent when he said her name always made Ma`ma's eyes shine. She adored her husband, and it was plain to see. Of course Alyssa wanted that in her life. Who wouldn't? It just didn't seem possible at this time.

"Well, that's not gonna happen to me," Alyssa said, raising her eyebrows. "I *want* to have a husband and children. But for now, I'll have to settle for this job until the right man comes along."

Vincenzo and Kate relented then, for they didn't want another disagreement brewing with their children. They would let God sort it out.

*****

Ben Simmons came to work for Noah in 1980. He was well educated and credentialed, and at the time Noah needed a foreman. Ben became Noah's assistant in 1987, shortly after Noah's abrupt breakup with Melinda. Ben was more than willing to fill the vacancy. Noah sensed that Ben was a good man, and he had proven himself dependable in Melinda's old position.

Ben would soon turn forty years of age, and had never taken a wife. He was tall, slender, dark and handsome, and always sharply dressed. Even when he worked on the sites with Noah, Ben's blue jeans and work shirts were clean and unwrinkled. There were times over the last few years Noah suspected that Ben did not *like* women. However, the last few months had started Noah guessing.

From Noah's office door, he watched the busy comings and goings of his large staff. If he sat just right in the chair behind his desk, leaned back a touch and slyly glanced to the right side of the office, Noah could see Lucy Davis' desk. She kept track of equipment orders, and was Ben's special assistant. Lucy was a sweet lady the same age as Ben, and had been married once before. She lost her husband in Desert Storm, and was raising three teenagers on her own. Lucy was a pretty lady with dark hair and shiny, blue eyes, but her expression was downcast and sorrowful — that is, until just a few months ago.

Noah spied on the romantic scene. Ben was seated on the corner of Lucy's desk, looking directly into her eyes and smiling. Lucy smiled in return, and for just the tiniest moment, Noah thought perhaps Lucy had blushed. After some time passed, she gave Ben a small stack of papers, and he thanked her and stood up. Noah hid behind a report Tessa had delivered to him earlier, hoping no one had caught him peeking.

Ben walked to Noah's office with the small stack of papers and laid them on Noah's desk. "Here are those equipment orders you wanted," he said with a smile.

Noah gave the papers a quick glance, as if they were important, and then he looked at Ben. His blue eyes danced with curiosity as he whispered, "So, are you guys secretly dating, or what?"

Ben's jaw nearly hit the floor and Noah almost laughed out loud. After a long moment of silence, and no response from Ben, Noah whispered, "Well, are you?"

"No," Ben answered, his eyes nervously darting all over Noah's office. "Whatever gave you that idea?"

Noah playfully frowned as he answered, "You seem to *really* like her."

Ben rolled his eyes and groaned, "She *is* my assistant. It is better if I do like her."

"Listen, Ben," Noah said with a lopsided grin, "there's nothing wrong with just asking her out. I think she really likes you. But, just remember what happened to me when I dated the help." He tapped his index finger on the small scar above his eyebrow where Melinda had hurled a picture frame at him on the night he ended it.

Ben laughed and shook his head. "I will keep that in mind, Noah."

*****

Schneider Rauwolf's eyes were deeply creased with age. He was exceptionally fair skinned, and his once fire-red hair and eyebrows had been taken by the chemotherapy. His lengthy illness had left him thin and weak. Occasionally a nurse took him for a ride in his wheelchair, but only on his good days. Most of the time, he wasted away in his hospital bed, watching the time pass on the clock on the wall.

He looked up in surprise when a tall, dark-suited man walked into his hospital room.

"Who are you?" Rauwolf asked, wondering if it was another cancer specialist making the rounds.

The man stood at the end of Rauwolf's bed, looking him up and down. His lip curled into a mocking sneer as he said, "Once so powerful and strong. Was it not you who stole my brother and his young son from the arms of our family?" He paused to pretend amusement. He took a deep breath and shook his head as he said, "And now look at you. It appears that the mighty Wolf has met his demise."

Panic rose in Rauwolf's heart. He took a breath and tried to get a grip on himself...*it can't be*, he thought. He studied the man's face, pausing at the scar on his left cheek. His heart skipped a beat. Just when he didn't think his life could get any worse, there stood Salvatore Ponerello at the end of his deathbed. "What do you want?" he whispered.

"Come now, Wolf, you know why I am here," he said.

Rauwolf shook his head as he answered, "I have no idea where to find it. Mario sent me away that night and he took care of it. The only other person that knew was his stepdaughter, and she's been dead for seventeen years. The secret died with her."

"She told Hansen."

"She didn't tell Hansen anything," Rauwolf lied.

Sal narrowed his eyes and questioned, "And how would you know?"

"Because he would have called the cops by now. There's not an unrighteous bone in that man's body."

Sal nodded. "That is what I understand...are you planning to contact the boy before you die?"

Rauwolf looked into Sal's dark eyes, but did not answer.

Salvatore laughed.

*****

During his investigation, Jason had managed to get together several files and reports on the various members of the Caselli family. For many years, Senator Caselli and his younger brother, Marquette, had made news in all major reporting services, so there was a lot of information available. Some of Marquette's cases, however, had been restricted by the United States government, as well as foreign governments.

Jason sighed and thoughtfully scratched his head as he frowned at the amassed collection of information on top of his desk. "So is there a connection here or what?" he said to himself.

Someone cleared his throat, and Jason looked up to see his father waiting patiently in the doorway of his office.

"Hey, Dad," Jason greeted with a tired smile. "Whatcha got?"

Joe gave the manila file in his hand a wave and stepped into Jason's small office to lay it on his desk. "M.E.'s report on Louis Mendoza."

Jason looked down at the file, slowly opening it up. "Is this about the North Rapid overdose I've been working?" he asked.

Joe nodded. "M.E. found strychnine in the kid. It's going to the press as a homicide this afternoon and the chief wants you to be ready with some kind of a report."

Jason looked up with a surprised expression. "I can't say anything, Dad," he said. "Mendoza was one of Andreotti's patients and you know I'm up to my ears in this nightmare."

Joe nodded, glancing at the many papers and files on Jason's desk. "Whatcha got so far?" he asked.

Jason took a breath and answered, "Well, the Casellis arrived in the United States in late November of 1956, except for the youngest sibling, Matilde, who was born in South Dakota in June of 1957. Guiseppi's brother, Angelo, had been in the United States for more than eleven years prior, and sponsored the family when they applied for work visas and residency. Guiseppi, his wife, Rosa, and all of their sons became citizens on the same day in 1962.

"Now, Vincenzo married an American, Kate Martin, in 1962. After a brief check on Kate Martin Caselli, I find that she has no family to reference, except for her brother who lives in Sioux Falls. Her other brother, Alex, is that guy who died in the Ben Stahlhiem plane crash in 1993. He was married to Matilde at the time —"

"They call her Angel or Tillie," Joe interrupted.

Jason nodded in acknowledgement and continued, "Senator Petrice Caselli also married an American, Elaine Netherton, in 1975. Her father was General Netherton, and high up in the Nixon Administration.

"Then there's the very famous duo of Marquette and Tara Caselli. Now those two are *extremely* interesting. Tara attended the same university in Chicago with Luigi Andreotti from September of 1960, until they graduated in May of 1964. It appears Marquette and Tara had no contact during the time she left Italy *illegally* with her grandmother in 1956, *which was the same year the Casellis left Italy*, until shortly before she and Marquette were married in 1968. Marquette and Tara are dual citizens, and they maintain three residences in Italy, and one in Washington, D.C. They are out of the country frequently and deeply involved in several politically controversial investigations. They have strong personal ties to the British prime minister and the Royal Family of Windsor, the Italian prime minister, the entire Reagan administration, the Swiss government, and the Pope."

Joe raised his eyebrows as he asked, "The Pope?"

Jason shrugged and replied, "They cracked an assassination plot a couple of years back, but the details were never released to the media."

"How did *you* find out about it?"

"Billy Holmes," Jason answered. "Remember him? We met in the Junior ROTC program, and then wound up at Ft. Riley together. He's CIA now." Jason took a breath and began again, "But what's really interesting, is this article I found in an old newspaper fiche." He quickly sorted through the files and papers on his desk, found the one he wanted, and handed it to his father. "I was cross-referencing newspapers from July of 1994 because that's when Luigi changed his address from Washington, D.C., to Rapid City, South Dakota, and I stumbled across the society page of the *Rapid City Journal*."

Joe looked at the copied article in front of him and grinned as he read it. It was a tiny announcement describing Noah Hansen and Tillie Martin's wedding. In the brief article, Marquette Caselli was listed as the best man, and it was also noted that Marquette and Tara had a residence in Washington, D.C. "Well, heck, Jason," Joe said with a chuckle, "I coulda told ya that."

"But you couldn't have told me *this*," Jason said, sliding his father two more copied articles. "Billy faxed me articles from the fiche of the 1994 *Washington Times* and *The Washington Post*. Both newspapers described Senator Caselli's sister's wedding in Rapid City, South Dakota — Luigi's abrupt change of address occurred only a few weeks after the date of the articles in the newspapers. Marquette, Petrice and Luigi all lived in Washington, D.C., from about 1990 until 1994."

Joe nodded, thoughtfully biting his lip. He took a breath and asked, "Obviously there's a connection between the Casellis and Andreotti, but what is it?"

Jason shook his head and answered, "I don't know yet, but I'm gonna find out."

The black Ford Taurus Jon Danielson drove to Rapid City was well hidden beneath the unkempt trees of an empty lot. Their position was just off Fifth Street, at the very bottom of Terricita Hills. Several hundred yards away was the business address of Luigi Andreotti. Jon and Alyssa watched his office window and the front door.

"The shades are closed, of course," Jon muttered, squinting through his binoculars. "But I haven't seen that fella with the birthmark come out yet." He lowered his binoculars and looked curiously at Alyssa, who was sitting in the passenger seat of his car. "Are we gonna follow him or do you want to wait for Luigi?"

"I want to wait for Luigi. I just want to see where he lives," she answered.

Jon nodded, putting the binoculars back to his eyes. "Here we go... Birthmark's leaving...and...I think another guy's coming in...you'd better take a look."

At his words, Alyssa lifted her own set of binoculars, focusing on the exchange just outside of Luigi's office. Tall, dark man in a nice suit. *That's odd*, she thought. *Everyone else who goes in and out of Luigi's office dresses like a gangster.*

"That's weird," Jon mumbled.

Alyssa watched the man with the dark birthmark on his face leave, and the professional entered.

"Hey, what's that shiny thing on his wrist?" Jon asked as he watched the suit open the door and step inside.

"A watch?"

"It's a strange color," Jon said. He bit his lip thoughtfully. Something about the glint of the piece of jewelry in the light was familiar. Suddenly he remembered. "It's copper."

"Copper?" Alyssa asked, watching the door close. She lowered her binoculars and looked at Jon.

Jon lowered his binoculars and answered, "My grandfather used to wear a copper bracelet for his arthritis."

"Professional looks a little young for arthritis."

Jon shrugged. "Whatever it is, it gives us a little bit of a description to file away for the future."

Alyssa reached for the small notebook on the seat. "Okay then. We've got *Birthmark* and *Bracelet*. Now, let's figure out how to get IDs on these two."

"After we follow Luigi home."

Chapter 5

"I understand the Casellis will be in the Black Hills at the end of June," Sal said with a frown, gazing at the professionally dressed man seated in front of his desk.

"Perhaps."

Sal turned to pour himself another snifter of brandy, then took a seat in his leather chair as he said, "I imagine Petrice will contact me when he arrives." In apparent uneasiness, he shifted his weight in the chair, and returned to his feet. "I need you to check on the shop tonight, Antonio."

Antonio touched the copper bracelet at his wrist as he mulled over his next words. "I want to know what happened to Mendoza," he said.

Sal pursed his lips together and said, "He was an addict and he overdosed."

Antonio frowned with suspicion. "That is not what the police think," he said. "I listened to the chief's conference —"

"The police are mistaken!" Sal barked. "Mendoza overdosed and that is that. Now, I need *you* to check the shop for *me*. Are you willing?"

Antonio nodded.

"Very good then." Sal exhaled through his nose. "Now, has Hansen been to see the Wolf?"

"Not that I know of," Antonio answered. "Either he does not know or he does not care. Chances are that Rauwolf will pass away shortly. He is on a waiting list for a marrow donor, and without such a donation, he cannot last much longer."

"When is the boy scheduled to return?"

"Noah will pick him up at the airport tomorrow," Antonio answered.

Sal grinned sardonically as he mused, "And there will be a flurry of news people. The Wolf will know when his son arrives. Will he contact him?"

"I do not believe that he will," Antonio assured.

Sal sighed. "It would be *most* unfortunate if he did, for we would certainly have our hands full with *that* mess."

Tillie stood ankle deep in Annie's blocks, which were spread out on the floor of the studio. She wanted to put some final touches on a painting, so Mona came over early that morning to help with Annie.

"Wow, Angel," Mona admired with a smile. "This one is really the absolute best. Is this the one that's going into the show during the Heritage Festival?"

Tillie nodded. "Thanks, Mona. It's my favorite too."

Tillie had become a fairly well-known artist in the Black Hills and surrounding area. She'd entered several contests over the last few years, and had even been able to sell a few pieces. Her favorite paintings were still the ones of Noah that she'd given to Maggie and Estelle, but those were off limits to the rest of the world. Their children knew of the paintings, and they were aware that Tillie had painted them when she was very young, but as far as knowing the romantic secrets of their parents, they were still in the dark.

"So, what are you calling this one?" Mona asked.

Tillie smiled thoughtfully. "*Family Time*," she replied.

"I love it —" Mona began, the sudden ringing of the telephone interrupting her. She picked up the cordless beside her and answered it for Tillie. "Hello, Hansen's." She smiled and said to the caller, "Of course." She covered the mouthpiece and whispered to Tillie, "It's some guy with an accent but it doesn't sound like anyone in your family."

Tillie frowned as she took the phone. "Hello?" she greeted.

"Hello, Mrs. Hansen," said an accented, male voice on the other end. "This is Luigi Andreotti."

Mona saw Tillie's eyes become big and round.

"Hello, Mr. Andreotti," Tillie politely greeted as she looked at Mona and suspiciously raised one of her eyebrows.

"I called your husband a few days ago," Luigi began in his smooth, smiling voice, "but since he has not gotten back to me. I decided to contact you directly."

Of course he hasn't called you back, Tillie thought. Noah had told her that he planned on pretending Luigi hadn't called at all and hoped he'd just give up and stay away from them. "Well, what can I do for you?" she continued in her polite tone.

"As you know," Luigi began again, "your family and I were well acquainted in *Italia* and I think it only right that, seeing how close you and I are living, I should get to know you and your family. I was wondering when you and your husband and myself could get together."

Tillie's mouth fell open. Mona squelched a giggle.

"I..." Tillie stammered and took a breath. "I'm sorry, but I have to check with Noah's schedule. He's very busy." She swallowed hard, hoping Luigi would say something next, because she was out of conversation.

"How about if we just plan a little something and surprise Noah," Luigi suggested.

Tillie was sure she could hear Luigi leering over the telephone. "I couldn't do that to Noah," she replied with feigned sweetness. *Who on earth would even suggest a wife do such a thing to her husband?* Tillie shook her head. *No wonder Marquette hates this guy.* "Hey!" Tillie suddenly exclaimed, attempting to sound surprised. "Somebody's at my front door! I gotta go, but I'll make sure that Noah gets this message. Thanks for calling, Mr. Andreotti." Before Luigi could respond, Tillie quickly turned off the phone.

"What was *that* all about?" Mona laughed.

Tillie laughed too and replied, "Patty ran into some long lost buddy from Italy. You know the one…that blackguard that kept Marq and Tara apart for so many years?"

Mona nodded. "Oh, yes. We know all about it."

"Well, the he was in New York at some sort of convention, and he looked up Patty." Tillie frowned. "I guess he thinks we're all gonna be friends again…or something."

"Well, what did the ole blackguard have to say for himself?"

"Just that he was very sorry and he's been asking the Lord for forgiveness," Tillie answered.

"So I suppose your brothers just up and forgave him?"

"Yep. And the whole deal was really awkward because for someone who was trying to sound and appear repentant, he drooled relentlessly all over the ladies, and now he's been calling Noah and me about getting together." Tillie laughed. "Just wait until Noah hears about *this* one. He'll feel like he's got his hands full of blackguards this week."

Mona chuckled. "Oh that's right. Tonight's the big dinner party with Laura's *friend.*"

Tillie sighed. "And that boy had better be on his *very best* behavior."

Alyssa and Jon had followed Luigi to a nice residence in Terricita Hills, only a few blocks from his business office. On the outside, it appeared to be a very well-cared for home: great yard, no weeds, blooming flowers in the pots on the porch. But, Jon had a hunch and decided to go back once they were certain Luigi was back at the office.

He slid into the passenger seat of the Taurus where Alyssa was still watching Luigi's office. "Who's with Luigi now?" he asked.

"Bracelet's been in there for quite a while," Alyssa answered. "What did you find at the house?"

"There was an electric bill in the mailbox addressed to Luigi Andreotti," Jon said, picking up his binoculars and setting his gaze toward Luigi's office. "But there's no furniture in the place, and no car in the garage."

"So it's just a front," Alyssa said.

Jon nodded and replied, "That's what I'd guess.…There goes Bracelet!" He opened his car door, glancing at Alyssa. "I'll see ya later."

"And I'll follow whoever else shows up today."

Jon got out of the car and walked in the shadows to where they had parked another rental. He got in, slowly started down Fifth Street, and Alyssa watched him fall into traffic behind Bracelet. She sighed and returned her focus to Luigi's office door.

*****

Noah had to pick up an equipment order at his office before he went over to his next work site. He was pleasantly surprised to see that someone had sent Tessa fresh flowers.

"Who sent 'em?" he asked as he went through the messages she'd handed him.

Tessa sighed with delight as she answered, "I went to the movies last week with Stan."

Noah's eyes danced as he quipped, "Ollie's friend?"

"Noah!" she quietly exclaimed, frowning.

"I know, I'm sorry," he apologized with a grin.

"I think your equipment orders are almost ready," she said, her eyes moving in the direction of Lucy's desk. Noah followed her gaze and saw at that moment Ben presenting Lucy with a vase of fresh daisies."

"Well, well," Noah muttered. "Everybody's gettin' flowers around here 'cept for me."

Tessa giggled. "If you're nice I'll put in a good word for you with the missus. Now, you'd better hurry up, Noah. Your big dinner is tonight and you don't wanna be late."

Noah slowly walked back to his office, being sure to keep a sly eye on the scene in the corner. "It's just one big *Payton Place* around here," he mumbled to himself as he cleverly positioned himself behind his desk. He opened the newspaper, peeking from behind it at Ben and Lucy. *I'm gonna have to spend more afternoons in the office*, he thought as he watched Lucy give Ben one of her glowing smiles.

In a few minutes, Ben strolled into Noah's office doorway, leaned against the frame and smiled. "The inspector is due at LaCrosse in about twenty minutes. Do you want me to do it?"

"No. That's the one for my relatives." Noah casually lowered his newspaper. "Did she like the daisies?"

Ben raised his eyebrows and replied, "Well, someone had to show the dear lady our appreciation."

"Oh, I see," Noah said, mischief dancing between his brows. "Did you ask her out yet?"

Ben sighed and shook his head. "Do not torture me with that. She is still grieving the loss of her husband and is not ready for any of that yet."

Noah couldn't hide the stunned look on his face. "Her husband's been gone for more than seven years," he said. "I'm thinkin' she's probably over it by now."

Ben laughed. "Come on, Noah. You must see the inspector and I have a mountain of equipment orders to go through."

Noah laughed and got to his feet, and as Ben turned to go, Noah asked, "I thought you were going to be out all day. Did you get to visit your sister and her mother this morning?"

"Yes, and it was a very good morning," Ben answered with a smile. "Thanks for allowing me the time off with them."

"No problem," Noah replied. "Whatever you need until she gets better. Just let me know."

Noah hurried home after the inspection to wash up and prepare himself for Laura's *friend*. He'd received mountains of advice from Vincenzo and, surprisingly, Marquette, on how to handle the young suitor. Marquette had dialed Noah's cell phone just as he was leaving the inspection, and they visited until Noah reached his driveway.

"Noah, seventeen years of age is far too young to date, and that is that," Marquette said. "Besides, this joker that she has picked up with is twenty-three years old. What on earth is he thinking? To take a young girl out away from her family and by herself? He is as crazy as the day is long."

"I know, Marq. I'm in total agreement with you. But what are we gonna do? She's gonna grow up sooner or later."

"You send Jake and A.J. to follow him around town for a few days," Marquette suggested. "Make sure that they are in disguise, and have rented an unfamiliar vehicle. Blackguards are oftentimes clever. He will know Jake and A.J.'s car by now and will be watching for it."

Noah laughed. "Okay, I'll get 'em right on that. But I'm just getting home now, so I have to go. I'm late the way it is."

"Many blessings, my brother," Marquette said. "And I will be praying for you."

"Thanks, Marq."

Noah took the front steps two at a time. He charged through the front door, meeting Laura in the foyer. She was dressed in a feminine, white lacey dress and her curly black hair fell gracefully on her shoulders. She looked so much like her mother at that moment that it took Noah's breath away. Suddenly, Marquette's idea of following the ole blackguard around town didn't seem like such a bad idea.

"Noah, you're late!" she gasped, her pretty brows wrinkling into a frown.

"I'm sorry," Noah apologized, backing toward the steps. "The inspector held me over and I couldn't get away. I'll shower right now."

"You don't have time for that," Tillie said, rushing from the dining room and into the foyer. She quickly kissed her husband, attempting to brush some of the dust from his shoulders. "Just put on a clean shirt and jeans —" She inhaled deeply through her nose and added, "You don't stink. It'll be okay."

"Papa!" Annie trotted in from the kitchen, followed by both of the dogs.

"Hi, Annie," Noah smiled, reaching down to pick up his daughter.

"Don't touch her!" Tillie scolded, softly laughing. She picked up her baby. "I've been able to keep her clean for nearly an hour."

Noah reached for one of Annie's hands, giving it a soft kiss as he said, "Papa's really dirty right now."

"Papa's late!" Annie exclaimed.

"Hurry and change," Tillie said, giving him another kiss. She caught the smell of Old Spice and dust, reminding her of how much she loved that part of her husband.

Noah hurried upstairs, and Tillie looked at Laura who was frowning by the door.

"We'll all be ready before he gets here," Tillie assured. "And you look really beautiful."

"Thanks, Mom." Laura allowed her mother a faint smile.

A.J. and Jake walked into the foyer, and A.J. said, "You look great, Laura."

"Thanks, A.J." She stole a careful glance out the dining room windows.

"When is he coming?" Jake asked.

"He should be here in a few minutes," Tillie answered.

"This is awkward," Jake said with a lopsided grin. "Are we supposed to be checking him out or what?"

"Jake!" Laura gasped, frowning at him. "We're just *meeting* him —"

"And making sure he's not a serial killer," A.J. interrupted.

"Where's Dad?" Jake asked.

"He's upstairs changing," Tillie answered.

"Papa's late," Annie added.

Jake's blue eyes danced and he sounded exactly like Noah when he said, "So, do you think *Papa* will let the young blackguard out of here alive tonight?"

A.J. laughed out loud and Tillie swallowed as hard as she could to keep herself from laughing.

Laura, on the other hand, did not find his comment amusing in the least. "Jake, you are such a *devil!*" she scolded, pointing her index finger at him. "Do you have any idea *how hard* this is for me? Every other girl I know is allowed to just go out with a boy. They don't have to schedule an inquisition with their male family members beforehand."

"Be good, Jake!" Annie scolded from Tillie's hip, attempting to snap her little fingers, and pointing at him.

A.J. giggled as he watched his little sister. "Wow...she looks just like Nonna when she does that," he said.

Jake put on his most serious and humble face and said, "I'm really sorry, Laura."

"Come on, Laura," Tillie said, slipping her free arm around her daughter. "Now don't get yourself upset before he gets here. This is just really strange for the rest of us because we love you so much and we care about your wellbeing." She looked at A.J. and Jake and said, "Why don't you two take the dogs outside so that they don't jump all over him when he gets here."

"Okay," A.J. replied. "Sparky. Vanilla. Let's get a biscuit."

A.J. and Jake proceeded to lead the dogs from the house and Laura sighed as she watched them walk away.

"What's *wrong* with them?" she scowled.

"Nothing," Tillie assured with a smile, giving her daughter a kiss on the cheek.

"I *never* act that way when Heidi comes over."

Tillie nodded. "But you've known Heidi for many years and she's also your best friend. They don't know anything about Elijah and we're all a little apprehensive. Besides, it could be a lot worse. I wish we had video tape from the night Billy Fairbanks took me to the prom." She rolled her eyes. "Your grandfather and your Uncle Marq were in *rare* form that night."

"What did they do?"

"Oh, my goodness." Tillie sighed and shook her head. "They trapped the kid in the entryway for starters. Then, while Grandpa circled him, Uncle Marq started asking him these terrible questions like, *I hope your intentions with my sister are honorable this evening.*"

Laura laughed. "But he *did* turn out to be a blackguard, didn't he?"

Tillie nodded. "And I knew it the moment he showed up in my driveway to ask Grandpa if we could go to the prom together."

Noah's boots stomped down the stairs behind them and they turned to see him hurrying down, dressed in clean clothes.

"Angel, can you button this stupid collar thing for me?" He asked in a desperate tone. "Why do I even *have* these shirts? I wouldn't be able to dress myself if you weren't here."

Tillie and Laura laughed as Tillie handed the baby to her sister.

"Here," Tillie said, reaching for the tiny button on Noah's collar. "You have these shirts because they look really great on you."

"Humph." Noah replied, waiting for Tillie to button the collar.

Laura couldn't help but giggle as she watched them together. Her mother had bought Noah some casual button-down collar shirts, just for everyday use, and Noah had been flabbergasted. He had never worn anything fancier than clean workshirts and perhaps a knit shirt with a collar. However, he'd eventually admitted that they were comfortable and that he enjoyed wearing them around the house and to church, but his thick, clumsy fingers could never manage the buttons on the collars.

"There." Tillie looked at him. "You look *great.*"

Noah took a breath and finally smiled. "Thanks, Angel."

"Papa." Annie said, reaching for her father.

Noah smiled, taking her into his arms as he said, "*Now*, I can hold you." At just that moment, Noah happened to glance through the dining room windows to see a red convertible Camaro pulling into a parking spot out front.

"Good grief," he groaned. "He's here." He looked at Laura with a frown and asked, "Why didn't you tell us he's a speed demon."

Laura almost smiled as she replied, "I don't think he is, Noah."

"Good grief," Annie echoed her father, putting her little finger into her mouth as she watched the young man park his car.

"Nice wheels," Tillie said, raising one eyebrow as she glanced at her husband. "He must be doing pretty good on the ole stock market."

The young man got out of the car and Tillie and Noah could see that he was tall and very blond. He was dressed in nice slacks and a shirt, but Noah noticed the collar didn't button down. His skin was tan, and Noah guessed that he'd been spending time on the golf course with his stock market buddies. Noah couldn't seem to help but roll his eyes as he thought, *golf is such a waste of time.*

As Elijah came up the steps, Noah reached for the door, opening it before the young man could ring the bell. "You must be Elijah," he said with a soft scowl, allowing Elijah to pass into the entryway.

"Hi, Elijah," Annie said with a sweet smile.

"Noah Hansen," he gruffly introduced, extending his free hand.

"Mr. Hansen," Elijah responded with a polite nod, extending his hand in greeting. "It's good to meet you."

Tillie just about laughed. That was the first time she hadn't heard Noah tell someone to call him by his first name.

Before Noah could introduce Tillie, Annie stuck her little hand out to Elijah in the same way her father had and repeated, "Hi, Elijah."

"Well, hello," Elijah said, smiling as he took the baby's offered hand. "You must be Annie Laurie."

Annie nodded her head, and her black curls bobbed on her shoulders.

"This is my wife, Mrs. Hansen," Noah introduced as he turned toward Tillie.

"How do you do?" Elijah replied, politely extending his hand to Tillie.

"Obviously, you and Laura are already acquainted with one another," Noah added, and Tillie almost laughed again. Had that been Noah's attempt at a joke?

"Hi, Laura," Elijah said with a small smile, and Noah thought perhaps he'd said her name just a little on the *breathless* side.

"Hi," Laura said, smiling in return, and Noah frowned again. They were obviously mutually attracted to one another. This was going to be a nightmare.

The sound of footsteps was heard behind them and they turned to see Jake and A.J.

"This is Noah's son, Jake," Laura introduced, and Jake reached for Elijah's hand.

"Nice to meet you," Jake said, frowning in the same way that his father had.

Elijah politely smiled and A.J. offered his hand in greeting.

"I'm Laura's brother. You can call me A.J.," he introduced, stepping a little too close to Elijah, apparently trying to intimidate the young man with his sheer size.

"Nice to meet you," Elijah replied with a nervous smile.

"Well, then." Noah abruptly turned and walked toward the dining room. "Let's eat. I'm starved."

Tillie smiled at their children and their guest, and followed her husband into the dining room. *This oughta be good,* she thought. She glanced at her husband as he carefully seated Annie in the high chair. *If he starts skulking around in the bushes after dinner, however, I'll put a stop to it.*

"You can sit here," Noah said to Elijah, indicating the place next to his own.

"Sure," Elijah agreed, and he politely pulled out the chair next to his own, smiling at Laura.

"Thank you," Laura responded. He waited politely for Laura to seat herself before taking his own seat.

Noah slid Tillie's chair out, waiting for her to seat herself before taking his own seat.

A.J. and Jake glanced at one another, digging deep for all of the self-control they possessed. The situation was intensely comical for some reason, and both of them had the urge to burst out laughing. Why couldn't they just sit ole Elijah down, *just the men that is*, and ask him what in the world he was doing trying to scam a seventeen-year-old girl? Why did everyone have to play nice and invite the blackguard over for dinner. Weren't they just gonna throw him out by his ear anyway? Wouldn't it save a lot of time and energy to just skip the nice dinner and have a meeting with him at a neutral location? Like, say, Canyon Lake Park after midnight?

Tillie's table was set like a beautiful picture. She'd used her favorite china, the set she'd purchased when they honeymooned in Italy. Each place setting was adorned with two forks, and Jake and A.J. wondered if Elijah would know which ones to use for what. A tall, crystal goblet of iced sparkling water and another of pink lemonade sat before each plate, while a colorful zucchini salad waited in the center.

Noah said a short, stressed-out prayer, thanking God for the food, family and the *friendship.* Everyone said 'Amen,' and the meal commenced.

"You set a beautiful table, Mrs. Hansen," Elijah politely complimented.

"Thank you," Tillie replied.

"Something smells great, Mom," A.J. said. "What did you make?"

"Stromboli," Tillie answered, taking a scoop from the large dish beside her place, then starting it around the table.

"Mom's a *real* Italian," Laura sweetly informed, and her pretty, black eyes sparkled when she looked at Elijah.

"Really?" Elijah replied. He asked Tillie, "When did you come to America?"

"I was born here," Tillie replied. "My family came to America in 1956. My parents live over in Sioux Falls, I have a brother in the Centerville area, and two brothers on the east coast."

"Well, sometimes Uncle Marq lives in Italy," Laura added. "He and his wife are dual citizens."

"Senator Caselli is our uncle," A.J. spat out the information more like a threat, rather than common conversation.

"And Marquette Caselli was Dad's best man," Jake added.

Elijah was obviously surprised. "So you guys are related to the famous Caselli brothers? What's that like?"

"It's great," Noah remarked. "Do you have family around here?" He was going to get down to the real business at hand, and that was finding out as much about this young man as he could.

Elijah nodded and answered, "My parents live up in Deadwood, but my grandmother lives here in Rapid City. Mr. Hansen, you probably remember her. Vivian Olson?"

Noah nearly choked on his fork full of zucchini. He struggled to swallow as he answered, "Of course I remember, Viv. How is she these days?" And the strangest feeling began in the pit of his stomach as he waited for Elijah's reply.

"She's doing really great for a woman of her age," Elijah answered. "She golfs most days now. My father checks on her properties for her."

"Is she a developer?" A.J. asked curiously.

Elijah shook his head and answered, "Grandmother has a lot of different businesses in the area. In fact..." and as Elijah took a breath to continue, Noah's heart began to pound because he knew what Elijah's next words would be even before he said them. "She once leased this house for one of her businesses."

Noah swallowed his food as he slowly nodded his head. Tillie saw the touch of pink on his cheeks, and the near-panic look in his eyes.

"Let's see now," Elijah reminisced, "what did she used to call it? Angel's Place?"

Tillie almost dropped her fork, and Noah could only look into his plate as he silently nodded. They both wondered what other information Elijah would offer. Their children knew only that Noah had built the house many years ago, but they didn't know *why*. It was a subject that had never been discussed...*until now*.

"We used to spend tons of time up here when we were kids," Elijah went on with a smile. Noah thought perhaps Elijah resembled the devil as his own past tumbled gracefully from the young man's lips. "Grandmother used to tell us this very dramatic story about a poor, uneducated peasant man who built this place for his only true love. Angel was her name, but she ran off with a rich Spaniard, and the peasant man wound up leasing the house out to Grandmother because he didn't want to live in it all alone."

Dead silence dropped over the dinner table.

Jake quietly cleared his throat, managing to croak, "Dad built this house."

"Oh. You were the builder?" Elijah asked, looking at Noah in complete bewilderment.

Noah took a breath, attempting a faint smile in Elijah's direction. Their eyes locked as Noah conveyed the message of *shut up about the house.*

Elijah got the message. "Well," he pretended to scoff with a smile, "so much for Grandmother's old stories."

Naturally, all three of Tillie and Noah's children gave each other questioning glances. *Angel's Place? Angel?* Only Noah and Tillie's family members referred to her as *Angel.* She signed all of her paintings *Angel...*

Tillie cleared her throat, giving Elijah a gracious smile as she asked, "So, Elijah, Laura tells us you work for Piper Jaffray. What do you do there?"

That was subtle. Elijah felt as if he'd been dropped directly into the Twilight Zone, with no hope of escape. "I'm a stockbroker," he answered.

"How long have you been there?" Tillie sweetly continued.

"Just about two years."

"He graduated from Black Hills State University in 1996," Laura added casually.

Jake and A.J. exchanged a short, but suspicious glance. Hadn't Laura *noticed* the uncommon stress surrounding the circumstances of the construction of the house where they were currently living? And was Noah, in fact, the poor peasant whose true love *ran off with a rich Spaniard?* Didn't she want to find out more about *that?* After all, her *father* was a direct descendant of the famous *Spaniard* Arturo Martinez. For a girl, she certainly didn't appear very interested in what was obviously the *coup de grâce* for Noah. A.J. softly touched Jake's shoe with his own and Jake gave him a soft touch in return.

"So how old are you?" Jake blurted. They might not find out at that moment what had happened between the *poor peasant and the rich Spaniard,* but some questions were going to have to get answered.

"Me?" Elijah asked with a stunned expression.

"Yeah," Jake said, narrowing his eyes. "You. How old are you?"

Elijah nervously cleared his throat and answered, "I just turned twenty-three."

"Did you know Laura is only seventeen?" A.J. asked, leaning across the table with a darkly serious expression.

Laura wanted to die, and if her skin color were any lighter they would have all been able to see right through her. *How could they behave this way?* She thought.

"I knew she was still in high school," Elijah admitted as he nervously looked from A.J. to Laura, and then at her parents. "And I'm sorry if you're offended by my interest in her. I assure you I have no dishonorable designs as far as Laura goes and I will submit to whatever rules you have." He smiled humbly at Noah and Tillie, waiting for their response.

Jake rolled his eyes and frowned. *What a performance.* He looked sideways at A.J. to see that he was frowning as well.

"Well," Noah said with a heavy sigh. He smiled at the nervous stockbroker seated next to him and asked, "What do you do for fun, Elijah?"

"For fun?" Elijah repeated, again surprised at the strange twist in conversation.

"Yeah," Noah replied. "You know, for fun. Golf's not that fun."

"I play on a men's fast-pitch softball team," Elijah answered. "A city league."

Jake and A.J. straightened in their chairs, and maybe even looked interested.

"We play for Post 22," A.J. said with a friendlier tone to his voice.

Jake nodded and his expression relaxed. *Might as well give the guy a chance.*

*****

During their dinner conversation Noah agreed to allow Elijah some time with Laura, *but not alone in a dark movie theater.* He explained that Jake had a special friend, Heidi, and the two of them were never allowed to spend time away from adults either. *Before* Elijah and Laura would be allowed to go anywhere together, Elijah would have to spend some time with Laura's family. He could start by coming over for dinner on a regular basis, and when Laura turned eighteen, which was the first week in November, Elijah would be allowed to take her out alone. Elijah was more than agreeable to the terms.

After Elijah left, Laura stormed past A.J. and Jake and up to her room, where she called Heidi and gave her the gruesome details of dinner. She also whispered about the strange announcement during dinner, highlighting the parts about the *peasant and the rich Spaniard.*

Jake and A.J. pretended to settle into the family room with Annie, turning on the baseball game, but were not really watching it. When Annie fell asleep, Noah and Tillie suddenly appeared. They took their baby upstairs and tucked her in.

While Laura was in her room on the phone, A.J. and Jake whispered about the strange twist of information...*especially when Noah didn't join them to watch the game.* It was obvious that their parents were hiding a peculiar secret.

Noah held Tillie in his arms on the love seat by the west window in their room. The Black Hills night floated in on the cool breeze, bringing the scent of pine into their room. They heard the soft noises of the crickets and frogs in the meadow below, and somewhere in the distance a coyote yipped his nervous cries. Soft rumbles of thunder signaled that the Black Hills would soon be soaked with a spring rain.

Noah whispered in the dark, "I just about died. I had no idea that ole Viv had that whole thing figured out."

"I don't remember ever being so surprised in my life," Tillie said with a giggle. "Well, except for finding out that I was pregnant with Annie."

"*Uneducated?*" Noah said in disbelief. "I've had my realtors license forever. It's not like I'm an idiot." He let out a heavy sigh as he asked, "Do we have to tell them?"

"I don't know," Tillie replied. "I thought maybe we should wait until they got a little bit older."

"It'll be pretty tough to explain," Noah said. "I leased the house about a month before I married the boys' mother."

"Well, they're gonna have questions," Tillie said. "And I don't how long we'll be able to avoid them."

"I'm sneaking out of here tomorrow morning," Noah whispered.

Tillie giggled. "And leave me holding the bag?"

"You sneak out with me," Noah offered. "Grab the baby and her diaper bag and we'll hang out with Maggie for a couple of days. You know, just until this thing blows over."

Tillie giggled again. "I love you. It's gonna be okay. We'll pray about this and figure out something profound to tell them. And remember, Ty comes home tomorrow. We'll have a huge distraction with that. They'll probably just forget about it."

Noah smiled and sighed with contentment. Angel loved him and that's really all that mattered in his world. He kissed the top of her head, catching the faintest whiff of her favorite fragrance.

"Oh, by the way," she added, "Luigi called today."

"No kiddin'?"

Tillie mimicked Luigi's soft accent as she said, "He wants to plan a little something to surprise you."

Noah laughed. "Like what?"

"Who knows, but I'm sure it involves a lot of leering and drooling."

Noah laughed again, shaking his head. "He must be so desperate."

"I hope he doesn't start calling me. I really don't wanna be that guy's friend. I've got a bad feeling about him."

"He'd better not make a habit of calling," Noah said with a solemn tone. "Or he *will* wind up spending time with me, and I'm sure it won't be what he had in mind."

*****

The drive was nearly three hours this time, in the pouring rain. The wheels of his car slipped in the mud as he pulled into the long drive. It was like driving on ice when it rained on the red mud. He slowed down again.

As he neared the barn he saw the familiar old cars. He parked next to one of them, getting as close to the awning as he could. He sprinted from his car to the doorway, almost slipping along the way. He worked the electronic combination, letting himself in. Several young men working around a table and an old stove looked up, recognized him, and went back to their duties.

"Hey, Tony. What took you so long?" one of them asked as he wiped off his hands, starting in Antonio's direction.

"The weather," he answered with a frown. "And I have an early day tomorrow, so let us get this over with, Ed."

Ed led Antonio into another room where there were plastic bags packed with a white substance stacked neatly on an old desk.

"This is it," Ed explained. "The drivers will be here tomorrow and they'll each pick up a load. They'll pay in advance and Sal will pick up cash tomorrow night. Tell him that you saw twenty-five bags, and you should count 'em before you go."

Antonio quickly scanned the bags on the desk. "It looks like twenty-five to me," he confirmed.

Ed took a hesitant breath, licking his lips as he asked, "Listen, Tony, we heard about Mendoza."

"What did you hear?"

"Cops say he was poisoned. What do you know?"

"He overdosed," Antonio answered.

Ed shook his head as he said, "I was really careful with how much I gave him. I don't see how that could've happened. The cops said they found rat poison in his system? Our stuff is pure. We're not mixing *anything* with it. That's why we get such a good price."

"Perhaps he mixed it himself," Antonio suggested.

Ed shook his head and lowered his voice to a whisper, "I got a bad feeling about this."

Antonio looked at Ed with disgust and bewilderment. *A bad feeling about this?* They were making and selling illegal drugs and he had a *bad feeling about this?* "Perhaps you should have considered that before you allowed yourself to become a part of this," he retorted.

"We think Sal did Mendoza," Ed whispered frantically. "We're afraid Sal's gonna do us all."

Antonio swallowed hard. "Do not take anything Sal gives you," he warned.

Chapter 6

It was the morning of the last day of school in Rapid City, South Dakota, and things were strained, to say the least, in the Hansen household. Tillie busied herself with rinsing and stuffing a turkey in preparation for Ty's homecoming. Noah pretended to pace agitatedly back and forth in Tillie's studio while talking on the cordless telephone. No one could hear what he was saying, but every now and then he waved his arms and stomped his foot. It *appeared* serious.

Laura was curt with her brothers as she announced, "I'm riding to school with Heidi today. And she'll be giving me a ride home, too."

"That's fine with us," Jake grumbled in response. " 'Cause we got practice over at Fitzgerald and we just as soon not have to run you clear back home."

"Is Heidi coming for dinner?" Tillie asked, placing a saucer of sliced bananas on Annie's high chair tray.

"Yes," Laura answered.

"Great," Jake muttered, rolling his eyes. He knew what that meant. Heidi would be *most unimpressed* with his performance from the evening before, and would, more than likely, give him the cold shoulder the same as Laura.

A car horn beeped and Laura grabbed her backpack. She hurried over to where her mother was working in the kitchen, kissed her cheek and whispered, "I love you, Mom. I wanna talk to you when I get home."

"Of course, dear," Tillie answered with a smile, but her heart plummeted to the bottom of her toes.

Laura hurried out of the house and A.J. and Jake stood from their seats at the table.

"We might as well get goin' too," Jake said.

"Ty will be home when you get here," Tillie said, perhaps too excitedly, smiling at Jake, and then at A.J. "Be sure to come straight home after practice." She gave them each a kiss on the cheek. "Have a great day, guys."

"You too, Mom," A.J. hesitantly acknowledged. *It's as if she's trying to get rid of us*, he thought.

They each gave Annie a kiss, picked up their backpacks, and left. Tillie gave a sigh of relief as Noah meandered into the kitchen and set down the cordless telephone.

"Anybody say anything?" he asked.

"No, but Laura wants to talk when she gets home from school."

"Well, we know what *that's* gonna be about," Noah replied.

Tillie nodded. "What would you like me to say?"

"Just tell her whatever you're comfortable with, as long as it's the truth," he said, slipping his arms around her waist. "What happened, happened. We can't go back, and that weekend we met is my dearest memory in the whole world. I wouldn't change it even if we could."

"Me neither," Tillie agreed, smiling into his eyes.

"And we already told them that we knew each other before, so it's not like they're in the dark about things. God will come up with the perfect explanation and we'll be off the hook."

"Okay," Tillie replied. "By the way, what time do you pick up Ty?"

"Three o'clock. And I'm sure he'll wanna get right home. When's the turkey gonna be ready?"

"About six," Tillie answered. "The boys have practice after school, so they won't be home until then, but Josh and Mona said they were coming over early this afternoon. Mona's making the sweet potatoes."

"Are you gonna make any of those little cranberry, fluffy thingies?" Noah asked.

"Just for you."

Noah kissed her lips and said, "I love you, Angel."

On the north side of Rapid City, at the same group of row houses, Detective Jason Patterson watched the county coroner's office wheel yet another black-bagged body into the back of their van. This made number three, and all in the last six weeks.

"Whatcha thinkin'?" Jason asked Todd Yearwood. Todd was the coroner's special assistant, and he and Jason had graduated together from Rapid City Central High School.

"I'm thinkin' it's another poisoning," Todd answered. "But we won't know for sure until we take a look. Might just be a regular overdose. He was still holding the syringe and there's a tourniquet nearby."

Jason took a deep breath, frowning at the notes he'd made. "Well, give me a call as soon as you know something," he muttered.

"Sure will," Todd promised as he got into his van.

"Hey, Jason," came the familiar sound of his father's voice, and Jason turned to see Joe.

"What are you doing out here, Dad?"

"Heard the call on the radio. Figured I could catch up to you. What happened?"

"Maybe an overdose," Jason answered. "But maybe not. He's one of Andreotti's patients, so I'm gonna bet they find poison in him."

"Who is he?"

Jason looked down at his notes. "Fred Michael. He's been out on parole for nine months. Busted for dealing coke in Sioux Falls, armed robbery, aggravated assault. Who knows how he got paroled."

Joe grimaced and said, "Listen, Jason, I came across some information on the Caselli family. I think it's gonna interest you."

"No kiddin'?"

"I was having coffee with an old timer, you know, Frank Morris?" Joe began, and when Jason nodded, he continued, "And he was talkin' about the good ole days and happened to mention that he'd worked with Marquette Caselli back in 1975."

Jason's mouth fell open in surprise. "Here? In Rapid City?"

Joe nodded. "Caselli was chasing this big mob family from Sicily and wound up with a lead that led him to Rapid. He had a friend working the case with him and they had to separate one night because of two different leads. Caselli went with Frank and Caselli's friend, a fella by the name of John Peters, went off on his own. Caselli's wife said she saw Peters that night and that he followed a guy by the name of Roy Schneider, along with a woman, out of some bar on the north side. At that time, they didn't know the name Roy Schneider, and when the trail ran cold, the Casellis never updated any of their records with the Rapid City Police Department. But, the peculiar thing about this is that John Peters was never seen again. And as far as Frank knows, nobody ever nailed down Schneider for questioning." Joe took a breath and smiled cleverly at his son, adding, "And all of that just sort of intrigued me, so I decided to see if I could pull any old records on a Roy Schneider."

"Find anything?"

"One *old* traffic ticket," Joe answered. "Dr. Roy Schneider was ticketed for speeding in 1974. Now, the really weird stuff starts here. The car Dr. Schneider was driving was licensed to a man by the name of Jack Nelson, who was squeaky clean. However, when I put Jack's name into the department's cross-referencing database, an old accident report popped up. Jack's wife, Della Nelson, took a fall down some stairs and passed away in 1980. Included in the list of survivors was a son-in-law by the name of Noah Hansen, who we know is now married to the senator's sister. In 1980, he was married to Carrie Miller, who was Della's daughter from a previous marriage."

"Marquette Caselli was Hansen's best man," Jason said.

"You might wanna think about looking at Hansen," Joe suggested.

"He's clean, Dad," Jason replied. "Except for some *ancient* drunk and disorderlies, Hansen's a model citizen."

Joe shrugged. "You never know, Jason. Hansen might have something that even *he* doesn't know about."

"Maybe. Listen, Dad, I'm goin' over to Andreotti's office and rattle his cage a little about Michael. Wanna come with?"

Joe shook his head. "Can't. I got a burglary. I'll meet ya downtown this afternoon."

Joe and his son parted ways, and Jason headed for the other side of town. He parked his car outside of Luigi's office, and strolled through the front door. As usual, there was no secretary to greet him. He waited patiently in the opulent lobby for Luigi to find his way up front.

Finally the tall Italian strode up the hallway, smiling with recognition as he greeted Jason, "Well, Detective Patterson, what a lovely surprise. What can I do for you today?"

"I'm here about one of your patients," Jason replied with a frown, hating the way Luigi's slippery smile spread from ear to ear.

"You know I cannot divulge any information on my patients," Luigi said. "That would be unethical."

Jason pretended to laugh, asking, "Is it unethical to poison them?"

Luigi's smile abruptly faded into a straight line. "Detective Patterson, shall we call your chief *again* and let him know that you are harassing me?" he retorted.

"Maybe you could tell him why your patients keep bitin' the dust," Jason answered. "We pulled Fred Michael out of North Rapid about an hour ago — still holding the syringe, just like poor ole Mendoza."

Luigi took a remorseful breath, lamenting, "It is sad to admit, but sometimes even *I* cannot help them when they are so disturbed." He gave Jason a steely stare. "Now, is there anything else I can help you with, detective, or shall we call your chief?"

"How come there isn't any furniture in your house?"

Luigi clenched his jaw, answering, "It is being cleaned."

The door opened behind Jason at that moment, and two rough-looking, leather clad young men entered. One of the young men had a snake tattooed on the entire left side of his face, and the other wore heavy black mascara and black lipstick.

"I must ask you to leave now," Luigi said with a scowl.

"Fine." Jason started to slowly back out of the office. "But I'll be back."

"Remember your warrant next time," Luigi taunted.

*****

Luigi took the painting from the wall, revealing a small wall safe. Quickly, he worked the lock, opening the door and removing two thick envelopes. He turned to face the young men with him.

"Clive, you do understand what I want you to do, do you not?" he asked with a very serious expression.

"Yeah, we get it," the young man with the make-up answered.. "We're not stupid."

"I don't know about this," the one with the snake said, slowly shaking his head. "I think it's gonna take more than just a warning to get the cops off our tail. Maybe we should just lay low for a while."

Luigi frowned at the young man as he replied, "I pay you well, Snake, and you never want for a thing." He handed them each their payment, and then reached into his inside breast pocket. Between his thumb and index finger, he held a small vial. He handed it to Snake. "Here. For free. So you know how much I appreciate your efforts."

Snake took the vial with a hesitant smile. "Thanks, boss."

"Do not mention it," Luigi said with a smile. "But be sure you warn the young detective *before* you partake in my gift."

The two young men nodded, and left Luigi's office.

Jason and his father met at the department that afternoon in order to reference any information on Noah Hansen and Carrie Miller they could find. They found Carrie Hansen's accident record of March, 1981, learning that she died in a car accident in Custer State Park. Survivors included her husband, Noah, two sons, Tyrell and Jacob, her stepfather, Jack Nelson, a stepbrother, Tony Nelson, and one sister, Charise Nelson. They looked for references to any of the Nelsons, but found nothing.

They looked for a listing on Dr. Roy Schneider, and couldn't find anything on him either. However, when they cross-referenced him through the city's computer, they found his name on the hospital's donor waiting list. Apparently, a man with the name of Dr. Roy Schneider was currently hospitalized in the Rapid City Regional Cancer Care Center, awaiting a bone marrow donor.

"I'll go over and see if this is our Dr. Schneider," Jason said. He got a file together, and headed for the door. "I have to follow up on a couple of things with Hansen first, but I'll let you know what I find out."

"Sounds great," Joe replied. They went their separate ways.

*****

Jason parked his car behind the Kicks 66 gas station, directly across the parking lot from Maggie May's. He'd followed Noah Hansen from his office downtown to two separate building sites, and then to this place. Strangely, this was the same little dive where Mrs. Caselli reported seeing Roy Schneider and John Peters in 1975. Jason waited patiently for Hansen to finish whatever he was doing in there.

After about thirty minutes, Hansen emerged, got into his pickup and drove away. Jason watched him until he was out of sight, and then he drove over to Maggie's and parked his car out front.

Maggie was cleaning off some tables when the nicely dressed gentleman walked in. He wasn't one of her regulars — she noticed that right away. He wore dress slacks, a shirt and tie, and a blazer. His shoes were clean and shiny and every hair on that man's head was in perfect place.

"What can I getcha?" Maggie asked in her gruff voice, taking her place behind the counter. "Directions?"

Jason smiled, walking to the counter and taking a seat. "Got any fresh pie and maybe a cup of coffee?" he asked.

"Sure do," Maggie answered, reaching for a cup and saucer, setting it before Jason. She reached for the pot on the hot plate and poured his coffee, asking, "Apple or blueberry?"

"Apple," Jason answered as his eyes focused on the painting hanging to the side of the old bar. He immediately recognized the work of the Black Hills artist who signed her paintings *Angel*. It was dated "75."

"Wow, that's an oldie," Jason commented with a smile. "My mother loves her work."

"Been hangin' there for twenty-three years," Maggie answered with a wistful smile. She reached beneath the counter for the envelope where she kept her favorite old snapshots, and delicately removed the yellowed photograph of Noah and Angel. "There she is. Best little artist I ever knew."

Jason was surprised to see the two of them together in such an old photo because he knew Tillie Hansen had been married to Alex Martin at one time. "When was this?" he asked.

"Nineteen seventy-five," Maggie chuckled. "What a crazy deal that was to get straightened out."

Jason smiled into Maggie's old, black eyes. "What deal?" he asked.

"It's the best secret I ever kept, but I'd love to tell it to ya if ya got the time."

Jason nodded. "I've got a few minutes."

From a window in one of the rooms at the Howard Johnson's, through a set of binoculars, Alyssa watched Detective Patterson go into Maggie May's. She'd followed him around town for a while before realizing that he was actually following her aunt's husband, Noah. She watched Jason hide his car behind the gas station, and then she quickly secured a room at the hotel. With her U.S. Marshal's badge she was able to obtain a room facing the east, giving her a bird's eye view of Maggie May's. She called Jon and told him to meet her there so they could exchange information from the day before.

Jon put the fast-food bags on the table beside Alyssa and said, "I brought you some lunch. I'm starved."

"Noah left now, and Patterson's inside," Alyssa replied, blinking at the paper bags on the table. "And you know I don't eat that junk. Where did Bracelet go yesterday?"

"Well you gotta eat something besides tofu," Jon retorted.

Alyssa chuckled and said, "I *never* touch tofu. I'm strictly a beef and veggie girl. I got something over at Albertson's earlier."

Jon shook his head as he took a seat at the table. "Bracelet drove out to a little hobby farm in the valley," he began. "Rapid Valley Quarter Horses. I've got a call into the Secretary of State and she's gonna call me back with the owner's name. He picked up a younger woman and a *really* old man, and they all drove down to Colonial Manor in Custer."

"What's *that?*" Alyssa asked as she watched Maggie's doorway.

"Nursing home. They went to see a woman by the name of *Della*

Nelson," Jon said with emphasis, and then was quiet.

Alyssa lowered her binoculars to look at him. "What's weird about that?" she asked with a frown.

Jon took a huge bite of his burger, answering through a mouthful of food, "Your aunt's husband used to be married to Della's daughter, Carrie."

Alyssa raised one of her black brows and stated, "Carrie's mother is dead."

"Mitzy over at the Marshal's office let me use their computer." Jon swallowed his food. "I accessed the South Dakota DMV's records and the car Bracelet drove this morning — all the way from Luigi's office to Custer, South Dakota — is licensed to Hansen Development, LLC."

Alyssa nearly dropped her binoculars. "Did you get an ID on Bracelet?" she asked.

"No. But I figured we could scope out Hansen's office and he'd be easy enough to recognize. It shouldn't be too hard to find out who he is." He took another bite of his burger. "And I pulled the accident report on Carrie Hansen out of the Custer County Sheriff's Office." He swallowed his food. "Did you know that her accident took place en route from that nursing home? I'll bet the ole gal's been in there since they purported her death in 1980."

Alyssa shook her head. "Ufdah." She sighed heavily. "So Carrie, more than likely, knew her mother was still alive. Then why has Noah led us to believe that she's been dead all these years?"

Jon shrugged. "Maybe he thinks she really is dead."

Alyssa bit her lower lip, wondering aloud, "Why would a woman let her husband believe that her mother had died if she was really still alive?"

Jon rolled his eyes and frowned. "Come on, Alyssa. It's the oldest trick in the book. Della was *hiding* from someone."

"How about Della's husband? Where is he?" Alyssa asked. "And didn't Carrie have a couple of siblings?"

"Jack Nelson was Della's husband," Jon answered. "And I couldn't find a listing, or *anything* for that matter, on him, or his son, Tony, or his daughter, Charise. They're all listed in the Custer County Sheriff's accident report as possible contacts…but it turned out they didn't need to notify anyone else because Noah was first contact, and he answered the call immediately. According to the report, the Custer County Coroner brought the body to the Rapid City facility because she'd nearly made it to the Pennington County line, and it was closer. She was identified by her husband, Noah Hansen, just a few hours after the accident." He took another huge bite of his burger, and washed it down with cola.

Alyssa grimaced as she watched him. She lifted her binoculars, noticing that Jason was still inside of Maggie's. "Well, I followed Birthmark over to a bunch of row houses not far from here," she said. "By the way, what we thought was a birthmark is actually a tattoo of a snake. Anyway, they hauled a dead body out of the same row houses this morning. I've been following Patterson ever since."

"Who was it?" Jon asked.

"I haven't gone to the city's police department yet, because you know I'll have to show my badge to get anything and I don't wanna tip off Patterson. Maybe Mitzy will let you use her computer again."

Jon smiled faintly as he replied, "Probably. I think we should go down to Custer tomorrow and see if we can talk to Della. Maybe she'll be able to shed some light on whatever it is that we're doing here."

"Agreed. Do you suppose this is all tied in with Noah somehow?"

"It's a weird deal, Alyssa," Jon answered, giving his head a thoughtful scratch. "But, everything is kinda pointing in that direction."

*****

Heidi and Laura arrived home shortly after school, and smelled the roasting turkey as they came through the front door.

"Wow!" Heidi exclaimed, inhaling deeply through her nostrils. "That smells *so* good."

"Ty comes home today," Laura said with a smile, drawing the delicious aroma into her nose. "And Mom always makes him a turkey."

"Hi, girls," came a feminine, Southern drawl. Heidi and Laura glanced into the dining room to see that Mona was setting silver around the table.

"Hi, Mona," they said in unison.

"How was your day?" she asked with a sweet smile.

"Good," they answered together.

"Where's Mom?" Laura asked.

"Angel's in her studio," Mona answered.

Laura raised a suspicious brow. *Angel. Mona and Josh always call her Angel.*

Laura turned to Heidi and whispered, "Go up to my room. I gotta ask my mom about something real quick."

Heidi saw the unusual expression in Laura's eyes, but she nodded and hurried upstairs. Laura went straight to the studio, where she found her mother working on her newest masterpiece.

Tillie looked up, greeting her daughter with a smile. "Hi, Laura. How was your day?" she asked.

"Good," Laura answered, set down her backpack and plopped herself into a white, wicker chair. "Where's Annie?"

"Believe it not, she's napping," Tillie answered with a casual tone, even though her heart was pounding about six hundred beats per minute. She and Mona had talked all afternoon, and had prayed about what she would tell Laura should the child ask. It wasn't so much the kids knew of Noah building the house for Tillie, but that Noah married Carrie because she was pregnant — *that* was the secret they didn't want to leak out.

"Mom," Laura said seriously, and Tillie looked at her daughter. "Could you sit down with me for a minute?"

"Certainly." Tillie set down her brush, reaching for a towel. She wiped off her hands and took a seat in the chair just across from Laura. "What's up, kid?" she asked.

"You know," Laura replied, lowering her voice to a whisper. "I'm gonna just ask you straight up...did you run off with Dad and leave Noah stranded with this house?"

Tillie raised both of her eyebrows in surprise. That wasn't *exactly* how she expected the question to be worded. She took a deep breath and answered, "I didn't know about the house, Laura."

Laura's tone was very serious as she said, "I *thought* you guys were just friends and that you couldn't really get to know each other because he wanted to start his business."

"Well, that's sort of true —" Tillie began.

"When *did* you run off with Dad?" Laura asked with a frown.

"I didn't *run off* with your father," Tillie clarified. "You know that story. I'd known him for all of my life."

"Come on, Mom," Laura coaxed. "*Please*, just give it to me straight and I won't say a word to the boys. You and Noah should tell them yourselves — *if* they even ask."

Tillie bit her lip, frowning thoughtfully as she replied, "Okay." She took a breath and continued, "Noah and I *thought* we wanted to get married, but we were too young. We had a terrible misunderstanding and I ended the relationship. As time went by, he decided to go ahead and build the house, but when he realized I wasn't going to marry him he leased it to Elijah's grandmother and she ran a business out of it."

Laura looked horrified. "He must have been just sick about that," she whispered.

"He was," Tillie said.

"Why didn't Noah and his first wife live in the house?" Laura asked.

"Because Mrs. Olson had a lease," Tillie explained. "By law, he couldn't just throw her out."

Laura nodded. "But *you* didn't know about the house?"

Tillie shook her head. "I didn't find out about it until the day that we got engaged. He'd saved it for a surprise."

Laura sighed, as if very disappointed. "I can't imagine having *that* big of a misunderstanding. *Especially* with Noah."

"Things are different when you're young," Tillie said. She playfully frowned at her daughter. "That's why we want you to be careful with your friend, Elijah. He's *a lot* older than you."

"We're the same ages as you and Noah when you first met."

Tillie's eyes opened with astonishment. "How did you know that?"

Laura laughed at her mother's expression. "Well, gee, Mom, those pictures you painted of Noah are all dated 1975, so you must have been about seventeen or eighteen, and Noah's forty-six now, so twenty-three years ago he must have been twenty-three."

Tillie nodded in silent amazement. "See. I know what I'm talking about."

Laura laughed again, getting up from her chair. "Okay...Heidi's up in my room. I better get goin'."

Tillie stood and put her arms around her daughter. "Please don't think I hurt Noah intentionally," she said. "It wasn't like that at all. We were just too young and probably a little rebellious."

"Probably *a lot* rebellious," Laura said, giggling. "Josh showed us pictures of the motorcycle and when Noah had long hair."

"Oh, goodness."

"It's okay, Mom. You probably really couldn't help yourself. I mean, he was really a hottie back then."

Tillie rolled her eyes. "Go see Heidi and don't be talking about boys."

"Okay," Laura promised, held up her crossed fingers, and giggled her way out of the studio.

Tillie sighed with relief. Thank goodness that was over...*and she hadn't even asked why Noah married the boys' mother*. Of course not. Why would she? She was more concerned with why her mother had left Noah at the altar with an empty house.

"How'd that go?" Mona asked. Tillie looked up to see that she was standing in the doorway.

"Great," Tillie answered. "I think she was more concerned with the jilting Noah took than anything else."

Mona nodded. "Good." The secret of Ty's biological father was still safe.

Ty and Noah arrived shortly thereafter and were overwhelmed with the delicious smells coming out of Tillie's kitchen. Mona and Tillie rushed out of the studio where they had been visiting and Josh pulled in at almost the same time. Heidi and Laura, along with an awakened Annie, joined the adults in the entryway downstairs. Everyone excitedly greeted Ty with hugs and kisses, and questions about his new draft. He relayed all of the details to them and that he would have to leave by Wednesday of the following week, but that was long enough to watch A.J. and Jake and the rest of Post 22 whip Bismarck.

When the clock neared six, Jake and A.J.'s car was heard in the driveway, and greetings and information were passed around once again. Conversation around the dinner table that night was cheerful and lively, and Noah was thankful that he didn't have to answer any awkward questions. Even after doing the dishes, there were still no questions. The boys headed for Whitehead Field to throw some balls and practice their batting. Heidi was very cool toward Jake, probably displeased with his reported behavior from the night before. She and Laura retreated to the bedroom upstairs.

Noah and Tillie were relieved. They relaxed on their deck overlooking the meadow, visiting with Joshua and Mona about the events of the last few days.

Tillie sat down a tray of iced teas, smiling at Joshua as she said, "Don't worry. They're all decaf."

"Oh, thank goodness," Joshua said, taking an icy glass from the tray.

He took sip of sweet oranges and spice and pressed his lips together, "Mmm. Nothing like it. Where did you ever come up with this concoction?"

"It's Ma`ma's recipe," Tillie answered, and took a seat beside Noah and Annie.

"So," Josh began, smiling at Noah. "You did some squirming during dinner the other night."

"Oh, Josh," Noah said with a sigh, rolling his eyes. "It was awful. It was like the devil himself was sitting at my supper table."

Tillie laughed, patting Noah's shoulder as she sweetly added, "Elijah's a really nice boy. I think it's gonna be okay."

"It was like one of those dreams," Noah went on, and the familiar sparkle of mischief danced in eyes. "You know, when you look down and all of a sudden you don't have any clothes on. That's what it felt like. Talk about spilling the beans."

Everyone laughed, including Noah.

"Well, nobody seems to be too worked up over the deal," Mona said. "The only one that had questions was Laura, and she was more worried about Angel mistreating you than anything else."

"What a good kid," Noah said with a smile. "Now if I could just get her to stay away from that boy."

Joshua laughed. "It's gonna happen sooner or later, Noah. Just be thankful that she's still young enough to be within *your* terms. How would you like to be in Patty's shoes?"

Tillie moaned and rolled her eyes. "I don't know how he lives from day to day. If the girl wanted to, she could just go off on her own and do as she pleased."

"She loves her folks too much to do anything like that," Mona sweetly defended. "Just like Laura."

"Thanks, Mona," Noah said with a smile.

At Whitehead Field, Jake was wrecking nearly every pitch. It was obvious that his mind was not on the practice at all. He dropped balls that should have been caught easily, and his curves were way off.

Ty finally scowled, walking to the pitcher's mound. "What's your problem?" he asked.

A.J. left his position behind the batter's box, meeting Ty on the mound.

"Nothin'," Jake answered.

"Oh, come on, Jake," A.J. barked with a frown. "Laura had this guy over for dinner last night and he dropped the bomb of the century."

Ty made a curious face. "What are you talking about?" he asked.

"Like Dad built that house for Tillie," Jake answered.

A.J. nodded. "Something's *totally* weird about that whole thing."

Ty frowned. "What the heck are you guys talking about?"

"This guy comes over last night —" Jake began, but A.J. interrupted.

"Elijah," A.J. added. "The stockbroker who golfs all the time."

"The *stockbroker*?" Ty's eyes were wide with curiosity.

"Yeah," Jake answered. "He works for *Piper Jaffray* —"

"But he plays on a men's slow pitch league," A.J. added. "So he *might* be okay."

"Yeah," Jake continued. "He plays on a men's league. Anyway, he starts talking about how his granny used to tell this story to all her grandkids about the *poor peasant man* who built our house for *the love of his life,* but she ran off with a *rich Spaniard* and left him with the house he named *Angel's Place.* I said, '*Dad built this house,*' and Dad shoots Elijah a really dirty look. So ole Elijah up and says, '*well so much for Grandmother's stories,* ' and the subject is dropped. Well, me and A.J. nearly fainted, 'cause you know Dad always calls Tillie *Angel* and her whole family calls her *Angel,* and Uncle Josh and Auntie Mona call her *Angel* —"

"And all those paintings down at Maggie's," A.J. interrupted with a pensive expression. "What about *that*? They're all signed *Angel.*"

"Here's my question, Ty," Jake went on, "that stupid house wasn't even finished until September of 1976, and I know that because of the date that's carved into one of the cement footings under the front porch —"

"Why were you under the front porch?" Ty asked with a frown.

"Sparky got stuck under there one day," Jake explained.

"But that's not the point," A.J. insisted.

"What *is* your point, guys?" Ty asked, trying his best to follow whatever conspiracy they thought they'd uncovered.

"My point *is*," Jake said, taking a deep breath. "Ty, you were born in June of 1977, which means that Mom and Dad would had to have been married the *moment* the house was finished so she could have been pregnant long enough to give birth to you by June."

Ty frowned, wrinkling up his nose. "I still don't get it." He quickly counted the time down on his fingers. "Nine months is all it takes. What are you saying, Jake?"

Jake moaned, rolling his eyes. "Ty, *listen* to me for once. Why would Dad build a house for the *love of his life* and then just up and marry Mom? And why didn't they ever live there? *That's* weird."

Ty laughed, slapping his little brother on the back as he said, "People do weird things every day, Jake. It's no big deal."

Jake frowned but said nothing. Ty didn't think it was that big of a deal, but he and A.J. *did*. Something weird went down many years ago, and the mysterious building of the house was only a part of it. Jake's father and A.J.'s mother were deliberately keeping something from their children, and Jake and A.J. were going to find out what it was.

*****

Jason awakened to the sound of breaking glass, feeling a heavy thud against his feet. He reached for the light next to his bed, simultaneously pulling his gun out from underneath his pillow. There was no one in the bedroom with him, but his window was shattered, the wind blowing the curtains crazily around the frame.

As he swung his legs out of the bed, he felt something weighting down the covers. He saw that near the footboard was a dead bird — a robin — tied to a brick. He took a closer look and groaned. A piece of paper was tied to the brick as well. He worked the paper out of the string, unfolding the message.

Jason was horrified to read the words: *Do you love your mother?*

He dropped the note, and reached for the telephone beside his bed. He dialed the number of his parents' home, and after a number of rings, his mother answered.

"Mom?!" Jason almost shouted into the phone. "Is everything okay?!"

"Yes, I think so," Jacqueline answered in a sleepy voice. "Jason? What time is it?"

Jason looked at his alarm clock and answered, "It's two-fifteen. Is Dad there?"

"Hold on," she replied.

"Who is it?" Joe asked groggily into the telephone.

"It's me, Dad," Jason breathed. "I think I just got a message from Luigi."

Chapter 7

Ty was sweating and out of breath. He sat down on the bleachers, picked up his water bottle for several large gulps, and dumped some of it over his head. He picked up his towel, and wiped the sweat from his face and the back of his neck. Jake and A.J. jogged off the diamond, grabbed their water bottles and gave themselves a good drenching.

"Great practice!" Jake breathed.

"You guys are *way* better this morning!" Ty exclaimed, taking another gulp of water. "I prayed for you last night."

"Thanks, Ty," A.J. said with a smile, breathing heavily. "And we'd love to practice some more, but we gotta get goin'."

"We promised Maggie we'd help her clean her floors this morning," Jake added. "Wanna ride along, Ty?"

Ty shook his head. "But tell her I said, 'Hi.'"

"How are you getting home, Ty?" Jake asked.

"I'll walk over and ask Dad for a ride…isn't he working just a couple blocks from here today?"

"I think so," Jake replied. He and A.J. began to back away. "We'll see ya later."

Ty waved as they hurried away. He took another gulp of his water and leaned back on the bleachers and took a deep breath of the cool Black Hills morning air. What a *great* morning at the park. No reporters and no questions. "They sure don't have air like this in Washington," he said aloud.

"Ty Hansen?" A voice called out from behind him.

Ty sat up to look around. He was surprised to see an old man in a wheelchair, being pushed by a young woman coming toward him.

"That's me," Ty said, getting to his feet.

The wheelchair stopped in front of Ty and the old man looked up at him. He was thin and pale, and his eyes were sunken into his slender face. In place of eyebrows and hair, shiny, white skin glistened in the morning sun. Ty wondered what kind of an illness this man bore.

"My goodness, but you've gotten so tall," the man said with a smile.

In that instant, Ty saw a strange familiarity in the man. "Do I know you?" he asked.

"You should have," the man answered. He took a breath, looking at the woman who pushed his chair. "Can you please leave us for a minute?"

"Certainly," she answered, setting the brake on the chair before she walked away from them.

"Sit down, Ty," the man requested with a gentle smile.

Ty smiled nervously, taking a seat on the bleacher.

"My name is Roy Schneider," the man said. "I have to ask you for a favor."

Alyssa and Jon walked the long hall in Colonial Manor. Even though they were dressed in casual blue jeans and dark jackets, their height alone made them stand out like the strangers they were. Their informal clothing had been Jon's idea. He said they'd look just like family members down for a visit. He carried a small potted plant.

They stopped at the nurse's station.

"Can I help you?" a nurse asked.

Alyssa smiled, glancing at the nurse's badge as she said, "Hi, Myrna. We'd like to see Della Nelson."

"Are you related?"

"Sort of," Alyssa answered.

"Della can only see immediate family members," Myrna respectfully informed. "And I don't recognize you."

"Please," Alyssa coaxed. "This is extremely important."

"No," Myrna said with a shake of her head.

Jon moaned, flipping his badge out of his breast pocket, laying it on the counter in front of the nurse. "Listen, Ma'am, we *must* see Della, and we don't want you calling anybody about this. Okay?"

The nurse was surprised, looking from the badge to Jon, and then at Alyssa.

Alyssa produced her badge, promising, "We won't hurt her and we'll be *very careful* with our questions."

The nurse looked at the two of them and began to nod. "Okay. But not for very long."

"Thanks, Ma'am," Jon said with a polite smile, putting his badge away.

Myrna led them down the hall, paused by a door and softly knocked. She opened the door, peeked inside and sweetly called, "Della honey? Are ya decent? You got some company."

"I'm here," came the reply in an old lady's voice.

Alyssa felt the strangest pain in her heart. She swallowed it away, determined to maintain her professionalism in whatever situation unfolded...*but more than likely, this is Noah's mother-in-law,* she thought.

As the nurse swung the door open, a little woman in a wheelchair came into view. She was seated by the window, bundled in a white sweater, with a bright blue afghan covering her legs. Her hair was as white as could be, and her gray eyes shown like marbles against her white skin. She smiled when she saw Alyssa and Jon in the doorway, waving them to come in.

"Who are you?" she asked excitedly. "Do I know you?"

Photographs of Ty and Jake, at all different ages, covered the walls around the old woman. Several shots of Ty in his Post 22 uniform were enlarged and framed, as well as photos of Jake with A.J. She also had photos of Laura and her friend, Heidi, and even a few of Annie Laurie. Several small, framed photographs were on the table beside the old woman's chair, and she was even holding one in her hands.

Alyssa drew in a quiet breath, realizing…*this woman is Carrie's mother.*

Jon smiled and presented her with the plant.

"Is it for me?" she sweetly exclaimed.

Jon nodded. "We thought you might like a little something." He glanced around for an empty place to set it, seeing only the ledge by the window. "Would you like me to put it here?"

"Yes, dear," she answered.

Alyssa knelt down in front of Della, impulsively reaching for one of the old woman's warm hands. "I'm Alyssa. You must be Della."

The situation appeared to be okay, so Myrna quietly backed out of the room, closing the door behind her.

Jon took a seat on the bed, still wondering if they had the right Della Nelson. After all, *Nelson* was a common name.

However, Alyssa already *knew* they had the right Della Nelson. "Look at all of these wonderful pictures you have," she said. "These kids are my cousins. How do you know them?"

"They're my grandsons, and their *new* family," Della answered with a proud smile.

Jon was stunned.

"Ty is one of my grandsons," Della went on, handing Alyssa the small framed photo she was holding. "Isn't he handsome?"

"He's wonderful," Alyssa said.

Della sighed with a smile, nodding her head. "Noah raised him you know. *All by himself.* My Carrie has been gone a long time."

"I know," Alyssa acknowledged. "Did she know you were here?"

Della chuckled as she answered, "She put me here! It was Jack and Tony's idea, but Carrie got them some money from Noah, but he *never* comes to see me. It would sure be nice to see Noah again."

"Does he know that you're here?" Alyssa asked.

"I don't think so. You see we're hiding from Sal, and Sal would be mean to Noah if he knew I was here."

"Who's Sal?" Jon asked with a frown.

"He's my Jack's brother, and he's tried to find us for years, but, we *always* get away."

Alyssa raised an eyebrow. "Tell me about Jack," she said.

"Well," Della whispered with a clever shine in her gray eyes. "He came from Sicily many years ago and his brother has always tried to find him. He did find us, *twice*, and that's when I fell down the stairs."

"Do you remember that?" Jon asked.

Della shook her head. "I don't remember very much anymore, except for my Carrie and Charise."

"Who's Charise?" Alyssa asked.

"She belongs to me and Jack."

"And Carrie doesn't?" Alyssa attempted to clarify.

"Carrie's father died before I met Jack. She was a very little girl when that happened and her and Jack never got along very well. I suppose that's why she took up with Roy."

"Roy?" Jon asked.

"He used to work for Jack," Della answered. She lowered her voice to a whisper again, saying "He's Ty's father you know."

Alyssa nearly fell on the floor. Slowly shaking her head, she said, "I thought Noah was Ty's father."

Della shook her head. "Noah knew it when they married. He's known all along."

Jon sat quietly on the bed, pondering what their next question could possibly be. Poor Alyssa was obviously dumbstruck by Della's words, unable to come up with additional queries. He cleared his throat, and asked, "Where's this Roy? Do you know how we can find him?"

"No," Della answered. "They tell me that he got mad when Carrie married Noah and left town. Nobody's even talked about him since then."

Alyssa swallowed, asking, "Did Roy know about Ty?"

"Oh, sure. Everybody in town knew about Ty, but nobody cared. We were all just so glad to see Carrie settle down and behave herself. She wanted to have an abortion, but Noah talked her out of it."

Alyssa was stunned, to say the least, at the news that Della was giving them. The poor, old woman was obviously mixed up about certain events, but some things seemed to be called from her memory with clarity.

"Can I see Charise?" Alyssa asked.

"I'm sure she'd love to meet you," Della answered with a smile.

"Where does she live?" Alyssa asked.

"In the valley. She sells horses."

Rapid Valley Quarter Horses, Alyssa thought. *Charise must live there.*

*****

Laura and Heidi had gone into town to do some shopping, and Tillie was home alone with Annie. Tillie had twisted her knee again, and the two year old was being her usual, rambunctious self. Tillie sat in a kitchen chair with the pack of ice on her knee, watching her daughter toddle by with two biscuits in her chubby hands, both dogs hot on her trail. Tillie groaned, praying for Noah to come home early.

Instead of walking over to ask Noah for a ride, Ty walked the entire way from Whitehead Field to their home behind the Fish Hatchery off Rimrock Highway. Along the way, he thought about the strange discussion he'd had with A.J. and Jake just the night before. *They were right…Dad was still in love with Tillie when he married Mom…had to have been….*

By the time Ty reached his front porch, he was more confused than when he'd started his long walk. He opened the door and was greeted by his little sister and the two dogs.

"Ty!" Annie exclaimed, dropping the biscuits as she reached for her brother. Sparky and Vanilla grabbed the treats and trotted away.

"Hi, baby," he said, scooping the pretty child into his arms. He found comfort in holding the baby, and Ty snuggled her close, giving her a soft kiss on the top of her head. "Where's Ma`ma?"

Annie shrugged her little shoulders. She put one hand on each of his cheeks, smiling into his eyes. "Let's play."

Ty smiled in return as he replied, "I can't play today, Annie." And then he called, "Tillie?"

"I'm in the kitchen," she answered.

"Let's go see Ma`ma," Ty said, meandering through the scattered toys in the entryway. He nearly tripped on a rubber dinosaur, managing to regain his balance before he fell. "Man, you can really make a mess."

"Let's play," Annie repeated, pouting.

Ty found Tillie still sitting at the kitchen table with her leg on a chair. She pulled the ice bag off of her knee and said, "I twisted my bad knee again." She gave the ice bag a purposeful toss, landing it expertly in the kitchen sink. She smiled at her perfect pitch and turned her eyes on Ty, seeing the grief on his face. "Ty, what's the matter?" She got to her feet, limping toward him.

Ty looked down at the pretty lady who'd married his 'father' nearly four years before, wondering if she even had a clue, or if it had been kept from her as well.

"Ty," she repeated, putting her hand on his arm, looking into his eyes for an answer. "Are you all right?"

"Are you alone?" Ty asked, tears falling onto his cheeks.

"Yes." Tillie's heart pounded with the fear of whatever was unknown. Something had gone terribly wrong, and Ty was bringing her a message of tragedy. She saw him trembling and so she reached for Annie, who willingly came into the arms of her mother.

Ty leaned against the door frame and slid all the way to the floor. Tillie sat Annie down beside him, and then herself, trying to look into his grief-stricken eyes. She took his shaking hand into one of her own and gave it a delicate kiss. "What happened, Ty? Is someone hurt? Where are your brothers?"

"They went to help Maggie and I walked home," Ty answered.

Tillie frowned. "You walked all the way home? Why didn't you ask Dad?"

Ty looked into Tillie's eyes and whispered, "There was a man at the park this morning — he says he's my *father*."

Tillie felt the floor beneath her begin to spin. She watched Annie go to the cupboard and fish out two more biscuits for the dogs. She tried to take a breath, looking back at Ty.

Ty saw the brief recollection in Tillie's eyes. Frowning he asked, "What do you know about this?"

She swallowed and whispered, "I think we should call your dad, Ty. You need to give him a chance to explain."

"Tillie, I'm nearly twenty-one years old. Dad's had plenty of time to *explain* things. What's going on?"

"Please, Ty. He loves you so much. I could never begin to explain things the way that he will. Let me call him." She looked earnestly into his eyes, and he finally responded with a nod.

Tillie took a deep breath, stood up and reached for the telephone hanging on the kitchen wall. She quickly dialed Noah's cell phone number, and he answered on the second ring.

"Hansen."

"It's me."

Noah heard the urgency in the tone of her voice. "What's wrong?" he asked.

"Where are you?"

"Just coming down Jackson. I was on my way home. Angel, what's the matter?"

"Ty needs to talk to you right away," she answered through the tears in her throat.

"I'm almost there. Can he wait for me? Is he there?"

"He's here with me and we'll wait for you," Tillie answered.

"Okay."

Tillie turned off the phone in her hand, resuming her position on the floor beside Ty. "He'll be here in a second," she said, lovingly brushing some of the tears from Ty's cheeks.

Annie noticed Ty's distraught appearance and wriggled into his lap, putting her little arms around his middle. Ty folded his arms around the sweet baby, holding her until they heard Noah's pickup out front. His boots clamored up the front steps, and down the hall to the kitchen.

Noah found his oldest and his youngest sitting together with Tillie in the doorway of the kitchen, and he knelt beside them. He attempted to look into Ty's pale expression, but his son wouldn't lift his eyes from the floor.

"Are you sick, Ty?" he asked, reaching for his son's forehead, wondering if they should be going to the doctor instead of sitting in the house talking about it.

Ty looked away from Noah as more tears fell from his eyes. Noah looked to Tillie for an explanation, seeing her tears as well.

"Noah," she said, reaching for her husband's hand. More tears fell from her eyes and she whispered, "Ty met Roy today."

Noah's eyes narrowed into an ugly scowl. "What did *he* want?" he growled.

"He told him everything," Tillie cried.

"Why didn't you tell me?" Ty whispered through soft sobs.

Noah swallowed hard and began to shake his head. Somewhere, in the back of his mind, he plotted Roy's demise. He'd warned Roy more than once to stay away from Ty, and yet the old derelict had finally done it. He'd pay dearly for this.

"Answer me," Ty demanded when Noah didn't respond. "Why didn't you tell me?"

Noah grumbled, "Because it wasn't important."

"Is that why you had to marry Mom?" Ty accused angrily. "Because Jake and A.J. told me about the house. Is that why Tillie wouldn't marry you and ran off with Alex Martin? Did you think that *you* were the one that got her pregnant, or did you know all along?"

Noah's heart raced, his hands trembling as he reached for the son he'd loved since before he was born. Ty fell against him, allowing Noah to hold him while he cried. It was a pitiful sight, and Tillie's tears were uncontrolled. Annie crawled from between the two of them and into her mother's arms, but stayed very quiet while they watched the scene before them.

"It wasn't like that at all," Noah assured as he held his son. "I knew I wasn't your father…but I'd lost track of Angel and I didn't know where she was. Your mom and I were both very lonely, and getting married was a good solution to a problem she didn't know how to fix."

"Did you love her? Ever?" Ty whispered.

"Of course I loved her —"

"*That's* hard to believe," Ty retorted. "She was *sleeping* with someone else."

Noah took a breath, vividly remembering all of the reasons he'd married Carrie. His eyes filled with tears. He wanted to cry — needed to cry — but Ty needed a decent explanation. Not some namby-pamby, gut-wrenching, tear-drenched melodrama, but the real reasons why he'd married his son's mother. *Suck it up,* he told himself. He set his jaw, explaining, "I watched you grow inside of your mother, and when I put my hand on her, and I could feel you moving, I couldn't wait to meet you. When you were born, there was this tiny, new life in my arms and I was *amazed* at God's creation of you. It didn't matter where you had come from, Ty, just that you were there and that you were *mine*. And God let something wonderful happen between your mom and me while she carried you and when you were newborn. Through you, God gave us blessing and love. You made us a *family*, Ty, and we were so happy that I don't think it ever really dawned on either of us that you didn't belong to me. We never talked about it, and so I don't think it mattered to your mother either."

"Did she love Roy?" Ty whispered.

"Oh, maybe she *thought* she did," Noah answered. "But she was young. It was probably more infatuation than love."

"He said that you forbid him to see me," Ty said. "Is that true?"

Noah nodded. "I had my reasons. He's crooked, and I didn't want you mixed up in that."

Ty looked at Tillie and asked, "Why did you leave Dad?"

Tillie sniffed, wiping away some of her tears as she answered, "We had a terrible misunderstanding — and it was *all* my fault. I was only seventeen years old, and I ran away. I didn't tell him where I'd gone, because I didn't want him to ever find me. By the time we ran into each other again, I was married to Alex and the twins had been born."

"What did Roy want anyway?" Noah asked. "Did he just come along to rattle everyone's cage, or was there a *real* purpose for this?"

"He's dying, Dad," Ty replied. "He needs marrow and I'm his only living relative."

Noah rolled his eyes as he replied, "Well, let him die."

Tillie and Ty were visibly surprised at Noah's reply, but Ty bit his lower lip, hesitating as he said, "I don't think he's saved. I'm afraid he'll go to hell."

"He deserves it," Noah growled.

Tillie felt as if she'd been dumped over a cliff. *That* didn't sound like her kind, loving husband at all.

"Why would you even want to help him?" Noah asked.

"Because he's lost," Ty answered. "Shouldn't we have a burden for the lost?"

Noah's expression twisted into an ugly scowl again, and he barked, "That poor, lost man wanted to abort you, Ty! I don't think I can ever get past that!"

Tillie and Annie shuddered at Noah's raised voice, but Ty was crushed, and could not reply.

Noah took a breath, lowering his voice as he said, "Listen, Ty, you're *my* son, *not* Roy's. Roy had his chance and he blew it. It's tough, but those are his consequences."

"It's not like I'll ever call him 'Dad'," Ty stammered, looking at Noah. "You're my only 'Dad.' Roy is just a lost soul who needs to hear the message, but he'll *never* take your place."

Noah shook his head and muttered, "If you decide to help him out, please let me and Angel know so that we can prepare the rest of your family." With that, Noah stomped away.

*****

The nurse reappeared in Della's doorway and the visit was ended without protest from either Jon or Alyssa. They left Colonial Manor, and headed for Rapid City on the route that Carrie more than likely took on that fateful day in March of 1980.

Alyssa sat in the passenger seat, biting the nail on her index finger.

"Whatcha thinkin'?" Jon asked.

"Eleven years ago, my Aunt Tillie was hit by a car and nearly died," she answered. "She suffered a head injury and lost the control of her arms and legs. During that time, a guy that worked for Noah told him about his stepmother and how she had fallen down some steps and suffered similar injuries. To aid in her rehabilitation, her daughter brought her a puppy. Anyway, Noah's employee brought a whole litter of his sister's puppies to the hospital."

"Hm. Do you think this employee is still around?"

"Could be," Alyssa answered. "*Somebody* from Hansen Development visited Della yesterday."

"Della said that the kid's name is Tony," Jon commented. "Does Noah have an employee by that name?"

"I don't know...and how about this Roy Schneider character? In what capacity did he *work* for Jack?" She shook her head. "And then she just mentions that Jack came from Sicily many years ago. Do you suppose he's an illegal alien?"

Jon shrugged. "If Jack's an illegal, then his son is, too. Do you remember the name of the guy that works for your aunt's husband?"

"I only met him one time." She suddenly snapped her fingers. "Ben! His name was Ben."

*****

Jason was sipping the pink lemonade his mother had brought to him, studying the painting hanging in her dining room. It was the depiction of a mysterious, hooded woman, leading a black horse through a canyon, a man trailing in the distance behind her. The caption beneath the portrait read *Hope*, and it was signed *Angel, '94*.

"Like it?" Jacqueline asked her son when she noticed he was eyeing the painting.

Jason nodded. "It's really good. I saw another one of her paintings just recently. It was dated 1975."

Jacqueline softly gasped. "Where did you see *that*?" she asked.

"A place on the north end. Maggie May's. It used to be a bar."

"What did the painting look like?" Jacqueline asked.

"A hooded woman with a horse."

Jacqueline smiled with a nod, hurrying from the room. In a few moments, she returned with a pamphlet. "I picked this up at her last show," she explained. "Originally, there were two of that particular painting, both done in 1975, and then a third in 1986. She gave one of the '75s to her first husband, Alex Martin, and he also got the one done in 1986." She snorted. "And he certainly didn't deserve them. *That's* for sure." She pointed to a photograph in the pamphlet. "Is that the one?"

Jason looked down at the photo. "That's the one," he replied. He frowned at his mother and asked, "Why didn't Alex deserve them?"

"Oh," Jacqueline groaned. "He was such a terrible husband to her. He was the attorney general for South Dakota, *briefly*, once. Let's see...when did he win the election?" She bit her lip as she recalled, "I believe it was 1986. He won by an amazing landslide, and then resigned less than a year later. He was a great attorney general, but he treated his wife and kids like dirt. He was especially cruel to Angel."

"What did he do to her?"

"She got hit by a car and was hospitalized," Jacqueline explained. "And Alex's best friend at the time was this man named Noah. And it's really an involved story, but Noah was terribly in love with her and Alex flipped out and served her with divorce papers, right there in the hospital bed. He served her with another separate lawsuit alleging pain and suffering, and served Hansen as well. I represented both Noah and Angel in the actions. Alex dismissed both of the complaints after a couple months."

"Did they have an affair?"

"Oh, heavens no," Jacqueline answered. "It wasn't like that at all." She took a breath and added, "They're married now you know…Angel and Noah. They live in that big house out on Rimrock." She giggled, "I've long suspected Hansen built the thing for her. It used to be called Angel's Place."

Joe's car pulled into the garage and soon he came through the back door. "Hi, Jacq," he said as he kissed her, and then caught sight of his son. They'd decided after Jason's threat from the night before, Jacqueline wouldn't be spending a whole lot of time alone. In fact, her meeting scheduled for that evening at the City School and Administration Building had been moved to their residence. "Hey, kid. What's up?"

"I have that meeting tonight," Jacqueline reminded before Jason could respond. "Dinner's in the oven. You guys can eat whenever you want."

"Okay." Joe smiled at his wife and gave her another kiss.

She blew a kiss at Jason, and headed for her office upstairs to prepare for her meeting.

Joe poured himself a glass of lemonade, joining his son at the dining room table. "You look like you're about ready to bust."

"I've been following Hansen."

"Is he interesting, or are we barking up the wrong tree?" Joe asked.

"Fairly interesting. He's been friends with this old bartender on the north end, Maggie May West?"

"Oh, Maggie May's," Joe acknowledged.

"That's the one. And Frank had mentioned to you that Marquette Caselli's wife saw something there back in '75. So, I'm following Hansen and guess where he goes? Maggie May's. So I waited for him to leave and I went in and there's an old, old Angel hanging in there. I got talking to Maggie about how my mother loves Angel's work and she spilled her guts. Turns out Hansen and Angel, who is actually Tillie Caselli, got together back in 1975. Tillie was seventeen years old and was visiting Rapid City for this young artists' convention thing and Hansen asked her out on a date. He was this mean, ole biker who couldn't say no to a drink if he tried, and I guess Tillie completely went *crazy* for him —"

"Are you talking about Senator Caselli's sister?" Joe interrupted with a frown.

Jason laughed. "I imagine her parents had a serious rebellion on their hands. Anyway, she was in town for a couple of days and they decided to get married. Well, she finally tells him that she's underage and he'll have to wait until she's eighteen. Hansen agrees to this and she promises to come back a couple of weeks later with her brother." He took a breath and continued, "Now, this is where is gets really interesting, and Maggie claims that she's never told another living soul. Marquette Caselli brings Tillie back to Rapid City, along with his wife, because he's following a lead on a case. And Maggie isn't clear on the details, but she remembers the night that Tillie claims to have returned and Carrie Miller, who was Noah's first wife, came into the bar really drunk that night. Apparently, Tillie saw Carrie kissing Noah and doesn't even come into the bar. A man, whom Maggie called Roy, came in and made Carrie leave with him." Jason paused and looked at his father. "Are you following me so far?"

"Yep." Joe took a sip of his lemonade.

"Okay," Jason continued. "The *next day*, Marquette Caselli waltzes into Maggie's place and says he's looking for two men. Caselli has photos with him; one is John Peters, Caselli's friend and associate, and the other is the man Maggie knows as Roy. And get this, Maggie lies to Caselli because she thought at the time Carrie's stepfather, Jack Nelson, sold illegal drugs and Hansen was a huge customer. Of course, by now, after meeting Tillie, Hansen has completely straightened out his life and was sober."

"Hansen did drugs?" Joe looked confused.

"Everybody did drugs in the seventies, Dad. Anyway, she sent Marquette Caselli on his way, thinking she was protecting Hansen."

"So, what's your connection there?" Joe asked.

"Carrie Miller," Jason answered. "Andreotti's got something on her and he's using the Casellis to get close to Hansen, maybe hoping that Hansen will just up and give him whatever it is that he wants."

"So you don't think the Casellis are involved with Andreotti?"

Jason shook his head, answering, "I think Andreotti's using the Casellis to get close to Hansen."

"You'd better have a talk with Roy Schneider," Joe suggested. "And then we're gonna have to pull Hansen in for questioning."

Jason sipped his lemonade, nodding in agreement.

*****

After a long afternoon with Ty, and a very stressed and quiet dinner with their other children, Noah went off to their bedroom alone while Tillie tucked Annie into her bed. As Tillie passed their other children's rooms, she noticed that Ty's door was closed. *That poor kid.* He wasn't speaking to any of his siblings and Tillie wondered when they would start asking questions about the sudden change in his mood.

Over the course of the afternoon, Ty explained that there would have to be some medical tests done to insure his blood and tissue matched Roy's. Noah wholeheartedly objected to the procedure, reminding Ty that Roy had wanted him dead before he was born. Noah tried to make Roy as evil and vile an enemy as he could, but Ty remained strangely compassionate toward the man. It cut Noah to his core. By the time the other children arrived at home, Noah and Ty were barely speaking.

Tillie slipped into her dark bedroom, closing the door behind her. Noah was sitting on the loveseat beneath the open window. How hard this day must have been for him. He'd explained everything to Ty the best he could, but the shock of the situation was still heavy within him.

"Hey," she whispered, padding across the floor.

"Hey."

In the darkness she saw his terrible frown. She sat down beside him and nestled herself in his arms. The moment she was with him, Noah held her tightly, and Tillie felt him begin to cry.

"I never wanted him to know," he whispered.

"I know," she whispered.

"I hate him."

"Don't hate him, Noah," Tillie said. "He's afraid to die."

"Ty's *mine*," Noah cried. "I don't want him giving any piece of himself to that evil man. I say let him die and burn in hell where he belongs."

Tillie could hardly disagree. After all, Roy had had the chance to be Carrie's husband and a father to Ty when she told him she was pregnant. He didn't want the responsibility then, but he was more than willing to take what he could get out of it now. How ironic. The very life Roy would have denied his own son before birth, he now asked for in the form of a *donation*.

Tillie touched the tears on her husband's face, whispering, "This is gonna be okay. We're gonna get through this and we'll be better people because of it."

"I don't want him in Ty's life," Noah cried.

"I know." Tillie lovingly dried the tears from his face. "But for some reason God chose this time to reveal this —"

"Satan did this," Noah protested.

"It doesn't matter, Noah. God will watch over us like He *always* has."

Chapter 8

Ty slipped out of the house before six o'clock the next morning. He wasn't speaking to anyone, except the Lord. Though he knew full well what Jesus wanted him to do, he ached with what he knew his dad would rather have him choose.

Tillie's old Mercedes was for his use while he was on school vacations, and he drove to Dr. Carlson's office at the Cancer Care Center. Maybe the tests this morning would be negative, and he wouldn't have to worry about making a decision to help Roy. Maybe he could just witness to the man and be on his way. After all, he didn't want anything to do with someone who once wished him dead.

After he'd finished with the doctor and the lab, Ty found Roy's room. He knocked on the door and waited for a reply.

"Come in," called the weak voice from the other side.

Rauwolf was sitting up in his bed, reading a newspaper. He looked up with surprise when he saw Ty. "Well, hello, Ty," he said with a smile.

"Hey, Roy. How are you today?"

"I'm still here, so it's a good day," he answered. "What are you doing up here so early?"

"I had to see Dr. Carlson and give some blood before breakfast, and I thought I'd stop by," Ty answered. "I guess they'll have the results in a few days."

"So, do you wanna go through with it?" Rauwolf asked.

"If the tests are positive I'll do it."

As Rauwolf looked at the tall, redheaded man before him, his heart softened. Shining out of Ty's expression was the perfect likeness of Carrie. She'd been beautiful, especially during the pregnancy, and the baby had looked like her from the moment he was born.

"You look like her," Rauwolf said. "You've got her eyes."

Ty nodded with a smile. "Dad says that, too." He took a breath and hesitantly asked, "Dad says that you guys wanted an abortion. Is that true?"

Rauwolf swallowed hard, answering, "It was your dad that talked her out of it. She asked him to borrow the money for it, and he wouldn't even discuss it with her."

"Why didn't *you* give her the money?"

"I was in some other trouble, so I ran away." Rauwolf frowned. "I thought she'd just figure everything out herself."

"Why didn't *you* marry Mom?"

Rauwolf took a deep breath, sighing as he answered, "That was the biggest mistake I ever made. But in the end, you wound up with the better man."

Ty nodded, swallowing away the strange lump in his throat. "He's good to us...he even loves Tillie's kids."

"Your mom loved him and being with him changed her," Rauwolf admitted with a sad expression. "I came back for her once, and she wouldn't leave him. She was pregnant with your little brother. Noah caught me there that day." He chuckled. "I thought he might kill me. I told him I had come to see *my boy*, and he hit me in the face...you know, Ty, your mom put *his* name on your birth certificate because she *knew* he was a good man." He shook his head and made a "tsk" noise. "I wish she would have loved *me* like that."

Ty's expression was thoughtful as he listened to the old blackguard's regrets. "Have you ever been to church?" he asked.

"Twice," Rauwolf answered. "The first time was to watch your mother marry Noah, and the second was the day of her funeral."

"Do you know about Jesus?"

Rauwolf rolled his eyes. "Everybody's heard of Him," he answered.

Ty took a seat on the edge of Rauwolf's bed, frowning as he said, "I'm going to tell you about Jesus —"

Rauwolf held up his hand, saying, "Please don't bother with that hocus pocus —"

"It's not hocus pocus." Ty frowned. "And if you want some of *my* marrow, you'll have to listen to what *I* have to say."

Rauwolf sighed. "Okay, it's a deal. I'll listen, but I'm not making any promises."

Ty smiled as he began, "My guess is that you've got a lot of sin in your heart, Roy, because Jesus has laid it heavily on my heart to make salvation clear to you."

"Salvation?" Rauwolf frowned.

Ty nodded. "Jesus will forgive your sins if you ask."

"Sins?"

"Things that you've done wrong...for example, your sin with my mother. You shared a marital relationship, though you were never married."

Rauwolf screwed up his face, asking, "And *that's* a sin?"

Ty nodded. "God intended that relationship to be only between a husband and a wife. The two of you made a child together, and you didn't take responsibility for that child. In fact, you would have rather murdered the child —"

"You weren't a *child*," Rauwolf interrupted. "You were an organism."

Ty shook his head. "That *organism* is sitting here on the edge of your bed, filled with marrow that you might need to live. Do you think maybe you should change your thinking on that issue?"

Rauwolf remained silent.

"And I have the feeling there are a lot of other sins in your heart, Roy, that Jesus wants you to confess to Him," Ty went on. "You don't have to tell me about them, and it's none of my business. Just take it all to Jesus. Lay them at the foot of His cross, ask for forgiveness and repent."

"I don't understand *the cross*," Rauwolf said.

"It's where Jesus died, becoming the ultimate sacrifice for our sin," Ty explained. "You see, in the Old Testament, God required animal sacrifices as an atonement for human sin. Every time the people sinned, they had to get an animal and offer it as sacrifice to God. But the people got so bad. So God offered His only Son, Jesus, to die in our place. Because if we don't atone for our sin, we will eventually die. And that death means an eternal life away from Jesus, and I think burning in the pits of hell itself. Why not just say you're sorry to the Lord Jesus so that when you do pass away you will have an eternal life of peace with Jesus? All you have to do is *ask* Him to forgive you. Ask Him to fill that empty place in your heart that makes you sin. Then turn away from those sins and commit them no more. Instead of having to run away from trouble, be *good*. Stop lying if you lie, stop stealing if you steal. Don't have sex with women you're not married to, and don't get drunk. Commit yourself to a life devoted to Jesus, sharing His message with other sinners, and helping other believers to obey and serve."

Rauwolf frowned, but it wasn't anger. He hesitantly asked, "Tell me, Ty, are there any sins that Jesus *won't* forgive?"

Ty shook his head. "When we sincerely ask for forgiveness, He forgives *all* our sins, removing them from us as far as the east is from the west, and then He *forgets* about them."

"How do you know all this?"

Ty held up his Bible. "It's all right in here...everything we need to know about Jesus."

Rauwolf winced. "Where did that come from?" he asked.

Ty grinned. "I've had it with me the whole time I've been here."

Rauwolf gulped as he looked at the worn book. "Read me something out of there," he said.

"It would be my pleasure," Ty answered with a smile.

*****

Charise peeked into her mother's room, and found the old woman sitting by the window.

"Hi, Ma`ma," Charise said.

Della turned her head and smiled, her eyes twinkling. "Hello...is it my Charise?"

"It's me, Ma`ma." Charise sat in the chair across from her mother.

Out of the corner of her eye, she caught sight of the new plant in the window, and she frowned. "New plant, Ma`ma?"

"Where's Antonio and my Jack?" Della asked, smiling into her daughter's eyes.

"Papa didn't feel very good today," Charise answered. "And Tony had to work. How are you?"

Della sighed contentedly as she answered, "I am having the *best* day, Charise."

Charise noticed the glow on her mother's face and she smiled in return. "Why are you having the best day, Ma`ma?" she asked.

"Do you remember Noah?"

Charise's heart skipped a beat and her face flushed hot. She glanced at the plant on the window's ledge. "Yes. I remember Noah. Why? Was he here?" she asked.

"Oh, no," Della answered in a peaceful voice. "It was a young lady. I think she called herself Alyssa and she was very tall."

Alyssa? Charise's heart pounded. "When was this?" she whispered.

"Yesterday I believe," Della answered.

Charise tried to remain calm so as not to alarm her mother. "What did she say?" she asked.

"We talked about your papa and Antonio. She says that Noah still builds things. I'd really like to see Noah again."

Charise's eyes began to burn with tears and she tried to blink them away. They hadn't had *this* discussion in so many years.

"We talked about Ty," Della went on, and Charise caught her breath again.

"What about Ty?" she asked.

"Well, Alyssa says that the boys are her cousins." Della's gray eyes twinkled.

Charise swallowed and asked, "Did she have a last name?"

"She didn't say."

Charise nervously licked her lips, standing from her chair. "I'm going to talk to the nurse. I'll be right back."

"Okay, my dear."

With that, Charise dashed from the room and down to the nurse's station. Several nurses were charting, and not one of them looked up to even acknowledge her presence.

Charise cleared her throat loudly and asked, "Did my mother have a guest yesterday?" She was more than just a little ticked off. These people had been given instructions, hundreds of them, with regard to who Della Nelson could and couldn't see.

Myrna looked up from her work and went to Charise.

"Who was here?" Charise asked with a frown.

Myrna let out her breath, answering quietly, "Look, there were a couple of U.S. Marshals here yesterday. I had to let them in."

Charise was aghast. "Did they have a warrant?" she asked.

The nurse shook her head.

Charise stomped her foot and growled, "Then you didn't have to let them in! They have no authority without a warrant!" She felt the room spin around her and she grabbed the counter to help her balance. Myrna rushed around to the other side, catching Charise before she fell.

"Get me some water or something," she called over her shoulder. "Are you okay, Miss Nelson?"

"I'm okay," Charise breathed, trying to regain her balance. "What did the marshals want?"

"Just to visit," the nurse answered.

"Did they have names?"

"They had badges...The tall one, the woman, was named Caselli."

Charise was spinning again, and then it went black as she slumped in Myrna's arms.

Sal stormed across his office, straight for the liquor. His regular graceful gait was gone, and in its place were the purposeful steps of a provoked man. His hand moved past the brandy, picking up the scotch. He poured himself nearly half of a tumbler and gulped.

"I did not want him to see the boy," he spat. He turned to look at the younger man seated in front of his desk. "And *you* should have been the one to bring me this information. Why did you not know?"

Antonio frowned, answering, "How was I *supposed* to know about this? I had no idea he could even leave the hospital, let alone be taken to a park across town."

"We have come too far to risk this," Sal ranted. "We still do not know how much your stepsister told Hansen before she died."

"I do not think he knows."

Sal searched Antonio's eyes, accusing, "You are getting cold feet."

"No." Antonio stood. "I just do not believe he knows."

"Perhaps he does not trust you," Sal said, gulping the rest of his scotch.

"He trusts me," Antonio reassured. "Perhaps you should let the thing go. This has become a futile search for something you will never find."

"Perhaps I should find *another* way to get close to Noah." Sal's mouth curled into an ugly sneer as he glared at Antonio. "It has become apparent that I cannot depend on you."

"You *can* depend on me," Antonio insisted with a frown. "Just give me some more time."

After they'd dropped Jacqueline off at her office downtown, Jason Patterson and his father spent the better part of the morning in the basement of the *Rapid City Journal* searching their archived microfiche. Earlier, they'd attempted to access information files on Marquette Caselli through the Police Department's computer. However, the only information of any use was simplified records outlining the Casellis' most astounding victories.

Everything else was restricted. They came across the old Ponerello mystery Marquette cracked in August of 1968, but found no details correlating to what was happening in Rapid City. That led them to the newspaper archives, and eventually the corresponding story run in every major newspaper in South Dakota at the time.

"Look at that hair," Joe murmured as they examined the photograph of Marquette Caselli getting into a limousine in Palermo, Sicily. At that time, Marquette wore a long ponytail.

"Must've been a hippie," Jason summarized, pointing to a section of the article. "It says here Caselli was on his way to Switzerland when this was written, but we can't find anything *after* that. This must have remained unsolved."

"But we know he had leads," Joe said with a thoughtful frown. "He followed one of them to Rapid City in 1975."

"And he had a photograph of Roy in 1975, when his buddy, John, followed him out of the bar. So we somehow Schneider was involved."

"I'd bet Schneider can lead us right to whatever is going on," Joe said. "You gotta get up there and talk to that guy."

"If it's even the same guy, Dad. It's been twenty-three years since Mrs. Caselli saw this happen. I'm more than just a little uncomfortable about questioning some guy on his death bed."

Joe nodded. "Okay, well, let's see what else we can shake out of the trees first. If we can't dig up another living witness, we're gonna have to go see the guy."

After a glass of water and several blood pressure checks, the nurses allowed Charise to go back to her mother's room. She stretched out the visit for as long as she dared and then told her mother that she had to be going, but would be back as soon as she could.

When she got to her car, she dialed Antonio's number on the cell phone she was never to use except in a dire emergency. "Antonio? Antonio?" she cried frantically into the phone. "Is it you?"

"Yes, it is me," came his familiar voice. "What is up with you today?" His tone was professional, so she knew he was with someone…probably Noah.

Charise lowered her voice, explaining, "One of the Casellis came to see Ma`ma yesterday — and she's a United States Marshall."

"Are you certain of this?"

"Who's Alyssa?" Charise asked, trying to pull herself together.

"I cannot say."

"Stay out of sight," Charise pleaded. "Are any of them in town yet?"

"Not that I know of."

"Ma`ma told this woman all about Papa and you," Charise went on.

"That is most unfortunate. I will learn what I can," Antonio responded.

"Come to the ranch tonight."

"I will. Thank you for calling."

After bringing Mitzy at the U.S. Marshall's office a dozen cookies from the Albertson's bakery, Alyssa and Jon convinced her to use her clearance to contact the Rapid City Police Department. Mitzy knew several secretaries in homicide, and knew who to ask. They conveyed to her that the body Alyssa saw being taken from the row houses had died of a suspected overdose. As of the last update, the M.E. hadn't finished with his autopsy yet.

"And like two previous deaths, in the same complex of row houses, this one was also a patient of Luigi Andreotti," Mitzy said.

"Does the P.D. think he's poisoning them?" Alyssa asked.

Mitzy nodded. "The lead detective has pulled in his father to help with the case. The Chief of Police has pretended to take Andreotti's side, but it's only a front. Department rumor is that it's not *if* it's *when*. Andreotti's going down."

Alyssa looked down at her notes, murmuring, "How does Schneider fit into this?"

"The first thing we're gonna do is find Schneider," Jon said. "Then we're gonna follow 'Bracelet' again and see if you can ID him."

"But I haven't seen him for eleven years, and I was only fifteen years old. I'll *never* recognize him."

"Well, we'll start with anybody named Ben, and work our way from there." Jon winked at Mitzy. "We'll probably be back."

*****

When Noah discovered that Ty had left the house early that morning, he went over to his brother's to tell him what had happened. Mona was at the grocery store, but Joshua was home and he and Noah visited on the deck. Joshua was horrified to hear that Roy had approached Ty, asking him for the lifesaving favor.

"I can't believe the old blackguard would come back after all these years and ask for the kid's marrow," Joshua said with a snort. "It just makes me sick."

"I just wanna kill him, Josh. I don't know what to do," Noah lamented. "I know Ty's at the hospital getting checked out by the doctor as we speak."

"I thought we were through with him." Joshua took a deep breath and slowly exhaled. "We haven't even had a sighting since…1993? Isn't that the last time you saw him?"

"Yep."

"Boy," Joshua groaned. "But, you know, Ty's a good kid, and he'll go through with this whether we like it or not, and it'll be the *right* thing to do…whether we like it or not"

"I don't wanna do the right thing," Noah complained. "I want my life to continue on as if nothing ever happened, and I don't want to have to tell the other kids. They're gonna think I'm weird."

Joshua chuckled. "They won't think you're *weird*, Noah. They love you."

Noah got to his feet as he said, "Listen, I gotta get home. Angel's twisted her knee again and it's Laura and Heidi's volunteer day at the shelter. The boys are going to Montana today, so I've gotta watch my little tornado."

Joshua grinned. "She was certainly full of vinegar the other day when Mona and I were over. Where does Angel come up with the energy?"

"Beats me. Thanks for listening, Josh."

Joshua put his arms around his younger brother, holding him close. "You're a good man, Noah, and this whole thing is gonna blow over in a couple of weeks. Just you wait and see."

*****

Noah found Angel and their baby playing on a blanket in the meadow, just behind the house he'd built for her. He felt relief in the precious scene before him, and felt his burdens easing.

Tillie looked up with surprise when she saw her husband meander into the meadow. Annie squealed with delight, jumping off the blanket, dropping her toy as she scampered to her father.

"Papa!" she yelled.

"Hello, my Annie," Noah said with a smile, picking up the child, snuggling her close. "What are you and Ma`ma doing today?"

"Ma`ma's knee hurts."

Noah sat Annie down on the blanket, and he took a seat beside Tillie. He kissed her softly and asked, "Does the ice help?"

She nodded. "I think we're making headway…at least the swelling is down." She reached for his hand, asking, "How are you, Noah? I've been praying for you all day."

"Oh, I'm fine," he grumbled.

Tillie sighed with a smile. "Ty's home now. He's down by the creek."

"He's home?" Noah was surprised and relieved at the same time.

"We talked for quite a while and I think he's feeling better about things. He's going to help the girls make dinner for us tonight, because I can hardly get around, *and* Elijah's coming for dinner again."

"*Again?*" Noah groaned, looking up into the sky. "Could You send me any more troubles, Lord?"

Tillie laughed, squeezing Noah's hand, "You should go talk to Ty. You guys haven't a chance to visit without Annie and I hanging all over you. Maybe you should be alone with him for a little while."

Noah looked into Tillie's black eyes, asking, "What would I say? He's thinking about saving a man I've *despised* for more than twenty years."

Tillie nodded. "But Ty is *your* son and you have a responsibility to love him through this. And if I know you, Noah Hansen, you'll never let him go through it by himself. That's why I love you so much."

Noah faintly smiled, attempting a joke, "I thought it was just my looks and my money."

Tillie laughed as she replied, "Well, that helps. But it's your *goodness* more than anything." She touched his face with her hand. "There is so much goodness in you that sometimes it amazes me."

Noah grinned and blushed. "Stop that."

"No," Tillie said with a smile. "I made up my mind about you years ago. Your goodness was especially plain to see when I got myself hit by that car. You didn't care about the way I looked or the fact that I couldn't even feed myself. You set your own needs aside in order to encourage my kids and me. And I probably never tell you as much as I should how much I love and appreciate the man that you are."

Noah laughed nervously. "Now quit that. You're embarrassing me."

"Only a perfect knight would be embarrassed by my words."

"Thanks," he said, leaning close, giving her a kiss. "I needed that." He got to his feet and said, "I'm gonna go see Ty." He glanced at her knee. "Can you manage yourself okay?"

"I'm fine. Me and Annie were just going into the house for a cookie break."

Noah helped her to her feet and Tillie reached for their daughter's hand, saying, "Come along, Annie. I've got some rainbow chip cookies just waiting to get dunked in a cup of tea."

Noah kissed her again. "I'll be back in a little bit."

Tillie nodded as she and their daughter walked off toward the house and Noah headed for the creek.

Sitting in a spot covered by the tall weeds bordering the bank of Rapid Creek, Noah found his oldest son. He was reading his Bible, but he looked up when he saw Noah approaching.

"Hi, Dad."

"Hi, Ty. Can I sit down?"

"Sure." Ty closed his Bible.

Noah took a seat on the ground near his son as he said, "I missed you this morning."

"I'm sorry," Ty replied. "I shouldn't have done that. Can you forgive me?"

"Well, it's okay. Forget about it."

Ty looked into the eyes of the only father he'd ever known. They were downcast and sorrowful today; an expression Ty didn't remember seeing on his father for a very long time. Dad's eyes always sparkled and danced with joy, especially when he was with Tillie.

"I went and saw the doctor today," Ty said. "We'll have the results in a couple of days."

Noah let his breath out.

"Dad," Ty said, reaching for Noah's hand. He saw the struggle and tears in his father's eyes and his heart broke for what the man was going through.

"And then what?" Noah asked in a gravelly voice.

"If everything is a match, I'm gonna do it."

Noah caught his breath, praying that Roy would just die before Ty had the chance to do it. "What's your brother gonna say?" he asked.

"I think he'll be okay. This thing that you've kept secret about Mom isn't really all that bad and you did it for all the right reasons." Ty hesitated. "I talked to Roy today and he told me that he came back for Mom once and you punched him. Is that true?"

Noah smiled with recollection. "I really let him have it. Of course, I was younger then and full of all kinds of fight."

"You must have really loved us."

"I did," Noah replied. "The two of you were the center of my world. My life was over until I married your mother and you were born."

"He told me that Mom put *your* name on the birth certificate. And then he said he wished Mom would have loved him like that."

"She might have —"

"I don't think so, Dad," Ty interrupted. "Roy says she changed after she was with you. Is that true?"

Noah took a deep breath, saying, "That's true. She was really mad when we first got married because she thought she had done a really stupid thing. But, then you were born and one thing led to another and pretty soon we had this great little life."

"Does Jake belong to you? Do you know?" Ty asked.

Noah chuckled, answering, "Jake belongs to me. That I know for sure. Your mother wasn't like whatever you're suspecting of her. After we were married, I was the only one she was with. She may have been a little goofed up when we first got together, but all of that changed about your mom and she turned into the nicest lady in town. She started sneaking into Uncle Josh's church on Sunday mornings, listening to his message and pretty soon she was reading the Bible."

"Did you think about Tillie when you were married to Mom?"

"At first I did," Noah admitted. "But then, time went by and I couldn't imagine myself with anybody else but your mom. I lost my heart to her during that pregnancy. And when you were born…" he paused, smiling at his sweet memories, continuing, "I'd see her holding you or feeding you, and she had changed so much that I just couldn't get enough of her. One day I finally kissed her and told her that I loved her. She just about fainted, 'cause that wasn't part of our little arrangement."

"What *was* your arrangement?"

"Well, I thought we'd just get married and raise you together," Noah replied with a grin. "I didn't want her to go off and have an abortion. You know how I hate that and I *always* have. And we were both so lonely. I knew all about Roy and she knew all about Angel, and we knew that it was probably gonna be awhile before either one of us would want anybody else. Anyway, she was gonna do the laundry and I was gonna do the cooking. Pretty soon, the little gal started surprising me with apple pies and roasts."

"She started liking you, too."

Noah nodded. "She *loved* us, Ty. She was a good woman and she wanted us to be a *real* family. And we were."

"We do not know the path of the wind, or how the body is formed in a mother's womb, so we cannot understand the work of God, the Maker of all things," Ty said.

Noah smiled. "*Ecclesiastes*. Except that I always thought Solomon should have added a verse that says, *So don't bother, 'cause you're never gonna get it anyway*."

Ty laughed and Noah took his son into his arms, saying, "I love you, Ty. You're a good man and you remind me *so much* of your mother. I don't know what would have become of me if God hadn't sent the two of you my way."

"I love you, Dad, and nobody's ever gonna take your place."

*****

Charise was moving straw with a pitchfork when she heard Antonio's car in the drive. She put her fork down and hurried over to greet him. He put his arms around his grief-stricken sister.

"Who's Alyssa Caselli?" she asked.

"She is the daughter of Mrs. Hansen's brother," Antonio answered.

"Which brother?"

"There is a brother who lives on a ranch located in the southeastern corner of South Dakota," Antonio answered. "Alyssa belongs to him. She works for the United States Marshal's Office in Denver, Colorado."

"How did she find Ma`ma?" Charise asked. "We've been *so* careful. Has Noah said anything about this?"

"Not a word." Antonio sighed with regret, shaking his head. "And something else you should know...Rauwolf went to see Ty yesterday."

Charise gasped, her black eyes flying open. "Does Sal know?"

Antonio nodded. "He knew before even me. And, poor Noah, he does not say anything, but he is sick over it. The expression on his face reminds me of when Angel returned to that wretched husband she was so long attached to."

"Oh," Charise growled through her tears. "Rauwolf has *no right* to that child. He *never* has."

"I agree. However, there now remains an even greater issue and that is the question of why a United States Marshal would be checking into things."

"That stupid Sal exposed himself needlessly," Charise snapped. "His greed blinded his ability to reason and now he'll have us all on the run."

Antonio nodded. "We will move your mother immediately, before Sal finds out about her. He will surely use the situation for leverage if this information falls into his hands."

"But she's been there for eighteen years. It'll kill her to move her."

"She may be uncomfortable if we move her, Charise." Antonio frowned. "However, if we do not move her, Sal will finish her off and then he will come looking for you."

Chapter 9

Bright and early Monday morning, Dr. Carlson called Ty and told him he was a *perfect* match and that he would like to proceed within the week. Ty told Noah and Tillie about the results, and the three of them decided to wait until after Monday's games to tell the other children. But, in the meantime, Ty had to notify the Orioles' team manager of the change in plans, and he made the call immediately.

"Hi Harry," Ty said.

"Well, Ty Hansen!" the manager exclaimed. "Great to hear from you! How's your little vacation going?"

"Okay," Ty answered. He took a deep breath and began again, "Harry, I guess I can't accept your offer after all."

After a long silence, Harry asked, "What's up, kid?"

"My biological father has leukemia and needs a marrow donation," Ty explained. "And I'm a perfect match."

Harry sighed heavily. "I'm sorry to hear about your dad, kid, but you risk being passed over for next year if you don't show up in time for training camp this year."

"I understand," Ty said quietly.

Harry sighed again, and after another long silence said, "I'll let everybody know. If there's anything I can do for you, let me know. I'll try my best."

"There is one thing," Ty said. "Please don't give this to the press until the end of the week. I have to talk to my siblings about it."

"Sure thing, kid," Harry said. "Good luck to you."

"Thanks, Harry."

*****

On the first Monday in June, Post 22 was scheduled to play their first doubleheader against the team from Bismarck, North Dakota. That day was also Tillie's forty-first birthday, and Jake and A.J. promised to win the game just for her. Post 22 was on an eleven-game winning streak and the boys just didn't see how they could be beaten.

Joshua and Mona came over in the early afternoon with not only a three-layer chocolate cake, but Guiseppi and Rosa as well. Noah asked them to fly in for Tillie's birthday as a surprise. When they arrived, they announced they would be staying over to help with preparations for the reunion, only a few weeks away.

Fitzgerald Stadium's parking lot was filled to overflowing, and it was hot on the blacktop. The early spring weather had warmed to nearly eighty degrees that day. Guiseppi donned the beloved *COACH* cap Noah had given him five years before, and he and Rosa shuffled to the stands behind Joshua and Mona. Jake and A.J. were already with their team, and Laura and Heidi took up their usual positions behind the fence. Annie skipped along between her parents, and Ty came along with them.

Just as they were about to enter the gate, a small crowd of reporters rushed Ty, stopping the group in their tracks. Ty put on his polite smile, waiting to begin the answering process, while his little sister danced gracefully between her parents. He noticed one of the cameras was directly focused on her, and he wondered if she would make the evening news as well. Since Noah and Tillie's marriage, the family had been in the spotlight. The mystique surrounding Tillie's brothers and the amazing way their children played ball was something the press could not resist. They called A.J. and Jake the *Gruesome Twosome.*

"How do you feel about your brother playing the same position you played for Post 22?" The first question.

Ty answered with a smile, "I'm very proud of him."

"Your stepbrother, A.J. Martin, has been predicted to break batting and catching records this year. Do you think he will?"

Ty nodded. "I'd guestimate that he's got about a one hundred percent chance at that."

"When do you leave for Baltimore?"

Ty's smile faded. "I have a few more days left in Rapid City, but my date of departure hasn't been finalized."

Guiseppi loudly cleared his throat, slipping his hand into Ty's, and said, "We need to find a seat because I am old. Could Ty perhaps answer questions *after* the game?" With that, they all began to turn away from the reporters, starting for the gate once again.

"Mr. Caselli," came a frantic reporter's voice, "do you hear anything from the Senator about impeachment?"

Guiseppi froze in his tracks, smiling maliciously.

"Do not *dare*, Guiseppi," Rosa warned.

Guiseppi turned and faced the reporters, beginning, "I do have news. Senator Caselli —"

"Will be answering questions on this very matter within the month!" Rosa pronounced loudly.

Noah covered his mouth with his hand in an attempt to hide his guffaw.

Rosa frowned at her husband, leaning close to whisper, "I do not wish to hear any more of your jokes."

The group of reporters chuckled.

Tillie smiled at the reporters, reaching for Noah's hand as she said, "You guys are great, but you need to let us find our seats."

The reporters nodded, allowing the Hansens to pass into the stadium. Joshua and Mona laughed as they walked along beside them.

Hansen Development, LLC, had a VIP box, which was cordoned off folding chairs with the company's name stamped on the backs of them. The box was situated behind the catcher, with an excellent view of the entire field.

Like her mother, Annie loved the hot dogs, nachos and cherry slushies sold at the concession stand, and Noah made sure they had plenty with which to indulge themselves. Guiseppi groaned when he saw the bad food being carried to the box, but Joshua laughed and slipped him a roll of Rolaids.

"They don't do it very often," Joshua assured. "But it *is* Angel's birthday, you know."

Guiseppi smiled and nodded, looking at his pretty daughter and the beautiful child on her lap. He'd never seen a child look more like her father *and* mother.

Ty and Rosa helped themselves to some of the junk food, and the announcer began his preamble: "It's a perfect, eighty degrees at Fitzgerald tonight. Post 22 has won their last eleven games with the deadly *Gruesome Twosome* starting in all. Pitcher Jake Hansen heads the league with strikeouts, averaging twenty-five per game. And don't plan on hitting any pop flies tonight, Bismarck, because catcher A.J. Martin is working on breaking the league's record this year. Out of his last ninety-nine innings, A.J. has caught one hundred and twenty-five pop flies..."

Guiseppi cheered something in Italian, and Rosa delicately tapped his shoulder. He glanced at her to see that she was frowning in disapproval, and to his surprise Tillie giggled.

"You do not know what I say," he stated in quiet indignation.

"I understood you, Papa," Tillie smiled. "Angelo's been teaching me Italian."

"Oh, dear," Guiseppi groaned.

Ty hurried to the locker room to visit with his brothers between games. It was loud and crowded, and Ty had to fight his way through reporters to get to where A.J. and Jake were drinking bottles of water.

"I knew you could hit like that!" Ty said excitedly, tussling Jake's sandy hair. He looked at A.J. and smiled. "Wonderful performance as usual," he said, referring to A.J. Martin's graceful bow before he batted. Pitchers hated him because he could send the ball anywhere he wanted it to go. No matter what they pitched him, he never missed.

Jake laughed. "Coach told him to knock it off."

"Well don't," Ty said. "You're awesome."

A.J. grinned. "Thanks, Ty."

They talked for a few minutes before everyone, except for players, were thrown out of the locker room, and Ty headed back to the VIP box. As Ty hurried along, a familiar face stopped him near the concessions.

"Hello, Ty. Do you remember me?"

"Mr. Andreotti," Ty said, politely extending his hand. "It's nice to see you again."

"You may call me, Luigi. Are your parents here this evening?"

Ty got the strangest feeling in the pit of his stomach, but he nodded his head, answering, "We have our own box."

"Would you mind taking me to them?"

Ty was hesitant, but he wasn't comfortable refusing the man knowing that Luigi was old friends with the Casellis. "Sure. Follow me," he replied.

Luigi fell in behind Ty, following him down the steps to the VIP box where the Hansens, along with Guiseppi and Rosa were still seated. Noah saw Luigi coming behind Ty, and he gave Tillie a soft elbow to get her attention.

"What's *he* doing here?" she whispered.

"Who's that with Ty?" Mona whispered into Tillie's other ear.

"That's the guy that called the other day," Tillie whispered in answer.

"Oh, dearest ones," Rosa moaned, reaching for Guiseppi's hand. "It is that dreadful Luigi Andreotti. Why has the Lord allowed him to find us?"

Guiseppi put his arm around Rosa and said, "Fear not, my love. I will protect you."

Rosa giggled.

Mona whispered to Tillie, "What did Noah say when he found out the little bugger called the other day?"

"He told me to pretend like it never happened."

Noah whispered something to Joshua and he nodded his head. Both of them got to their feet as Luigi approached and Ty took a seat behind Mona and Tillie.

"Hello, Luigi," Noah said in a gruff voice.

Luigi extended his hand in greeting, and Noah shook it.

"Hello, Noah," Luigi replied with a smooth smile. "What a surprise to see you here! I did not know your sons played ball."

"That's funny," Noah said with a frown. "Everybody else in South Dakota does."

Joshua gave Noah an elbow.

Noah turned to Joshua and said, "This is my brother, Josh." Joshua extended his hand.

Luigi took Joshua's outstretched hand and said, "It is nice to meet you."

"Likewise," Joshua answered.

Noah and Joshua had positioned themselves in such a way that Luigi could not see who was seated behind them. He attempted to peak through their shoulders and a very curious Annie waved at him from her mother's lap.

"I see your wife and your little one are with you this evening," Luigi said.

"Yep," Noah answered.

"I was speaking with your brother-in-law the other day," Luigi went on. "Petrice invited me to your reunion. Thank you very much. I am looking so forward to the event."

Tillie's jaw nearly fell to the pavement below. Mona put a gentle hand upon her knee.

Noah didn't flinch. "You're welcome," he replied.

"Well, I should be moving along," Luigi said politely. "It was nice to meet you, Joshua." He turned and walked away, leaving the Hansens dumbfounded at what he'd told them.

Noah turned to Tillie with wide open eyes. "Your brother did *what*?"

Tillie shook her head, her dark eyes as big as saucers looking back at her husband. She wasn't aware that Petrice had invited Luigi.

"I don't want that *freak* at my family reunion," Noah said with a frown. "He's just coming for a peak at the women."

"I'll be sure to wear my best then," Mona said, smiling with mischief, and Joshua laughed.

"Come on, Noah," Joshua said, patting his shoulder. "Forget about it. He probably won't even show."

*****

Alyssa and Jon went over their notes in the small office they'd been granted for use at the Federal Building in Rapid City.

"And I forgot to tell you," Jon added, "The secretary of state got back to me on Rapid Valley Quarter Horses and they don't have a business listed with that name. So, apparently, whoever's operating out there, isn't collecting sales tax."

"But we know that Charise sells horses there —"

"Well, Della *told* us she sells horses," Jon corrected. "But we don't *know for sure*. Some of Della's info was a little scrambled."

"But they would have needed something to support them all these years," Alyssa argued.

"Nobody by the name of Jack Nelson in the Rapid City area has paid taxes *ever*." Jon said. "So whatever they're doing out there is under the table."

"That's nothing new. People evade taxes every day, and if they were trying to hide from this Sal character they would take every precaution, including not filing their taxes. Obviously they have friends in our government. Filing your taxes would make you an easy find."

Jon scratched his chin as he said, "It's funny, though, Della didn't mention Luigi."

"Maybe she doesn't know him," Alyssa suggested. "He may have gotten into the picture after she fell."

"Maybe his drug business is part of how they're supporting themselves," Jon suggested.

Alyssa shrugged. "I wonder if Schneider will be able to give us anything on Luigi."

"I hope we can *find* Roy Schneider."

*****

The third day of June dawned with snow on the ground, which was fairly typical for the Black Hills of South Dakota. One day it could be warm and sunny, and the next day would bring a drastic change in the weather. The night before, Post 22 played in a very cold, windy rain, losing their first game to Bismarck, but beating them in the second. Their next games would be played in Omaha, Nebraska, the coming weekend, and, despite their one loss, the boys were excited to make another out-of-town trip.

Dr. Carlson scheduled the donor procedure for early the following week. Between Ty, Tillie and Noah, they decided it would be best to tell their other children on Wednesday night. Jake and A.J. would have some time to absorb the information before leaving for Omaha. Noah and Tillie were thankful that her parents were there because they didn't know how everyone would react. Joshua and Mona said that they would be there as well.

*****

Rauwolf was watching television from his bed when the young detective walked in. He looked up with surprise at the unfamiliar face.

Jason pulled out his badge and said, "Detective Patterson. Rapid City Police Force. Turn off the television, we've gotta talk if you can."

Rauwolf turned off the television, wondering what in the world the young detective had uncovered. *Maybe Noah called him.* "What do you want?" Rauwolf asked.

"What do you know about Jack Nelson?" Jason questioned.

"Who?" Rauwolf asked, appearing completely baffled.

"Don't do that," Jason warned. "You were driving a car in 1974 that was licensed to Jack Nelson. Obviously you knew him, unless you stole the car, and *that* certainly didn't come up in your record."

Rauwolf rolled his eyes and answered, "We were friends years ago. So what? I haven't seen him in a long time."

"How long is a *long time*?"

"I don't know, maybe twenty years or more."

"What was Jack Nelson up to at the time?" Jason questioned.

Rauwolf shrugged. "Mostly stocks and investments. He wasn't into anything shady if that's what you're implying."

"Where did he come from?"

"Florida. He had a fishing company that he sold and shortly after that he moved to the Rapid City area."

"How 'bout John Peters?" Jason asked.

Rauwolf almost choked. He hadn't heard *that* name since…"I never knew the guy," he replied.

"But you obviously recognize the name," Jason prodded.

"A couple of terrorists hassled me about it several years ago," Rauwolf replied, involuntarily reaching for his throat as he remembered how Tara Caselli used her switchblade knife to coerce the information they wanted. "I never saw them again."

"How do you know they were *terrorists*?" Jason asked.

"They were Middle Eastern," Rauwolf lied.

"And what kind of questions did they ask you with regard to John Peters?" Jason continued.

Rauwolf scowled. *Where did this punk kid detective come up with all of this?* He pretended to cough, adding weakness to his tone as he replied, "I don't remember."

"Oh, baloney," Jason growled. "I've got two witnesses who watched John Peters follow you and a girl named Carrie out of Maggie May's the last night Peters was ever seen."

Rauwolf was confused as he snapped, "So somebody followed me. That doesn't mean anything."

Jason frowned. "Did Noah Hansen know any of these people?"

"Well, he married Carrie in 1976."

"Carrie was Jack's stepdaughter?" Jason questioned. Rauwolf nodded and so Jason continued, "So, Noah knew Jack?"

Rauwolf gave Jason a coy smile, answering, "He was his son-in-law. I imagine he knew the man."

"How about Luigi Andreotti?" Jason asked abruptly. "How long have you known him?"

Rauwolf relaxed. He'd *never* heard that name before in his life. *The kid's not as smart as he thinks he is*, he thought. "I don't know any Luigi," he replied.

"Did Nelson or Hansen or Carrie know a Luigi?"

"Not that I know of," Rauwolf answered.

Jason frowned at Roy, "I know you know something about what's going on —"

"What *is* going on?" Roy barked. The place where his eyebrows used to be, furrowed into an angry crease. "I don't have any idea what you're talking about. My time is taken up with trying to keep myself alive these days and then you stomp in here, waving your badge, thinking you can squeeze me for something. You're barkin' up the wrong tree, pal."

Jason clenched his jaw as he said, "I don't think so. You're connected to too many people here. You claim you don't know Luigi Andreotti, but I think you do."

"How?"

"I don't know that yet, but I'll find out. I *always* find out," Jason answered.

Rauwolf nodded. "Tell your hot-shot mother good-luck on the election."

"I'll do that. And I'll be back to see you in a couple of days."

"You do that," Rauwolf smirked. "You come on back if you wanna find out anything else I *don't* know."

Jason clenched his jaw again, making a hasty exit.

Rauwolf shook his head, reaching for the t.v. remote as he said to himself, "Who's Luigi Andreotti?"

In a nearby doorway, Alyssa and Jon waited to make their own appearance, wondering if Patterson had already tipped off Schneider. Mitzy had gotten a call from one of the secretaries in Homicide. She'd given them the location of a Dr. Roy Schneider, who'd become a person of interest in Detective Patterson's case.

Jon pulled his baseball cap down over his eyes, peering out at Alyssa. "He's gone," he whispered. "Let's go." As he moved out of the doorway, a man walking down the hall ran right into him. Alyssa nearly fainted. *It's Noah.* She turned around, entering the room of the doorway they'd waited in.

"Excuse me," Jon apologized, pretending to be just a befuddled stranger. "I'm very sorry. I seem to be lost."

"No problem," Noah answered. "Can I help you find something?"

"Ah..." Jon stammered. "I'm looking for the nurse's station. I need to find a patient."

Noah turned, pointing to the nurse's station, which was in clear view of where they stood. "It's right over there," he said.

"Thanks," Jon said with a smile. He turned and started down the hallway.

Noah continued on his way, entering the room Jason Patterson had just left. Alyssa emerged from the room where she'd hidden, and Jon joined her.

"Schneider's room is a busy place today," he commented.

"Like a revolving door."

"I think we're gonna hit the jackpot on this one," Jon said, raising one eyebrow as he eyed the closed door of Roy's room.

When the door of his room opened again, Rauwolf thought the young detective had returned. He almost lost his breath when he saw Noah Hansen stroll into the room.

The last few days hadn't been easy for Noah. His expression was angry and weathered, and Rauwolf knew he had it coming. *He looks like the wrath of the Almighty*, Rauwolf thought.

Noah walked to the end of the bed, pointing his index finger at Rauwolf as he barked, "I told you to stay away from him." He crossed his arms over his middle and scowled.

Rauwolf didn't remember Noah ever being that large of a man, but he looked huge at the end of his bed. "I know," Rauwolf replied. "But a funny thing happened. I'm dying Noah, and Ty is my only living relative."

"You selfish blackguard," Noah said through clenched teeth.

"Please," Rauwolf said, holding up a shaky hand. "Save the lecture. I just wanna know if you're gonna turn me in now." He sighed heavily, whispering, "Did you tell Ty?"

"My wife doesn't even know," Noah muttered, setting his jaw.

"There's no statute of limitations on murder," Rauwolf informed. "I could still go to jail. But without an eyewitness, I doubt they'll put me to death, even in South Dakota. And let's not forget, Noah, you've kept the body hidden for how many years? You'd be prosecuted as an accomplice at this point, and I wouldn't go to jail alone."

Noah slowly nodded his head in angry agreement.

"Why didn't you ever turn me in?" Rauwolf asked.

"Because I was afraid I'd be the next one to wind up dead. I did a selfish, stupid thing. Have you killed anybody else?"

"I don't remember. Now how 'bout just telling me where the body is."

Noah snorted and replied, "Like you're in any kind of shape to go and move it now. You must be nuts. I'm not telling you anything."

"Come on Noah," Rauwolf begged. "I need that body to tie up some loose ends. Even if I survive this donation from Ty, I'll be in a lot of trouble with —"

"I don't care, Roy," Noah interrupted, shaking his head with disgust. "I don't give one rip about whatever trouble you *might* be in. You were a liar twenty years ago, and you're still a liar today."

"Ty's *my* boy," Rauwolf spat. "And it was wrong for you to raise him like your own. He's gonna give me *his* own marrow and I'm gonna live and I'm *always* gonna be in his life."

"He's a man now and that decision was his own," Noah said, "But I'll guarantee one thing, he's *nothing* like you, Roy, and you won't be like him even with part of him inside of you. He's a good person and he'll do whatever it takes to get another soul into heaven."

"Don't you think I'm going to heaven, Noah?"

"I *know* you're not going to heaven," Noah snapped. "And I don't care if you *do* burn in hell. Unfortunately, *my* son is different."

Rauwolf looked into Noah's eyes. For more than twenty years he'd watched Noah with those two little boys, loving them from the tiniest of human beings into full-grown men. Then along came Caselli's sister and her two children, and Noah was just as tender and loving with them. The newest member of Noah's clan, the pretty curly-haired baby girl, who looked just like her mother, had not been spared the slightest of Noah's gentleness. He shook his head as he said, "I can't believe this is the person you really are. You haven't taught your family any of these things so why do you behave this way with me?"

"Because I *hate* you." Noah was cold. "The boy you wanted to kill before he was even born was *my* gift and now you want him back. I can't get past it."

"You're big on forgiveness, Noah," Rauwolf said. "Ty has already shared your beliefs with me and I know all about your Christianity. Why don't you just forgive me?"

"You never asked," Noah answered.

"Well," Rauwolf said, hesitating. "Would you forgive me Noah?"

Noah drew in a sharp breath, holding it for a few moments before he answered, "I *hate* you for doing this to my life."

"But I'm sorry."

Noah shook his head and stormed out of Rauwolf's room. He was so upset and distraught, that he didn't notice the mysterious couple waiting only a few doors down the hall.

"Poor Noah," Alyssa whispered.

"I betcha Roy asked the kid for some marrow," Jon guessed as they started for his room.

"None of us knew about Ty," Alyssa replied. "So, I imagine Ty didn't know either."

"What a selfish person," Jon mumbled as he turned the latch on the door. "I hope we can nail this guy for something."

He opened the door to Rauwolf's room, flipping open his badge.

"Oh, brother," Rauwolf moaned as his door closed behind them. "Now what?"

"You've had a busy day, Mr. Schneider," Jon said with a coy smile. "How 'bout you tell us what Detective Patterson wanted and then what Noah Hansen was doing here?"

"Why are the two of you here?"

"We're checking into some strange things that happened in Rapid City about twenty years ago," Alyssa answered.

Rauwolf rolled his eyes. "Everybody is, but I don't know nothin'."

"Why was Patterson here?" Jon asked.

"He wanted to know if I knew a Luigi Andreotti and I *don't.*"

"We wanna know if you helped hide Della Nelson," Jon said.

Rauwolf's mouth opened in surprise and he couldn't answer. The look on his face was all that they needed to know.

"Why?" Alyssa pressed.

Rauwolf took a deep breath and whispered, "They had to hide her from one of their psycho relatives."

"Who's the psycho relative?" Jon asked.

"I don't know," Rauwolf lied.

"How is Noah Hansen connected to all of this?" Alyssa questioned.

"He's not," Rauwolf answered. "He's just mad at me because I told his son something that he never wanted him to know."

"Why'd ya do that?" Jon asked.

"It seemed important at the time." Rauwolf sighed. "Now, listen, I've had a really busy day and I need some rest. So unless the two of you have a warrant or something, our little feel-good trip down memory lane is over."

Alyssa nodded. "We'll probably be in touch."

"I'll be really busy for the next few weeks," Rauwolf said. "I'm having some surgery in a couple of days and, hopefully, I'll be unconscious."

Alyssa felt the hair on the back of her neck prickle. The old blackguard *had* asked for Ty's marrow.

"We'll be around after your recovery," Jon said, stepping toward the door, holding it for Alyssa. "Good luck to you."

"Thanks, pal."

Alyssa and Jon started down the hallway.

"What Noah must be going through," Alyssa pondered. "I'm glad my grandparents are out here to help them all through this."

Jon took a deep breath. "So, do you think the old blackguard knows anything?"

"Yes, but we don't have nearly enough to connect the two situations and serve him with a warrant."

"He says he doesn't know Luigi," Jon said.

"And that's weird. Luigi's the focus of Patterson's investigation."

"The only people familiar with Luigi seem to be your uncles."

Alyssa nodded. "Well, we'll go out and question Charise tomorrow and see what she has to say about things. Maybe she'll be able to connect the dots for us."

*****

Antonio ascended the wooden steps of his sister's porch where she was watering her plants. She attempted a smile as he approached, but the expression he wore was so grim it made her frown with worry. *Now what?*

"Noah has been to see the Wolf," he breathed.

Charise gasped. "Do you think he knows?"

"Carrie did not tell him everything," Antonio answered.

"Will you tell Sal?"

Antonio shook his head. "But he already knows about Ty."

"There must be someone else working for Sal."

"No. There is no one else working for Sal, except maybe for some street hoodlums. He has gotten information from someone other than me. But, I promise you, Charise, I will do everything I can to convince Sal that Noah does not know anything."

*****

Tillie made sure that dinner was served promptly at six o'clock that evening. Her parents were there, and Joshua and Mona *just happened* to stop over. Conversation around the dinner table was tense, and no one could help but notice how distracted Noah was. He seemed able to communicate only with the baby, and occasionally Tillie. He didn't look at their other children, and A.J. and Jake were beginning to wonder if they were in trouble.

Guiseppi's heart went out to Noah with what he had to tell them that evening, and he prayed silently through the entire dinner. Noah was concerned the most with how Jake would react, but Guiseppi assured him that Jake was a kind, loving child and he would understand.

After dinner, Noah ushered everyone into the family room, preparing to make the announcement.

He waited for everyone to be seated and he sat down next to Tillie and Annie. He looked at the family he and Angel shared and his eyes started to burn with angry tears. How could he even begin to do this? He tried to swallow his emotions away. "I don't even know how to tell you guys this," he started. Tillie reached for his hand and Noah swallowed again. He looked at Jake, who seemed to be on the edge of his seat, and he smiled faintly at his son. "When your mom and I married, there was an unusual set of circumstances, but we wanted to be a family and we decided to work with what was available to us." His eyes turned toward Ty and then back to Jake. "Your mom was pregnant when we got married and the man she was involved with sort of up and left her."

The room was deftly silent and all eyes dropped to the floor except for Jake's. He looked at his father with a soft frown, quietly clearing his throat, managing to ask, "Who got Mom pregnant?"

Noah swallowed hard. "The other guy."

Ty put his arm over Jake's shoulders in an effort to comfort him.

"How do you know?" Jake whispered.

Noah took a deep breath, answering, "We just know."

Jake shook his head, bewildered and unbelieving as he asked, "Why tell us this now?"

"Because he's come back," Noah answered, trying not to look angry but the reality of the situation still infuriated him.

"He's dying," Ty explained. "He has leukemia and he needs some of my bone marrow."

Jake began to nod as if he understood. He took a deep breath and angrily accused, "So *that's* why Tillie wouldn't marry you."

Laura and A.J. couldn't hide their surprised expressions as they watched the situation unfold. Laura was about beside herself with confusion. Her mother hadn't told her *any* of this. A.J. could only think, *no wonder nobody wants to talk about the house.*

"No, Jake," Tillie said, smiling at her confused stepson. "It wasn't like that at all —"

"Oh, come on," Jake interrupted with a frown. "He builds you this huge house and then he goes off and marries somebody else." He looked at his father with a disgusted expression. "How could you do that?"

"It wasn't like that at all, Jake," Joshua said in a serious voice. "Don't forget, your Auntie Mona and I were there for the whole thing, and it's nothing like what you're assuming."

"Well then what was it?" Jake snapped.

"Your dad and Angel had a terrible misunderstanding," Mona offered. "He couldn't find her —"

"Oh this is *so stupid.*" Jake got to his feet, shaking off his brother's arm. "Alex Martin was your best friend for *how many years*? I find it hard to believe that you *didn't* know. In fact, I think it's really weird that nobody wanted to talk about this last week when Laura's stockbroker came over for dinner —"

"So what are you assuming, Jake?" Noah demanded.

Jake shook his head, answering, "I don't know what I think of this." He took a breath and looked at Ty. "So are you gonna give this old derelict your marrow or what?"

Ty swallowed, slowly nodding his head.

Jake 'humphed', shaking his head. "Wow. What about the Orioles?"

"I'm not going."

Jake shook his head again and frowned. "This is *so stupid* that I can't even believe it." He looked at Noah and demanded, "Who do *I* belong to?"

Noah was surprised at the question and couldn't bring himself to answer.

"Jacob Hansen!" Tillie gasped with admonishment in her tone. "Now that will be enough! I can't believe you said that, young man!"

"Oh, please," Jake replied, rolling his eyes. "I can't believe you actually married him."

"All right," Noah growled with a frown. "It doesn't matter where Ty came from, he's still your brother and I'm still your father."

Jake was backing out of the room, shaking his head and frowning at Noah. "The two of you are still lying about something," he accused. "Who knows what it is."

"We're not lying about anything," Tillie said. "You're misunderstanding this, Jake. Please —"

"No," Jake interrupted, still shaking his head, moving closer to the doorway. "I've gotta think about this for awhile." And with that, he bolted from the room. They heard his footsteps down the hall, through the entryway and out the front door.

A.J. sighed, getting to his feet. "Can I try to talk to him?" he asked.

Noah nodded, and A.J. quickly followed his angry stepbrother out of the house.

Poor Noah looked as if someone had knocked the wind out of him, and Tillie softly kissed his hand. Joshua frowned and Mona shook her head. Guiseppi was also frowning and he even made a soft "tsk" noise when Noah allowed Jake to stomp out of the room. Rosa was crying and Laura reached for her hand.

"Don't cry, Nonna," Laura said with a sweet smile. "A.J. will fix him up." She looked at Noah with tenderness. "I think you did a very brave thing for Ty's mom. You're even *cooler* than I thought. We're so lucky to have you."

"Thanks, Laura," Noah said.

Laura looked at Ty. "You know, Ty, it really *doesn't* matter where you came from, just that you're here with us now. You belong with *us*."

Ty nodded and looked at his father. "I know *exactly* where I belong."

Chapter 10

Noah was lying on their bed, staring up at the ceiling when Tillie came into their room. Everyone had gone to bed, including Annie. A.J. and Jake hadn't yet returned from wherever they'd gone. Shortly after leaving the family meeting, everyone heard the old Impala's engine revving as it peeled out of the gravel driveway.

Tillie sat down close to her husband, putting her hand on his chest, looking into his sad blue eyes.

"Should I go out and look for them?" Noah whispered.

Tillie shook her head. "Where would you go? I'm sure they'll be home soon."

"I *never* wanted them to know," he breathed, a tear rolling from the corner of his eye. "He's the worst kind of slime you could ever imagine, Angel."

Tillie lay down beside him and whispered, "It's gonna be okay, Noah."

"They're *my* boys," he cried. "They've always been *my* boys. Roy doesn't have the right to do what he's done to *my* family."

"No he doesn't," Tillie agreed. She softly kissed his face. "I love you, Noah and we can lead our family through this. God will make it better again."

*****

In the parking lot of the fish hatchery, two young boys turned off the engine of their old car, coasting it into the driveway. They put it into park, creeping out of the automobile without closing the doors. It was late, hours past their curfew. They hoped everyone in the house would be sleeping so they could move on with the next phase of their plan.

With great stealth, the two gathered their packages, making their way to the guest house behind their home. Guiseppi and Rosa were in the guest room of the main house, so no one would even know they'd been there.

The guest house was unlocked, and they let themselves in.

"Whew!" Jake breathed with a smile, closing the door. "I thought we'd be caught for sure."

"Me, too!" A.J. laughed, pulling a six-pack of beer from a paper sack. "You know, if we get caught, Post will suspend us."

"Nobody's gonna catch us," Jake goaded, pulling out his own six-pack.

They each cracked open a bottle and relaxed on the furniture in the small greeting room of the cottage. They took long gulps from their bottles, pretending to enjoy the taste.

"Can you believe this story they're trying to sell us?" Jake smirked.

A.J. shook his head and made a "tsk" noise. "I can't believe it. He must have still been in love with Mom when he married your mother."

"No wonder Tillie wouldn't marry him," Jake muttered, taking another long pull from the bottle. "He probably *thought* he was the baby's father. He must have been fooling around with every chick in town."

"What really ticks me off is how they throw around the word 'blackguard'," A.J. added.

"Yeah," Jake sneered. "Like it *means* something."

A.J. shook his head. "Mom up and marries one."

Jake's eyes opened wide with sudden recollection. "Remember when your mom got hit by that car?"

"Yeah," A.J. acknowledged, taking another glug of the beer.

"Remember how your dad stayed away for a really long time?"

A.J. frowned. "*You don't suppose?*"

"Oh, yeah, I suppose," Jake said, exaggerating a nod. "They've probably been fooling around for years."

A.J. screwed up his face. "Mom? *My* mom?"

"Well, she *did* marry a blackguard," Jake reasoned, finishing off his first bottle, reaching for another.

Laura heard the sound of gravel crunch beneath the wheels of the car. From her bedroom window she watched Jake and A.J. sneaking into the guest house. She'd expected them to come into the house, but when they did not, she decided to investigate. She crept from the house and hurried down the short path to the guest house.

She paused at the closed door, listening. Loud jeering and obnoxious laughter came from the other side. She snorted and flung open the door, staring in silence at what was happening. Empty beer bottles were lying everywhere, and Jake and A.J. were laughing hysterically.

Jake suddenly noticed Laura in the doorway and got to his feet.

"Well, hello, Laura," he slurred. A.J. was still seated and Jake gave him a slap to the side of head. "Don't you appreciate Laura? On your feet, boy!"

A.J. giggled and staggered to his feet. "Sorry, Laura," he apologized. "I didn't see you there."

"Want a beer?" Jake asked, burping.

"What have you done?" Laura gasped.

A.J. laughed. "You sound like Mom!"

Jake laughed too, slowly staggering to where Laura stood. He put a friendly hand on her shoulder, coaxing, "Come on, Laura. Why don't you have a beer with us and we'll explain the *whole thing.*"

Laura frowned as she stepped away from him. "You stink."

Jake's jolly expression changed to one of hurt. He asked, "What do I stink like?"

"Like beer!" Laura scolded.

Jake frowned thoughtfully.

"Are you gonna tell, Laura?" A.J. asked with a hint of concern in his tone. He attempted to stay standing without wavering, glancing at Jake with a burp. "Because, you know, Jake, she always told when we were little. She was *always* the one to tell. Girls are like that...they tell everything —"

"Who got this for you?" Laura interrupted.

"Jake has a friend," A.J. answered.

"Shhh," Jake whispered. "She'll tell."

"Oops," A.J. mumbled, taking a pull from the bottle he held.

"What's going on in here?" thundered a deep voice from behind Laura, and the three of them turned around to see Noah standing there in nothing but his pajama pants. Tillie was beside him, and her expression was nothing less than astonished.

He looks just huge, Jake thought as he sized up his father in the doorway.

A.J. frowned as he thought *I don't remember Noah being that red.*

"Hi, Dad," Jake giggled with a silly smile.

"What are you doing?" Tillie gasped.

A small burp fell from A.J.'s lips as he smiled and carefully explained, "Mom, we're *real* sorry...I don't know what came over us —"

"We been talkin'," Jake slurred, staggering backwards a few steps, thinking *Dad can't reach me from here.*

"Go into the house, Laura," Noah commanded.

Laura hurried from the guest house, leaving Noah and Tillie alone with their sons.

Tillie had never seen Noah angry with their children. They'd surprised him of course, but had *never* made him angry. Then again, their children had never done anything *like this* before. This was new territory for both of the them and she wondered how either of them would deal with it. She wanted to put her six and a half foot son over her knee and give him the spanking of his life, and she thought perhaps Noah should hold him. Jake, on the other hand, reminded her so much of his own father's rebellion twenty-three years before, she could hardly find the words with which to correct him.

"If I were a bigger man, I'd pound the both of you," Noah growled, and Tillie looked at him with surprise. She put her hand on his bare arm, hoping to remind him of a better way to deal with this, for instance, replacing the word *pound* with *spank.* He briefly glanced down at his surprised wife and returned his attention to their sons. "Why on earth would you do something like this?"

A.J. cleared his throat, attempting a charming smile as he answered, "Well, it was kind of an accident."

"An *accident*?" Tillie was incredulous. "You call *this* an *accident*?"

"Who got this for you?" Noah pointed to the empty bottles strewn around on the floor.

Jake shrugged and answered, "I have a friend."

Noah shook his head and exhaled. "I'll deal with whoever that is tomorrow. It's after one o'clock and I've got an early day. You'll clean up this mess before the three of us leave in the morning."

Jake looked horrified. "Where are you taking us?" he asked.

"You're coming to work with me," Noah snapped. "Obviously, the two of you have too much time on your hands. Now try to find your beds and get some sleep. We'll be talking more about this when you've sobered up."

The boys nodded obediently and headed for the house.

Noah looked down at Tillie, noticing the concerned expression in her eyes.

"Don't work them to death," she said.

"They'll just *wish* they were dead," he replied.

*****

Noah shook the boys awake at five-thirty a.m. They hadn't heard their alarm clocks. Noah was surprised they'd remembered to set them. The last four and a half hours had slept away *most* of the effects of the alcohol, but both boys were miserable with intense headaches.

"Hurry up and get yourselves dressed," Noah growled. "We've got a lot to get done today."

They didn't dare disobey, and got ready to leave with a very angry man.

The sun was just rising over the Black Hills and Tillie had been up for a half hour. She'd prayed for their sons and that they would come to an understanding with Noah that day. When Noah came downstairs, he saw her faithful pot of coffee and poured himself a cup. He went into her studio, her favorite place in all the house, and sat down beside her in the comfortable wicker love seat.

"Good morning," he said with a soft kiss on her cheek.

"Hi," she replied with a sweet smile. "I've been praying for you."

"Thanks." He took a sip of his coffee. "I'm gonna need that. In fact, why don't you call Josh and tell him to get the whole church prayer chain going."

Tillie chuckled, laying her head on his shoulder as she asked, "Where are you guys going to be today?"

"The concrete contractor on your family's new project is short a couple of laborers," Noah explained, "so I'm gonna take 'em over there. They're gonna strip forms. I've gotta be down there for most of the morning anyway so I can keep an eye on 'em."

"Is that a hard job?" Tillie asked.

"It's a *terrible* job," Noah answered, taking another sip of his coffee. "But, it's just across the street from Maggie's so I thought we could have lunch over there, you know, maybe talk about things."

"Are you going to call their coach?"

"Yes. They can't just waltz out of here and do whatever they please without consequences."

"They'll be suspended," Tillie said.

"That's just too bad. They'll be lucky if they don't get kicked off the team altogether."

Jake and A.J. appeared in the doorway of the studio and looked at Noah.

"We're ready to go," Jake said.

"Get some water jugs for yourselves," Noah barked with a frown. "You're gonna need it. And have you cleaned up that guest house yet?"

The two hungover boys shook their heads, backing out of the studio.

"We'll do that right now," A.J. said, and he and Jake headed for the mess they'd left behind the night before.

Noah shook his head and said, "Ty *never* did anything like this."

Noah took their sons to the job site across the street from Maggie May's. His old friend, Leonard, was the concrete contractor and Noah told him he had two *free laborers* for the day. Leonard was delighted to have the help, promising Noah the two would be worked most strenuously.

Needless to say, it was a terrible morning for A.J. and Jake. A.J.'s head would not stop pounding, no matter how much water he drank. Jake made several trips to the outdoor toilets with an upset stomach. However, they worked hard, without words between them, stripping forms from walls and footings that had been poured the day before. It was the most horrendous job they'd ever performed, but there was a part inside each of the boys that was fearful of not doing it. Noah was mad, that was easy to see, but the disappointment in Tillie's eyes from the night before weighed heavy on their minds.

Even so, they thought Noah had some explaining to do. They hoped at the end of their sentence he would give them some sort of reason for why what had happened, happened. After all, the house was *clearly* built for Tillie, Noah was *not* Ty's father, and yet he married his mother, and what, *exactly*, happened that made A.J.'s father stay away for so long?

Noah spoke few words to the boys all morning so they were surprised when he came to them around noon and told them to walk over to Maggie's for lunch. They gladly dropped their tools and followed.

Maggie must have known they were coming because she had heaped plates of barbecued ribs and baked potatoes waiting at the counter. A.J. and Jake grimaced when they saw the food.

Unbeknownst to Jake and A.J., Noah had informed Maggie of their drinking episode. She couldn't resist just a little jeering.

She smiled devilishly, watching them take seats before their plates. "You're lookin' a little green around the gills today, boys," she said.

A wave of nausea hit Jake, and A.J. stared into the unappetizing plate.

Maggie laughed, leaving them to wait on some other customers.

She's mean, A.J. thought, gingerly attempting a small forkful of the baked potato Maggie had doused with butter and sour cream. A small slice of dried toast would have gone down easier than the rich dinner before them, *that* he was certain of.

Jake carefully flaked off a few pieces of the ribs and gave the fork a cautious smell. He was immediately woozy and thought maybe he'd have to dash into Maggie's restroom. *How could I possibly throw up anything else?* he thought, *I must have run out of fluids hours ago.*

"Just try a couple bites," A.J. whispered. "It seems to help."

Jake nodded, and with one eye on the restroom, he tried a small taste of the ribs.

Noah, however, wolfed down his food in about five bites. Then he asked Maggie for a slice of pie and a cup of coffee.

Anger makes him ravenous, the boys were thinking, astonished he would even request dessert after the gargantuan meal he'd just devoured.

Noah's pie went down in a single gulp. As he began to sip at his coffee, he glanced at the weakened young men seated at the counter with him. They'd managed some of their food, but about three quarters of it still remained on the plates.

"How are you feeling?" he asked with a frown.

"Better," Jake answered, attempting another bite of his potato.

"Me, too," A.J. said.

Noah shook his head. "I can't believe the two of you —" He stopped himself, taking a deep breath, announcing, "I called the coach this morning and the two of you have been suspended."

His words fell upon them like boulders. Their eyes dropped sadly into their laps. Baseball was their life. How could he do this to them?

Noah sighed. "Listen, guys, the coach is gonna release it to the press this afternoon, after Ty makes his announcement about his stupid father. You're not off the team forever, just for a month, and they're gonna let you play in the Firecracker Tournament over the Fourth, as long as you tell the cops where you bought the beer. And the cops will go easy on you as long as you tell the truth. You'll have to work for me during the entire suspension, forty hours a week, and there will also be ten nights of community service. You're gonna coach a pee-wee team over at Timberline. They're short-handed."

The boys were quiet, surprised at the relatively light punishment. Boys caught drinking on the Post team were generally kicked off for good. No one they were aware of had ever been given a second chance.

Noah saw Maggie heading back their way and he lifted his empty coffee cup. She nodded with a smile, hurrying over to give him a refill.

She grinned demonically, and asked, "Anybody want pie?"

Noah almost laughed as he asked, "Do you still have that old envelope under the counter, Maggie?"

Maggie reached below the counter, sliding an old, yellowed envelope at Noah. "You mean this one?" she asked.

"That's the one." Noah reached for the envelope. "Thanks, Maggie."

"You bet," she said, walking away.

Noah opened the envelope and pulled out the old snapshots. He smiled with a wistful expression in his eyes, tenderly setting the old snapshot of him and Tillie on the counter. "These pictures have been around for a really long time. Maggie and Estelle used to keep this photograph tucked into the frame of that painting right over there." He pointed to Tillie's first portrait entitled *Obedience*, and continued, "It was taken on the last night of a trip she made to Rapid City in 1975. Shortly before Angel and I were married, I had Maggie put it away with these others I'm gonna show you because I didn't want you to misunderstand things. And I think in order to answer all of your questions, you might as well know *exactly* how it happened."

Noah took a deep breath and smiled. The boys saw the familiar dancing in his blue eyes as he looked back at the old photograph. "She was only seventeen years old, but *I* didn't know that," he began. "She came over to Maggie's to *save* some of her drunk little classmates and I couldn't keep my eyes off of her. I was an awful person back then, but the strangest compulsion came over me that night. It was like I knew we were meant for each other, though I didn't how I was gonna swing it. I remember thinking, *what's a nice girl like that gonna want with a ratty, old biker like me?* But, I asked her out and to my complete and utter delight, she said yes. We went over to Mr. Steak, you know, that little place down on Haines that's a Mexican restaurant now. She told me all about how she was gonna go to school and become an art teacher, and then she asked me what I wanted to do with the rest of my life. Well, of course, I didn't have any kind of a plan, but she recommended I get one and I knew then if I wanted her to get interested in me, there would have to be some kind of a plan for my life."

Noah took a breath and continued, "She gave me quite a little lecture the next day about my drinking, too. She told me to drop my loser friends and get a real life, finish school and straighten myself out. Well, I could hardly say no to the girl. She was smart and pretty and the first one who ever made me feel like I could take on the world and make a difference.

"We drove my old Harley all over the Hills and hiked in Spearfish Canyon. We stopped at The Sluice that night for supper and there was this little cowboy band playing a few tunes and she was so excited because her papa loved old cowboy music. They played *Annie Laurie* and we danced together for the first time." Noah closed his eyes at the memory. "I *loved* her and I *knew* we were supposed to be together." He opened his eyes and grinned as he said, "So I asked her to marry me that night and that's when she finally told me she wasn't old enough. I said *that's okay, I can wait*, and she promised to come back when she was eighteen.

"A couple of weeks later, we had a terrible misunderstanding and I lost track of her. I prayed for a second chance, finished school, got a new job, got some more school and about a year later I prayed some more and started building the house for her. I thought for sure God would bring us together somehow, and I wanted a really nice place for her and all of our kids to live."

Noah paused, laying the rest of the snapshots on the counter as he explained, "My father left this land to me and so that's where I decided to build. I took pictures as I went along so that I could show them to her someday, but the someday just never came. I went to every art show I heard of and drove all over the state of South Dakota trying to find her. By September of '76, the house was finished and I had no bride to put into it. A few weeks later, I leased the thing to Elijah's grandmother because I couldn't bear to live there without my beautiful Angel. Obviously, God wasn't going to let me find her, or at least that's what I told myself. Anyway..." Noah paused and looked at Jake. "This is where *your* mother comes in. Your mom and I had been friends for a couple of years, and we had done quite a bit of drinking together. To make a long story short, I hadn't seen her for a real long time. I had cleaned up my act and was waiting for Angel to come back. But, Jake, your mom called me one night to bail her out of jail and I went down and got her. *That's* when I found out she was pregnant and she was threatening to abort the baby. We had lots of fights about it because, of course, I don't believe in abortion, and she was into that whole feminist movement thing. Anyway, this guy — his name is Roy — ditched her and she didn't know what she was gonna do. She couldn't take care of a baby on her own, and so her only reasonable solution to the problem was abortion. I thought maybe there was another solution and so I asked her to marry me. It was obvious Angel wasn't coming back and I decided maybe I should go ahead and save the baby's life at the very least.

"And I still don't know how I convinced her, but she agreed to marry me." Noah laughed as he remembered, "She was so mad at me on our wedding day she could have spit nails. She didn't want to be married, and to this day I can't help but wonder what made her go through with it. And she was just a devil to live with...*at first*. But when the baby started to grow and move around inside of her, she started going to church and reading the Bible. Pretty soon she was picking up books on how to take care of newborns. After Ty was born, it was like some kind of a miracle between the two of us. We started taking care of the baby together and I fell in love with that woman. She had changed so much it was amazing." He paused, looking at Jake and A.J. with a soft smile. "We had a really great life together and I've never regretted what I did."

"Why didn't you ever tell Ty?" Jake asked.

"Because I loved your mom, Jake, and I think it made me see Ty as *my own*."

It was quiet for a long moment and then A.J. quietly cleared his throat and asked, "Did my Dad know?"

Noah slowly nodded his head, admitting, "Your dad and I were friends for probably ten or eleven years before I realized he was the one who'd married Angel. Boy, was I mad. I thought she'd dumped me for a Harvard Law graduate. By this time, Ty and Jake's mother had been gone for five years and I was very lonely. Of course, when I saw your mother again, I *totally* lost it. I tried to control myself, and she told me to stay away, but I couldn't and eventually your father found out."

"Was he mad?" A.J. asked.

"Furious," Noah answered. "I had deceived my best friend and it hurt him. He told me I could never see her again, and so I stayed away. He forgave me, and we were good friends again by the time he died."

The boys sat quiet, looking into their partially emptied plates, trying to absorb all Noah had told them. They couldn't help but feel a measure of compassion for the man and all that he'd experienced. They regretted what they'd done the night before.

"I'm sorry," A.J. blurted. "We should have given you a chance to explain."

"I'm sorry, too, Dad," Jake said, looking at his father. "I acted like an idiot."

Noah laughed and nodded. "Yeah, you did. You should have seen yourselves last night. You know, for years I thought I could solve my problems with drinking, but it only made me and Josh and Mona's life a nightmare. That stuff will wreck you."

A.J. rolled his eyes. "I can't even believe we did it."

"I can't either," Noah replied. "I know we have a hard thing to go through with Ty, but getting drunk and acting stupid won't make it any easier."

*****

"Detective Jason Patterson," Jason repeated into the telephone. Joe walked in just in time to see his son roll his eyes, shake his head and say, "No. Mr. Caselli *does not* know me, but it's very important for you get a message to him so we can discuss an old case of his." Jason paused, obviously listening to whoever was speaking on the other line. "Well, can I please have his number overseas?" Another short pause and Jason frowned. "Well, jeez lady, I didn't realize I was dialing Fort Knox —" He was quiet. "Hello?" Jason sighed and hung up the phone.

"What was *that* all about?" Joe asked with a curious smile.

"Oh, brother," Jason moaned. "I'm trying to reach Marquette Caselli and it's like trying to call the president. Apparently he's overseas right now and the ole gal that works for him wouldn't give me his number. Hopefully, she'll get a message to him and he'll call me back."

"Why are you trying to call *him*?"

"I thought maybe he'd give me some information on his old Ponerello case," Jason answered. "When I questioned Schneider he said two *terrorists* hassled him about John Peters several years ago. I think they were actually Marquette and Tara Caselli. And I also think that whatever is going on here in Rapid City, has to do with whatever happened in 1975. The only problem is I'll have to contact Caselli directly because anything he's ever worked on is completely off limits to the rest of the world."

"Why don't you give that nice Mrs. Hansen a call? She probably knows how to reach him," Joe suggested.

"I can't do that, Dad," Jason protested. "I'm still thinking about pulling her husband in for questioning and if he got wind of what was happening and *does* happen to know something, it'll tip my hand for sure. I gotta keep that guy in the dark for just a little bit longer."

Joe nodded. "Well, what happened with Michael's autopsy?"

"Strychnine, just like the other two. Todd says it looks like an identical dose —" Jason didn't finish what he was about to say because the phone on his desk rang. "Patterson here," he answered. There were a few moments of silence and Jason looked grimly in his father's direction as he said, "I'll be down in a few minutes." He hung up and got to his feet. "They're pulling another body out of that same bunch of row houses on the north end."

"This thing is gonna get worse before it gets better," Joe grumbled, following his son out the door.

Noah left A.J. and Jake in the very apt care of Leonard. He'd promised Ty he'd be there for him when he made the announcement to the press with regard to the marrow transplant, as did Joshua and Guiseppi. The women stayed at home that day because it didn't seem necessary to put them through the media circus Ty's announcement would certainly bring. They promised to watch the event on television.

The press had set up a long table in the parking lot at Fitzgerald Stadium, where Ty and Noah sat together in the middle, Guiseppi next to Ty and Joshua next to Noah.

"Thank you all for coming here today," Ty began with a polite smile. "I know you have several questions for me, but I have to read a statement first and then we'll see if you still have questions." He took a deep breath, looked at his handwritten notes, and began, "Baseball has been my life for as long as I can remember. The Baltimore Orioles have given me an excellent invitation, but I regret that I must decline at this time." Quiet hushes were heard at his words, but Ty swallowed and continued, "My biological father is dying of leukemia and my marrow has proved a perfect match for donor transplant. My recovery period prevents me from reporting to the Orioles within the required time frame. As well, I must stay close to my biological father should he need additional treatments. These circumstances prevent me from playing ball for the rest of the season. The Orioles have already chosen another pitcher, and I understand I may be passed over next year." He took a breath, smiling at Noah, and then he returned his eyes to the cameras before them. "This man beside me you all know as my dad, because that's who he is. And though he is not my biological father, he's the man who taught me right from wrong and how to make a good decision, rather than a bad one I might regret. Dad lives with no regrets and neither will I." Ty paused and looked into the small crowd of very quiet reporters. "I will take a few questions at this time."

After a few moments, a young lady cleared her throat and asked, "If Noah Hansen isn't your biological father, who is?"

"He's requested I not divulge his identity," Ty answered.

"Will you play for George Washington next year?"

Ty nodded.

"Will Baltimore give you another chance next year?" another reporter asked, but his heart wasn't into it. Ty felt sorry for the hush that had fallen over the usually anxious press.

"I don't know," Ty answered. "Maybe."

"Are they upset about the turn of events?"

"A little," Ty answered. "But they have another pitcher they'll be announcing tomorrow, so their bases are covered so to speak."

"Mr. Hansen," a young lady questioned, looking directly at Noah. "What do you think of all this?"

"Me?" Noah asked with surprise, pointing to himself, looking wide-eyed into the camera. The young reporter nodded and Noah quietly cleared his throat. "Ty is making the decision God would want him to make." He smiled at Ty and added, "Ty's a good man."

At home in their family room, Tillie, Rosa, Laura, Mona and little Annie watched the announcement on the local television station. Tillie smiled at what her wonderful husband had just said, and she felt Rosa put her hand into her own.

"You are married to such a good boy," Rosa said, sniffing away a tear.

Tillie sighed with a smile and squeezed her mother's hand.

They turned their attention back to the televised press conference, where Senator Caselli's father had suddenly taken center stage.

"Oh, no," Rosa groaned. "Why can they not leave him alone?"

Guiseppi was leaning forward with his ear cupped as if he were hard of hearing. "I am sorry, Missy, I did not hear the question."

"Mr. Caselli, your son is a senior senator. Certainly there have been words between the two of you with regard to the president's situation."

Guiseppi frowned with a nod, answering, "I understand that the president's missus is very upset about things."

"Would you care to give us any opinion?"

Guiseppi moaned, reaching for his chest, pretending to cough.

At that point, the press began to laugh. Senator's Caselli's father was known for theatrics.

Tillie was aghast. "Is he *still* doing that old trick?"

"Yes, my Angel," Rosa admitted. "I cannot convince him to stop because it works so well."

Mona and Laura burst into laughter.

Rosa took a soft breath, smiling at her husband of sixty-two years. She shook her head and whispered, "What an old codger."

Alyssa and Jon knocked on Charise Nelson's front door and waited. No one came to the door right away, so Jon knocked again.

"Maybe she's not home," he suggested, peeking through the lace curtains in the windows next to the steps. "I can't see any lights or anything."

Alyssa shook her head. "She's hiding from us. By now her mother and probably the nursing staff at Colonial Manor have told her we were there. We'll have to find another way to question her."

"Okay then." Jon turned around, heading down the porch steps. Alyssa followed. They got into their black Taurus and pulled away.

Charise crouched in a corner, holding her breath, praying every moment they would just leave. Nothing could be said to them that wouldn't compromise her situation and send it spiraling further out of control. When she heard the engine of their car start and the wheels begin to crunch away on the gravel, she let out her breath, her eyes burning with tears. It wouldn't be much longer now and everyone would know where they were.

*****

It was six o'clock when Tillie heard Noah's pickup in the drive out front. She was setting the table and had been just wondering when they'd be back from their first long day. Guiseppi and Rosa were enjoying the late spring afternoon in the porch swing, and Tillie heard them teasing the boys.

"There are those two rascals!" Guiseppi said, laughing and making a "tsk" noise. "If I were a betting man, I would bet the two of you do not look for fun near the bottom of a bottle again."

Tillie saw Jake and A.J. smile politely, but their embarrassment was plain to see.

"I still love you," Rosa proclaimed, shuffling her way from the porch swing to the boys to put her arms around both of them. She smiled into their tired eyes and tittered, "But there will be no more of that nonsense. Right?"

"Right," both boys agreed at the same time.

Tillie stepped out onto the porch, looking them over with a gentle smile. They were covered in dirt, dust and dry concrete from head to toe. Poor Jake had a scrape on his cheek where something had caught him during his labor.

"Hi, guys," she greeted.

"Hello, Angel," Noah said, reaching for Tillie's hand. He gave her a soft kiss. "Did you see our press conference?"

Tillie nodded. "It was awesome. You guys were great."

"Especially me," Guiseppi chided from the porch swing.

"Especially Papa," Tillie agreed. "Now, you guys better get washed up because Nonna's made some of her special fried chicken and I'm about starving to death."

Noah looked at their sons and smiled curiously. "Are you guys up for it?" he asked.

"I think so," A.J. answered, giving his stomach a rub.

"I can eat," Jake said, and he looked at Tillie. "But first I have to apologize to you, Tillie. You're the greatest lady in this whole town and I'm really sorry for being such an idiot. Can you ever forgive me?"

"Of course, Jake." Tillie put her arms around the dirty boy and gave his dusty cheek a kiss. "I love you."

Jake sighed with relief. "Thanks, Tillie."

A.J. put a hand on his mother's shoulder. "I'm really sorry too, Mom," he said. "I was a total jerk. Please forgive me."

"It's okay." Tillie put her arms around her tall son. "I love you, A.J. Please don't ever do this again."

A.J. shook his head. "We won't. I promise."

Chapter 11

The early light of dawn eased into the sky above the Black Hills. Just above the ridge, the expanse melted from deep blue to pale pink in barely the blink of an eye. Noah sighed with contentment, watching the colors pass before the window in their bedroom. He was already up and dressed and ready to get the boys rolling for work.

He set two cups of coffee on the nightstand beside their bed and gently nudged his sleeping wife. It wasn't very often he saw her sleeping — she was usually up before everyone else. He brushed the curls away from her face and gave her a soft kiss. She took a deep breath, opening her eyes.

"Good morning," she said with a surprised smile. "What are you doing up already?"

"Early start. I thought maybe we could have a cup of coffee together before I go."

"Oh, I *do* smell coffee." Tillie sniffed the air and smiled at Noah. "I thought maybe I was still dreaming."

Noah helped her into a seated position in the bed, handing her a cup of her favorite hot brew.

"Where are you taking them today?" she asked, sipping carefully.

"Same place," Noah answered. "Leonard's gonna work 'em over at your family's project for probably a good couple of weeks. After that, Ben scheduled him to do footings and basements on about sixteen places. That should take us through June."

Tillie grimaced and asked, "What will they do about practice?"

Noah raised his brow. "They should have thought about that before they decided to tie one on —" Tillie giggled, and Noah smiled into her black eyes. She was still the *best* part of his life and not a day went by that he didn't thank God for the beautiful woman he was married to. "They can find time to practice in the evenings, after they're done coaching their pee-wee team," he continued. "They'll be as strong as a couple of oxen by the time the Firecracker Tournament opens."

Tillie laughed again and said, "Those two. They sure looked beat when they got home last night."

Noah laughed too, saying, "Oh, man, you should have seen them when we went over to Maggie's for lunch. Jake was sicker than a dog. But, then they had some lunch and that seemed to straighten them out for the rest of the afternoon." He took a sip of his coffee and said, "Marquette and Tara fly in today. You gonna pick 'em up or do you want me to swing over and get 'em?"

"I'll go," Tillie answered. "Laura doesn't have to work today and she promised to watch Annie for me."

"How about the rest of your clan? When does everybody else get here?"

"Tomorrow," Tillie answered. "Patty's flying into Sioux Falls and then he's riding out with Vincenzo and Kate in their new conversion van. He thought it would be easier to hide from the press if he did it that way."

Noah laughed as he remembered Guiseppi with the press from the day before. "Your father was so funny yesterday."

"Oh, he's terrible," Tillie giggled.

"You know, he used to pull that old trick with his heart on me. He could make me do whatever he wanted."

Tillie chuckled and gave Noah a soft kiss on his cheek. "Ma`ma says you're a good boy."

Noah laughed. "A *good boy?* I haven't been called *that* in a terribly long time."

Jason arrived at the department before his father. He retrieved a book of old mug shots and got himself a cup of coffee. Todd had called the afternoon before to let him know that the last death was looking more and more like another poisoning. However, they hadn't been able to identify the victim. Chances were, the dead man they found yesterday had a record.

As Jason began his search of mug shots, Joe arrived, taking his morning seat in front of Jason's desk.

"Dropped your mom off at work again this morning," he said. "Boy, she's really getting sick of that."

"When does she go to Georgia?" Jason asked, paging through the photos on his desk.

"She flies out on Monday," Joe answered.

"I'll be really glad to get her out of town." Jason turned the book of mug shots toward his father, pointing as he said, "This is the guy they pulled out of North Rapid yesterday."

Joe squinted for a better look. "Have you seen him up at Andreotti's office?" he asked.

Jason shook his head, answering, "I don't know if he's a patient or not, but he's got a record."

"Who is he? And what's that mark on his face?"

"Delvin Mixon," Jason answered. "And it's a tattoo of a snake."

"Are you sure?" Joe frowned at the photo.

"I took a good look at it yesterday," Jason answered.

Joe sighed and shook his head. "Wonder where *this* guy came from," he mused.

*****

Jon produced his badge, introducing himself to the morgue official, "United States Deputy Marshal Jon Danielson, sir."

"Special Assistant to the County Coroner, Todd Yearwood," the man replied, "What can I do for you folks this morning?"

"You pulled a body out of North Rapid yesterday," Jon began, tucking his badge back into its place at his waist. "We need to take a look at it."

Todd nodded and turned, saying, "Follow me. He's right over here." He led them to a table where a body draped in a white sheet waited. "I'm not quite finished yet, but it looks like a poisoning to me. I think he died about a week ago, but we didn't get the call until yesterday. I've got some lab work out, but I should have it back by this afternoon." He lifted the sheet from the body's face and Alyssa and Jon leaned in for a good look.

"You got an ID on him yet?" Jon asked.

"Just this morning," Todd answered. "His name is Delvin Mixon. The detective is pulling his record, but I'm sure he won't be any different from the others."

"The others?" Jon raised an eyebrow.

"This is the forth poisoning we've had in about a month. All drug dealers with prior felony records. All with the same dose of Strychnine in their system, along with cocaine. Normally, there's always a little something else in cocaine, especially from cheap dealers, but the doses I've seen appear to be deliberate. You'll have to talk to the detective for more details. I only work on the bodies."

"Patterson's the detective?" Jon questioned.

"He's the one, and I know he's over at the shop right now. You can probably still catch him."

"Thanks," Jon answered. "Can I call you this afternoon about that lab work?"

"Certainly. I'm here all day long, unless we get a call."

"Thanks, Mr. Yearwood, we'll be in touch." And with that, Jon and Alyssa left.

Outside in their car, Alyssa scribbled down notes as fast as she could recall them. "Four poisonings in the last month," she murmured. "I wonder if they've all been Andreotti's patients."

"Let's assume for just a moment they *are*," Jon suggested.

Alyssa raised a curious brow. "Okay. So?"

"Well, the most logical question, of course, would be *why is Andreotti poisoning his patients?* Unless they're not really his patients at all and they've obtained certain information about Andreotti he doesn't want to share with the rest of the world. Maybe they threaten him or whatever. Think about how easy it would be to get a dope fiend to take something, especially if it was free. Andreotti pretends to be his buddy, slips him the poison and sends him on his way. The addict dies when he does the drugs, and the body is found in a location completely disconnected from Andreotti. He doesn't have to lift a finger in the murder, and there won't be a trace of him at the crime scene. No fibers, no hair, no prints —"

"Maybe prints," Alyssa interrupted.

"How?"

"If your theory turns out to be truth," Alyssa answered, "Andreotti would have to physically *give* the addict the drug. Cocaine has to be transported in *some kind* of a container, like a bag or a vial for instance."

Jon thoughtfully mused, "So, how do we get a hold of crime scene evidence? You'll be exposed and you didn't want to do that yet."

Alyssa took a deep breath. "We're gonna have to think of something. Today's Friday and my family reunion starts tomorrow. My Uncle Marq will be here this afternoon and my own parents will be here in the morning." She rolled her eyes with a sigh. "And *that's* gonna be a huge mess when my folks find out I'm working."

Jon laughed. "Oh, what a tangled web we weave."

Alyssa smiled. "Come on, let's get out of here. We still have time to follow Bracelet and make an ID on him."

*****

Antonio usually didn't come to see Charise in the middle of the day, but he made an exception today. Too many things were happening and she needed to know.

"Have those marshals been back?" he whispered to her while they stood near the horses' corral, watching the older stallion prance around, tossing his head. Antonio could tell the poor devil wanted out — he felt much the same about his own circumstances.

"No," she answered, noticing the unusual slump in his posture. She frowned into his eyes and asked, "What have you come to tell me, Antonio?"

"Sal knows," Antonio answered. "Somehow he learned that Noah went to see Rauwolf. He desperately wants to find the stiletto and he is determined that Noah knows its location."

Charise sighed heavily as she said, "This is bad."

Antonio nodded and added, "I will try to see Rauwolf this afternoon if I can get away." He took a breath and continued, "And you should know something else, Charise...Marquette Caselli arrives today. Should his niece question him about these things, or should Noah even mention the name of his son's father, Mr. Caselli will *instantly* know what has happened. He knows every detail and will quickly be able to put things together. It is time to move your mother. Within the next few days, Charise, our identity will be compromised and we must be ready to move."

*****

Detective Patterson stopped at the county coroner's office to see if Todd had anything more on the overdose from the day before. Hopefully the thumbprint on the vial matched with the ones retrieved from Andreotti's INS records.

"Not even close," Todd said. "There were two different prints on the vial we found near the body. One of them, of course, belonged to the victim, but the others were *not* Andreotti's, or at least didn't match the prints you got from INS."

Jason frowned.

"My lab work came back," Todd went on. "And that did show the same dose of strychnine I found in the other three victims. Someone is going to a lot of trouble to exactly mix this stuff."

Jason's frown deepened. "Of course it's Andreotti," he said. "Who else could it be?"

"But if Andreotti slipped the victim the vial, something would show up on it, unless he was wearing gloves, and who's gonna take something from a guy wearing rubber gloves? That would be suspicious *even* to a hardened addict."

"I'm calling INS," Jason said. "Maybe they sent us the wrong set of prints."

"Or maybe the prints belong to someone else," Todd suggested. "We still haven't run 'em through on a general search. And how about the Marshal's Service? Wouldn't they have access to a lot of FBI files?"

Jason started to nod his head, thinking it might not be a bad idea to contact the United States Marshal's Office. He was suddenly struck with a suspicion and asked, "Why would you think of the U.S. Marshal's Service?"

"Well, they were here this morning," Todd answered. "Didn't they catch up to you?"

Jason shook his head.

"Well, they knew about Mixon and they knew that you were the detective on the case," Todd continued. "They told me they'd be contacting me this afternoon about my lab work, but they haven't called yet."

Jason rolled his eyes. "How many of them were there?" he asked.

"Just two. Did you know they were involved?"

"No," Jason moaned. "What did they look like?"

"Tall man, blond. He showed me his badge and said his name was Danielson. The other one was a real tall lady. Good looker, short black hair, black eyes. I could see her badge and a gun, but she didn't speak and she didn't identify herself."

Jason snorted and clenched his jaw. *Alyssa Caselli.*

Todd saw the anger flash in Jason's expression. "Do you want me to stall 'em?" he asked.

Jason shook his head and answered, "Give 'em whatever they want and if they mention something new, I want you to call me as soon as you can. Don't let on that we've talked."

Tillie waited at the gate for the Northwestern Airlines flight from Minneapolis, Marquette and Tara's last connecting flight. It was almost four o'clock in the afternoon in Rapid City, South Dakota, and that made it nearly eleven p.m., on Como Lake in Italy. By now, Marquette and Tara had been traveling fourteen hours.

Behind what seemed like hundreds of people, Tillie could just make out Marquette's profile. His head was turned, as if he was talking to someone, and he appeared to be laughing. Soon, Tillie saw that it was Tara he was speaking with and she was smiling at him in return. Tillie waved to get their attention, and in a matter of moments, they cleared the gangway, greeting Tillie with hugs and kisses.

"How were your flights?" Tillie asked.

"Long," Tara answered, rolling her eyes and shaking her head. "It is getting to be about too much."

"I received a message during the last flight," Marquette said. "I must give my liaison a call as soon as possible."

"Well, I promised Noah we'd stop by before taking you home. Is that okay?" Tillie asked.

Marquette nodded. "That is fine, Angel."

"He's had a terrible week," Tillie continued as they began to walk the short concourse. "I have so many things to tell you."

After loading their luggage into Tillie's Suburban, she drove to the work site where Noah was building the Casellis' new hotel complex. Black clouds were rolling in from the west, and lightning strikes could be seen in the distance.

Along the way, Tillie explained all that had happened and that Ty's surgery was scheduled for early the following week. She told them about how the other children were informed of the unusual circumstances which had prompted Noah to marry his first wife. As a result, Jake and A.J. had *tied one on*.

"So, they've been suspended from their team," Tillie went on as they drove onto the work site, the boys coming into view. They were dutifully pulling forms from concrete walls and Tillie shook her head, adding, "Noah's working them forty hours a week during the suspension, which will last an entire month."

Marquette laughed. "That reminds me of our brother, Vincenzo," he said.

"Oh, do not tell on your dear brother," Tara said. "He would be so embarrassed."

Tillie put the Suburban into park, looking at her brother and sister-in-law with a curious smile. "What did he do?" she asked.

Marquette laughed again. "When we sailed for America on the *Alexandria*, we were allowed attendance at a formal ball. We had stopped in Cannes, France, earlier in the day, and Papa bought us all smart clothes. We looked quite dapper. We had watched the movie *Giant* and Vincenzo wanted to be James Dean, and so he wore dark pants and a white sport coat and slicked back his hair. He *was* most stunning. Anyway, at the ball, they offered free champagne and we decided to try some. Naturally, we had had wine before in the valley, however, champagne is nothing like our *Moscato d'asti*, which does not have very much alcohol in it. The champagne was wonderfully bubbly and I remember thinking it would be difficult to discern whether or not I had had too much, so I decided to have just the one glass. Vincenzo, on the other hand, tore into it like a crazy man. I told him to be careful with it, but he lived it up, dancing with the ladies and inviting many of them back to our quarters —" Tillie and Tara laughed. Marquette smiled and continued, "It took nearly two days for Vincenzo to recover from the episode and I do not believe he tasted champagne for another twenty years, and even then it may have only been a swallow."

"Poor Vincenzo!" Tara laughed. "He still does not like to remember it, and is very embarrassed when you bring it up around Lovely Kate."

"I won't even mention it," Tillie assured with a chuckle.

Noah saw them park, and he left what he was doing. He reached the truck just as they were getting out, and Marquette put his arms around Noah, holding him close.

"Angel told us of your dreadful week. I am sorry that we were not here for you," Marquette said.

"Well, we're getting through it," Noah said with a faint smile. "I guess it could've been a whole lot worse."

Tara reached for Noah as well, embracing him tightly. "Angel told us of the shenanigans of your sons."

Noah smiled, pointing to the two young men working in the distance. "They're working their tails off."

"It is good for them," Marquette said.

Ben walked up to the group, extending his hand with a smile to Marquette as he said, "Good to see you again."

"And you as well," Marquette answered.

"Mrs. Caselli." Ben politely extended his hand to Tara.

"Mr. Simmons," Tara acknowledged with a smile.

Ben looked at Noah and said, "Leonard will be pulling the men off of the site shortly because of the lightning. And I need to get to an appointment. Would you like me to check on the Sheridan project tomorrow morning?"

"Tomorrow's Saturday, Ben," Noah reminded.

"Oh." Ben chuckled, backing away from them. "I forgot. This week has been so busy for me."

"We'll see ya Monday," Noah said.

"I will meet you and your in-laws here early," Ben replied. "Have a good weekend."

"You, too, Ben," Noah said with a wave, and Ben turned and walked quickly to his car.

Noah sighed as he watched Ben walk away. "That poor guy," he said. "His stepmother is really sick right now and they've about got him run ragged."

Marquette frowned. "What is wrong with her?" he asked.

"Oh, she fell down some stairs quite a few years ago and has been in a wheelchair ever since," Noah explained. "Now she's been diagnosed with lupus and they're trying to treat her for that. She's not very old either. Something like sixty-five."

Without any of them knowing, Alyssa and Jon watched Ben leave the work site, determined to identify him.

"He's the one with the bracelet. Follow him," Alyssa said, watching through her binoculars. "I want to see where he's going now."

Jon threw the car into gear, taking up a secretive tail on the tall, dark man who worked for Noah. Alyssa put down her binoculars and dialed Hansen Development, LLC, on her cell phone.

"Hansen Development."

"Good afternoon," Alyssa said in a professional voice. "I'm looking for Noah Hansen."

"He's on the LaCross site this afternoon. Can I take a message for him?"

"How about his foreman?" Alyssa asked.

"Ben Simmons?"

"Yes, Ben," Alyssa acknowledged. "Is Ben around?"

"He's also on LaCross today."

"Thanks anyway," Alyssa said quickly. "I'll call back later." And she turned off the phone.

"Ben Simmons," Alyssa said to Jon as they drove along. "Noah's right-hand man."

Jon took a quiet breath as he carefully followed Ben through the winding traffic on LaCross. They turned right on East North Street, following the gentle curve into East Boulevard where Ben turned right on Omaha. They continued following until they reached Fifth Street. Ben turned left and Jon began to nod his head.

"He's headed in the direction of the hospital," he surmised.

"Is he going to see Schneider?" Alyssa asked.

"I think so," Jon answered.

In just a few minutes, Jon pulled into the parking lot of the Rapid City Regional Cancer Care Institute.

Alyssa grabbed her binoculars. "I can see him getting out of his car," she said. "He's going inside." She put the binoculars down and unbuckled her belt. "Let me out, Jon," she said. "I'll follow him just to make sure."

Jon slowed down the car, suggesting, "I'll make a few passes through the parking lot and pick you up in the back."

"Sounds good." Alyssa exited the car. From there, she hurried into the building, attempting to reach Schneider's room before Ben could get there. She found the inner stairwell she and Jon had used before, taking the steps two at a time. With her long legs, it didn't take much time to reach the floor where Schneider's room was located. She stepped out of the stairwell just in time to see Ben walk by, and she fell into a casual pace behind him. Sure enough, he headed down the hall, stopped beside Schneider's door, knocked and went inside. Alyssa continued on her way, attempting to gulp away the pounding of her heart in her throat. *Ben Simmons isn't who he's portrayed himself to be all of these years*, she thought. *He's Jack's son, Tony!* The question of *why* was probably the reason Luigi Andreotti had so suddenly dropped back into the Caselli's lives.

"If he knew you were here, he'd kill you himself," Rauwolf rasped from his bed. He was very weak today and had developed a heart murmur.

Antonio took a seat on the edge of the bed. He looked into Rauwolf's aged and tragedy stricken-eyes, noticing the flicker of an unfamiliar light. "But I had to talk to you," he said. "Does Noah know?"

Rauwolf frowned as he asked, "Are you here for Sal or yourself?"

"Charise sent me."

Rauwolf nodded. "He won't tell me where it is."

"Is the stiletto with the body?" Antonio questioned.

Rauwolf shrugged. "That I *don't* know. I used it that night, but Carrie was able to get it away from me before they sent me away."

Antonio sighed as he said, "You should not have approached the boy. Noah is sick at heart over it."

"I was afraid to die. He's my only living relative, Antonio."

"I understand all of that," Antonio acknowledged. "But you only make matters worse, and put yourself in peril."

Rauwolf took a raspy breath and asked, "A Rapid City detective and two United States Marshals were here asking about an Italian named Andreotti. Do you know anything about that?"

Antonio nearly fell off the bed. "What did they want to know?" he asked.

"Just if I knew him. I told them I didn't, because I don't. Who's Andreotti?"

Antonio hands shook, sweat beading up on his forehead. He rose from the bed and went to the window, watching the darkness of the impending thunderstorm move closer. He saw the lightning strikes closing in on Rapid City, briefly wondering if Leonard had gotten the men off the site in time.

Rauwolf saw the alarm in Antonio's expression and his mouth went dry. "It's Sal, isn't it?" he whispered.

Antonio took a deep breath, answering, "And he has killed at least four of his own people."

Rauwolf swallowed and closed his eyes. "Antonio, you've gotta go to the cops with this —"

"I cannot," Antonio said, turning quickly from the window to look at Rauwolf. "If I do, I risk unleashing whatever evil the man has been able to restrain so far. He threatens me with your son's demise on an almost daily basis, and I am terrified of what he will do if I back him into a corner." He sighed heavily. "One of the marshals that visited you the other day was more than likely Mrs. Hansen's own niece. She and her partner have already found my sister and her mother. Their God only knows when this thing will be completely out in the open and our identities will be exposed. And it is not the police I am afraid of, but whoever Sal sends to eliminate us."

Rauwolf let out his breath as he looked into Antonio's sad, dark eyes, remembering the fire of youth burning there years ago when he'd vowed his very life to protect the family he loved. "You are the Elder Son, Antonio," he reminded. "You've done the *best* job you can and your father must so proud of you."

Antonio's eyes shined with tears, but only for one uncontrolled moment. He took a breath and asked, "Are you afraid?"

"Petrified. But I no longer *fear* my death, whether Sal does me or the Lord takes me home. But, it is the *way* I will die that frightens me the most."

Chapter 12

Jason sprinted from his car to the shelter of the awning where his father was waiting. It was raining in sheets, with lightning crashing all around them. A small restaurant on Mt. Rushmore Road had been robbed at gunpoint, and Jason's father had been dispatched to the scene. No one had been hurt, although the manager, several waitresses and a handful of customers were shaken by the incident.

"I remember noticing their shoes were covered with tons of that red mud you see in the hills," the manager explained to Joe in a teary voice, shivering in the storm.

Joe nodded sympathetically, jotting down notes. "Did you see what they drove away in?" he asked.

"It was an old, gray pickup," she answered with a sniff.

"Gray in color or gray because it had been primered?"

"There was lots of rust," she answered with a confused expression. "And I don't know what primer is."

Joe smiled at the young lady and spoke into his radio, "We're looking for an old, gray pickup with lots of rust." He paused and looked at the manager. "How *old* is this pickup?" The manager slowly shook her head in response and Joe questioned further, "Is the hood flat or domed?"

"Domed," she answered.

"Any markings on the hood or the grill, or anywhere on the doors?" Joe questioned.

"There was small lettering on the side," she answered, and then she shook her head. "No...there was one letter and some numbers...like F-1-0-0...does that make sense?"

"Perfect," Joe answered, nodding with an approving smile. He said into his radio, "On that old, gray pickup we're looking for...it's a fifties Ford. It's probably gonna be primered." He paused and looked at the manager. "Flat bed or box style?" he asked.

"It was a wooden bed," she answered.

Joe spoke into his radio again, "That Ford has a wooden bed and I think it's headed north. There's a lot of red mud at the scene." Joe smiled at the distraught manager, giving her a gentle pat on the shoulder as he said, "Why don't you get yourself a drink and have a short rest. I have to talk to someone and then I'll ask you a few more questions."

"Okay," she said, sniffing again as she walked back into the restaurant.

Joe turned to Jason and said, "Couple of punks robbed the place about an hour ago. They pulled out the telephone lines *before* they came in and 9-1-1 didn't get called until just a few minutes ago. They tied up the help and whatever customers were in the place, but apparently forgot to lock the door before they left. Somebody happened to come in for coffee and found everybody. He had a cell phone and called the cops."

"Were you able to get any good descriptions?" Jason asked.

Joe looked at his notes and answered, "One man in particular, but I don't know if we can go on it or not. He was wearing that Gothic, black makeup you see the kids with these days. Black hair, but it could have been colored that way, and he was wearing those funny, green Halloween contact lenses on his eyes. He *might* be a white guy, but it was hard to tell because he was wearing gloves. Long, black trench coat and knee-high boots pulled over his pant legs. The manager thinks the pants were leather, but she couldn't be sure. The guy with him was definitely white, blond hair, but he wore sunglasses to cover his eyes, and he was wearing just some blue jogging shorts, a t-shirt and some tennis shoes. They're both in about their mid-twenties and short, like five and half feet or so, and the gal I interviewed said their shoes were covered with red mud." He took a breath and added, "There's a bunch of dried mud in the restaurant and I'm having forensics take a sample of the stuff. Whether or not it'll do any good, I don't know."

Jason frowned, scratching his head as he said, "I've seen a couple of Gothic characters coming out of Andreotti's office."

"Are they living up in those row houses with the rest of them?" Joe asked.

"No. I've never been able to place 'em." Jason raised one eyebrow and smiled at his father. "But guess who I followed out of Andreotti's today?"

"Who?"

"A guy named Ben Simmons, and he went from Andreotti's down to Hansen Development, out to a couple of sites with Hansen himself, and then he went up to the hospital to see Roy Schneider. A couple of people in a black Taurus with government plates followed him up to the hospital. I think they're United States Marshals."

Joe looked surprised. "When did *they* get involved?"

"Probably right after Caselli caught me on her uncle's boat," Jason answered. "And they were down to see Yearwood and the most recent body this morning. They said they'd call him back this afternoon, but he hasn't heard from them."

"Were you able to get a finger print match from Andreotti's INS records?" Joe asked.

Jason shook his head. "The prints didn't match. INS is reworking the identification just in case they made a mistake." He rolled his eyes. "Can you believe that? They don't even trust themselves."

"Good grief. Well, where are you going now?"

"I'm goin' up to the hospital to see what Simmons and Schneider talked about," Jason answered. "Maybe he'll be able to give me something."

By the time Tillie, Marquette and Tara reached the Hansens' home on Rimrock, the Black Hills was experiencing the worst thunderstorm of the spring. Lightning and thunder crashed and the rain fell so hard it appeared as sheets of water. Sparky scurried upstairs, beneath a safe bed, but Vanilla was content in her regular place on the kitchen floor.

It stormed through dinner, and even hailed, dropping the temperature several degrees. Noah lit the fireplace in the family room to take off the chill in the air. Rosa whipped up a batch of hot chocolate, and everyone gathered around the fire to enjoy a tasty cup.

"And what is this I hear about a *boyfriend?*" Marquette asked, suspiciously narrowing his eyes as he questioned Laura.

Laura giggled, but Noah frowned.

"He's a crafty stockbroker," Jake teased, and A.J. laughed.

"Don't tease Laura," Noah admonished with a pretended serious expression. "Besides, I hear he plays ball so he can't be *all* bad."

"When will we meet him, Laura?" Tara asked.

Laura smiled as she answered, "He's coming over for Sunday dinner, and you're really gonna like him."

"And someone else of interest will be here this weekend as well," Rosa tittered with a sly expression.

"And who is that, Ma`ma?" Marquette asked.

"Luigi Andreotti," Guiseppi whispered.

Everyone laughed — except for Marquette. "Why on earth will *he* be here?" he questioned.

"Your brother *accidentally* invited him," Noah answered with a grin. "Patty's supposed to go over and try to talk him out of it tomorrow, but we'll see how *that* goes."

"Oh, goodness," Tara said with a sigh and a shake of her head. "Has the old boy been around quite a bit?"

"He calls constantly," Tillie informed. "And he even showed up at the Bismarck game last week."

"He wants to be my best friend so that he can date my wife," Noah said, raising his brow with a smile. "But I'm on to him."

Everyone laughed.

Guiseppi decided to change the subject. He looked at Marquette and Tara, asking, "And where have the two of you been?"

132

"Indonesia," Marquette answered with a heavy sigh. "And that is a place I do not *ever* wish to return."

"I thought you guys were in Italy?" Tillie frowned.

"We were," Tara smiled. "But we were only able to spend a few days there before it was time to leave for South Dakota."

"We are selling our place at Tyson's Corner," Marquette suddenly blurted, and Tara giggled. Everyone looked at the two of them with surprise.

"What are you talking about?" Rosa asked.

Marquette took Tara's hand into his own, looking around the room as he answered, "The two of us are crowding the sixty years-of-age mark and that has prompted us to make a certain decision."

Everyone was quiet as they watched Marquette and Tara look into each other's eyes and smile.

"We are retiring," Tara whispered, and they looked at the surprised faces sitting around the room.

"No kidding?" Noah said, looking stunned.

Marquette nodded. "The only problem we are struggling with at present is who to turn this business over to. The work we do is unending, but it is terribly difficult to find someone with a passion such as ours."

"So, why are you selling your residence in Washington?" Rosa asked.

"We would like to be closer to home," Marquette answered.

Guiseppi's heart jumped. *Can it be? Is my Marquette moving back to South Dakota?* He quietly cleared his throat, getting to his feet as he said, "My Marquette." Shuffling to where his youngest son was seated, he dropped into the cushion beside him. He looked into Marquette's eyes. "Are you *finally* coming home to me?"

Marquette reached for his father's hand and answered, "I think it is time, Papa."

Everyone in the room gasped.

Tears sprang from Tillie's eyes. January of 1964 was still a vivid memory for her, even though she was only six and a half years old at the time. Marquette had packed up his belongings, explaining that he had a *purpose* and that was why he was leaving. It was cold the day they'd taken him to the airport, and their father wept so terribly that Uncle Angelo had to drive them home.

"We would like to have a little place out here in the hills, as well as a residence in Sioux Falls," Tara explained. She rolled her eyes as she looked at everyone's surprised faces, adding, "I imagine the press will have a feast with the information once they find out what we are up to."

Rosa cried and Jake put a tender arm around the old woman as he said, "Isn't it great, Nonna? They'll be right here with us."

"It is wonderful," Rosa agreed.

"We will tell everyone at the reunion," Marquette said, smiling at his mother and sister. "We should not have stayed away for so long."

*****

Jon watched Alyssa pacing back and forth in the room at the Howard Johnson's. She wore a dreadful frown between her pretty brows.

"But don't tell him yet," Jon warned. "Let me follow Ben this weekend and then you can tell Noah what's going on next week."

"But what about Della? Doesn't he have a right to know?" Alyssa questioned.

"We haven't finished with our investigation, Alyssa," Jon reproached. "If you weren't related to the man, you'd never dream of telling him until you absolutely had to."

Alyssa let out a breath and sat down on the bed. "I have to *pretend* I'm just getting here tonight," she said. "I'm meeting my brother for dinner, and then we're getting our rooms at the Plaza."

Jon nodded. "That's right. Stay focused, Alyssa. And I'm not gonna tell you that this will be easy, but you need to be among them right now for their protection. I'll follow Ben and get a hold of you if something comes up. And don't forget, we're still on duty. And by the way, I called for a backup team. We're not doing this alone anymore."

*****

Jason was shocked when he reached Roy Schneider's room and learned that he wasn't there.

"He's been moved to Intensive Care," the nurse explained. "He developed a heart murmur and we're trying to stabilize him before his surgery next week."

"Can he have visitors?"

The nurse shook her head. "I'm sorry. Only family can be with him right now."

*****

Early Saturday morning, Dr. Carlson called Ty to inform him that the surgery might be delayed by a few days the following week due to Roy's heart murmur. However, Roy had asked specifically to see Ty. Dr. Carlson relayed the message, and Ty left for the hospital while his family began preparations for the reunion.

Noah angrily stuffed wood into the barbecue pit he and Vincenzo had built last summer. He hadn't so much as shared a cup of coffee with his wife before he slipped from the house, unobserved by the rest of the family.

Guiseppi made his way down the gentle incline behind the magnificent home dear Noah had built for his Angel all those years ago. The early June morning was so cool Guiseppi could see his breath. He deeply inhaled the pine fragrance. *No wonder Noah and Angel love these hills so much.*

"Do not hurt yourself," Guiseppi warned, easing himself into a chair beside the table near the pit.

"I won't hurt myself," Noah retorted, stuffing another log into the pit, kicking it into place just for good measure.

"There is enough wood to burn a small country in that pit, Noah Hansen," Guiseppi declared. "Perhaps you should start it now so that some may burn off before we put the meat on this afternoon — or are you planning burnt sacrifices?"

In response, Noah picked up another log, throwing it as hard as he could at the perfectly positioned stack he'd worked so hard to achieve. The logs tumbled haphazardly around in the pit. Noah frowned, growling as he threw another log into the mess.

Guiseppi rolled his eyes and sighed. "Come, now, Noah," he said, giving the chair beside him a soft pat. "Sit with me for a moment so that we may talk about this."

"I don't wanna sit."

"Well, then, you may stand," Guiseppi said in a tone that sounded like, *I give you permission.*

"I *hate* him."

Guiseppi nodded. "I understand. But let us not waste your energy on hating the man, for we both know he is not worth it. God will deal with him, be it ever so severely, and we have nothing to gain by stomping around and ignoring our wives."

"I didn't mean to ignore Angel this morning. I just don't want her to see me like this."

Guiseppi chuckled. "No one *wants* to see you like this, but everyone *saw* the madman in the back, throwing his wood around, tossing out miscellaneous curses. Just because we cannot hear you, does not mean we do not know what you are saying to yourself."

Noah swallowed a small measure of his anger and said, "I don't want Ty around that man and I can't believe he keeps going back up there to see him. Ty's *my* son, Guiseppi. Why do I have to put up with this?" He pointed to himself as he said, "*I'm* the one that actually *wanted* the kid. Roy would have rather seen him thrown out with the trash. There are so many things wrong with this situation, I can't even begin to count them, and everybody wants me to just sit around and pray about it."

Guiseppi nodded again and said, "You have incredible strength, Noah. If God had called on *any other man* for this particular duty, *that man* would have surely failed."

Noah melted at Guiseppi's kind words. "Thanks, Guiseppi," he said.

"You are quite welcome, Noah Hansen." Guiseppi got to his feet, reaching for Noah's hand. "Come along. Your brother and his wonderful, redheaded wife have arrived with many things I must sample." He gave Noah's hand a gentle squeeze, but did not let go of it. Instead, Guiseppi pulled on it as if he were leading a rebel back to obedience.

From the kitchen window, Mona and Tillie were watching. Guiseppi's old, slightly stooped body shuffled along next to Noah's younger, stronger frame. Guiseppi's black eyes sparkled with delight as he talked, nodding his shiny bald head, obviously continuing Noah's instruction as they made their way. Noah appeared to be respectfully listening to every word Guiseppi offered, and by the time they had made it to the steps on the deck, Noah wore a faint smile.

"That's the dearest thing I've ever seen," Mona whispered.

Tillie sighed with a smile at her old father. "Papa's words are *always* the best."

Marquette borrowed Noah's pickup, and was out of the house before seven o'clock that morning. Through dispatch, he learned that Jason was scheduled to have the day off. But any detective in the middle of a mystery, *and worth his salt*, would be working on his day off. Marquette made his way to the Law Enforcement building on Kansas City Street, downtown Rapid City.

Everyone Marquette approached was friendly and professional, especially when he identified himself, announcing that he was there to see Detective Jason Patterson. He was pointed in the direction of Jason's humble office, where the young detective was bent over his desk, studying a myriad of papers and files.

Jason heard the soft knock on his open office door, and he looked up with a curious frown. In his doorway stood a slender built, dark man, dressed in a sharp, blue suit and a matching hat. There was something eerily familiar about him, but Jason couldn't quite place it. "Can I help you?" he asked.

Marquette extended his hand in greeting, stepping forward, introducing himself in his soft accent, "Marquette Caselli. I received a message from my liaison that you wanted to speak with me."

Jason's mouth fell open in surprise as he shook the hand of the world's most famous investigator. "I'm sorry...I didn't recognize you," he stammered. "I thought you'd just call me or fax me or something."

"I prefer to make my contacts in person," he said, politely removing his hat. "Now, my young friend, what is it that you have discovered?"

Jason took a breath, looking from Marquette to his desktop, and back at Marquette. "Umm..." He hesitated, pointing at a chair in front of his desk. "Please, have a seat." He shuffled through some papers until he found a page from a legal pad.

Marquette took a seat and politely waited for Jason to get his documents in order.

Jason sat down, looking from the yellow page of notes back to Marquette as he said, "I understand that you worked on a case here in Rapid City some years ago."

Marquette nodded with a smile, answering, "Ponerello. The second most difficult case of my life. Do you believe yourself to have found something?"

"I'm not sure. I do have a location on a man named Roy Schneider, but he claims to not know anything. When I questioned him the other day, he said two terrorists hassled him several years ago about the disappearance of John Peters. Could that have been you and your wife?"

136

"Most certainly," Marquette answered. "We let him go that day because he claimed to have the ability to find the location of John's body. He also admitted to us he was John's killer. At a later date, we learned that he only masqueraded under the name of Roy Schneider, but in actuality he is Dr. Schneider Rauwolf, more commonly known as '*The Wolf*' within his circles. He helped the Ponerellos escape *Sicilia* in 1964, when they deserted their family."

"He's up at the Cancer Care Institute and he's in real bad shape," Jason said. "I went up to talk to him again last night and he's been moved to Intensive Care with a heart murmur. Only family can see him right now."

Marquette was taken aback. He frowned as he asked, "Is Mr. Schneider awaiting a bone marrow donation from Ty Hansen?"

"Yes," Jason answered with a serious expression. "And I have several questions I'd like to ask your brother-in-law, but I wanted to speak with you first."

Marquette was horrified at the personal turn his professional life had suddenly taken, but he maintained his composure as he said, "Let us start from the beginning, detective, for I have the feeling that there are many things you will teach me this day."

Shortly before noon, Vincenzo parked his new conversion van beneath the awning at the Rushmore Plaza. His children, Angelo and Alyssa, were waiting there for their family, and they came to the van to greet them.

Petrice was in the passenger seat and he frowned curiously at Alyssa. "She must be on duty," he murmured.

Vincenzo saw the flicker of the metal badge at her waist.

"She is *so* cool," Gabriella said from one of the seats in the back, admiring Alyssa's long gate and the discreet way she wore her holster beneath her black, leather jacket. "Maybe I should be a United States Marshal."

Michael snorted, teasing, "I think you're too short."

Kate sighed, glancing at Ellie. "She promised to take time off for this," she whispered. "I wonder what came up."

Vincenzo and Petrice greeted Alyssa and Angelo with embraces and kisses. Vincenzo didn't comment on Alyssa's obvious *on-duty* status, and neither did Petrice. They slid open the side doors so the rest of their family could get out, and to Alyssa's surprise, Uncle Sam and Aunt Becky-Lynn stepped out with them.

"Oh, you *did* decide to come!" Alyssa exclaimed, embracing her uncle and aunt. "Auntie will be so surprised!"

"Well," Sam said with a smile and a sigh, "We thought it might be fun. We haven't been out to the hills since Thanksgiving of '93."

"Now," Vincenzo said, looking at his son and daughter. "Are we all still staying here?"

"And our rooms are all next to each other," Angelo answered.

"Well then," Vincenzo said with a smile. "Let us get ourselves checked in." He looked at Petrice and winked. "And the Senator has a short meeting to get to I believe."

"Hopefully, the car I ordered is here by now," Petrice said.

"And we all meet at Angel's Place by three o'clock," Vincenzo instructed. He gave his tall daughter a serious look, adding, "Do not any one of you be late, for your Auntie would surely be disappointed."

*****

Sal scowled into his snifter of brandy, swirling the liquid around in the glass before taking a sip. He looked at the young man seated in front of his desk, admiring his black makeup. "And you are most certain of this?" he asked.

"Positive," the young man answered. "They followed your partner all the way back to work. He works at Hansen Development, right?"

Sal ground his teeth together, managing only an acknowledging nod. He took several agitated breaths, looking around the room as if in thought, then slid open his desk drawer. He retrieved a small vial of fine powder from the tray inside, handing it to the young man with a pretend smile. "Here is a gift," he said. "Thank you for your excellent work. You have proven yourself adequate for my needs. I have one more favor I wish to ask of you. Now, do not partake of my gift until you have completed this favor. Listen carefully, my friend, the mayor is taking a trip...."

Petrice Caselli had never been to Luigi's office, but he knew the city well enough to find it. He attempted to look up Luigi's home address in the phone book, but found only a listing for his office and drove to that location.

It was a nice enough office, located in the professional buildings just across the street from Rapid City Regional Hospital. He found Luigi's name on the Directory in the lobby and made his way from there.

The door was not locked and Petrice let himself into what appeared to be a waiting area. He saw a receptionist's desk with all of the usual equipment: telephone, blotter, computer terminal and keyboard, printer, and calculator. The blinds were closed and the lights were off, but somewhere from down the hall just behind the waiting area, Petrice heard muffled voices. He assumed Luigi must be counseling someone, so he took a seat in one of the available chairs.

Soon Petrice heard the sound of footsteps approaching in the hall, and he stood. Luigi appeared with a young man about Petrice's height, wearing black makeup and black, leather clothing. Luigi, on the other hand, was impeccably dressed in a sharp, gray suit.

Luigi flashed a smooth smile, extending his hand as he said, "Petrice. What a delightful surprise."

Petrice took Luigi's hand, giving it a shake, but the appearance of the man with Luigi more than unnerved him.

138

"Allow me to introduce my friend, Clive," Luigi continued, glancing at the young man with him. "Clive, this is a dear childhood friend of mine, Senator Petrice Caselli."

Clive awkwardly offered Petrice his greeting.

It nearly took Petrice's breath away when he touched Clive's hand. It was all Petrice could do not to jerk his own hand away from Clive's grasp. Instead, he followed through with the greeting, putting on his best politician's face. "How do you do?" he said with a polite smile.

Clive said nothing, hurriedly exiting the office.

Luigi smiled as he asked, "And what do I owe this unexpected surprise?"

Petrice pretended to smile as he answered, "I am in town for my sister's get-together."

"Well, it is so good to see you, my friend," Luigi replied. "I just finished with my last counseling session for the day. Normally I do not see patients on Saturday, but today I made an exception. The dear youth is so troubled. Shall we go for a cup of coffee?"

Petrice nodded. "A cup of coffee would hit the spot."

*****

Antonio turned on his ringing cell phone, but before he could even say 'hello,' a familiar, angry voice shouted, "Those idiots are already in town?! Why did we not know about this?"

Antonio gulped.

"You are an idiot as well!" Sal stormed. "Did you know you were followed from my office to Hansen's?"

"No one has followed me," Antonio protested.

"My source says otherwise!" Sal yelled. "And that idiot Petrice Caselli showed up in my office this morning. Dadeleas only knows who is watching me! And just because you had to be *so sloppy!*"

"I have not been sloppy," Antonio defended.

"Go to the shop this minute!" Sal screamed at the top of his lungs. "Get up there and change that electric lock."

"I was just up there last night."

"Do as I say!" Sal demanded. "Or I will allow the family to find you. It only requires one phone call and they will be on their way. If you do not help me, I will protect you no more!"

"Fine," Antonio relented. "I am on my way." And with that, he turned off the phone.

*****

Another two and half hours of his life. How he hated the drive and what it was associated with. Antonio parked his car close to the barn, noticing the old, white pickup parked along the side. He wondered who'd left it there, but then, he'd never been there during the day, and so any vehicle would look different in the sunlight.

He went to the door, worked the electric combination, and let himself into the barn. To his surprise, the place was dark and empty. Ed should have at least been there.

"Ed!" he called, switching on the lights, looking around. No reply. Antonio went into the back room. "Ed!" he called again. Still no reply. "Where is he?" he wondered aloud. Ed would certainly have to be made aware of the change in the electric combination, and Antonio didn't have any other way to reach him.

As Antonio rounded the corner, he caught sight of what appeared to be a man's boot. He frowned, stepping closer for a better look. As his eyes adjusted to the dim lighting of the room, Antonio gasped at the sight before him. It was Ed, staring blankly up at the ceiling, lying in the darkness of his own blood. Antonio reached for the pulse in Ed's neck, but Ed's skin was already cold and hard.

Antonio swallowed away his nausea, backing away. Only one person he knew of was capable of slitting another's throat in such a fashion: his uncle, Salvatore Ponerello.

Chapter 13

Upon his return to Angel's Place, Marquette sequestered Tara to the guest house. Their family didn't notice them rush away because Ty had returned from the hospital and everyone wanted an update on the "old blackguard."

"Sit down, my love," he whispered to Tara. He locked the door and made sure the windows were closed.

Tara sat down on the couch, watching her husband pace nervously back and forth in front of her. "What is the matter, Marquette?" she asked.

"I have so much to say, my love," he answered, throwing one arm into the air. "I do not know even where to begin."

Tara took a soft breath, looking questioningly at her husband. "How about at the beginning?" she suggested.

Marquette stopped pacing, leaned against the small stone fireplace and took a deep breath, whispering, "Roy Schneider is Ty's biological father."

Tara gasped, reaching for her chest. "How did you learn this?" she asked.

Marquette threw his arm into the air again, explaining, "Our liaison gave me a message to seek out Detective Jason Patterson, and that is where I was this morning. My Tara, that is not even *the half* of it." He took a breath, continuing, "This particular detective was aboard Patty's boat the night we had the birthday party for Vincenzo. He says he followed Luigi all the way from Rapid City to Cape Vincent. He has been looking into Luigi's history as he is investigating Luigi on suspicion of drugs. *And,* as of yesterday, they have found four bodies at the same location, all poisoned with the same dose of strychnine. He thinks Luigi is behind it."

Tara took a calming breath and said, "My Marquette, dearest, please sit down with me and settle yourself. I do not understand what you are saying. You are giving me a lot of information and none of it is making any sense."

Marquette knelt quickly before her on the floor, taking her hand into his own, beginning again, "Listen to me, my Tara, everything leads straight back to Noah. The night we brought Angel to Rapid City in 1975 was the same night John Peters disappeared from the globe. Maggie May watched John follow Roy Schneider and Jack Nelson's stepdaughter from her bar —"

"Jack Nelson?" Tara interrupted.

"Please remember with me, Tara," Marquette pleaded, looking frantically into his wife's eyes. "When we were in Miami trying to find out who effected the sale of the small fishing business —"

"Oh my goodness," Tara breathed. "I remember now. The owner of the hotel found John's file and called us."

"Jack Nelson was Noah's father-in-law," Marquette blurted.

Tara gasped again, feeling as though she might faint. "Noah?" she whispered.

Marquette nodded. "Schneider Rauwolf, whom we learned used the name of Roy Schneider, worked for Jack Nelson. In what capacity, I do not know, and neither does the young detective —"

"Where does Luigi fit into all of this?"

Marquette swallowed, closing his eyes for just a moment as if to collect his thoughts. He opened them again, and looked into Tara's eyes as he continued, "I think this man we are calling Luigi could actually be one of the Ponerellos."

Tara frowned. "Mario would be nearly eighty by now, Marquette!" she softly scolded. "And Antonio is closer to forty. The only other Ponerello not accounted for was Salvatore, and he killed himself upon the rocks at *Ustica*. You witnessed the suicide *with your very own eyes*."

Marquette nodded. "Yes, but, my love, I think it is possible Salvatore survived the attempt and has somehow assumed Luigi's identity. Detective Patterson also tells me that this man, whom we will call Luigi for convenience sake, listed his address as Washington, D.C., from sometime in 1990 until July, 1994, when he moved to Rapid City, South Dakota. Patterson says the change of address happened *after* Noah and Angel were wed. Now, we both know that our newspapers in Washington wrote small stories with regard to the wedding. After all, Angel is the sister of a very famous senator, and I was Noah's best man. Luigi probably saw the stories and began his plot from there. Patterson thinks Noah has something on Luigi and Luigi is just using us to get close to Noah."

Tara's eyes were huge and round as she stared back at her husband, unable to respond to all of the information he had given her. "We must contact our liaison for the Ponerello file," she whispered.

"There are a few more things," Marquette began again.

Tara was taken aback. "More?"

Marquette swallowed and started again, "Ben Simmons has been seen by Patterson at Luigi's office. He has also been up to the hospital to see Ty's biological father." Marquette took a hesitant breath, pondering, "I think Ben is actually Mario's son, Antonio."

Tara gasped. "But how could he fool Noah all these years? Or do you think Noah has known all along?"

Marquette shook his head. "I do not believe Noah is aware. Remember, my Tara, the Elder Son takes an oath to protect the family. At the time they left Sicily, Antonio was Mario's only son. That would automatically make him the Elder Son — even if Mario had other children. Now, if Jack Nelson is actually Mario Ponerello, and he took an American bride, with an existing daughter, those two women would fall under the protection of the Elder Son. Noah married the existing daughter and had children with her, one of them being fathered by a friend of Mario's. That would then place Noah under the protection of the Elder Son as well, even though Carrie died many years ago. Even if they were *divorced*, once Antonio took the oath, Noah and his sons would still fall under the purview of the Elder Son. I think it is safe to assume Antonio has placed himself close to Noah in order to protect him."

Tara nodded. "And perhaps Luigi found out about that somehow."

"Undoubtedly. Remember, Mario took Antonio from Sicily after the child's mother died in 1964. Tara, if you will recall, Mario's wife was found at the bottom of a staircase, *with her throat slit* — and as I recall from our first meeting with Mr. Simmons, he spoke of his sister's mother taking a fall down some steps —"

"Which is how Noah's mother-in-law died," Tara blurted.

"Yes, my Tara. *However*, Carrie's mother died during the summer of 1980, according to an accident report Detective Patterson showed me, and Simmons spoke of her in 1987, and Noah mentioned her yesterday."

"That would mean that she is still alive," Tara murmured.

Marquette nodded. "I am thinking that they have been hiding from Salvatore, but now he has found them. And I have many guesses, but Salvatore probably found them as soon as the late sixties or early seventies, for instance when Jack Nelson sold his fishing business in Miami. One of Luigi's old addresses is Jacksonville, Florida, but not until 1985. So, they have successfully hidden from him for a number of years. They are probably still under the impression that the Ponerello Family could be called upon for their demise at a moment's notice. Perhaps they are not even aware that there are no other family members besides themselves."

Tara took a deep breath, letting it out slowly. "We must begin work on this as soon as possible. Noah probably knows more about the situation than he even realizes."

"We must be very careful, Tara," Marquette warned. "If this man who is portraying himself to be Luigi is actually Salvatore Ponerello, we have an extremely dangerous situation on our hands. Thirty years ago, he was known for being easily provoked and I cannot imagine that age has mellowed him at all. Also, before I forget, our niece, Alyssa, has been looking into the case. Patterson says she caught him on Patty's boat, but let him go once she realized that he was police. However, he believes that she, along with her partner, have been in Rapid City for at least a week, maybe more, looking into the same circumstances."

"First, my Marquette," Tara began, "We must get close to Luigi and figure out a way to question him without provoking him."

"I agree, but how do we do that? Certainly he will be suspect to our every question. After all, my love, we do have a reputation."

Tara nervously smiled. "Yes we do." She paused with a thoughtful frown and softly gasped, "I know! If Luigi shows up today, *and he probably will*, we will set up someone with fragmented information to ask him some questions — someone he does not know. *Someone who likes to have a little fun.*" Tara giggled. "And I know *exactly who!*"

As Marquette and Tara left the guest house, they saw that Vincenzo's van-load had arrived, and greetings had already commenced.

Marquette took a deep breath, held tightly to Tara's hand and smiled into her eyes as he said, "We must put on our *very best* demeanor for this, my Tara. God has sent us this divine chance to solve our oldest mystery, and we must not let Him down."

"Agreed." Tara took a deep breath, smiling back at her husband.

"My Angel," Petrice said, putting his arms around her.

"Hi, Patty," Tillie said, smiling at her brother and giving him a kiss on his cheek.

"Uncle Patty." Annie reached for her uncle, and Petrice took the baby into his arms.

"Well, hello Annie," Petrice smiled. "How are you this day?"

"Ma`ma's party," Annie replied, putting her hands on Petrice's face to give him a kiss, as she had seen the rest of the family doing during their greetings.

Petrice nodded. "Today is Ma`ma's party." He looked at Tillie, adding, "And I did meet with Luigi this morning, Angel. Apparently, he misunderstood something I said to him in New York, and I did not have the heart to *uninvite* him."

"Oh, Patty," Tillie groaned. "He's just *so weird.*"

Noah frowned and Sam looked curious.

"Who's Luigi?" Sam asked, looking from Petrice to Noah.

"An old lecher," Noah grumbled.

Tillie chuckled. "We'll fill you in later. It'll be okay. We'll get by."

Marquette and Tara seized an opportunity with Alyssa the first moment they could, stepping away from the rest of the family.

Marquette put his arm around his tall niece's shoulders, pretending to kiss her cheek as he whispered in her ear, "We know about your investigation."

Alyssa's eyes flew open with surprise and she replied, "How?"

"Detective Patterson sought me out."

Alyssa frowned. "Why?"

"We must speak as quickly as we can," Tara whispered, purposely smiling at Alyssa as if they were visiting about something else. "And you must give us whatever knowledge you have gleaned during your time in Rapid City. This is an emergency of intense proportions, Alyssa, and we must act with as much stealth as possible."

Charise saw the familiar car speeding up the gravel driveway. Had it not been for the heavy rain from the night before, he would have been kicking up dirt and dust along his way. She came out onto her porch just as his car stopped in the drive. The driver's door flew open, and Antonio dashed up the porch steps, two at a time. When he reached the top, he threw his arms around his sister, holding her tightly. He shook with sobs as he held her, and that was a thing Charise had *never* seen her brother do. The hair on the back of her neck prickled.

"What's the matter, Antonio?"

He took several deep breaths, and after some moments was able to calm down. "I went up to the shop today," he began, "and there was a dead man waiting for me. I am certain that it was a warning. He sent me deliberately."

Charise was hit with a wave of nausea. "A dead man?" she asked.

"His throat was cut. Sal said that I had been followed from his office to Noah's office. He thinks I have been found out and Petrice Caselli showed up in his office this morning." Antonio took a breath. "Oh, Charise, this is such a mess. I was supposed to have changed the lock on the door, but I do not remember even closing it. Sal has finally unleashed whatever evil lies within him. I am afraid that Papa will want me to kill him."

Charise held her brother, taking quiet breaths as she processed the information he'd just given her. She had deep compassion for what he was going through, remembering vividly the day he took his oath, vowing to always protect their family.

"Did the doctor say if your mother could be moved?" he asked.

Charise nodded. "We can move her, but she still needs so much care. Antonio, I'm afraid to take her away from Dr. Benson. He's used to all of her crazy stories and he never asks questions. What will happen when we start taking her to someone else? I can't make her go to Custer twice a week."

"We cannot risk leaving her there," Antonio said with conviction. "Sal will find her for sure. We will move her tonight and bring her here for now."

Maggie and Estelle arrived at Angel's Place, and Noah got them seated in the comfortable furniture on the deck with Sam, Becky-Lynn, Guiseppi and Rosa. He and Tillie's brothers then made their way to the pit, where their meat had been roasting since early that morning. On long tables on and near the deck, Tillie and the other ladies set out their salads, pies and breads.

Everyone had a specific duty for the reunion, so no one noticed Marquette, Tara and Alyssa having several private conversations. As well, no one noticed when the redheaded southern belle was drafted into their ranks.

Maggie, as always, stayed close to Estelle, helping her to understand the different things that were going on, attempting to gently prod her memories. Estelle's condition had deteriorated more slowly than their mother's had, and she enjoyed the social functions Noah and Tillie invited them to. Over the past several years, Maggie and Estelle had been included for birthdays, Sunday dinners and holidays. The two were a part of the family, and Guiseppi and Rosa had grown quite fond of them.

Annie had her little hard hat on, and followed her father around the smoking pit. She seemed to be trying to get as close to the pit as she possibly could, but Noah scooped her up and gently instructed the child to stay back. She frowned dreadfully at her father, squirmed to get down, and the whole episode started all over again.

Guiseppi laughed as he watched. "That little thing is giving her father a hard time," he said.

"She's certainly busy," Maggie frowned. "But it's good for Noah. Somebody's gotta keep him in line."

Annie took another step closer to the pit, and Noah picked her up again. He looked around with an exasperated expression on his face, saw Tillie and called to her, "Angel, help me!"

"Annie will give him a heart attack," Guiseppi laughed.

Tillie looked up from what she was doing and hurried to help Noah.

"She wants to jump *directly into the pit!*" Noah exclaimed, his baby daughter fussing and squirming to get out of his arms.

"Down!" Annie demanded, pushing away from her father, attempting to drop her body to the ground.

"*See!*" Noah exclaimed with wide-open eyes.

Tillie laughed at the two of them, taking the squirming baby into her arms. "Okay. Come on you, little stinker. Let's go see Nonna."

Noah sighed with relief. "Thanks, Angel."

"Don't mention it," Tillie said, snuggling her bundle as she headed toward the deck.

Annie was placed into the capable arms of Rosa and given a delicious Popsicle to enjoy.

"There!" Rosa exclaimed with a soft sigh. "Now we do not have to watch poor Noah die of fright!"

Tillie smiled and asked, "Is it okay if she sits with you for just a couple of seconds, Ma`ma? I forgot my salt and pepper shakers in the house, but I'll be right back."

Rosa gave the quieted baby a gentle hug and assured, "She will be fine with us."

Before Tillie left the kitchen with her shakers, she remembered the panettone cake, deciding she'd better take it out of the pantry before she forgot. After all, it was Papa's favorite. With her back to the entryway of the kitchen, she searched her pantry for the box, wondering what shelf she'd placed it on. A voice behind her made her jump with a start.

"Hello, Mrs. Hansen," it said.

Tillie turned abruptly, nearly bumping her head on the shelves of her pantry. Luigi Andreotti stood in the middle of her kitchen, smiling like the cat that swallowed the canary. Her heart pounded. *Why does he smile like that?* She thought. *And how in the world did he get into the house?*

"Hi, Mr. Andreotti," she politely greeted, taking an instinctive step backward. "The meat is just about ready...everyone is out back...there are some appetizers out there."

"That sounds lovely," Luigi replied, smiling eerily as he took enough steps toward Tillie to close the gap between them. He reached for her hand, lifting it to his lips, placing a soft kiss on top of it.

Tillie was horrified at his overture. She jerked her hand away from him, glancing at the fire extinguisher near the stove...*Come a little closer, pal, and I'll drop you like a hot rock.*

Luigi smirked, stepping closer still, whispering, "Now why would I want an appetizer when you are right here." He clicked his tongue and chuckled. "Noah Hansen is a *very lucky* man."

"Blessed man," came a deep voice from behind Tillie, and she startled again, turning around to find her husband standing just inside the door.

Luigi seemed startled as well, instantaneously stopping his encroachment.

"Go outside, Angel," Noah said, taking a few aggressive steps toward Luigi.

Tillie swallowed hard, wondering if it was the wisest thing to leave Noah alone with the man. Noah had been more than provoked by the events over the past couple of weeks, and Luigi's poor manners might be just enough to send him over the edge. Even though Noah was a kind, Christian man, he was a *man* nonetheless, and he did not like Luigi Andreotti.

Tillie nervously rambled, "Noah, is the meat ready? Do you want me to find the platter? Because I forgot to put the platter on the table by the pit and I know Vincenzo likes to have one handy." She swallowed, took a breath and continued, "So, maybe I should just find the platter and we can eat."

Noah frowned at Tillie and was just opening his mouth to respond when Mona dashed through the open deck door, heading straight for Luigi. She smiled as if they were old friends, reaching for his hand.

"Mr. Andreotti!" she gasped a bit too breathlessly. "Everyone's been asking about you! Why are you hiding in here?" She began to lead him outside, smiling at Tillie and Noah along the way. "You'd better hurry with that platter, Angel, 'cause Vincenzo says the meat is pert-near ready."

"Okay," Tillie managed to croak.

"Oh, we're so excited to have you here today!" Mona said with enthusiasm, leading Luigi out the deck door. "I've been hearing all sorts of great stories about *Chianti*..." And the rest of her words were lost to Tillie and Noah. They stood there looking confused at one another, wanting to say *something*, but not knowing exactly where to begin.

Noah let out the breath he didn't realize he was holding and impulsively put his arms around Tillie. "You okay?" he asked.

Tillie's eyes were filled with mischief. "He just kept getting closer and closer," she said. "I thought I might have to whack him with the fire extinguisher."

"I should've just punched him," Noah grumbled. "Why did you let him come through the house? Why didn't you just send him out back?"

Tillie shook her head. "I didn't. He just appeared."

"Sorta like a bad smell," Noah replied.

Tillie chuckled with a nod.

"Well, I *did* come in for the platter," he said. "Do you have one handy?"

"It's in the pantry. Now, let's get our stuff together and get back out there before he grabs somebody."

Noah nodded, starting for the pantry. "You know, I've heard about stuff like this at family reunions," he commented dryly. "There's *always* one who can't behave himself." He had a wildly funny thought then and laughed. "Hopefully he'll grab Alyssa. That'll teach him."

Joshua watched his normally reserved wife from a distance. He was down at the pit with Tillie's brothers, listening to them argue about the doneness of the meat, but he could see Mona near the stairs of the deck. He couldn't hear what she was saying, but she was up to something. She had managed to get Mr. Andreotti off by himself, and seemed to be flirting with him most shamelessly. She bobbed her head, laughing uproariously at his comments, obviously purposing to keep him busy with her for a time.

Joshua frowned, squinting for a better look. For a woman of sixty-six years of age, she was still an attractive lady. Mona had no wrinkles to speak of, and, of course, she still had her gloriously red hair.

"Do not fear this thing with Luigi," Marquette whispered in Joshua's ear.

Joshua turned and saw Marquette watching the situation as well.

"Turn this way, Joshua." Marquette took Joshua by the elbow, turning him away from the scene. "I have asked your wife for a certain favor."

Joshua raised a brow. "A *certain favor*? What in the world have you set her up to?"

"To ask our dear friend, Luigi, some questions," Marquette answered, "Do not worry, Joshua, Mona will be quite safe." He looked in the direction of Alyssa, who was leaning against a tree, pretending to have a conversation with her brother and cousins. "See my niece over there? She is tops in target practice. In fact, she has a better aim than even me." He turned his eyes in the direction of his own wife, who was seated comfortably at one of the long tables, laughing and talking to her sisters-in-law. "But no one is as quick as my Tara."

"And it is such a lovely shade," Luigi gushed, referring to Mona's hair.

"Well thank you, Mr. Andreotti." Mona batted her eyes.

"And your accent is so lovely. Where are you from again?"

"Atlanta...Georgia, that is." Mona was sure to over accentuate the way she spoke.

"How long have you been here in Rapid City?" Luigi asked.

"Oh let me think." Mona batted her eyes as she pretended to recall. "I came to Rapid after Joshua and I were married. Let's see, that's been just about forty-five years ago. How long have you been away from *Castellina?*"

Luigi appeared to be caught off guard for the moment, but he quickly recovered his composure, answering, "Thirty years."

"Thirty years?"

"Well, off and on," Luigi answered, casually pulling a cigar from his inside breast pocket, placing it between his teeth. "I used to go home and visit my family, but they were all killed in a fire at the winery fifteen years ago."

"I'm very sorry," Mona said with a compassionate expression in her eyes. "That must be so difficult for you to be alone in this world."

Luigi lit his cigar and nodded. "At times it has been quite lonely. However, now that I have found my dear friends again, I am relieved of some of my pain."

"That was so brave of you to ask Marquette and Tara for forgiveness like you did," Mona went on, feeling a tight ball begin in her stomach. She could see that Luigi was tensing up, and he was having a difficult time hiding it. This reaction in him made Mona self conscious about what she was doing, but she prayed for strength.

Luigi took a deep draw from his cigar, let the smoke out and nodded his head as he replied, "Thank you for saying so. It took every ounce of courage I have."

"I could have *never* taken the hit like you did on that one," Mona declared. She rolled her eyes, leaning close enough to whisper, "You know, just between you and me, I don't think it was right of them to carry that grudge for such a long time."

Luigi's expression said that he was pleased with her words, and he said, "After all, it was my right as the Elder Son —" he suddenly cleared his throat, pretending to cough.

Mona frowned. "The Elder Son?" she questioned. Marquette and Tara hadn't said anything about that.

Luigi smiled openly, apologizing, "Pardon me, I misspoke —" he pretended to cough again. "Excuse me, dear lady, but I must get a drink." And without waiting for Mona's reply, Luigi hurried to a cooler away from the crowd.

He fled the party shortly after that. No one noticed him leave, only that he was gone and Tara sought out Mona for an explanation.

"He's in a huff about some Elder Son rights or something," Mona informed in her Southern drawl, making a soft "tsk" noise and shaking her head. "He didn't mention once his blackguardly secret of your location and how he never told Marq you had survived the crash."

Tara softly gasped. "Elder Son?"

"Well, he said he misspoke, and then he pert-near coughed out a lung and had to go."

Tara was alarmed, but she forced a smile as she said, "Thank you, Mona. You have helped us considerably."

Mona nodded with satisfaction. "Maybe I could help you with some more cases sometime," she offered.

"Perhaps," Tara replied.

*****

They drove through the Black Hills and Custer State Park for hours, waiting for it to get dark enough to bring her back to the ranch without being spotted. It was well after ten o'clock when the threesome pulled into Charise's long driveway. Antonio turned off the headlights and the engine, coasting to a stop.

Antonio came around to the back door where Della was seated. They'd made her comfortable with blankets and pillows, and she was still in a cheerful mood. She spoke several times during the trip about not riding in a car in longer than she cared to remember, and that surprised Antonio and Charise.

"Here, Della," Antonio said, slipping his strong arms beneath the tiny lady. "I am going to carry you just a short way."

"So that my wheelchair doesn't make too much noise," Della whispered.

"Yes," Antonio answered. Obviously she knew something of what was going on. To what extent still remained to be seen.

As Antonio lifted Della from the car in the cradle of his arms, she looked into his eyes and sweetly smiled, saying, "You look so much like your papa. Handsome like him."

"Thank you, Della," He replied, trudging up the steps and to the open door where Charise waited.

"You're moving me at night," Della whispered as Antonio carried her into the dark house.

Charise led the way to the room she'd readied for her mother's arrival and Antonio set her down on the bed. Charise turned on the soft light on the nightstand and Della smiled with pure pleasure.

"Jack?" she softly exclaimed.

The old, white-haired man reached for the hand of his wife. "Hello, my love," he whispered.

Charise began to work the slippers off of her mother's feet, saying, "It's late, and Ma'ma should get some rest."

"I will not keep her up too long," Mario promised.

Della smiled into her husband's eyes and asked, "Will you be here when I wake up?"

Antonio swallowed away the lump forming in his throat. He should have done things differently from the very beginning. It was wrong to have kept them apart for so long. He slipped out of the room and down the hall. He couldn't bear to hear anymore.

"Yes, my love," Mario answered. "I will be here every day."

Della sighed with a peaceful smile. She looked at her daughter and said, "Thank you, Charise."

"You're welcome, Ma`ma." Charise left her parents, and went to find her brother.

Antonio was in the kitchen, sweating profusely, drinking a bottle of water.

"Are you going back tonight?" she asked.

He set down the emptied bottle and replied, "I will take care of it tonight."

*****

"I had Jonathon check telephone listings in *Castellina,*" Tara whispered to Marquette as they meandered toward the guesthouse that evening. "There is still a telephone registered in Lorenzo Andreotti's name."

"It may just be an oversight," Marquette replied. "As we know that the vineyard is still up and running. Perhaps they just never got around to changing the name on the telephone."

"Marquette," Tara began, "I wish to go to *Italia*...to *Chianti* and learn what has *really* become of the Andreottis."

Marquette inhaled deeply, as if considering her offer. "By yourself?" he questioned.

"I will be quite safe," she answered. "The real danger is *here*, where this purported Luigi has been attempting to make himself welcome. And we know how vital personal contacts are...these circumstances require visual confirmation. You will stay behind because you know the situation better than anyone else involved."

Marquette was quiet as he considered his wife's plan. "But the trip is so long, my love. Perhaps we will unravel this debacle before you even return, making your solo travels for naught."

Tara smiled and replied, "There is an available seat on the Concorde on Monday."

Marquette smiled at his wife. "You are the smartest lady I know," he said. He inhaled deeply again, nodding his head. "*Excellent*, my Tara. This is an *excellent* plan."

Chapter 14

Alyssa returned to her room at The Plaza at nine-thirty. As she slid her card into the lock, she heard footsteps approaching.

"Hey Alyssa."

She looked up to see Jon sauntering down the hall.

"What's up?" she asked, opening her door, allowing him inside.

Jon lowered his voice to a whisper, "Listen, I followed Ben Simmons up north, to a little town called Mud Butte. It's very small and rural, absolutely no cover, so I wound up breaking off the tail. I think we need to go back up tonight."

Alyssa nodded. "Darkness is always the safest. Besides, I've got a ton of information for you...we can talk on the way."

They left Alyssa's room, heading down the hall. Angry voices from behind a door along the way made Alyssa stop in her tracks.

"That's coming from my parents' room," she whispered.

Behind the door they heard Vincenzo scolding, "But, Angelo, your service is up in 1999! You *promised* me that you would leave the military, come home to Reata, and have children."

"Papa, I don't even date!" Angelo retorted. "For now, I believe my purpose to be in the military."

"Your purpose is to serve God," Vincenzo replied.

"And what if I choose to serve God through my military service?!" Angelo replied, sounding exasperated. The door suddenly opened and Angelo stormed into the hallway, slamming the door behind him.

Angelo was surprised to see his sister and her partner standing there.

"Hey, Angelo," Alyssa said, reaching for her brother's hand. "How's it going?"

Angelo humphed and replied, "What do you think?" He looked at Jon and then back at Alyssa. "Where are the two of you off to?" he asked.

Jon looked at the giant of a man in front of them. Angelo was well over six and half feet tall, and his shoulders were very broad. As he sized him up, Jon began to smile, and said, "Angelo, we could really use you tonight."

*****

Shortly after midnight, Jon parked the black Taurus on the main street of Mud Butte. The small town consisted only of a shack labeled, "UNITED STATES POST OFFICE," a tiny grocery store, and a bar with a neon sign that read, "Circle Q Bar & Grill."

"This is one hoppin' little town," Angelo murmured.

Alyssa smiled faintly, glancing at her brother.

"Let's go see if they know anything," Jon said. He turned in his seat and looked at the huge man folded into the back of the small car. "What I want you to do is stand directly behind us and appear as threatening as possible."

Angelo raised one eyebrow. "How does one *appear* threatening?"

"Pretend you're a Marine," Jon answered.

Angelo grinned.

They got out of the car and Alyssa and Jon took off their jackets. This way, their guns and badges would be immediately visible when they went into the little bar. Intimidation was always a helpful tactic.

They walked toward the double wooden doors of the bar and Angelo pulled one open, allowing Jon and Alyssa to pass through first. He thrust his shoulders back and frowned.

The inside of the bar was just as dingy as the outside, like stepping into a scene from the past. It was dimly lit, but when their eyes adjusted they saw a long counter with beer taps. Several small tables were scattered around the room, where a few cowboys sat, sipping frosty mugs of beer. The floor in the bar was covered with muddy red footprints. Country music played in the background. A few customers looked up at the armed Marshals momentarily, but after a few surprised seconds, returned to their beer and conversation. An overweight man with a greasy t-shirt stretched over his belly was wiping glasses at the counter.

Alyssa and Jon stepped up to the bar, while Angelo followed behind them. He held his shoulders back, scowling at the bartender.

Jon and Alyssa put their badges in front of the man at the counter, and Jon began to speak, "United States Marshals Service, sir. Can we ask you some questions?"

"What can I do you for?" The bartender asked, returning Angelo's scowl. He set down the glass he was wiping, and reached for a cigar. Tucking it between his front teeth, he lit it and took a deep draw.

"We're looking for someone," Alyssa said, showing no emotion on her face as she bored her eyes into the expression of the man at the bar.

"Who ya lookin' for?" the bartender asked.

"Tall man," Alyssa answered. "As tall as me. Dark skin, dark hair and eyes. He wears a copper bracelet on his right wrist."

The bartender nodded. "Tony. He ain't been in tonight though. Used to meet with another fella. He's dark too."

"Do they live around here?" Jon asked.

The bartender shrugged. "Don't know. He comes in a couple of times

153

a week, has a drink or two and then he leaves. Sometimes we visit. Heck of a nice guy, but he's lonesome."

"What do you talk about?" Alyssa questioned.

"Poor devil's mother was murdered when he was kid and I don't think he ever got over it. He'd like to marry and have some kids, but he says he's too obligated to his family and doesn't have the time."

"Obligated how?" Jon questioned.

"Doesn't say and I don't pry." The bartender frowned at the trio at his counter. "Are you guys gonna buy anything to drink, or are ya just in here to hassle me?"

Jon gave him a coy smile as he said, "We're just in here to hassle you. Do you have anything else you can tell us about this guy? Do you know what he does up here for instance?"

"Not a clue. All I know is he's a good customer. Pays with cash and doesn't get drunk. It's none of my business where he comes from or what he does. Just a heck of a nice guy."

Alyssa nodded. "Thanks."

"You're welcome." The bartender took another draw from his cigar. "Do you guys got a card or something? I could tell him you were looking for him."

Jon winked. "We'd rather he didn't know we were here."

*****

On Sunday morning, the Pattersons enjoyed their usual brunch at the Radisson. Jacqueline excitedly relayed her schedule for the following week, explaining that she was meeting with her sisters in Valdosta, Georgia, to plan the Holliday Family Reunion. She loved traveling down south and looked forward to it every time she made the trip. "I should land in Valdosta at nine o'clock tomorrow night and I'll give you guys a call when I get to Mother's," she said.

"Wish I could go with you, honey," Joe said, taking a bite of his food. "But with this unsolved armed robbery, and Jason's north-end homicides, I can hardly justify leaving."

Jacqueline smiled at her husband, giving his hand a soft pat as she said, "I'll just have to get by without you."

Jason breathed a sigh of relief. Thankfully, she was getting out of town before anything could happen to her.

Antonio stormed down the hall, heading for Sal's office. The old drunk was always there in the mornings, meeting with his various henchmen, and beginning his all-day drinking. The thin Sicilian was sitting behind his desk in a gray suit, sipping what appeared to be brandy, smoking a cigar. Antonio burst through the door, surprising Sal, but he was already inebriated and couldn't get from his chair to his feet before Antonio stood before his desk. Antonio's black eyes burned with fury. He came around the desk, shoving Sal up against the wall, chair and all.

"You killed him!" Antonio shouted, grabbing Sal by the knot in his tie. "You killed them *all!*"

"It could not be helped," Sal slurred. "I had no choice. Had you not been such an idiot and let on to who you really were, none of them would have had to die."

Antonio spit in Sal's face. "How many more untruths must I listen to?!" he shouted.

Sal's black eyes narrowed and he stared hard into the expression of the younger man who held him. "And how many untruths have you told me, Antonio, in order to protect the stiletto?" he asked. His upper lip curled into a smile as he said, "Perhaps if we ask your sister —"

"My sister left us years ago and cannot be found!"

Sal laughed. "Hansen will be asking you some very difficult questions. What will you tell him?"

Antonio suddenly shoved Sal away from him. "I am not going back to Noah." He began backing toward the door as he said, "I will find another way to protect them."

Sal laughed again. "Oh, the oath…I took the oath once myself."

"You will stay away from Noah and his family," Antonio warned, continuing to back toward the door.

Sal looked at Antonio, smiling as he lifted his feet to rest upon his desktop. "I will do as I see fit," he said, reaching beneath his pant leg for the knife holstered at his ankle. He flung it at Antonio.

Antonio dodged the blade as it sailed past his neck and into the wall behind him. He produced his own knife, rushed Sal, and held the blade firm against his throat. "Do not ever try that again," he snarled.

"Are you going to kill me?" Sal whispered.

"What did Ed say before you killed him?" Antonio asked.

"Nothing…he was dead before he realized that he had been cut."

Antonio pressed his blade against Sal's throat as he said, "You will stay away from Noah Hansen and his family. And if you do not, I will kill you myself. Do you understand this?"

Sal swallowed and nodded his head.

"Good." Antonio released Sal and started backing away again. He stared hard into Sal's eyes as he said, "I cannot believe you are the brother of my father. Surely it was hell itself that spawned you and that is why your mother died at your birth."

Sal began to laugh, softly at first and then it grew until his voice rang off the walls in the room. Antonio backed out the door, and Sal's insidious laughter rang behind him as he made his way out of the building.

*****

Angelo and Alyssa slipped into the back of the church, hoping not to raise any family eyebrows. They hadn't gotten back to Rapid City until shortly before three o'clock a.m., and they were exhausted. They'd slept through their wake up calls, and their parents had left for church without them.

They slid into the back pew next to Ty and his brothers. Vincenzo turned around and frowned.

"Where were you guys?" Ty whispered.

Angelo swallowed. He still hadn't thought up an excuse and he didn't want to lie.

"We played Scrabble all night long," Alyssa whispered. "We didn't hear our wake up calls."

Angelo frowned as he thought, *apparently she doesn't have a problem with lying, while sitting in the back of a church, almost related to the pastor.*

Kate was ticked off, her children could tell, and Joshua's sermon didn't last nearly long enough. After church ended, the Casellis and the Hansens filed past the pew in the back, smiling mischievously in Alyssa and Angelo's direction. Noah even gave them a sly wink. Obviously, Kate had already voiced her disappointment to the relatives and Alyssa and Angelo were hanging their heads by the time they reached their parents' van in the parking lot.

"We thought it might be fun to hit the late show last night," Kate sounded off when she had them alone. "But the two of you were *nowhere* to be found."

Vincenzo put his arm on Kate's shoulder, attempting to smooth things over as he said, "Now the two of you are well into your twenties and we know you can take care of yourselves."

"But you promised to take time off," Kate scolded.

"I know, Ma`ma," Alyssa replied. "But something's come up and I had to be somewhere."

"I heard you lie to your cousin," Kate accused.

Alyssa frowned, whispering, "It's not everybody's business what I do for a living. I didn't cancel on you and I'm coming over to Noah and Tillie's for Sunday dinner."

"You're just like your uncle," Kate snapped.

Alyssa bristled. "No, I'm not. If I was like Alex, I wouldn't have even shown up." She stomped off in the direction of her car.

Kate shook her head, got into the van, and slammed the door.

For Sunday dinner following church services, Tillie and her mother had prepared their famous Stromboli recipe, along with giant zucchini salads and focaccia bread on the side. Tillie's most treasured times were spent in her kitchen, preparing huge meals for her family. It had always been such a wonderful time when they came together, *except this time.* Tillie sensed the tension between Kate and Alyssa and she hoped they could put things in order before the end of the day.

Laura's friend, Elijah Olson, had been invited, as was Jake's favorite young lady in the whole world, Heidi Romanov. The two "couples" were sitting together with A.J. and Ty, enjoying heaping plates of their favorite pasta beneath the pine trees behind the house.

"That's the one," Noah whispered to Marquette, looking sideways at Elijah so Marquette would know whom he was getting ready to talk about. "He's a stockbroker." He shook his head, rolling his eyes. "Twenty-three years old. He must be nuts to think he can just close in on a seventeen year old girl."

Marquette narrowed his eyes in the direction of the young suitor, and frowned. The young man appeared to have manners, as he hadn't touched Laura inappropriately during his entire visit. As well, he had already agreed they would not go anywhere together alone until she was eighteen years old.

"He could be very clever," Marquette whispered. He looked at Noah and his eyes began to shine. "Now, how old were you when you asked Angel for her hand in marriage?"

Noah frowned. "*That* was completely different."

Marquette laughed. "Okay, my friend, if you wish it to be."

"It was," Noah persisted. "People got married when they were younger back then. Besides, I didn't know she was only seventeen."

"All right you two," Tillie was suddenly beside them. She had Annie on her hip and a plate of food in her free hand. "I know you're talking about Elijah. Don't do that." She handed Noah the plate of food and Annie reached for her father. "Now you guys go sit down and put some of this food into your mouths so you won't be tempted to gossip."

"Angel, I *never* gossip," Noah defended.

Tillie laughed. "I'll get us some more food. Save me a place." She raised her eyebrows and giggled as she said, "And hopefully I won't find any more spooks in my kitchen!" With that, she hurried inside.

Marquette laughed and patted Noah's shoulder as he said, "I think I will get some food as well."

Noah looked at the pretty baby in his arms and said, "Well, I s'pose we'd better do as we're told then."

Annie smiled up into her father's eyes and Noah couldn't help but smile back. Despite how crummy things had been recently, there were still many blessings.

Alyssa sat down with her uncles, Sam and Patty, but was only half-listening to their conversation. Her mind was still on the night before and what they'd learned in Mud Butte. In her heart, she wanted to tell Noah about Ben, but on a professional level she could see that now wasn't the time.

Her eyes drifted around the large gathering, coming to rest on Tillie and Noah. They were sitting by themselves with little Annie perched on Noah's lap, feeding her mother bites of the focaccia. Noah looked into Aunt Tillie's eyes when he spoke to her, and he must have said something funny because she was laughing. Alyssa couldn't help but smile at the sight.

Her eyes moved on to Ty, who visited with her brother and Gabriella and Michael. It was funny how inseparable the three who attended George Washington had become. Alyssa wondered about Rauwolf as she looked at Ty. Besides Tara Caselli, Schneider Rauwolf and Carrie were the last two people to see John Peters alive. Her thoughts progressed from there and she was suddenly wondering if Carrie had ever said anything at all about John Peters to Noah. Certainly, Carrie had kept many things from Noah, including the existence of her own mother. Perhaps Noah didn't know anything at all.

"So, where did you go last night?" Marquette said, taking a seat beside her. Alyssa suddenly realized that Sam and Petrice had moved on without her even noticing.

She forced herself from her thoughts, answering, "My partner followed Ben up to a little town north of here. We drove up there last night and had a look around. It's called Mud Butte, and there isn't a thing there except the post office, a little grocery store and a bar."

"Were you able to interview anyone?"

"The bartender. When I gave him Ben's description, he called him 'Tony,' and said that his mother was murdered when he was still a child."

Marquette nodded. "Antonio Ponerello."

"And my partner just called me a couple of minutes ago," Alyssa continued. "Apparently there was a fire down at Colonial Manor last night. That's the place where they've been keeping Della Nelson, and she's missing. All of the other residents are safe and accounted for, but the facility lost its entire records storage room and their computer system was completely wiped out. It will be weeks before their back-up systems are restored and up and running."

"They have decided to run again," Marquette said.

Alyssa frowned. "What I don't understand is why they want to hide from Luigi or Salvatore, or whoever he is. And why does Luigi want them so bad in the first place?"

Marquette shook his head and replied, "Perhaps Tara will be able to fill in those blanks when she flies to Italia."

"Jon and I need to get back up to Mud Butte, no later than sometime tomorrow. Jon says there are a couple of back roads up there he wants to check out. Maybe that's where they're making the drugs or something. Why don't you and Patterson come along with us?"

Marquette nodded. "I will contact him. He has been trying to stay very close to his mother due to what he considers a threat on her life. She will board a plane tomorrow for Valdosta, Georgia, and then he can relax a bit."

"Jon called in senior backup and a task force and they'll be here tomorrow. He wants them around when everything starts coming apart, which I think is going to happen in a couple of days…I just want to tell Noah and Auntie everything."

"Well, you cannot." Marquette smiled. "Not just yet, anyway. Perhaps tomorrow, and after we have learned Luigi's true identity and purpose, we can sit down with Noah and ask him what he knows of Rauwolf." Marquette smiled in the direction of his best friend as he said, "I think it's safe to assume that Noah knew Ty's father only as Roy Schneider. And, knowing Noah's character, I cannot imagine he will be able to give us much more than that on Mr. Schneider's account."

*****

The hospital called Ty early Monday morning. Roy had asked for him and requested that he come up for a short time. Ty promised his family that he'd be back to spend the day with his cousins as planned.

The team Jon had called for arrived at the Plaza early, and Jon ushered them into a conference room. Alyssa planned on touring the Black Hills with her cousins in the afternoon, so Jon scheduled a briefing with the team before she left.

After leaving Sam and Becky-Lynn at the airport, Vincenzo and Kate made their way to Angel's Place, where Petrice and Ellie were waiting for them. The ladies, along with Mona Hansen, were planning a relaxing day with Tillie, visiting and putting together a scrapbook. Tara had still not figured out a way to tell Tillie she would be leaving that night, but she prayed God would send her the words. She didn't want to lie to Tillie about their suspicions regarding the alleged Luigi Andreotti; on the other hand she didn't want to alarm Tillie, either.

The men had planned to meet Ben at the construction site that morning, and Marquette wondered if Ben would appear. If Ben Simmons was actually Antonio Ponerello, Marquette guessed that he knew by now his identity was compromised.

Guiseppi and his sons followed Noah around the progressing framework of the building, complimenting Noah's hard-working construction crews at every turn, especially when they came to Jake and A.J., who were laboring very hard.

"It is a tough job," Guiseppi declared, slapping A.J.'s broad back. "But you know someone has to do it, and your youth and strength will sustain you."

"Thanks, Grandpa," A.J. replied, smiling politely.

"Work the devil out of you is what it will do," Vincenzo said, giving Jake's shoulder an encouraging pat.

Jake smiled, but looked embarrassed.

Noah led Guiseppi and his sons along, explaining in detail how the finished building would look, using the blue prints and an artist's rendition to give them better understanding.

"I wish Ben would have showed up this morning," Noah said with a frown. "He can explain these drawings better than I can. He's had formal training you know."

"Where is he this morning?" Vincenzo asked.

Noah shook his head. "This isn't like him at all. He probably got held up over on St. Pat. We've had some trouble with a little warehouse we're putting up over there —" Noah was interrupted by the ringing of a gunshot. "What in the world?" He looked around and saw a man dressed in black leather dashing out the front door of Maggie May's.

"Maggie," he whispered. He dropped his blueprints and ran across the street.

"Noah, wait!" Marquette yelled, breaking into a run behind Noah.

159

Vincenzo and Petrice helped their father through the rest of the construction site, while Marquette quickly closed the distance between himself and Noah, reaching him in the middle of Maggie's parking lot.

"Wait, my friend!" Marquette breathed heavily, taking a firm hold of Noah's shoulder.

"But Maggie's inside!" Noah panted.

Marquette produced a pistol from beneath his suit jacket and Noah looked at him with surprise. "Let me go in first," Marquette whispered.

Noah nodded, and followed Marquette as they approached the glass entry doors of Maggie May's. Marquette peered into the glass doors and saw a body lying on the floor inside. He drew in a surprised breath, pulled the door open and stepped inside with his weapon drawn. Noah followed, and saw the body on the floor. The young man lying before them had been shot once in the shoulder. His hand was still clutched tightly around a gun of his own, though he was obviously disoriented. Marquette and Noah wondered if he had shot himself.

Marquette knelt beside the young man and took his gun away.

"Oh, brother," Maggie grumbled from behind the bar. "I just winged him. And he looks like he's coming out of it. Humph."

Marquette and Noah looked up in surprise. Maggie was standing with her own pistol still drawn.

"Maggie?" Noah gasped.

"The little derelict tried to shoot me," Maggie explained. She pointed her gun at the mirror behind her, and Noah and Marquette saw the bullet hole.

"But I heard only one shot," Marquette said with a confused expression.

"He's got a silencer, Smarty Pants," Maggie retorted.

Marquette looked at the retrieved weapon in his hand, nodding.

Maggie rolled her eyes. "I've already called the little creep an ambulance. Thankfully, I'm a darn good aim. He's gonna be okay."

Guiseppi, Vincenzo and Petrice burst through the door, breathing heavily from their jaunt across the construction site. They surveyed the unusual scene inside of Maggie's place.

"Did *you* shoot him?" Guiseppi asked, wearing a horrified expression.

Maggie nodded with a frown, looking over the pistol in her hand as she said, "That's the first time I've ever had to actually shoot a customer." She looked thoughtful for a moment and added, "I've threatened quite a few of them, but I've never actually had to shoot one. Little Lucky here was closer to my reach, otherwise the toad over there would've gotten it with my old Remington."

Noah went to where Maggie stood behind the bar and threw his arms around her. "I'm so glad you're okay," he said.

"Now don't get all mushy on me," Maggie groaned, giving Noah a friendly pat on the back. She chuckled, backing out of his arms. She reached beneath the counter and tossed some towels at Marquette. "You're gonna need to put some ice on that," she suggested. "I'll get a bag from the back."

They put the towels and ice on the young man's wound while they waited for the ambulance to arrive. He asked for water, and they provided him with that as well. Marquette attempted to question him, but he wouldn't speak.

Within a matter of minutes, an ambulance, along with Detective Patterson and squads of Rapid City Policemen, were on the scene. They asked for Maggie's weapons and concealed weapon permit, and she turned them over.

"This is my regular beat," Jason explained to Marquette. "I always work the north end." He looked at the young man they'd loaded on the stretcher and frowned. "You ready to answer any questions?" he asked.

"Not until you guys get me a lawyer," he answered.

"Figures," Jason replied, looking at the ambulance attendants. "Take him to ER, but I want a uniform on him at all times." Jason looked at a young officer standing near them and said, "Go ahead and ride along — don't leave him for anything."

The attendants loaded up the young man, and the officer climbed into the back of the ambulance with him. They closed the doors and were soon speeding away from the scene.

Alyssa's partner, Jon, pulled onto the scene at about that time. He flashed his badge at the police officers blocking off the parking lot, making his way to the inside of the old bar. He walked to where Jason was standing, held up his badge and said, "I'm United States Deputy Marshal Jon Danielson. Deputy Caselli is on her way."

Jason frowned. "Why?"

"I heard the call and we think it's related," Jon replied.

Jason shook his head. "This is totally *unrelated*. We just had an armed robbery by the same two guys last Friday."

"Deputy Caselli says there's a correlation," Jon insisted.

Jason sighed with disgust as he retorted, "Listen, Mac, I know the two of you have been looking into my investigation, but don't try to make this a federal case because it's not. The two of you need to go back to wherever you came from, and let me do my job. You're wasting a whole lot of government money spinning your wheels up here."

Jon wrinkled his brow, obviously taken aback by the young detective's brusque attitude. "We've already called in our own team and we've got authority to take over jurisdiction if you want to make this some kind of a contest," he said. "The best thing to do here is get everyone downtown for questioning."

Maggie couldn't help but smirk at the comical theatrics playing out before her. It was obvious that Petrice and Marquette seemed to know something of what was going on, but Vincenzo, Guiseppi and Noah were completely in the dark. Maggie, for her own part, was very surprised to realize that the young man who'd questioned her about Angel's portrait only a week before, was actually a detective. When he was through questioning her, she was going to have some questions of her own.

"What in the world is going on here? What is *correlated*?" Guiseppi demanded.

Marquette put a friendly hand on his father's shoulder, explaining, "We cannot say, Papa."

Guiseppi looked questioningly at his youngest son. "You know of this Marquette?" he asked.

"Yes, Papa. And I will try to explain everything as soon as I can," he replied. At that moment, Alyssa walked in and Detective Patterson groaned.

Alyssa gave Jason a coy smile as she said, "Detective Patterson. How in the world are you?"

"Deputy," Jason replied, politely nodding in her direction.

Maggie watched the exchange with intense interest. *Those two have met before.* "Hey, let's get this show on the road," she said with a sardonic grin. "I don't know about the rest of you, but I'm curious. For starters, Detective, why didn't you tell me you were a cop when I spilled my guts to you about Angel's portrait?"

Maggie's words fell on Jason like a giant brick. He needed to get everyone out of here before the old gal started making mincemeat out of his case.

"Okay," Jon said, taking the lead. "Everybody out — except for Hansen and Marquette Caselli."

Alyssa looked at Jon. "Did somebody pick up my aunt?" she asked.

Jon nodded. "I had a couple of our deputies pick up Mrs. Hansen. I thought we'd take everyone downtown, but I can have 'em bring her over here. It might be a whole lot safer at this juncture not to start moving folks around too much."

Noah and Vincenzo's mouths fell open at Jon's remarks.

"This is ridiculous!" Guiseppi suddenly snapped. "Marquette, submit to me and tell me what is going on here! And why has someone gone to pick up Angel?"

"Papa," Marquette said, attempting to calm down his father, "please be patient. The answers will come shortly. Now, if you and Vincenzo and Petrice could go back over to the construction site and tell A.J. and Jake that Maggie May is fine, I think that would be a very good thing."

Petrice put his hand upon Guiseppi's shoulder, saying, "Come along, Papa. Let us be on our way."

"Nearly eighty-one years have I lived upon this earth," Guiseppi complained. "And yet you do not count me worthy to listen to your secrets."

Vincenzo forced away his smile. "Come along, Papa," he said, "Should we not speak with A.J. and Jake? They must be very worried by now."

Guiseppi threw his arms into the air, snorting as he started for the door. "I suppose!" he exclaimed. "Keep the old man in the dark! See if you do not regret this as I lay dying in my bed." And as he passed through the door, he groaned and clutched his chest.

"Take care, Marquette," Petrice said as he and Vincenzo showed their father through the door.

With the exception of Jon's cell phone conversation ordering the deputies to deliver Tillie to the scene, tense silence filled the small restaurant.

"Anybody gonna say anything?" Maggie cackled.

Noah's eyes were huge. "Well I'd sure like to know how come my wife is on her way," he said.

"You and Angel are witnesses," Marquette explained. He smiled at his brother-in-law. "When I brought Angel to Rapid City in 1975, it was only because I was going to be here anyway. The night she came to Maggie's was the last night anyone saw my associate, John Peters, alive." He raised his eyebrow and looked at Maggie. "And I know now that you lied to me all those years ago because you believed yourself to be protecting Noah. However, the case still remains unsolved and the crimes associated with the people I have been looking for have escalated."

Maggie pursed her lips tightly, looking hard at Marquette. She remembered the day vividly. He'd strolled into her bar in one of his fancy suits and hats, wearing an elegant ponytail and speaking in his romantic accent. She'd recognized him as one of the *Refugees* in Angel's painting, but when he started to ask questions about the two men following Carrie, she'd lied.

Maggie cleared her throat, attempting to explain, "Noah had just cleaned up his life and was gonna get married. I couldn't let anything happen to him." She looked at Noah and smiled. "You were sitting right there with that little diamond in your pocket and when she didn't show I thought you were gonna die."

Marquette sighed heavily, "In the meantime, I continued to search for two men. One of them was my associate, John Peters, and the other was a man whom you know as Roy Schneider."

Noah thought perhaps he'd misunderstood Marquette. "Did you say Roy Schneider?" he asked.

Marquette nodded. "Yes. The very man who fathered your son."

Noah glanced around the room, seeing that everyone seemed to be familiar with the information.

"Noah," Alyssa took a few steps in his direction, trying to smile. "Jon and I figured it out during our investigation." She took a deep breath and was about to speak again when two United States Marshals, dressed in suits, escorted Tillie into the restaurant.

Noah went to her, reaching for her hand.

"What's goin' on?" she asked with a nervous smile, glancing at the puddle of blood on the floor in the middle of the room. She looked at Maggie. "Are you okay?"

Maggie nodded. "How 'bout some coffee, Angel?"

"Okay," Tillie answered, her tone still unsure. She took a tight hold of Noah's hand and looked into his eyes. "What's going on?" she asked again.

Noah looked away as he led her to the counter, answering, "Beats me." Though, deep down inside he knew why Marquette Caselli was looking for Roy Schneider. It was a secret he hadn't even shared with his own wife and now it was coming back to haunt him in a way he'd never imagined. Not even Maggie knew Noah's secret.

Maggie poured a cup of coffee and set it before Tillie. "This is really getting awkward," she said with a frown. She glanced from Alyssa to Jason, and back at Alyssa. "So let's get the ball rolling. I'm terribly curious as to what ole Roy was up to twenty-three years ago and how Noah fits in to all of that."

"First, I've gotta ask Deputy Caselli why she thinks this whole thing that happened here today is correlated," Jason said.

"One of the robbers was described as wearing black make up and black leather clothing," Alyssa explained. "Jon and I followed a man with a similar description out of Andreotti's office last week. He's staying in the complex of row houses here on the north end and I'm gonna chance a guess he's the next one you'll find."

Jason frowned. "Why?"

"Detective, where's your mother today?" Alyssa asked.

"I was leaving her off at the airport just as the call —" Jason suddenly stopped speaking and Alyssa nodded.

"When Jon called me about the attempted robbery and resultant shooting," Alyssa said, "I tried to call you, but couldn't. I got a hold of your father and told him that I suspected whatever happened here may have been staged to pull you away from your mother. He's on his way to the airport to make sure she boarded her plane."

Jason was hit with a wave of nausea. He swallowed hard, sitting down in one of the stools next to Tillie. She saw the sweat beading up on his forehead and instinctively put her hand on his shoulder.

"Are you okay?" she asked.

Jason could only nod, wiping the sweat from his forehead, taking a deep breath.

"His mother is the mayor of your city," Marquette smiled.

"Oh, Mayor Patterson," Tillie said. "Nice lady."

"Thanks," Jason managed to croak.

Tillie smiled nervously at her husband. "You remember Jacq?" she asked. "She represented us...." Tillie hesitated, adding, "You know. Remember?"

"Oh, yeah," Noah recalled.

"Noah," Marquette said, taking a breath and trying to smile. "We have come to a point in our case where we find it necessary to question you and Angel about your knowledge of Roy Schneider."

"Don't be afraid," Alyssa added. "We can promise you immunity. Nothing you tell us can harm either you or your family."

Chapter 15

Joe Patterson paced nervously in the control tower at Rapid City Regional Airport. Via the controller's radio, United States Marshal Cameron, who was in charge of the senior support team in Rapid City, was relaying information to the captain of Jacqueline's flight. So far, they'd been able to verify her boarding pass, but it was uncertain as to whether or not Jacqueline actually *boarded* the flight. They were nearly ready to land at the Minneapolis terminal, but under the direct request of Marshal Cameron, the captain of the flight sent an attendant to visually confirm Jacqueline's presence on the plane.

"Marshal Cameron?" asked a male voice from the radio speaker, and Joe stopped pacing to listen.

"Cameron here," he answered, giving Joe a glance.

"Captain Jackson here," he said. "We cannot visually confirm Mrs. Patterson's presence on this flight. I repeat, we cannot visually confirm Mrs. Patterson's presence on this flight."

Joe's heart stopped as he sank into a nearby chair.

"Thank you, Captain," Marshal Cameron answered. He handed the radio back to the controller, taking a seat beside Joe. "I have to call the FBI, and Caselli and Danielson. Maybe you should give your son a call first."

*****

"And you didn't have any idea that Carrie's mother was still alive?" Alyssa was questioning Noah, after briefing him on what authorities had learned.

Tillie sat at the bar, thunderstruck, sipping coffee, and nibbling Maggie's pie. She couldn't have been more amazed than at what had been brought to light about Noah's past.

Noah shook his head. "Not a clue," he answered. "We went to a funeral and everything. Jack wouldn't let anybody view the body, and I thought *that* was a little weird." He shook his head and smiled as he said, "And all these years I was afraid that Carrie might have been seeing

165

somebody on the side down in Custer. The day of her accident my accountant was trying to get me to explain the sale of a quarter of million dollars in stocks. She must have given the money to her family so they could take care of Della."

Marquette suddenly snapped his fingers. "We monitored the transfer of a quarter of million dollars from a Carrie Miller!" he exclaimed.

"That was Carrie's maiden name," Noah said.

Detective Patterson's cell phone rang, and he answered it quickly. "Patterson." A short moment of silence, and then Jason said, "Did you find her, Dad?" A longer moment of silence, and before Jason could respond, Alyssa's cell phone went off.

"Caselli." Alyssa swallowed hard, listening. She glanced at Jason, realizing by the look on his face that he was receiving the same news. "Thanks, Marshal," she said. "Keep us posted." She turned off her phone.

Jason turned his back on the group as he finished his conversation. Everyone waited quietly.

As Alyssa glanced around the room, she saw that the forensics team had started to scrape red mud samples from Maggie's floor. She frowned and looked at Jon. "Where have we seen that before?" she asked, pointing at the floor.

Jon looked at the chunks of red mud and clicked his tongue. "Are you thinking what I'm thinking?" he asked.

"What is it?" Marquette asked.

"That stuff is all over the floor at the Circle Q," Jon said with a grin. He looked at Jason and said, "Hey, Patterson, get off the phone. We've got a lead."

Detective Patterson called in the lead, notifying his chief that he would accompany the two deputies to Mud Butte for a look around. Noah and Tillie were allowed to go home. Marquette went to find Tara so that they could discuss a few of the old facts, and then he was taking her to the airport so that she could travel to *Italia*.

Noah drove along in dead silence, hoping his wife didn't ask too many questions on the way home. He couldn't help but wonder if John Peters was the guy Jack and Carrie had buried out behind the Harney Little League Complex in 1975. He'd decided early into Alyssa's questioning *not* to divulge that information. He'd have to have a good, long talk with Marquette before risking being accused as an accomplice in a murder. After all, he barely understood the word *immunity*, let alone about how far reaching it would be once they realized he'd purposely purchased the land where the body was buried.

Tillie sat in quiet amazement in the passenger seat, until she finally blurted, "The whole thing is unbelievable…and how about Ben? What do you think of all this 'Elder Son' stuff?"

Noah shook his head and replied, "It's really weird. I never met Tony, but he was always talked about. You know, I should have guessed something about that. Even though Ben never had an Italian accent, I've always noticed how he doesn't use contractions when he speaks. You know, sort of like your family, except that he doesn't have the same accent. Although, Alex noticed it years ago — I thought it sounded a little like Lakota, and he is fairly dark-skinned."

"I'd like to know why he's been seeing Luigi."

Noah frowned with contemplation. "You know, from the time we met him on Patty's boat, I always thought Luigi looked a little familiar."

"Familiar how?" Tillie asked.

"Like I had met him somewhere before," Noah murmured.

Tillie sighed. "Well, I s'pose he's Jack's brother and we've just had a family reunion with a homicidal maniac."

"Listen, Dad," Jason said, talking on his cell phone, while Jon drove, "we're on our way up to Mud Butte to have a look around. We should get up there around three-thirty or four o'clock." He took a deep breath, promising, "We're gonna find her, Dad. There's about a billion people looking for her."

"But what if he's killed her," Joe whispered.

"He won't kill her," Jason replied. "Good grief, she's the mayor. He's going to hold her hostage or something. She's leverage."

"I wanna come up there with you —"

"No," Jason interrupted. "Stay put. He'll be sending a letter or making a phone call. Put a bug on your phone."

"Who are you with, son?" Joe asked.

"I'm with Caselli and Danielson."

"Son, be careful."

"I will, Dad."

"Call me."

"I will," Jason promised. "We're gonna find her, Dad, and she's gonna be okay."

Charise hung up the phone, and returned to her mother's side. Della was in her wheelchair on the front porch, enjoying the early afternoon sun.

"Who was on the phone?" Della asked.

"That was Antonio," Charise answered, trying to hide her anxiety.

"Will he be coming to see us?"

"I don't know."

Della slowly nodded her head, looking at Charise with forethought and purpose — as if that part of Della that had been broken for so very long had suddenly come back together.

Charise was startled to see the deep expression behind her mother's eyes, and she asked, "What is it, Ma`ma?"

"You have moved me because of Sal."

Charise swallowed hard, looking back into her mother's eyes. For years, Charise assumed Della remembered only fragments of her life with her father, but lately, ever since her visit with Deputy Caselli, Della remembered more and more.

"What do you remember about Sal?" Charise whispered.

Della shrugged her old, thin shoulders, smiling faintly as she answered, "That he is an evil man, and that your father is afraid of him."

"Why?"

"He controlled us with threats," Della answered. "He said he would contact the family and have us all killed if we didn't do what he wanted." She paused. "Your father wanted to start a new life with me and Carrie, but Sal just wouldn't hear of it. He was obsessed with bringing justice to the imprisoned family in Sicily..." Della's voice trailed off and she stared at the landscape around them, watching the horse prance in the distance and the long grass blow gently in the breeze.

Charise waited for her mother to continue and when she didn't, she gently prodded, "And what else, Ma`ma? Why is Papa afraid of Sal?"

The familiar veil dropped over Della's eyes. She had been there for a few, precious moments, and was gone again.

"Ma`ma?"

Della nodded, watching the horse in the distance, whispering, "I don't remember anymore."

Jacqueline Holliday Patterson heard the buzzing of insects when he pulled her from the back of his car. She couldn't see where they were because he'd kept the blindfold on for what seemed like hours of driving.

"Come along, darling," he said in an overly polite tone, leading her from the car.

"Where are you taking me?" she asked.

"You have asked that question for the last time," he warned. "Ask it no more."

She was dressed in shorts, and felt long grass brushing against her bare legs as he led her. *No sidewalk*, she thought. *We must be out in the country somewhere.*

They stopped suddenly and she heard him working the lock on a door. It squeaked open, and she was led inside. He slammed her down on a hard seat. He secured ropes to her ankles and wrists around what felt like the wooden brackets of an old-fashioned chair.

Sal removed her blindfold at last, and as her eyes adjusted to the dim lighting, she saw the inside of what appeared to be an old gardening shed. The shelves were sparsely supplied with fertilizer, but there were no tools at all — nothing she could use for a weapon. The small windows were covered with newspaper. There was an empty seat across from her. Sal sat down and smiled.

"You have a spoiled, rotten son," he said, his greasy smile turning eerily into a frown. "But, *all* sons have a special place for their mothers."

"What do you want?" she asked.

Sal laughed. "Even though your son is very spoiled, he does happen to have some vague smarts about him. Very soon now, he will stumble upon treasure I have sought for nearly thirty years. However, I do believe he will trade *his* treasure, *that is you*, for *my* treasure, and all will be resolved rather quickly."

Sal stood up and went to the door. "I have a few things to take care of which will prompt events to unfold as they should," he said. "And I will return with some company for you."

He smiled with a polite bow and left Jacqueline, locking the door behind him.

*****

Petrice had someone bring his plane from the hanger in Vermillion to the Rapid City Regional Airport. It would take less than an hour to fly Tara to Denver, and then he would return to Rapid City.

From Denver, Tara had chartered a flight to New York City, where she'd board the Concorde for Paris. From Paris, she'd chartered a flight to Florence, where Jonathon, their helicopter pilot would take her to *Chianti*. If everything went as they'd planned, Tara would be at the Andreotti Winery by nine-thirty a.m., Italian time.

While Petrice checked everything for the flight, Tara and Marquette quickly reviewed their oldest case.

"You go carefully, my love," Tara said. "For if this man *is* Salvatore Ponerello, he is capable of profound evil. And do not forget his father's curse on you."

"I do not fear whatever witchcraft they *may* possess," Marquette scoffed.

"I know that, my love, however, I do not doubt that Salvatore would be willing to help the curse along a bit."

"No doubt," Marquette agreed.

Tara took a deep breath and asked, "And what if I learn that this man *is* Luigi Andreotti?"

Marquette shook his head. "Then we have a mystery of substantial proportion. We must pray God allows us to put the pieces in order."

"And I understand that our old file should be here within a day?"

Marquette nodded. "Our liaison says that there are several photographs and I will show them to Noah. Hopefully, he will recognize at least Mario and be able to give us a positive identification."

Tara frowned as she said, "I think Noah is hiding something from us, Marq."

"I have sensed it as well. But what can it be?"

Tara shook her head. "I do not know, but perhaps you can coax it out of him. He is probably so afraid of whatever it is he has not been able to bring himself to speak of it even to Angel."

"I will speak with him as soon as I have the chance," Marquette promised.

*****

Marquette arrived at Vincenzo's hotel room, and found him and Guiseppi sitting on the balcony. Guiseppi sat still, staring hard at his youngest son as if waiting for an answer to the strange events of the morning, while Vincenzo puffed nervously at his pipe.

"Our wives are at Angel's Place," Vincenzo murmured. "We are expected for dinner there this evening."

Marquette nodded.

Guiseppi frowned. "And where is your brother?" he asked Marquette.

Marquette took the last chair available on the small deck, looking from his father to his brother. "He is flying my Tara to Denver as we speak," he answered. "He will return in a few hours."

"And what is in Denver, Marquette?" Vincenzo asked, holding his pipe tightly between his teeth, raising one eyebrow.

"I have arranged a private charter to take her to New York City, where she will board the Concorde. She will be in *Chianti* by their morning. She will then visit Andreotti Vineyards & Winery to learn what she can with regard to Luigi."

Guiseppi's frown deepened as he asked, "Do you believe him to be a phony?"

"I do, Papa," Marquette answered. He leaned back in his chair. "Do you remember my Ponerello case?"

"How could we forget?" Vincenzo replied, taking a puff of his pipe. "It has been your obsession for many years."

Marquette smiled. "I suspect that the man we have been calling Luigi is actually Salvatore Ponerello."

"The man *you* watched *kill himself?*" Guiseppi barked. "Marquette! And you have sent your beautiful wife this great distance, *alone*, because of a *suspicion?*"

"She is the only one I completely trust," Marquette defended. "And I also think Noah has information on the whereabouts of my old colleague, John Peters. Things will be happening very quickly now and the two of you would do well to listen to what I must tell you."

Guiseppi sighed. "Very well then, my Marquette, keep us in suspense no longer. Fill us in on all of your gory details."

*****

After hiding the black Taurus with government plates safely behind a stand of trees not far from the barn, Jon, Alyssa and Jason slipped through the heavy overgrowth of weeds and bushes, making their way to the front door. After driving just a short distance down a gravel road north of Mud Butte's main street, the barn came into view and the threesome decided to check it out. An old white pickup was parked along the side of the barn, but other than that there didn't appear to be any activity. Tire tracks were everywhere in the dried, red mud, which was consistent with Alyssa's theory the robbers were in *this* area before coming to Maggie May's. What was most unusual about the barn was that the front door had been left wide open, even though there was an electronic combination lock available.

Jon caught the smell of a decomposing body as they entered the barn.

He politely handed Alyssa his handkerchief. "We're gonna find somebody," he murmured. He swallowed hard as they crept through the front door.

"I can't get service on my phone," Jason whispered, clipping his cell phone on his belt, drawing his weapon. "We can't even call for backup until we get back on the main road."

"We don't need back-up," Alyssa whispered with a frown. She looked at Jason, raising her eyebrow. "Unless you expect the dead body to rise up and come after us."

Jason frowned. "What makes you *so mean?*" he retorted.

"I'm not mean."

"Knock it off!" Jon growled in a whisper. "Let's just go in and take a look around, find the body and get forensics up here."

Alyssa and Jason nodded in submissive agreement, following Jon into the dark building.

Jon brushed his index finger along the top of a table, turning it over to show Alyssa and Jason the powdery substance he'd collected. "You got a bag?" he asked.

Jason reached inside his jacket pocket and pulled out a small, clear plastic bag. He handed it to Jon, who scraped a little of the white powder into it and sealed it.

"I bet it's coke," he said, slipping the bag into his jacket pocket.

He led them around a corner and into a dark room, nearly stumbling when his foot came into contact with something on the floor. Jason reached for the small flashlight on his key chain, shining the light on the dead body before them.

"There's a switch over here," Alyssa said, flicking the switch on the wall near her. She swallowed away her reflexive gag, shaking her head. She'd never get used to decomposed bodies.

"He's been dead for awhile," Jason said.

"At least two or three days," Jon agreed.

The front door suddenly slammed and the three of them looked at one another with surprise.

"You just could not wait!" An accented man's voice shouted from the outer room.

"Come on, Boss," begged the voice of a younger male. "What's one old lady gonna say? So, we missed."

"She was part of my plan!" The accented voice was more of a hysterical scream than a regular shout. "Now I will have to think of something else!"

The three in the back room looked intently at each other, drawing their weapons. Jason took a breath, leading them into the outer area of the barn where they saw Luigi Andreotti forcing a man, whose hands had been bound, to bend over the table. He flicked open the blade of his knife.

Jason leaped into the center of the room. "Freeze!"

Jon and Alyssa followed his lead, stopping just short of rushing Luigi in order to save the life of the man he threatened.

Luigi didn't even startle. He kept his hand firmly against the back of the man he held, the knife at the man's throat. Luigi slowly turned his head in the direction of Jason, smirking as he said, "Hello, Detective. What brings you this far north?"

"Drop your weapon," Alyssa commanded.

"Certainly." Luigi dropped his knife to the floor.

"Now kick it over here," Jon growled.

The knife skittered across the floor.

Jason saw Luigi flick his wrist, and out of nowhere, a small knife flew in Alyssa's direction. Jason shoved her to the floor and the knife's blade caught him in the shoulder. He winced as the muscles in his hand involuntarily relaxed, letting go of its grip on his gun.

Alyssa jumped to her feet as Jon rushed Luigi, who fled for the door. Jon brought him down with a single blow of the handle of his pistol to the back of his head. Jon cuffed Luigi who was lying nearly unconscious, face down on the floor.

Jon stomped back to the young man who was still bent over the table. He pulled him up by the back of his shirt, scowling into his eyes as he demanded, "Who are you?"

"Marty McGuire," the young man answered quickly.

In the mean time, Alyssa took Jon's handkerchief and was trying to figure out how to place it over Jason's wound. The knife was securely imbedded in his shoulder muscle, blood quickly draining out around it.

"Just pull it out," Jason urged her. "It'll be better if we pull it out."

"I don't know about that." Alyssa shook her head.

"Listen," Jason said, taking a deep breath. "Sturgis is over an hour away and this thing will do a lot more damage if we leave it in there."

Alyssa let out her breath, looking at the wound again. She reached for the handle, hesitating.

Jason knew he should look away, but his eyes were glued to the procedure at hand.

"Okay," Alyssa whispered, "I'm gonna do it."

"Come on," Jason coaxed. "Just pull it out." He hesitated, trying to smile. "I promise not to cry."

Alyssa was breathing heavily, her hand resting on the handle.

"Pretend you're a Marine!" Jon shouted.

Alyssa nodded and quickly slipped the knife from the wound, pressing the handkerchief against Jason as hard as she could.

Jason took a deep breath, clenching his teeth. "Ufda," he groaned. "But, it's feeling better already."

There was the sound of tearing material and Jon produced a wadded up piece of Luigi's suit jacket, pushing it against Jason's wound.

"How did you know he was going to do that?" Jon asked.

"I saw him do something strange with his wrist," Jason answered. "But before I could warn you guys, the knife was in the air."

Jon nodded. "Well done, Detective. I'm impressed."

Jason looked at Luigi, who was coming to and trying to move. "Let's get these two over to the Meade County Sheriff's Office," he said.

"I'll call forensics when we're back on the main road," Jon offered.

"And let's get a chopper up here," Alyssa suggested. "I'd bet we're not very far from wherever he's stashed Mrs. Patterson."

*****

An hour later, Alyssa pulled into the parking lot of the Meade County Sheriff's Office in Sturgis, South Dakota. Six deputies surrounded the car with their weapons drawn. A team of paramedics waited behind them. Jason was riding in the front seat, while Jon had stayed in the back with the two bound prisoners, holding them at gunpoint all the way to town.

Luigi still appeared to be dazed. Two officers took him out of the back seat of the car and into the small holding facility. Another set of officers escorted Marty McGuire, while paramedics came to Jason's aid.

"It's only a flesh wound," Jason insisted with a frown.

"I'm gonna take forensics up to the barn," Jon said to Alyssa as they stood on the sidewalk outside of the Sheriff's Office. "I'll get a ride back to Rapid with somebody else if you wanna take the detective home. He's gonna have to have some stitches and he won't be able to drive himself anywhere after that."

Alyssa nodded. "I need to call my uncle and tell him that we've got Andreotti, or Ponerello, or whoever this guy is."

Jon raised an eyebrow, smiling at Alyssa. "And it's after six o'clock, so you need to give your mother a call. They'll be wondering where you are by now."

Alyssa groaned. "I've gotten into the wrong line of work."

"It couldn't be helped this time," Jon said, giving Alyssa's shoulder a soft pat. "I mean, come on, how many family reunions do you think will be spoiled by something like this?"

"Not many I hope."

Jon chuckled and said, "Get diehard over there into a car and take him home. I can run the show from up here until we find Mrs. Patterson. I don't think this is gonna take much longer."

The commotion from near the ambulance drew Jon and Alyssa's attention. Detective Patterson struggled off the stretcher and backed away from the paramedics, saying, "Listen, you guys have done a great job, but I don't need any stitches."

Jon smiled and shook his head, murmuring, "He should probably have some stitches."

Alyssa nodded, trying to think of some encouraging words to say to Jason, when the sheriff ran out the door of his office. "Marshals!" he shouted. Jon turned as the sheriff came to a stop in front of them. He was breathing hard and his hands were covered in blood. "I've got two dead deputies back there and Andreotti is gone!"

Chapter 16

Rauwolf sighed with relief. He reached for his remote, and turned on the television. Dr. Carlson had announced that his heart could tolerate the surgery and preparations would begin the next day. Ty had been up to see him, and they'd prayed together. Rauwolf smiled, resting against his pillows. "Things are looking up for me," he murmured.

His door opened and quickly closed, and Rauwolf turned his head to see Sal, disheveled and bloodied. A portion of his suit coat had been torn away, and his dressy slacks were covered in mud and blood.

"Look what the cat dragged in." Rauwolf snickered.

"I have come to give you one more chance," Sal whispered.

Rauwolf shook his head. "I told you before…Mario sent me away that night and he and Carrie took care of it. I tried to get the truth out of her years ago, but she refused to tell me."

"Hansen knows, I feel this within my very being," Sal declared. "I would imagine if his precious Angel were threatened, he would tell me *immediately* where to find my treasure."

"You leave my son's family alone," Rauwolf said, reaching for the nurse's light. "I'm tired of your threats. I'm calling Caselli *tonight.*"

Sal laughed. "I have been worried about that."

*****

Tara stomped to a clear area outside of LaGuardia, dialing Angel's phone number on her cell phone. Laura answered when the call went through, and after a few moments, found Marquette and put him on the line.

"Why are you still in New York?" he asked.

"Our flight has been postponed due to an equipment failure!" Tara growled. "I must now decide whether or not to take an overseas charter, or wait for the Concorde to be repaired. They have promised us a minimal wait, but we are several hours behind."

"I see," Marquette acknowledged. "You should be aware, my love, things are heating up here. Alyssa and her partner, along with Detective

Patterson were in Mud Butte this afternoon where they found the drug facility and a dead body."

Tara gasped. "Who is it?"

"We do not know at this time," Marquette answered. "However, they were able to apprehend Luigi for a short time. He escaped two deputies at the Meade County facility." Marquette took a deep breath, lowering his voice as he said, "Tara, their throats were cut."

Tara gasped again. "He *must* be a Ponerello."

"Agreed. Deputy Danielson has taken over the investigation in Meade County and Alyssa is returning to Rapid City with Detective Patterson. They will attempt to question the man we believe to be Schneider Rauwolf this evening and..." Marquette hesistated and whispered, "I will have to question Noah as soon as I get a chance."

"I will pray for you, my love. Please be careful."

"I will," Marquette promised.

*****

It was nearly eight o'clock in the evening when Alyssa drove into the parking garage beneath the Pennington County Courthouse. Jason's right arm hung limp in the sling paramedics had provided at the scene. She knew he was hurting, but he said nothing. And, just as he'd refused medical treatment beyond cleaning and dressing of the wound, he'd also refused to be taken home. Instead, Jason insisted he be taken directly to his office where he and Alyssa could go over his investigation notes. Alyssa couldn't help but agree with him. After all, his mother was still missing and if it were one of her parents at risk, she wouldn't have behaved any differently.

"Did your uncle say whether or not his old files were coming?" Jason asked as they went up the steps to his office.

"They should be here tomorrow," she answered. "His liaison is having them sent by way of an overnight delivery service."

They reached the top of the steps and Jason opened the door for Alyssa with his good arm. "Imagine that," he said as they continued down the hall. "A guy like me gets to work with someone like Marquette Caselli —" he was interrupted when a tall, lanky man dressed in blue jeans and a t-shirt started for them from the end of the hall.

"Hey, Patterson! Wait up!" he called, hurrying toward them.

"Hi, Steve, what's up?" Jason asked. He turned to Alyssa and said, "Detective Steve Nichols." He turned to Detective Nichols and said, "United States Deputy Marshal Alyssa Caselli. She's on the Andreotti case with us."

Detective Nichols smiled politely, shaking Alyssa's hand as he said, "How do you do?"

"Very well, thank you," Alyssa replied, noticing the abrupt and hurried nature of his pleasantries.

"Listen," Detective Nichols said, looking more at Jason than Alyssa. "Rapid Regional just called and they've got a dead body in their cancer care center. I know it's not your area, but I think it's connected to what you're working on. Wanna come along?"

Jason raised one eyebrow. "Homicide?" he asked.

"Oh, yeah," Detective Nichols answered. "Somebody slit his throat."

*****

Tillie and Noah, along with her parents, her brothers and their wives were seated on the comfortable deck furniture. Annie had finished her meal just a little earlier than everyone else and was enjoying a Popsicle on her grandfather's lap. Marquette had gone inside to take a phone call.

Everyone had returned to Noah and Tillie's home for the meal, except Tara and Alyssa. A.J. and Jake excitedly relayed the events at Maggie's to their cousins while they ate their dinner beneath the pine trees in the backyard.

Everyone was uneasy, to say the least. They were given some *sketchy* details about the United States Marshal's Office chasing an illegal alien — Luigi Andreotti — and how Tara had gone to Italy to learn the whereabouts of the *real* Luigi.

Ellie, bless her dear, sweet heart, tried to keep conversation going with her lively chit-chat about the President's latest scandal and how she planned on reporting more of it in the *Washington Post*. Petrice made some silly jokes in Italian quietly to his father, and when Vincenzo accidentally laughed, Rosa glared at the two of them.

The deck door slid open and Marquette stepped outside. "That was my Tara on the phone," he announced. "She has been delayed in New York and there is no telling what time she will arrive in *Chianti*." He looked at Noah and said, "Perhaps, Noah, you and I could take a walk down to your lovely creek and have a private visit."

Noah gulped. "Sure," he said, getting to his feet. He and Marquette walked away from the small group on the deck.

"What is *that* all about?" Vincenzo asked as they watched the two of them follow a path to the creek.

Tillie shook her head. Noah had been quiet and thoughtful all day. She had the feeling that whatever was keeping this mystery a mystery lay within Noah's heart.

The early spring evening in the Black Hills was very cool. The sun had started to set behind the ridge, showing its graceful, beautiful streaks of pink and yellow in the meadow. The creek was high, and Marquette and Noah heard the rushing of the strong current before they were close enough to see it.

"Do you know what your spiritual gift is, Noah?" Marquette asked as they walked along. Noah shook his head and Marquette continued, "Goodness and mercy. Two qualities I tend to see only in a knight."

"Come on, Marq, you know I'm not perfect or you wouldn't want to get me off away from everybody else," Noah grumbled.

Marquette nodded, taking a deep breath. "My strongest spiritual gift is discernment," he said.

"So what are you *discerning*, Marq?"

"I *discern* that my dear brother, Noah, knows more than he is willing to share in the presence of his Angel. Perhaps you can share it with me now."

As they neared the banks of the creek, Noah motioned toward the trampled spot in the grass where he and Tillie had often sat and talked. "Why don't we sit down for a second?" he suggested.

Marquette took a seat in the grass and Noah seated himself across from him.

"First," Noah said with a heavy sigh, "tell me about *immunity*."

"It means that you cannot be prosecuted for your involvement in a crime if you volunteer information that helps Detective Patterson or Deputy Caselli in their investigation."

Noah frowned. "Well, what if I'm not involved in the crime itself, but I knew about it and helped to cover it up? Will immunity still cover that?"

Marquette nodded. "You will be completely safe, Noah."

Noah sighed and began, "I've never told another soul about this, Marq, and I don't know how I'm gonna tell Angel."

"First of all, *nothing* will make her leave you. Certainly you must know this," Marquette assured.

Noah grimaced, looking away from Marquette, watching the creek flow by. "I didn't find out until 1980. I came home from work one day and Roy was pushing Carrie around in the backyard. I slapped him up a little bit and told him to never come back. After he left, Carrie told me that he had killed a man in 1975. She said he 'lost his cool' and slit the guy's throat and he died before they could get him to the hospital. So, Jack told Roy to leave them, and he and Carrie buried the body."

Marquette's mouth fell open in surprise.

Noah continued, "She told me it was an accident. Carrie's stepfather never intended to kill the guy, he just wanted to scare him away. Carrie told me that Jack and Tony were both from Sicily and that their family there was always trying to find them. They thought that this man who'd been following them around had been hired by their family in Sicily."

Marquette frowned and scratched his chin. "Undoubtedly, the man they buried is my friend, John Peters," he said. "Did Carrie ever show you the location of the burial?"

Noah took a deep breath, hesitating before he said, "I bought the land, Marq."

Marquette's face was ashen with surprise as he whispered. "What?"

Noah swallowed. "I own the land. Ty was little and Carrie was pregnant with Jake. Marq, I was afraid. I thought that if I bought the land and kept it all from being disturbed, I could keep my family safe —"

Noah was interrupted by approaching footsteps on the path and he and Marquette looked up in surprise. Detective Patterson and Alyssa had arrived. Marquette and Noah got to their feet.

"Mr. Hansen," Jason said with a frown. "Roy Schneider was murdered earlier this evening. We need you to tell us everything you know about him."

*****

After they'd told Alyssa and Detective Patterson all of the gruesome details, Noah and Marquette made their way back to the house. It was agreed that no one would speak of Roy's murder until further details were uncovered. Ty and the other children would simply be told that Roy had passed away.

Jason stepped into the driveway by himself to dispatch Pennington County deputies and Rapid City police officers to patrol the grounds around Noah and Tillie's home. If the killer was aware of Noah's knowledge of the body's whereabouts, it only made sense that he would come for Noah.

Alyssa called Jon and updated him with the details Noah had given her. "I called Cameron, and he'll have a team over there to dig up the body tomorrow," she said.

"And I was able to get a little bit of information out of that kid that we grabbed this afternoon," Jon said.

"What does he know about this whole thing?"

"He says that he and the guy that got shot this morning were supposed to hit Noah's friend, Maggie," Jon answered. "Deputies searched him and found a vial of coke on the guy. Forensics is doing a field test on it, but I'm betting it's laced with strychnine."

"Did he say where he got the stuff?"

"Says Luigi gave it to him and told him he couldn't use it until after he finished his job."

"That's the first statement that corroborates my theory," Alyssa replied. "I'll tell Patterson and he'll probably want prints off the vial."

"How is 'Old Diehard'?" Jon asked.

Alyssa watched him pacing slowly around the parking area, talking on his cell phone. "He's in a lot of pain," she answered. "But he's so worried about his mother I could hardly say no to the guy. He's taking quite a bit of Advil, but I think he'll be okay. I guess his dad's a basket case. He's getting ready to meet us back at the station in a few minutes."

"How 'bout your aunt and Noah? How's all that going?"

"Noah hasn't told Aunt Tillie yet," Alyssa answered. "I'm gonna give him some time to straighten things out with her before we spill the beans to the rest of the family."

"Good plan."

From one of the windows in the formal parlor, A.J., Jake, Michael, Laura, Gabriella and Ty watched the authorities with great curiosity.

"Something *huge* is going on," Michael said.

Gabriella nodded. "Something they don't want us to know about yet."

"Like what?" Jake frowned.

Michael shook his head as he said, "I don't know, but look at all of the cops in the parking lot of the fish hatchery."

Everyone squinted through the window for a better look, surprised to see the number of squad cars.

"And look at Papa pace," Gabriella observed as she watched Petrice on the porch. "He only acts like that when he's got something on his mind."

"And Ma`ma is nervous," Michael added, glancing at Ellie on the porch swing with Kate, smiling and visiting in a very animated way.

"She's probably just trying to make Aunt Kate feel better," Laura suggested. "Aunt Kate's been acting worried all night long."

Ty bit his lip. "*Especially* when she found out that Alyssa wasn't coming for dinner."

A.J. frowned. "Somethin's goin' on."

"Somethin' big," Laura agreed.

Shortly before ten o'clock, Alyssa and Jason had to leave for a meeting, but left behind several officers to keep an eye on the grounds around Angel's Place. Petrice and Ellie, along with their children, went back to the hotel and Vincenzo and Kate went for a drive in the hills.

Guiseppi and Rosa were exhausted from the long day's events and fell asleep when their heads hit their pillows. Little Annie started falling asleep while Tillie got her ready for bed, and Ty, A.J., Laura and Jake decided to pray together before they turned in. They were huddled in Laura's room when Tillie came to say goodnight, and she decided not to disturb them. She was more interested in speaking with her exceptionally quiet husband. What in the world had transpired between him and the police?

As Tillie came down the hall, she paused by the paned window facing the west. Marquette and Noah were on the sidewalk outside of the guest house. Marquette gave Noah an embrace and patted his shoulder. Noah nodded his head, turned and headed for the main house. Marquette went into the guest house. Tillie's stomach fluttered with anticipation...*this is it. He's coming to tell me something terrible.* Her stomach lurched.

She went into their room and closed the door. For a few seconds, she paced back and forth by the loveseat by the window, wondering what she had gotten herself into. Obviously, whatever was going on with Noah had something to do with his past, *that* she was certain of. They had *never* discussed his past — it had never seemed important. She knew that he'd been in Vietnam, and like Marquette, he just didn't talk about it. She knew that he'd been a drinker, but that he'd kicked the habit more than twenty years ago. What about *those things* could bring about these current events? And how on earth was Noah's past connected to the lecher that had attended her family reunion?

The door to their bedroom opened and Tillie stopped in her tracks, looking at her husband. He smiled faintly, closing the door.

"Hey," he greeted in his most casual tone.

"Hey."

Noah took a deep breath and went to his nervous wife, reaching for one of her hands. "Can we sit down for a second?" he asked. "There's something I have to tell you."

Tillie gulped as they sat down together on the loveseat.

Noah held her hand and looked into her eyes as he began, "You're all I ever wanted, Angel, and that's the truth. From the time I first saw you at Maggie's until this very moment, I just wanted to share a life with you." He kissed the top of her hand and whispered, "Angel, I gotta tell you something and it's gonna be hard to hear."

Tillie swallowed hard as she looked back into her husband's eyes. "It can't be that bad, Noah," she whispered, though she had started to shake with anticipation.

"It's pretty bad, Angel." He hesitated and began again, "I sorta forgot about it for the last twenty years, but now stuff has started to happen." He took a breath and whispered, "Ty's father was murdered this afternoon."

Tillie gasped in response, searching her husband's expression for an explanation.

Noah continued, "It's all tied together, and I didn't even find out how connected everything was until Marq and I talked earlier. Back in the early seventies, Ole Roy used to keep tabs on Carrie for Jack. She was really wild. Poor Jack couldn't risk her leading his estranged family back to him and his son, Tony."

"His *estranged* family?" Tillie frowned.

"Marq's about ninety-nine percent certain that Carrie's stepfather is actually this Ponerello guy that he's been chasing for thirty years."

Tillie's eyes opened wide. "I remember this!" she gasped. "Marquette has talked about it for years. I was probably only ten or eleven when he started looking for the missing members of that family. He's never been able to nail them down."

"Until now," Noah said. "And I still don't know where he is. The last time I saw Jack was at Carrie's funeral and he told me then that he and Charise were leaving the area. Marq thinks they stayed here. They had been able to hide from this wacky brother of Jack's for quite awhile. He probably just recently tracked them down."

"And how does Roy fit into all of this now?"

"*That's* what I have to tell you," he replied. He hesitated, swallowing hard, drawing every ounce of courage from within himself. "Back in 1975, Marq had a friend named John Peters."

"Yes," Tillie said, nodding with recollection. "I remember John."

"Well, John caught a lead on a man whom he believed to be Mario Ponerello and tracked him to Rapid City," Noah continued. "Marq thinks John must have recognized Roy right away and decided to keep tabs on him. John was following Roy the night he disappeared. Anyway..." Noah took a deep breath, continuing, "Jack thought that John was working for his family back in Sicily and he sent Roy to scare him away, but Roy lost it and slit the guy's throat —"

"What are you saying, Noah?" Tillie gasped.

"Jack and Carrie tried to get him to the hospital, but he died before they could make it and so Jack decided to bury the body —"

"Oh, my Jesus!" Tillie gasped again, putting her hand over her heart as her body began to shake, nausea creeping into her stomach.

Noah felt her trembling as he continued the story in a very quiet voice, "Carrie took me out there once and showed me where they buried the body."

"Noah! Why didn't you ever tell me?!" she spat.

"I didn't tell you, Angel, because I sort of forgot about it."

"*People don't forget things like this!*" Tillie exclaimed with a frown.

"I really did," Noah insisted.

"Is this what you and Marquette and the cops have been talking about all night long?" Tillie demanded.

Noah nodded. "Marq and I and the cops are going out to the location tomorrow so they can dig up the body. Marq thinks that this is what brought Luigi, or whoever he is, into their lives."

Tillie didn't want to ask, but she couldn't seem to help it. "*Where is this place?*" she asked.

"It's that fairly large piece of land down behind the Harney Little League Complex," he answered.

"Oh, brother," Tillie groaned. "What will the owner say?"

"Well, I actually own the land," Noah stammered.

"*You what!*"

"It was for sale when Carrie told me, and so I bought it," Noah explained. "I thought maybe I could keep everything from being disturbed."

Tillie didn't know whether to be angry, afraid or shocked. "And Marquette knows about all of this?" she asked.

"And so do Vincenzo and Petrice and your father," Noah said.

Tillie shook her head disgustedly. "If I didn't love you so much, I'd get up off of this loveseat and punch you in the nose for keeping this from me!" she scolded. " I can't *believe* you didn't tell me!"

Well, she still loves me, Noah thought with relief. "Angel I'm really sorry," he said. "But I think everything's gonna be okay now. They'll grab Luigi, or whoever he is, and everything will be put to rights. I didn't know your brother back then, and Carrie might have gone to jail if I called the cops. She was pregnant with Jake and I was afraid. I had to do whatever I could to protect my family."

Tillie took a deep breath, calming down somewhat as she asked, "Is there anything else that I should know?"

"No, that's about everything. Please forgive me." He gave her one of his lopsided grins, and his eyes danced as he whispered, "Please."

Tillie nodded and smiled with a heavy sigh. "You don't even have to ask."

Vincenzo pulled into the parking lot of the hotel. After they'd talked, prayed and drove for hours, Kate fell asleep in the passenger seat. She was so worried about their daughter, Vincenzo hated to wake her. He got out and went around to Kate's door and quietly opened it. "Wake up, my love," he whispered.

Kate's eyes opened and she looked at her husband. "I'm sorry, I didn't mean to fall asleep," she said.

"We are at the hotel," Vincenzo said. "Let us get you into a soft bed where you can sleep a little more comfortably." He gave her his hand, but it was gone suddenly from hers, and Vincenzo fell to the ground.

"Vincenzo!" she gasped. As she reached for her husband, she suddenly realized that there was someone there with them. Her hair was pulled from behind, and searing pain sent Kate tumbling to the ground beside Vincenzo....

Chapter 17

Petrice awakened with a start, feeling a hand upon his shoulder. "Yes, Ellie," he mumbled in the dark. No response came from his wife's side of the bed so he rolled over to make sure she was still there. Her familiar shape lay next to him, rising and falling to the rhythm of her breathing. "Ellie?" he whispered. Still no reply. Elaine was sleeping deeply. *How odd. I am certain I felt her hand on my shoulder,* he thought. His heart pounded as he felt a wave of goosebumps cover him. *It was just a strange dream.* He attempted to calm himself, but the uneasiness he'd awakened with would not leave him.

He took several deep breaths and closed his eyes, trying to get back to sleep, but something tugged at his very soul. He swung his feet to the floor and padded over to the adjoining room's door where his children were sleeping. Very quietly he opened the door, peeking inside. Michael was sleeping in the bed closest to the door, and Gabriella slept peacefully near the window. Petrice shook his head, closed the door and stood still in the dark silence; his heart pounded.

He slowly crossed his dark room, pausing at the balcony overlooking the parking lot. He slipped between the heavy drapes, and out the sliding glass door. He breathed in the Rapid City night air, gazing into the parking lot below. Petrice squinted in the dark, noticing that someone had left his dome light on. *That looks like Vincenzo's new van,* he thought. *But what is that thing next to it?*

He raced for the door of his suite, his heart thumping. In his panic-stricken determination to reach Vincenzo's van, he neglected to awaken his wife.

In nothing but pajama pants, Senator Caselli sprinted down the corridor. He found the inner stairwell and galloped down the steps two at a time. In only a matter of moments he reached the door at the bottom and tore into the parking lot. He ran as fast as he could until he reached Vincenzo's van and dropped to his knees beside Kate's still body, reaching for her hand. Her skin was already cold.

"Vincenzo!" He cried out in anguish for his brother, but no one answered. "Kate!" Petrice cried again, hearing footsteps behind him.

"What's wrong here?" The security guard asked with authority. He stopped in his tracks when he saw the pool of blood surrounding the body on the ground. He gasped, backing away from Petrice. Reaching for his radio he shouted, "Call the cops!"

"*Aiutilo!*" Petrice cried for help in Italian as he watched the young security guard back away from him.

The security guard shook his head, turned around and ran for the hotel lobby.

Petrice turned his face to the heavens and shouted, "*Si prega Dio di inviare qualcuno che mi aiuti!*" (*Please, God, send someone to help me!*)

"What's going on over here?" a voice behind him questioned. Petrice saw another young man running toward him.

"*Aiutilo!*" Petrice cried again.

As the young man got closer, he recognized the Senator and knelt beside him and Kate. He reached for the pulse point in her neck, only to find a terrible gash where it should have been. He reached instead for her wrist.

"She's still alive, Senator," he whispered.

Petrice cried, "*Dove `e il mio fratello?*" (*Where is my brother?*)

The young man shook his head in confusion, getting to his feet as he said, "Senator, I know you speak English. I'm gonna go in and call an ambulance. Where's your wife?"

Petrice held onto Kate's cold hand, sobbing. The young man ran for the front door, running into the security guard along the way, who had already called for an ambulance and police.

"Keep everyone in the hotel!" the frightened security guard yelled, running through the lobby.

"It's okay, Larry!" the young man shouted, grabbing hold of his arm. "Stop screaming like a lunatic and calm down!"

Larry looked into his shift manager's angry frown, yelling, "What do you mean, Scott?! There's a nut in the parking lot and he's already killed once —"

"Shut up!" Scott yelled, giving Larry's arm a hard shake. "It's Senator Caselli in the parking lot, and I can guarantee that he didn't kill anybody! Now, we gotta get his wife and his brother out of their rooms. They're all on the fifth floor." He turned his eyes toward the nervous desk clerk, shouting, "Look up the Casellis' room numbers and give 'em to Larry!" He looked back at Larry and said, "I'm goin' back out to be with the senator until the ambulance gets here, and you get his wife and his brother."

Larry pulled himself together and trotted toward the desk clerk. Scott took a deep breath and sprinted across the lobby to the parking lot. Petrice was still beside Kate's fallen body, and Scott heard sirens in the distance.

"There's an ambulance on its way," Scott said, dropping to his knees beside Petrice.

"*Lei è l'amata moglie di mio fratello!*" (*She is the beloved wife of my brother!*) Petrice sobbed. "*Potete aiutarli?*" (*Can you help me?*)

Scott took an uneasy breath. "I can't understand you, Senator," he said, putting his hand on Petrice's shoulder.

An older gentlemen rushed to the scene with towels and dropped to his knees beside them. "I'm a doctor, let me help!" he breathed heavily as he packed the towels around Kate's neck and throat.

"*Potete aiutarli?*" Petrice cried, kissing Kate's hand.

"*Non so,*" the doctor answered in Italian, and Scott felt relief.

Petrice let loose with a mournful wail, bowing his head all the way to the pavement.

Elaine heard the insistent knocking on their door. She forced herself from her sleep and sat up in the bed, rubbing her eyes. "What in the world?" she mumbled, and that's when she realized that Petrice's side of the bed was empty. "Patty?!" she called out with alarm. Fumbling for the lamp beside the bed, she called, "Patty?!"

"Mrs. Caselli!" Larry called from the hall. "Mrs. Caselli!"

Her children burst suddenly through the adjoining door.

"Where's Papa?" Michael asked.

"I don't know," Elaine answered, getting out of the bed, struggling into her robe as she hurried to the door. "Who's there?" she asked.

"Hotel security, Ma'am, and there's an emergency."

Elaine opened the door to find the young, disheveled security guard. He panted, "There's been an accident, and you have to come with me." Elaine and her children hurried along with him.

"What's goin' on?" Michael asked.

"Someone was attacked in the parking lot," Larry answered as they took the inner stairwell Petrice had galloped only moments before. "The Senator is with her, but he's not speaking English."

"Who got attacked?" Gabriella asked as they hurried down the steps.

"Some lady," Larry answered. "My boss told me to get the Senator's wife."

Elaine's heart dropped into her stomach...*something's happened to Kate.* They hadn't returned to the hotel by the time Petrice and Elaine went to bed, and Petrice had been *extremely* anxious about it. He had even asked Elaine to pray with him about it before he let her fall asleep.

Within minutes, they came out the door leading into the parking lot. Elaine gasped, sprinted to her husband and knelt beside him and Kate.

Petrice looked into Elaine's eyes and wailed, "*Sta morendo, il mio amore!*" (*She's dying, my love!*)

Elaine put her hand on his shoulder, looking at the crumpled body of her sister-in-law. "Oh, Kate, what happened?" she whispered in anguish.

"We don't know," Scott answered, "and your husband can't tell us."

"He found her like this," the doctor offered. "He says that he's afraid she's dying, and that he can't find his brother...she's not dead yet. Whoever

185

attacked her was interrupted, but I don't think she'll make it. She's lost too much blood."

Michael and Gabriella were not far behind their mother. Suddenly Michael grabbed Gabriella's hand before she could get any closer. He turned her head into his chest, holding her there. "Don't," he whispered. "I can see. It's Kate. She's bleeding...don't look, Gabby."

"What's happening, Michael?" she cried.

"Somethin' bad."

Jon was driving Alyssa down Fifth Street, on their way back to the hotel, when sirens behind them made him pull off to the side of the road. Jon allowed several police cars to scream by them, and when they were safely past, he returned to the driving lane.

"Hey, they're going to the hotel," Jon observed as he drove along. "Wonder what's going on over there tonight."

Alyssa's heart started to pound and for an instant she thought she might throw up. "Jon, please hurry," she said.

"Okay. What's wrong, Alyssa?"

"Something."

The palms of Jon's hands started to sweat as he gave the Taurus a stomp on the gas pedal. They caught up to the police cars, turning in just behind them at Rushmore Plaza Civic Center. Alyssa saw paramedics already loading a body into an ambulance, and her Uncle Petrice sobbing uncontrollably in the arms of his wife.

Alyssa gasped. "It's Ma`ma!"

Jon felt a lump in the pit of his stomach as he rounded the corner into the parking lot and came to an abrupt halt behind several squad cars. He was waving his badge out of his car window, yelling, "United States Marshals!"

Alyssa didn't wait for the barricade to clear. She leaped from the car, waving her badge at anyone that tried to stop her. Her long legs sprinted swiftly to the back of the ambulance.

"I'm her daughter! Let me ride!" she shouted.

The attendant in the back of the ambulance drew Alyssa up by the arm, into the vehicle. The rear doors were slammed, and the ambulance screeched out of the parking lot.

*****

"They're pullin' in the choppers for the night," Jason said, setting a cup of fresh coffee in front of his father. In all of his life, Jason had never seen his father so upset. He took a seat across from Joe.

Joe's eyes were downcast and sullen. "What's happened to her, Jason?" he wondered aloud, rubbing his tired brow.

"He's gonna keep her alive, Dad," Jason assured, with all of the professionalism required of a police officer during an unknown situation. He took a deep breath. "He's taken her hostage and he'll keep her alive. We're gonna hear from him really soon."

Joe nodded, but for the first time in his life Joe had no one else to lean on...*that was Jacq's department.* She comforted and encouraged *him.* Never once had he looked to his son or another human being to figure things out for him.

"Hey, guys," Detective Nichols said, striding toward them with a frown. "You better get up to the hospital ER. Deputy Caselli's mother was attacked in the parking lot of the Civic Center. Somebody tried to slit her throat."

Shaking off their disbelief, Jason and Joe rose from their seats, reaching for the holsters on the table in front of them.

"We'll get right over there," Joe replied, strapping on his holster. He checked his gun. "Her poor husband."

"Her husband is missing," Detective Nichols went on. "Can't find hide nor hair of the ole boy. Deputy Danielson tried to reach you on your cell, Patterson, but you must have turned it off."

Jason reached for the cell phone attached to his belt and moaned. "This thing is out of battery."

"Get it charged up," Detective Nichols snapped. "I gotta feeling you're gonna need it."

The phone beside Noah and Tillie's bed was ringing and ringing. Noah thought it was just part of his dream.

Tillie heard the ringing, and when Noah didn't move, she reached over him, grabbing the receiver. "Hello," she mumbled.

"Angel?" Petrice asked with a shaky voice.

"Patty?" Tillie came to a straight-up seated position in the bed.

"Oh, Angel," he cried, "I am sorry, very sorry to awaken you —"

"What's the matter, Patty?" she demanded, feeling a lump swell in her stomach.

Noah heard Tillie's voice, sat up and turned on the light. He looked at the clock and frowned. It was only two a.m.

"Kate has been brought to the hospital," Petrice explained through mournful tears. "She has been cut very bad, Angel, and our brother is missing —"

Tillie gasped. "*Which* brother?" she whispered. "Is Ellie there with you?"

"Yes, my Ellie is here," Petrice confirmed. "Michael and Gabby are with us as well and we have been praying. It is Vincenzo, Angel. We cannot find him."

"You can't find him?"

Petrice swallowed his tears. "Please send Marquette. Alyssa believes this to be related to the case they are working on. She says that you and Noah and the children should not leave and that Marquette should only come to the hospital with police escort. Please awaken our parents so they might pray for Kate. Angel, she is very bad."

"Okay, Patty," Tillie replied, tears burning her eyes. "I'll do everything I can. Has someone called Angelo?"

"Alyssa called him and he is on his way," Petrice answered. "Pray for Kate and Vincenzo."

"We will," Tillie assured her frightened brother, and they hung up. She looked at Noah. "Vincenzo's missing, and Kate's been taken to surgery for a bad cut." She took a shallow breath as tears rolled down her cheeks. "I imagine that means he slit her throat."

*****

Awaking from a deep sleep, Vincenzo could tell that he was traveling in some kind of a vehicle. His hands and ankles were tightly bound. Despite the sluggishness of whatever drug he'd been given, he attempted to struggle free. He was exhausted in a matter of seconds. As his eyes adjusted to the darkness around him, he realized that he was in the back seat. By the light of the dashboard, Vincenzo saw Luigi behind the wheel. "Luigi? Is that you?" he asked groggily.

"My name is not Luigi."

Vincenzo snorted. "I knew you were not Luigi when we met on Patty's boat. I should have trusted my instincts."

"But you were too polite," Sal replied. "As I knew you would be, and just as your brothers were."

"Salvatore Ponerello."

"So, they have already found my treasure?"

Vincenzo frowned. "They have found no treasure, only a dead man in a hospital bed." He took another breath, trying to clear his mind from the weight of his skull. "Did you drug me?"

Sal laughed, replying, "Barely."

"Why did you take me?"

Sal laughed again. "For the same reason I took the mayor. Your spoiled daughter and the equally spoiled son of the mayor will soon stumble upon a mystery I would rather leave unsolved. However, I am quite certain they will not trade the lives of their parents for the solution to my puzzle."

"My Kate will call my brothers when she realizes that I am missing, and you will be a *sorry devil*."

"My dear Vincenzo," Sal cackled, "by the power of Daedlalus my own father cursed the very ground your brother Marquette has walked upon for the last thirty years. You and your brothers and your wives will all suffer at my hands, for the time has come for me to avenge my family. By now, your Kate has gone home to your Lord. I killed her before I even took you —"

Sal's speech was interrupted by Vincenzo's uproarious laughter. "You fool!" he exclaimed. "Nearly thirty-six years have I shared my body with Kate Martin. She is *not* dead for I did not feel her go."

"She is quite dead, my friend," Sal argued.

"You may have left her for dead, but she is not dead yet." Vincenzo laughed hysterically.

Sal drove along in the dark, *certain* he'd cut deep enough. Her death was instantaneous, and Vincenzo's denial was nothing more than the effects of the drug.

Noah awakened Marquette, who left immediately for the hospital, escorted by the Pennington County Sheriff. Marshal Cameron called in more deputies, stationing them in the parking lot of the fish hatchery, along with local police.

Tillie awakened her parents, explaining the horrible turn of events. Tillie feared for her father's health. *He's too old for all of this anxiety*, she thought, wondering how he would bear up under it. Her mother, on the other hand, appeared to thrive on the intensity of the situation. After they'd prayed together, Rosa worked busily in the kitchen for the remainder of the early morning hours. She baked fresh cinnamon rolls, brewed espresso and steamed milk, while Noah and Guiseppi watched in awe. They sat with Tillie at the kitchen table, where she'd packed her knee in ice after twisting it, *again*, when she got out of bed.

"It's pretty bad this time, Angel," Noah said with a frown, adding a fresh pack. "You gotta stay off that thing today or you're gonna be in trouble with it."

Guiseppi nodded. "I have never seen something swell so much in such a short period of time."

Tillie was amazed as she looked down at her knee, wondering why in the world it was so bad this time. "You'd better get my cane, Noah," she said with a sigh.

At the hospital, Marquette and Petrice led everyone in prayer, including Joe and Jason Patterson. While the Casellis *always* called upon the Lord for help during their trials, this practice was completely foreign to the Pattersons. Alyssa and Angelo wept their prayers in petition for their parents, but Jason and Joe sat quietly until they were finished. They didn't believe in God, much less the saving knowledge of Jesus Christ. However, they weren't about to trample on this grief-stricken family's feelings. They had a right to their beliefs.

Just as they finished, Detective Nichols appeared and took a seat beside Jason in the waiting room. By this time, it was nearly five o'clock in the morning. "How's things goin'?" he asked.

"She's still alive," Jason answered under his breath. "Still in surgery, and we haven't gotten a report in quite a while."

"Do you have anything on our brother's whereabouts?" Marquette asked with a tired sigh.

Detective Nichols shook his head. "I was at the scene up until the time I came over here. We found a man's handkerchief, heavily soaked with what the field agent thinks is chloroform. That's probably how he was able to subdue Mr. Caselli. There's quite a bit of blood on the handkerchief. Forensics is gonna run some tests on that."

"Is Jon running the crime scene?" Alyssa asked.

"Yes, ma'am," Detective Nichols answered with a faint smile. "And I don't think any of us have worked this hard in a long time."

"He's taken Mr. Caselli wherever he's taken my wife," Joe lamented, shaking his tired head. "We've gotta find 'em, boys —" He was interrupted when a doctor walked into the waiting room.

"Dr. Stattler," Petrice acknowledged, and he and his family rose to their feet. "How is our dear Kate?"

Dr. Stattler took a deep breath and answered, "Well, she did arrest during surgery, but we were able to bring her around, and stabilize her. We repaired her vessel and tissue damage, but there's been significant damage to the larynx. It's too soon to tell if it will heal properly, but her esophagus is intact. She's been able to breathe on her own, but she hasn't regained consciousness." Dr. Stattler paused to take another breath. "And I gotta be up front with you...she's lost a lot of blood. Her pressure isn't even close to normal. The next twelve hours will be critical."

Angelo put his arm around his sister and asked, "Can we be with her?"

"Certainly," Dr. Stattler answered. "But only her children for now."

Alyssa and Angelo followed the doctor down the long hall to their mother's room. Neither of them were prepared for what they saw. Their dear mother was lying flat on her back, with a swollen and bruised face. Her neck was completely covered in bandages, and plastic tubing brought oxygen to her nose. One of her arms was bound with more gauze and tubes, while the other lay lifeless on the bed sheets. Her usually dark skin had a strange, yellowish tinge, and her lips were ashen.

"Ma`ma!" Alyssa gasped in a whisper as she dropped to her knees beside her mother's bed. Angelo knelt beside his sister, and they began to pray.

Marquette put a hand on his brother's shoulder, gripping it firmly as he said, "We must pray, Patty."

"But what if he has done this thing to our brother?" Petrice whispered.

"He will keep Vincenzo alive," Marquette answered. He took a breath, looking at Joe Patterson and his son, offering them a faint smile. "Just as he will keep your Jacqueline alive. He needs them for something, and it is only a matter of time before we figure it out."

Jason slowly nodded. "It's amazing to me this case that's been driving me crazy for months now is related to a case of yours," he mumbled.

Marquette replied, "It is not amazing at all to me, my young friend. Emmanuel has put us together so that we might figure this thing out."

Joe frowned. He'd been around grief-stricken families before and he didn't want this thing getting out of control. Caselli was probably getting ready to drop to his knees in front of everyone and speak in tongues. "Pull yourself together, Mr. Caselli. We don't have time for that nonsense."

Marquette faintly smiled at the tense man, while the rest of his family waited politely for him to continue. More than Marquette loved his job, he loved to share the Gospel. His black eyes shined with delight and his voice was gentle as he began, "I have prayed for this opportunity for more than half my life. It is finally upon me, and I want to share it with the rest of the world."

"What opportunity?" Jason asked. He was just about ready to bolt for the nearest exit. He'd been with Christian people during traumatic events as well, and had always been a gut-wrenching experience. They wailed and prayed like nobody's business, and he didn't want to stick around for a session of *that*.

Detective Nichols watched the scene with amusement. He was a Christian and he understood. The prayers Mr. Caselli referred to were obviously those regarding his old and unsolved Ponerello case. He smiled, waiting patiently for Marquette to continue.

Marquette took in a breath and began again, "You see, my friends, I was so stumped on this case in August of 1968. My colleague John Peters and I went to *Sicilia* in pursuit of diamond thieves. We found, instead, the greatest mystery of a lifetime. However, Emmanuel intervened and sent me on the trail of my beloved wife, Tara. John and I broke off our search for the Ponerellos in order to find Tara. The trail of the Ponerellos was lost, and I have prayed since then for God to show me where they are."

"Allow me to explain, Marquette," Petrice quietly interjected. "*Emmanuel* means *God with us*, and He is with us as we speak. We gathered in this small waiting room while we wait for Kate, and we gathered in His Name. He promises that wherever two or more are gathered in His Name, He is there with us."

Joe rolled his eyes. "And what on earth does that have to do with our situation?" he grumbled, rising to his feet, and his son followed. "I've got work to do."

"Please wait," Marquette said with a smile. "Before you continue on this adventure, I am prompted to share something with you."

Joe sighed. He'd heard the *Salvation Message* about a million times. "Hurry it up, Caselli, I gotta find my wife," he barked. "I know the basics of the thing. Jesus was born, died on a cross to forgive my sins, and was raised on the third day. It's the most sadistic story I've ever heard, so give me some kind of an abbreviated version."

Marquette was hardly surprised for he'd been snubbed by the best of men. "Very well, then, Detectives, an abbreviated version," he continued. "Well, since you are already aware that Jesus died for our sins, you must also be aware that *you must ask for forgiveness of those sins*." He mysteriously raised his brow. "I note your exclusion of the *Comforter*. Do you have a particular reason for that?" There were heavy sighs from the Patterson's, and a moment of silence. Marquette went on, "The *Comforter* comes after Jesus leaves his disciples for the last time, and that is the Holy Spirit. It is the Holy Spirit that dwells within a Christian, and He only comes into that person when he or she submits to the forgiveness of the Lord, Jesus. It is the Comforter that is with us when we are troubled and when we need to make decisions. The Comforter speaks to the Father for us, when we have no words."

Petrice politely added, "The Comforter holds us while we wait for

Kate and my brother and your dearest wife and mother. You see, we know that whatever happens to Kate and Vincenzo, they will be safe with our Lord. Even though we shed tears and we worry, in our hearts we know the Truth. You do yourselves a dreadful disservice by denying yourselves the comfort only the Holy Spirit can give."

There was another long moment of silence, until Joe sighed and spoke in a more friendly tone, "Listen, guys, I know what you're sayin', but we been livin' like this for a long time and the only thing that's ever gotten us outa tight spots is our wits and common sense. Emmanuel didn't lead us together to solve a thirty-year-old crime, and He's not gonna lead us to my wife. We have to put our marbles and our common sense together —"

At that moment, Deputy Danielson dashed down the hall, stopping just in front of Marquette. "Judge Mitchell just called," he panted. "He's sighed a warrant to enter Charise Nelson's residence on suspicion of harboring illegal aliens."

"And that's what *I'm* talkin' about," Joe quipped. He looked at his son, asking, "What time is it?"

"Six o'clock, a.m."

"How long to get a team together?" Joe questioned.

"About an hour."

"I've already got a team on stand-by," Jon informed. "All we need is backup and the paddy wagon."

*****

Tara sprinted to the designated helipad at *Amerigo Vespucci Airport* in *Firenze, Italia.* She'd made several phone calls while in the air, but had not been able to reach Marquette. It was already two o'clock in the afternoon in *Chianti,* and Tara was exhausted. She'd been awake for the better part of twenty-four hours and her patience was wearing thin. The delays in New York had put her schedule significantly behind. She should have had this information to Marquette by now.

Jonathon pulled her up into the helicopter, and she took her seat. As she reached for her headpiece she said, "Acquiring your license to fly this thing is the best idea you have ever had."

"Thank you, Signora Caselli," Jonathon acknowledged, preparing for takeoff. "However, it was Signor Caselli who thought of it."

Chapter 18

Dawn broke over the beautiful Black Hills, spilling into the valley below Angel's Place. Tillie sipped at her coffee, watching God's creation come to life from the window of her studio. *And if you can do all this Father*, she prayed, *You can straighten out the mess in our family*. She caught the heavy smell of cinnamon from the kitchen, inhaling it deeply. She bit her lip as she glanced down at the purple and swollen joint, wondering why, after all these years, her knee had started to act up now.

"How ya feelin', Angel?" Noah asked from the doorway of her studio.

Tillie turned her head in surprise. "Like I could use a nap," she answered with a faint smile. "How 'bout you?"

"Guilty." Noah moaned as he strode to where his wife was seated, sitting down beside her.

Tillie looked confused. "Why?"

"Because there's a maniac running around slitting everybody's throats and I could have had him put away years ago."

Tillie rolled her eyes as she replied, "If my brother Marquette couldn't nail him down, what makes you think you could have? Good grief, Noah, you've probably saved a lot of lives, including the lives of your sons." She sighed and asked, "Did you talk to Ty?"

Noah nodded. "I told him just a few minutes ago. I just said that Roy passed away during the night…I didn't tell him about the murder or anything like that. Ty told me that he prayed with Roy when he was up to see him last night." He sighed, shaking his head. "I guess the old blackguard took Jesus for his Savior, so he's in with the rest of us now."

Tillie took a deep breath, tenderly reaching for Noah's hand. "I love you, Noah."

Noah tried to smile as he said, "Thanks, Angel. You're a great gal."

"Thanks."

"Josh offered to do a little funeral when they're done with the autopsy," Noah continued. "And he's on his way over to the hospital. He and

Mona are gonna stay with Petrice and Kate and everybody, and Marquette's gonna bring Ellie over to help you a little bit while I go with 'em over to the…" Noah hesitated to swallow, and finished, "you know, the burial site. That way, your parents can go be with Kate and you don't have to be left alone."

"But the kids will be here," Tillie pointed out.

"I know, but I want you to be with another adult. Federal forensics is gonna meet us over there, and then we'll pick up a package at the airport. Marquette's liaison, or whatever she's called, overnighted his Ponerello file from D.C. He thinks Jack's picture will be in there and hopefully I'll be able to identify him."

Tillie nodded. "I'll pray for you all day."

"Thanks, I'm gonna need it."

Marquette and Ellie left the hospital shortly after Joe Patterson and Detective Nichols left to question Charise Nelson. Joshua and Mona were with Kate, who was still unconscious, and Petrice and his children dozed in the uncomfortable waiting room chairs. Angelo and Alyssa had been with their mother since the doctor led them to her room, and were relieved to see Pastor Hansen and his wife allowed to be with them.

Alyssa's guilt was tremendous. The last words she'd had with her mother were not friendly. *All Ma`ma wanted was for her daughter to marry and raise babies. Is that such a bad thing?* Alyssa was convinced it wasn't, and she expressed her regrets to Pastor Hansen and his wife.

Angelo was beside himself with guilt and regret as well. He hadn't gotten along with his father since his birthday in New York. However, he couldn't get out of what he'd done now, and his hitch with the Air Force would not conclude until April of 2003.

"We never know what's coming around that corner next," Joshua said with a smile. "You know, I lost my parents when I was about your age — actually a little younger. I was twenty-four years old, and Noah was only four. Mona and me didn't know what we were gonna do. Dad and I *never* saw eye to eye, especially about the ministry, and when he died he wasn't a Christian. I don't regret preaching the Gospel to him, but I regret the manner in which I delivered it. I was haughty because I knew I was going to heaven and Dad wasn't. He was wrong, and he was going to find out some day. In fact, I even told him that the week before he died." He paused to swallow his tears as he looked at Kate and Vincenzo's children. "Sometimes our folks *are wrong*, but we still have to be kind."

"Papa's not wrong about wanting me home," Angelo whispered.

"And Ma`ma's not wrong about wanting me to have a family," Alyssa cried.

"Then let's pray about this," Mona said, taking each of their hands into her own.

*****

After they'd prayed together, Alyssa offered to get them all some coffee. She went to the machine in the waiting room. To her surprise, Jason was still there, fumbling with the coffee pot with his good arm.

"Here, let me help you," Alyssa offered, taking hold of the pot and filling his Styrofoam cup. She looked at the blood-encrusted bandage on his bicep and shoulder. "You need stitches…before it's too late."

"Maybe," Jason replied, taking a sip from his cup. "How's your mom?"

"She's still alive. By the way, where is everybody?"

"Your uncle Marquette took the Senator's wife over to your aunt's house. My dad and your partner went over to see if they can get into Charise Nelson's house." Jason rolled his eyes and shook his head. "I can't imagine what they think they're gonna find over there."

Alyssa glanced at her sleeping uncle and cousins. "I can't believe they stayed all night. They're so awesome."

"Your whole family is amazing, Alyssa," Jason said. "And they even had time to lecture us on the finer points of Christianity before they passed out."

Alyssa had to smile. As long as she'd known the Casellis, and that had been all of her life, they'd never resisted an opportunity to talk about salvation. She looked questioningly at Jason, asking, "Why are you still here?"

He took a deep breath, whispering, "Listen, I got an idea, but I'm gonna need some Advil and a little help."

*****

"They are denying me permission to land," Jonathon informed Tara as they hovered above the helipad at Andreotti Vineyards & Winery.

"Tell them it is a life and death emergency," Tara instructed.

Jonathon relayed the message to the Andreotti controller, waited politely for a reply, and said, "They have requested we leave the area immediately or police will be dispatched forthwith."

Tara growled. "Tell them I have news from Luigi and I must speak with them at once."

Jonathon raised a suspicious brow, but again conveyed her message. There was a long moment of silence before a response finally came. Jonathon politely acknowledged, "Thank you, sir, we shall land in the designated area." He glanced at Tara. "They will allow us to land now."

As the blades were turned off and began to slow, several men and a woman came from the building attached to the helipad. Tara looked at the forming crowd with nervous apprehension. Judging by expressions, they were significantly distressed, which made her wonder what kind of a situation she was stepping into. Jonathon left his seat, opened the door of the helicopter and stepped onto the pavement. Tara rose from her seat and Jonathon helped her to the ground.

"Stay here," she instructed, "but be ready to leave in an instant."

"*Si, Signora.*"

Tara walked quickly to the small crowd waiting for her near the doorway of the building.

The woman held up her hand, frowning as she said, "Come no closer. Are you Tara D'Annencci, and what news do you have from Luigi?"

Tara stopped in her tracks, answering, "I am Tara D'Annencci Caselli. I saw Luigi only a few days ago in America."

The woman drew in a sharp breath, bringing her hand to her chest. Her skin was gray and wrinkled, her silver hair drawn back in a tight knot at the base of her skull. A man beside her put his arm comfortingly over her shoulders, and Tara recognized something familiar in his black eyes. She squinted, focusing on his expression.

"Pietro?" she whispered, holding her breath. Luigi's brother-in-law was *old* — much older than he should have been. His hair was white, as were the bushy eyebrows upon his dark face. His eyes were heavily lined with grief, his body stooped with age.

Pietro slowly nodded. "You have barely changed, Tara," he said.

"Why have you come here?" The woman demanded angrily.

Tara's attention was drawn to back to her. "Marsala?" she whispered in disbelief. Luigi's younger sister was beautiful when Tara left Italy in 1956, but time had drastically changed her appearance.

A commotion behind the door turned their heads, and an extremely elderly man and woman shuffled through the crowd.

"Is it Tara?" the old man asked, he and his wife hobbling toward her. He reached for her hand, smiling into her eyes. "Is it really you, Tara?"

Tara hesitantly nodded. "Signor Andreotti?"

Luigi's parents smiled, nodding their heads as tears sprang from their eyes. Lorenzo, Luigi's father, squeezed Tara's hand. "Your father would be so proud of you."

"What is this news of Luigi?" Marsala barked in interruption.

Luigi's mother, Marie, gasped, whispering, "What news would you have of Luigi?"

Tara took a breath, explaining, "Marquette and I have happened upon a case and we think someone is pretending to be your son, Luigi. Do you know where Luigi is at this time?"

The Andreottis' eyes filled with tears as they nodded.

Lorenzo put his arm around his wife, whispering, "Our Luigi has been gone for nearly fifteen years, Tara. He was killed in a fire at the winery." He broke into quiet sobs as he held his wife.

Tara caught her breath, apologizing, "I am so sorry. I had no idea."

"He was *not* the blackguard you thought him to be," Marsala scolded. "He saved all of us that day, Tara. When he went back in for a slow servant, he gave his life so that the servant's could be spared."

Lorenzo and Marie nodded, tears flowing from their eyes.

"He was always sorry for what he had done to you and Marquette," Pietro went on, holding his wife. "He did not mean any harm, he only wanted to obey to his father."

"He was a good man!" Marsala barked through her tears. "And he *loved* you, Tara —"

"Do not hold this thing against Tara any longer," Lorenzo softly snapped at his daughter. "She did what she felt was right at the time, as did Luigi." He looked into Tara's eyes, asking, "Will this information help you?"

"I do not know," Tara answered, "but I promise that my family will know of Luigi's sacrifice —"

"Please forgive us," Marie whispered. "We are so very sorry."

Tara's eyes filled with tears as she looked at the tiny people before her. This man had been her father's best friend — they'd fought side by side in a war against a dictator more than fifty years ago. How could she possibly refuse? "You are completely forgiven," she replied. "Please, regret the thing no more, because I do not."

*****

"This is the mayor of Rapid City," Sal introduced, pulling off Vincenzo's blindfold, pushing him into a chair across from a woman.

Vincenzo smiled and said, "How have you been, Mrs. Patterson?"

Jacqueline frowned and looked confused.

"You are the delightful woman who defended my sister during her… her…um…unfortunate marital mishap," Vincenzo explained. "Do you remember me now?"

Jacqueline nodded and politely returned his smile. If circumstances had been different, Jacqueline would have had a good laugh. *Marital mishap? That's rich.* "It's good to see you again, Mr. Caselli," she said.

"Well is that not just the nicest thing of me?" Sal crowed, making sure that Vincenzo's bounds were secure. "I am glad to know at least you will have the old times to catch up on. Now," he said, taking a breath as he went for the door. "I have one more piece of bait to collect, but I shall be back shortly." He bowed slightly as he left through the door, locking it behind him.

"Jason is your boy?" Vincenzo asked.

Jacqueline nodded with a frown. "How did you know that?"

"He was at the home of my sister last evening," Vincenzo answered. He smiled and made a "tsk" noise as he rolled his eyes. "There are several dreadful things afoot in Rapid City, South Dakota, Madame Mayor, and your Jason is working with my Alyssa to solve a grand mystery."

Jacqueline raised her eyebrows and said, "Well, we've got some time on our hands. Why don'tcha fill me in?"

Deputy Danielson was surprised, to say the least, when he and his team pulled into the yard at Rapid Valley Quarter Horses. Charise Nelson and her mother were on the front porch, drinking coffee as if they had not a care in the world. Jon hesitated in the car, while the rest of his team took their positions.

"Okay, don't anybody approach. I'll go up first," he said into his radio. He took a thoughtful breath, glancing at Joe Patterson, who was seated in the passenger seat. "The two of them don't look like they have many worries today."

"I hope we're not walking into an ambush," Joe said with a frown.

Della cheerfully waved from her wheelchair, but Charise didn't move at all.

Jon glanced at Joe questioningly, speaking into his radio again, "Keep your eyes peeled and your weapons drawn."

They got out of the car, slowly approached the porch and ascended the steps together.

"Charise Nelson?" Jon asked, opening his badge for identification.

"Yes," she answered.

"United States Deputy Marshal Danielson," he introduced. "This is Detective Joe Patterson from the Rapid City Police Department." He glanced at Della. "Della Nelson I presume?"

Della chuckled. "You know me! Don't you remember?"

Jon was embarrassed, but he quickly recovered, saying, "We have some questions for the two of you. First of all, do either of you know anything of the whereabouts of Antonio Ponerello or Mario Ponerello?"

"We do not," Charise answered.

"How about Luigi Andreotti?" Joe questioned. "Your step-son, Antonio, has been meeting with Mr. Andreotti for several months now. Were you aware of this?"

Della shook her head in confusion, and Charise quickly answered, "We don't know anybody by the name of Luigi Andreotti."

Jon pulled the judge's warrant from the inner breast pocket of his jacket and handed it to Charise, explaining, "I've got a warrant that says we can enter and search your home."

"Be my guest," Charise replied, taking a deliberate sip of her coffee. She lifted her mug into the air, saying, "Make sure you grab yourself a cup on your way through. It's kinda early."

"Are they here, Ma'am?" Joe kindly asked.

Charise shook her head. "And I don't expect to ever see them again."

"Do you have any idea where they went?" Jon questioned.

"Not a clue," Charise answered.

Jon decided to try a threat. "Aiding and abetting illegal aliens is against the law and you could go to jail for that," he said.

Charise maintained her stone-face as she replied, "Why don't you just round up your boys and check the place out then? If you're planning to arrest me, you'd better get yourself some proof together."

Jon took a quiet breath, collecting his thoughts. He had no idea they'd be so cooperative. He bit his lip, turning on the porch and summoning the senior officer of the team. "Go ahead and have the guys check the house and outlying buildings," he commanded.

"Yes, sir," the officer replied, leaving the porch to collect his team.

Jon looked back at Della and asked, "Mrs. Nelson, did you help to fake your own death?"

"Yes, I believe so," Della answered, and Jon noticed Charise's mouth fall open in surprise.

"You did?" Joe asked, raising his eyebrow.

"Well," Della sighed with a smile. "It was only to get away from Sal."

"Salvatore Ponerello?" Jon asked.

"He's Jack's brother," Della kindly informed.

Charise's eyes were as big as saucers.

"You mean Mario?" Jon questioned further.

"Now we're getting somewhere," Joe commented, taking a small notebook from his shirt pocket, scribbling notes as fast as he could.

"Well, I never called him Mario," Della went on. "He always wanted to be called Jack."

"I see," Jon said, looking to Charise for further comment. "Ms. Nelson, have you seen your father recently."

"No," she answered.

Dead silence followed, as the two women looked back at their interrogators. Charise appeared to be fairly frightened, and Jon felt sorry for her. Her mother, on the other hand, seemed happy and jovial about the whole episode — as if she were *pleased* to have company on the front porch.

Joe touched Jon's sleeve, pulling him back a few steps. "So, are you gonna haul 'em in or what?" he whispered.

"What for?" Jon asked with a frown. "Della's too nuts to take into custody. Charise won't leave her here, and she won't move her again so soon. We can set up a watch from the road. Maybe Antonio and Mario will be back."

Joe slowly nodded his head. "Agreed."

The Ponerellos were not located anywhere on the small ranch, and Joe and Jon dismissed their men. They put two agents on the road at the entrance of the ranch, leaving Charise and Della to finish their coffee on the porch.

"They probably know something," Jon said as they drove away.

Joe shook his head as he replied, "I don't know, Deputy. I don't think those two women know anything right now."

*****

Angelo awakened with a start, feeling the early morning sun warm upon his face. He looked around the hospital room, reorienting himself. His beloved mother was still sleeping peacefully in her bed, but Pastor Hansen and his wife were nowhere to be seen.

Angelo yawned, scratched his head and remembered that Pastor Hansen and his wife had gone to check on Alyssa and that coffee she'd promised. He must have fallen asleep. He stood and went to his mother's side. He carefully took her hand into his own and whispered, "Even if you should leave us, you will still have the victory." He softly kissed her hand and laid it back on the sheets. He sighed heavily and left the room.

199

When Angelo came into the waiting room, he found his Uncle Petrice, along with Michael and Gabriella, visiting with Deputy Danielson and Joe Patterson. Pastor and Mrs. Hansen were with them. Everyone was wearing a frown. They looked at Angelo when he came into the small room.

"Where is your sister, Angelo?" Petrice questioned.

Angelo shrugged. "Beats me," he answered, "I thought she was gonna bring us some coffee."

Petrice's brow was knit with confusion. "It seems she has slipped away with the young Detective Patterson," he said.

"While we slept," Michael added disgustedly.

"*Slipped* away?" Angelo asked, raising a black brow.

"She was long gone by the time Josh and I came out to check on her," Mona answered.

"And Patterson's in no shape for backup," Jon dryly commented. He was already assuming that Jason and Alyssa had conjured up some plan to take out the elusive Luigi/Sal figure, not bothering to wait around for help.

"I can't reach him on his cell," Joe said, turning off his phone. "We told that kid to get the battery charged."

"How 'bout Alyssa's cell," Angelo suggested.

"You mean this one?" Petrice retorted, holding up the cell phone he'd found discarded beside the coffee machine.

Jon tightly pursed his lips together. She'd done that deliberately. There was no telling now what would become of Salvatore Ponerello.

When Marquette arrived at Angel's Place with Elaine, Guiseppi and Rosa took a police escort back to the hospital to be with Kate. Tillie called Sam and Becky-Lynn to tell them what had happened to Kate during the night, and they promised to be in Rapid City as soon as they could.

Patrol cars were still in the fish hatchery's parking lot, and everything seemed to be under control for the moment, but Noah had the strangest feeling about leaving his family. Tillie's knee was increasingly swollen, forcing her to use her cane to get around.

"There are armed police walking the premises," Marquette encouraged his brother-in-law. "Everyone will be quite safe. Besides, we need you at the site in order to find the precise location. Whoever has gone to these lengths to capture the mayor of Rapid City and my brother, I believe has a dreadful secret hiding in that old grave —"

Marquette was cut off when the telephone rang, and Noah reached for it, "Hansens'."

"Oh, Noah!" Tara gasped into the phone. "May I please speak with my Marquette?"

"Sure." Noah handed the phone to Marquette. "It's Tara."

"My love, what have you found?" Marquette asked.

"That man is *not* Luigi Andreotti!" she exclaimed, swallowing away her emotions to continue as rationally as possible. "Luigi was killed in a fire at the winery nearly fifteen years ago, *not his family!* In fact, Luigi gave his life so that a servant might live. I have visited with his entire family. This man calling himself Luigi must be either Mario or Salvatore —"

"He is too young to be Mario," Marquette objected. "But you watched Salvatore take his own life. How can it be Salvatore?"

"I do not know," Marquette said, taking a deep breath. "Where are you now, my love?"

"I am on a charter en route to Paris." Tara answered. "Have you exhumed the body yet?"

"We were just on our way," Marquette said, hesitating for a moment. "My Tara, there is something you need to pray about while you are on your way. My brother, Vincenzo, is missing. It is believed that the person we know as Luigi has taken him."

"Oh my goodness! How long has he been gone?"

"Sometime after midnight," Marquette answered. "And Lovely Kate has been cut. She did survive, but she is still in the Intensive Care Unit."

"Oh, Marquette, how are her children?"

"Angelo is with Kate, and he is holding up rather well. However, Alyssa has slipped away with Detective Patterson. I am quite certain they share a vengeful spirit. One can only imagine what they are up to. How long before you return to Rapid City?"

"I do not know. We will land in Paris in ninety minutes, but I will have to secure another flight from there."

"We will pray for you."

"I love you, Marquette." Tara began to cry into the phone. "I will be so happy when this last adventure is over. I want nothing more than to retire and spend the rest of my life in your arms."

Marquette smiled at his wife's words, whispering, "I love you my Tara and I will pray for you each moment you are away from me." He took an excited breath, adding, "Our oldest mystery is nearly solved, my love. It will not be long and we will have laid to rest the grandest puzzle of our lives."

Tara nodded on the other end, wiping away the emotion trickling down her cheeks.

Marquette heard her sniffing and he smiled as he said, "My love, try to nap on all of these flights. You will be of no use to me if you come to Rapid City exhausted."

"Yes, my love," Tara agreed with another sniff. "I must hang up now. Goodbye."

"Goodbye." Marquette hung up the phone with a smile. He looked at Noah and raised his eyebrow. "Luigi Andreotti has been dead for nearly fifteen years. This imposter I believe to be a Ponerello. Let us go now, Noah, so that we may solve this nightmare before it gets worse."

Upstairs in Laura's room, and just above the kitchen, was a heat duct. Laura lay on the floor with her ear pressed to the vent, listening to what transpired below. *An imposter? That scary, old Mr. Andreotti? Is that what*

201

they were talking about? When Laura heard footsteps leave the house and the front door close, she knew the *good stuff* was over. She sat up, leaning against the wall. *Ty's father was murdered last night* — that much she knew to be an absolute. Aunt Kate had been *cut*, and Uncle Vincenzo was missing. Then there was the matter of *the burial site*, and Noah had to give Uncle Marquette and the Feds its *precise* location. *How in the world does Noah happen to have that kind of information?* Laura's black eyes flew open with sudden amazement. *He's some kind of spy!*

She reached for the notebook and pencil under the bed, reviewing her notes. There were sketchy things here and there that she hadn't been able to fill in, and was hesitant to question her stepbrothers about. For instance: *Is Della Nelson Noah's first mother-in-law? If so, didn't she die many years ago? Even before Ty and Jake's mom died? How could the cops have questioned her that very morning if she's dead? Also, why didn't Noah know that she was still alive, and why does everyone keep asking about Ben? Are they talking about Ben Simmons? What does he have to do with all of this? Is he friends with Mr. Andreotti, and is Mr. Andreotti actually one of Uncle Marquette's elusive Ponerellos?*

Laura sighed heavily as she looked at her notes. *Something strange is afoot in the Hansen household and those boys are just going to have to tell me what it is!*

Chapter 19

"I think we got somethin' here," a Federal forensics specialist murmured to his partner as they brushed dirt away from a protruding object. His partner nodded, reaching over to clear away the excess dirt with another soft brush. Wire-rimmed spectacles with cracked lenses rested on what appeared to be part of a skull.

Noah swallowed to keep from getting sick to his stomach.

"John wore similar spectacles," Marquette said.

"The skeleton seems to be fully intact," the specialist confirmed as they continued to carefully dig away at the earth.

"What's that?" Deputy Danielson asked, frowning as he squatted next to the grave, pointing to another protrusion.

"I can't tell," the specialist answered. He took a plastic bag, gently pulling the protrusion from the side of the grave. As the object came into view, they saw that it was a knife with a very large, ornate handle. Most of the handle was packed with hard dirt, and the long blade was rusted and blackened in spots.

Marquette raised his eyebrows. "May I see that?" he asked.

The specialist looked to Jon for permission, and he nodded.

"Try not to touch it with your hands," the specialist said, handing the knife to Marquette.

Marquette took the knife in his hand, careful to keep the bag around the handle. He smiled with recognition.

"What is it?" Noah asked, watching Marquette's expression.

"That, my brother, is *Il Dagger Del Dinastia*," Marquette answered. "*The Dynasty's Dagger*."

"What's the *Dynasty*?" Noah asked.

"I remember this," Jon murmured. "*Dinastia* was the only case you ever left open, at least the only case the public knows about. Alyssa told me about this."

"Once an obsession of mine," Marquette admitted, looking intently at the dagger in his hand. "I was called to *Sicilia* to investigate a diamond robbery in 1968 and uncovered one of the biggest Mafia families their country had ever known. By the time we arrived, however, we learned that two of the members had escaped four years prior. I was never able to catch up to them." He pointed to the dirt-encrusted symbol on the handle of the dagger. "This marking will identify the Ponerello family. They put their family shield and patriarchal symbol on each handle — some said that you would be dead before you realized that you had been cut. I suspected it was a Ponerello doing the cutting, but our Luigi imposter is too young. Mario would be nearly eighty years of age by now, if he is even still alive, and far too old to be doing the cutting. As outlandish as it appears, I must suspect the Elder Son, Salvatore, at this point, though I believed to have watched him take his own life the day we imprisoned the entire Ponerello family. Our imposter *must* be Salvatore."

"What's he want with the Casellis?" Jon questioned.

"His father cursed me before I left *Sicilia*," Marquette answered with a grim expression. "It could be that Salvatore survived his suicide attempt and has now decided to take revenge. His aged father died in prison about ten years ago, and the rest of the family passed on shortly thereafter. If the three missing Ponerellos are still alive, they are the *only* members of that family that are left."

"And you think my first father-in-law — Carrie's stepfather — was a Ponerello?" Noah asked.

"I believe it," Marquette acknowledged. "Did you know of any strange religious practices, Noah? Do you remember?"

Noah nodded. "I remember Carrie telling me about Jack's faith in this Greek god, or something like that."

"The Ponerellos were pagan," Marquette explained. "They built their lives and faith around the Greek myth of Daedalus. Daedalus was an inventor and builder of sorts who killed his young worker, Talos. Daedalus then left Greece for the island of Crete. There he built the Minotaur's Labyrinth. King Minos would not allow him to leave. So, Daedalus fashioned himself and his son, Icarus, wings of wax and feathers. Supposedly, they attempted to fly away together. Icarus flew too close to the sun and his wings melted and he fell to his death. Daedalus, however, escaped to *Sicilia*, where he changed his name to Ponerello, and planned his revenge. When we imprisoned Salvatore Ponerello, Sr., he vowed to fly on the wings of Daedalus from his prison and take revenge for the death of his son. Poor Salvatore never flew from the prison where he died." He looked into the shallow grave and the skeleton that was taking shape, shaking his head with remorse. "I think this will be my associate, John Peters, who has been missing since 1975. Schneider Rauwolf confessed to the murder, but said that he did not know where the body was buried." Marquette thoughtfully rubbed his chin, frowning as he said, "It is quite unusual they left the dagger behind. Daggers were never left behind, unless they had been used to spill innocent blood...*or* if the Ponerellos wanted to flaunt power...and it would be difficult to flaunt power from a grave."

"Salvatore must have tried to get close to you and your brothers in order to take revenge," Jon said.

"That is the part I do not understand," Marquette replied. "It almost seems to me that Salvatore was trying to get close to Noah, perhaps in order to find this missing dagger."

"Why would he want it?" Jon asked.

"That, my friend, is an excellent question," Marquette answered. "Perhaps we will learn more when forensics is done with their examination, and I have retrieved my file from the airport."

*****

"How will you get all of the way to Angel's Place without being caught?" Charise whispered. During the brief search of their home and grounds, Antonio had hidden in a tunnel beneath the barn — something their father had designed several years ago — just for that purpose.

"I can make it," Antonio insisted. "I have vowed to protect them, and Sal will hit there next."

"Maybe not," Charise disagreed. "They left two Marshals by the road, and you can't go out on foot…you'll never make it."

"Charise, I *have* to make it. You will be safe because Sal does not know of your existence. Noah's family, on the other hand, is at risk and it is my job to protect them. You know this to be true and you must allow me to be a man. We all knew this could happen someday."

Charise clenched her teeth together, fighting the urge to beg her brother not to go. He was right, of course, and she *had* to allow him to fulfill his vow.

*****

"Come on, kiddo," Tillie gently coaxed the baby. "It's way past your naptime and somebody might as well get some sleep around here." She tried to pick up the child, but Annie squirmed to get away.

"No!" the baby screamed in a shrill voice.

Tillie frowned, wanting to give the little stinker a spanking. As she bent over to pick up the child again, her knee gave way, and she tripped. She caught her balance on the hallway wall, steadying herself. She frowned at her precious baby again, watching as the little devil slowly backed away. As Tillie began to limp after the child, she felt a friendly hand upon her shoulder.

"Let me take her," Ty offered. "Aunt Ellie was going to come up when she heard Annie giving you a hard time, but I volunteered. Do you think you can get downstairs okay?"

"I'll be fine," Tillie answered, relieved that he was taking over. "Are you sure you wanna wrestle with her? She's really a little grouch this morning."

"I'm sure," Ty said with a smile. "I can get her settled down, and you need to get some ice on that." He bent over his little sister, and Annie went into his arms without hesitation. She cuddled close to his chest, giving him the sweetest kiss on his chin. Tillie frowned and headed for the stairs.

Ty chuckled, snuggling the baby in his arms. "You're a little devil to do that to Ma`ma," he said. "She has a bad owie on her knee."

In response, Annie snuggled him closer, laying her head on his chest. As Ty walked toward her room, A.J. and Jake's bedroom door opened, and they, along with Laura, quietly stepped into the hall.

"Where's Mom?" A.J. whispered.

"She went downstairs," Ty answered.

Jake's eyes were suspicious. "We gotta talk. What are you doing?" he asked.

"I'm gonna rock Annie to sleep," he answered with a curious expression. "What's going on?" He continued toward Annie's room, the three teenagers following.

"Laura's made some pretty peculiar observations," A.J. whispered. "She's been eavesdropping —"

"Eavesdropping?" Ty whispered.

Jake nodded. "Her room is right above the kitchen and she can hear almost everything through the vent —"

"You shouldn't be doing that," Ty quietly scolded as they went into Annie's room. He sat down in the rocking chair.

"Listen," Laura said, closing the door, taking a seat on the floor with A.J. and Jake. "Do you wanna hear some really good stuff, or not?"

While Petrice paced nervously in the hallway outside of the waiting room at Rapid City Regional Hospital, Michael and Gabriella played a quiet game of chess. Guiseppi and Rosa had arrived, and they were allowed into Kate's room to be with Angelo. No one had heard from Alyssa or Detective Patterson, and Marquette had yet to contact them with any additional information. Pastor Hansen was allowed in and out of Kate's room, but only if Guiseppi and Rosa left. Petrice and his children requested to see Kate, but the doctor wouldn't allow it. He promised if Mrs. Caselli showed any improvement by that afternoon, perhaps they could see her for a short time. However, she was still unconscious, her vitals were exceptionally low and erratic, and her condition remained unstable. Only her immediate family, her son and her husband's parents, were allowed in the room. The only exception would be the pastor.

"Poor Papa," Michael whispered to his sister as they watched him pace past the doorway. "He's a nervous wreck."

Gabriella watched her father pass the doorway again. "He must be sick over this," she said. "We'd be a mess, Michael, if we were in this situation. I can't imagine how horrible it would be if somebody bagged you and tried to kill your wife."

Michael slowly nodded. "And I wonder what became of Alyssa," he said. "Why hasn't she called or anything?"

"Who knows," Gabriella replied, rolling her eyes. "You know darn good and well her and that detective are gonna kill Luigi, or Sal, or whatever his name is. They've *totally* lost it."

"Do you think she'll go to jail?"

Gabriella frowned. "You're gonna be the big JAG lawyer, what do you think?"

Michael shrugged. "Depends…if she commits a crime of passion, say the murder of the man who attempted to kill her mother and kidnapped her father, and if she gets a good lawyer, she might be able to get off, but…" he hesitated, taking a deep breath. "But, I think her and that detective she likes are just gonna bring him in. Alyssa's got Caselli blood. She doesn't have a vengeful bone in her body."

"You think she likes the detective?" Gabriella asked with surprise.

Michael nodded. "Oh, yeah. She thinks he's hot stuff."

Gabriella giggled. "Alyssa? Get real, Michael. She doesn't look at men, she doesn't even date. She's a career junkie like Uncle Alex used to be."

Michael shrugged again. "It just takes the right kinda guy, and the next thing you know, you're in love and it's all over."

Alyssa drove Jason's car into the long grass of the ditch. She carefully inched it under a tree, turning off the engine. She sighed as she looked at her accomplice in the passenger seat. He downed another Advil, followed by an enormous gulp of Coca-Cola. "I can't believe I'm doing this," she muttered. At the very least, the hot engine of the car might set the grass of the ditch on fire. At worst, their parents' captor could come along with a bunch of his hooligans and they'd be outnumbered. "We need backup…we need a chopper —"

"We don't need anybody for this," Jason gruffly interrupted. "We'll do just fine on our own." He pulled a map out of the glove box. "Now, open this up for me."

Alyssa swallowed. Jason's arm, *his firing arm*, was useless, and he was still losing small amounts of blood. The dressing the EMTs had fit over his wound the night before was horribly soiled. Bright red drainage was seeping out onto his torn shirt. He'd purchased gauze and tape at the same convenience store where he'd picked up Advil and Coke. He needed a doctor, but he was bent on finding his mother.

Alyssa hesitantly submitted to his request, unfolding the map on the seat between the two of them. Hopefully he'd make it through this fiasco without a serious infection — or worse.

"Okay," Jason continued, looking down at the map. "We're right about…here." He pointed to an area just north of Mud Butte, South Dakota. "We gotta go the rest of the way on foot."

"Why?"

"Because there isn't any cover besides the ditch," Jason answered. "But, lucky us, the county must have decided to save money and skipped mowing this spring."

Alyssa shook her head as she looked out the car window at the waist-high weeds. "I can't believe I got roped into this," she groaned. "He won't take them back to the original scene of the crime. This *never* happens."

"They might not be at the *exact* location of the crime scene, but they're gonna be close," Jason insisted. "He's probably been hiding out up here for months, or maybe even years. He knows this territory like the back of his hand. Besides, he'd see anybody coming for miles. He'll never suspect two people on foot, coming at him through the ditch, because that's not how the law does things. He's counting on us to behave like regular police." He smiled and confidently raised one eyebrow. "But I'm not your ordinary cop, and neither are you." He stopped to take a gulp of his Coke. "By the way, I read your dossier. You're a martial arts expert?"

"Yes," she replied, overwhelmed by his confidence. She was compelled to go along with his plan...*but to crawl through a ditch with a useless and bleeding limb? Can he do that?*

"Whatever got you into that stuff?" Jason queried, as if they had the entire morning to chat about personal information. "You don't need that stuff when you got your trusty Smith & Wesson." He patted his holstered weapon.

"It's a long story," she answered. "Can you fire with your other hand?"

"Expertly," he bragged. "How many rounds you got with you?"

"Fifteen loaded, and another forty-five in my pockets," Alyssa answered.

"Holy buckets, you're ready to start a war. How do you handle that thing?"

Alyssa raised one black brow. "Expertly," she said with a grin. "Now, let's at least camouflage this car before we just leave it sitting here. I don't want to take the chance that he'll come by and follow us in, because it'll be months before they find our bodies."

*****

After they'd finished exhuming the body, Marquette and Noah went to the airport to retrieve Marquette's file. Included in the file were John Peters' medical and dental records, and Marquette told Deputy Danielson he would take it directly to Todd Yearwood in the Medical Examiner's Office.

From photos in the file, Noah was able to identify his first father-in-law, Jack Nelson, as Mario Ponerello. The photo of young, Antonio Ponerello, on the other hand, had been taken when the child was perhaps five years of age. It was impossible to tell if Ben Simmons was actually Antonio. Salvatore's photo was extremely old, but there were enough similarities to believe he was, in fact, the man who was pretending to be Luigi Andreotti.

"And this is interesting," Marquette said, squinting at a yellowed page of notes taped to the inside of the file. "Tara wrote that we interviewed a gentleman by the name of Dean Jasper in 1980. He could not identify Mario from his photo, but his description matches Salvatore. There is a special notation here about the *scar on his left cheek.* Our fake Luigi has a mark on his left cheek." He sighed and looked at Noah. "Let us visit forensics now."

*****

Deputy Charlie McGregor was a Federal forensics specialist and he was examining the dagger that had been unearthed earlier that morning. He carefully cleaned the debris away from the symbols on the handle. Marquette was compelled to have just a peek at the ancient piece of history, as he had only looked upon one once before in his life.

"It was 1968," Marquette explained as they watched Charlie. "It had been the only one I have ever seen, until now." He looked closely at the handle of the knife. "An eagle, just as I suspected."

"It's really incredible," Charlie commented, continuing to scrape away at the knife. "I've never seen anything quite like it." At that moment, the knife made a popping noise, and Charlie startled. "I hope I didn't break it." He touched the handle with the delicate tool in his hand, and to their surprise, it snapped open to reveal a glittery compartment. "What's this?" Charlie murmured, carefully moving the shiny stones with his tool.

Marquette laughed. "*That* is what Salvatore wants."

The morning sun had warmed the small shed hiding Vincenzo and Mayor Patterson. They were extremely uncomfortable by now, and Jacqueline was thirsty.

"My back is killing me," she quietly complained.

"My Alyssa is very smart," Vincenzo said with a faint smile. "They will be along soon and we will be out of this mess."

"Come on, Caselli, *we* don't even know where we are. How are the cops going to find us? We're done for."

Vincenzo raised his eyebrows, encouraging, "I do not believe so. Now, let us speak of more pleasant things until help arrives. For instance, my sister tells me you have started to collect her paintings."

Jacqueline sighed and tried to smile. He was such a positive guy. Didn't he realize that even if Sal didn't come back to finish them off, dehydration would? Her heart softened as she looked at him sitting across from her...*he must be so worried about his wife.* The least she could do was humor him during their last hours. "I have all of the paintings in her new series, *The Greatest of These*," she said.

Vincenzo smiled and took a deep breath. "Ah, yes, our father's favorites," he said. "You know, there will be a new painting added to the series, and she will debut it at the Heritage Festival. I believe she has entitled it *Blessing*."

Jacqueline wore a curious expression and, deciding to go for broke, she asked, "So, I always wondered if Hansen built that place out on Rimrock for Angel. Did he?"

"Yes," Vincenzo answered. "Dear Noah loved her from the moment he set eyes upon her, and always believed they would be together one day."

Jacqueline wrinkled up her nose and asked, "How in the world did she ever wind up with Alex Martin?"

"That is a very long and unfortunate story," Vincenzo said with a soft frown. "Would you care to hear it?"

Jacqueline *almost* laughed. "Well, we're not going anywhere. Why don't you go ahead and tell it to me."

Elaine tucked a light blanket over the sleeping baby, giving her a delicate kiss on the top of her head. Ty said that he had rocked and rocked the baby before she finally gave in and decided to take a nap. She glanced across the hall at the rest of Tillie and Noah's children as she made her way for the stairs. The four of them were huddled around Laura's desk, and it appeared that Laura was showing them some kind of a trick with recipe cards. Elaine continued down the steps without another thought about it, intent on her duty to somehow keep Tillie off her feet until the police deemed it safe enough to take her to the doctor.

"Okay, I think I've got this thing figured out," Laura breathed after Elaine passed the door.

"Lay it on us, Laura," Ty goaded, stretching out on her bed.

"First of all, there's Luigi Andreotti," Laura began. "He claims to be some long lost friend of our uncles, but Alyssa discovers that he's meeting with Ben Simmons and Ty's biological father. Now, who are these two gentlemen connected to? Both of them have ties to Noah, and the Casellis also have ties to Noah." She paused to place several cards on her desk in an attempt to diagram the relationships between all of the men involved. "And Noah knows about this murder way back when, and I'm gonna bet when that body comes up, a knife is gonna come up with it."

"Why?" Jake frowned. "Nobody's said anything about a knife."

Laura began, "Uncle Marquette said the Ponerellos' family identification is on the handle of their dagger —"

"What does that have to do with anything, Laura," Jake interrupted.

"Well, if you'd listen for once," Laura snapped with a scowl, "maybe I could get a little farther and we'd already have this thing figured out!"

"Okay, Jake, be quiet for a minute," Ty commanded from his lounging position on the bed.

"Thank you, Ty." Laura took a deep breath. "Now, from what I've heard, Luigi Andreotti is dead and has been for about fifteen years. The other things I've heard are that Jake and Ty's grandmother is still alive, along with her daughter, Charise, and her stepson, Antonio. Deputy Danielson thinks he saw Jack Nelson, or Noah's first father-in-law, the day he followed them to Custer to visit Della. Jack was *old*. In fact I heard Deputy Danielson say that *his hair was white as snow*. Now, if Mario is still alive, according to what I've been able to piece together, he'd be practically eighty years old. His hair could definitely be as white as snow." Laura covered the name *Jack Nelson* with a new recipe card entitled *Mario*. "Luigi's dead, but he'd be about the age of Salvatore Ponerello, and Salvatore needed a way to get to close to Noah." Laura covered Luigi's name with the name of *Salvatore*. "Mario escaped Sicily with his young son, Antonio, and he'd be the age of Ben Simmons." Laura covered his name with a card labeled *Antonio*. "Uncle Marquette said when the Ponerellos reach a certain age of maturity, they must take a vow to protect the family. Noah and his children, and even his new wife and the rest of us, would fall under the protection of Antonio's vows. That's why he went to work for Noah all those years ago."

"Okay, that all sounds really great, Laura, but why does Salvatore want to get close to Noah?" A.J. questioned with skepticism. "I just don't see the connection."

"Roy Schneider murdered someone in 1975," Laura answered. "Ty and Jake's mom told Noah where the body was buried. Noah kept it secret in order to protect his family —"

"But there's something more important than an old, dead body in the ground!" Ty exclaimed, snapping his fingers and sitting up. "It's *gotta be* the knife!"

Laura nodded at Ty. "It's gotta be."

"But what about the knife and why does Salvatore want it now?" Ty thought out loud.

Laura took a deep breath, continuing, "In 1968, Uncle Marquette went to Sicily because of a diamond theft. Fifty loose diamonds were never recovered. How much do you wanna bet those diamonds are in the knife?"

"Oh, come on," Jake scoffed. "You said Mario and Antonio left Sicily four years *before* Salvatore escaped. How did he get the diamonds into the knife? Transcendental Meditation?"

A.J. laughed.

"Uncle Marquette said something about catching a lead on the Ponerellos in the mid-seventies or early eighties," Laura continued. "He and Tara discovered that Jack Nelson owned a small fishing company in Miami Florida. He sold it in 1972 and never resurfaced again. He thinks Jack Nelson, aka Mario, was hiding from Salvatore after that —"

"Because Salvatore caught up to him in Miami," Ty excitedly interrupted. "Salvatore was probably looking for a way to fence the diamonds and Mario was afraid he'd draw too much attention. Mario swiped Salvatore's knife, which would have identified them *all*, and high-tailed it out of town. Salvatore's been searching for it ever since."

"And we can't forget that Salvatore must have found them in Rapid City," Laura reminded. "Because of Della's *purported death*. Della told Alyssa she and her family hid from Salvatore for many years, but they always got away. Alyssa thinks Salvatore may have pushed Della down the steps and left her for dead."

"So how did Salvatore figure out that Noah knew where the body was buried?" A.J. questioned.

Laura shook her head. "I'm not sure. Maybe just a lucky guess. Maybe not. He took the mayor, I think, because he's trying to scare Detective Patterson into handing over the knife if he finds it. He took Uncle Vincenzo and tried to kill Aunt Kate because he wants Alyssa to be afraid as well."

"Then he'll probably try to take Tillie next," Ty speculated, and they turned their eyes on him. He raised his eyebrow. "Dad would do anything for us. If he finds a knife with fifty diamonds in it, he'll gladly turn it over to Salvatore to save one of us...but I think it will be Tillie."

"But we've got half of the Rapid City police force stationed in the parking lot of the fish hatchery right now," A.J. pointed out. "Salvatore's gonna get pretty frustrated."

Jake frowned. "So where's this vent, Laura?"

"Right over here," Laura pointed. "And Uncle Marquette and Noah should be back pretty soon. We should be able to fill in the details once they return."

*****

Noah was driving while Marquette read from the file they'd retrieved at the airport that morning. Noah's cell phone rang.

"This is Noah."

"Well, hello, my American friend," came a sinister voice on the other end.

"Sal?" Noah asked with astonishment, and Marquette looked up from his file.

Sal laughed. "So, you know who I really am —"

"What have you done with my brother-in-law and what do you want?" Noah barked.

"I want my treasure."

"I don't have it," Noah answered.

"Well I have yours," Salvatore daunted. "Perhaps we could make a trade?"

Noah felt as if someone had punched him in the stomach. "What are you talking about?" he asked.

"Your precious Angel is with me now."

Noah nearly drove off the road. He looked into Marquette's curious expression, whispering, "He says he's got Angel."

"Yes my friend, I have your Angel." Salvatore laughed heartily. "You see, my whole plan came together when I saw a wonderful little story about you on the social page of the *Washington Times*. How convenient for me when you took your Italian bride — a bride from the very family I have vowed my father's vengeance upon."

"You're insane," Noah said, throwing his phone at Marquette. "Clear that call out and call my house. Tell 'em we're just about there."

Tillie was at the kitchen table when Elaine came downstairs. Her leg rested on one chair, while a bag of ice covered her knee. Her cane sat close by. Elaine carefully lifted the ice bag for a better look, grimacing as she said, "Good grief, I never even saw my kids get this black and blue. What have you done to yourself, Angel?"

Tillie softly frowned down at her knee. "It started out with just a little twist at the airport a couple of weeks ago, and I haven't been able to walk it off."

Elaine carefully placed the bag of ice on Tillie's knee. "Well, can I get you anything?" she asked. "Might as well relax for awhile. Ty got your little one to sleep."

"I'd love a cup of coffee and one of my delicious little Darvocets," Tillie murmured.

"Just made a fresh pot," Elaine said, turning for the kitchen counter. "Where do you keep your delicious little Darvocets?"

"In the cupboard above the microwave," Tillie answered.

Elaine went to the cupboard, found the prescription bottle, and fished out a pain pill. "You know, you're so good-natured about this whole thing," she said. "I'd be a big *pain* about it." She snickered at her own joke, reaching for a coffee cup. Tillie was strangely quiet, so Elaine turned to glance at her sister-in-law. She gasped when she saw a young man standing next to Tillie, holding a small gun at her temple. He was dressed in dirty, baggy clothing, his blond hair long and stringy. His face was covered with scruffy whiskers. Obviously, he had slipped in through the open deck door.

"Don't speak," he instructed with a strange smile. "I gotta take Mrs. Hansen now, and you're gonna help me get past the cops."

Tillie sat very still, a thoughtful expression between her brows. She didn't look afraid, but she didn't look very happy either.

"How did you get past the police?" Elaine whispered.

"It was incredibly easy," he answered. "And your dogs didn't seem to mind me either — especially when I gave 'em a handful of biscuits." He looked down at a very quiet Tillie. "Now, if you could just get up, we'll go to your car and you'll drive us out of here. You'll tell the police there's no reason for an escort because you're only running an errand."

Tillie looked at Elaine and sighed. The pain in her knee was excruciating, and anger began to burn within her. There was no way she could leave the house, unless this fellow wanted to carry her, and then who would drive? "I just can't," she murmured. "My knee is in really bad shape."

"That's not all that's gonna be in really bad shape if you don't come with me." He gave Tillie's temple a soft tap with the muzzle.

Tillie wanted to take the gun away from him and give him a good smack with it, but she took a deep breath and said, "Well, then I suppose we oughta go. Ellie, I'm gonna need *my cane*." She looked into Elaine's eyes, narrowing her expression.

"Okay, Angel," Elaine replied, reaching for Tillie's cane.

"Don't try anything stupid," the young man warned.

Elaine slowly handed the cane to Tillie. Tillie eased her leg off the chair, put her full weight on the cane, and slowly got to her feet.

"Now," the young man went on, tossing a folded piece of paper onto the kitchen table. "These are your directions. Read them over and do what it says. I'm sure Mrs. Hansen will be returned in one piece — at least that's what I was told." He aimed his gun at Elaine, reaching for the deck door beside the table. "We're going to the garage through the back way."

As the young man pointed his gun at Elaine with one hand, and opened the deck door with his other, Tillie saw an opportunity. She swung her cane above her head, and as hard as she could, brought it down on his forearm. His gun flew from his hand, firing when it hit the wall on the other side of the kitchen. Tillie fell to the floor without the balance of her cane, and the young man attempted to make a grab for her. Elaine took the glass jar of biscotti on the counter, and in a panic, smashed it over his head. He was instantly dazed and staggered into the table, where he fell and struck his head against a leg. He lay motionless beneath the table, and Elaine and Tillie could only stare.

"What a *jerk*," Elaine muttered, reaching for Tillie, helping her back into the chair.

All four of the youngsters that were upstairs were suddenly in the kitchen. They'd heard the gunshot, as had the police officers pouring through the front door.

Several officers rushed to the unconscious young man beneath the table. Someone checked for a pulse, and when they found one, he was cuffed and rolled over onto his side.

A.J. and Laura went to their mother.

"What happened, Mom?!" A.J. exclaimed.

"That guy!" Tillie gasped, looking around at the mayhem. "He wanted me to go somewhere with him."

"There's a note," Elaine said, reaching for the folded paper left on the table.

"What happened?" an officer asked, taking the note from Elaine's hands.

"I hit him with my cane," Tillie began, her eyes big and round. "And Ellie got him with the biscotti." Tillie looked at the smashed glass on the floor and worriedly bit her lip as she said, "We gotta get this cleaned up before Annie wakes up from her nap." Annie's cries were suddenly heard from the upstairs and Tillie made a "tsk" noise. "Too late."

Elaine suddenly laughed out loud, and everyone looked at her. She couldn't help herself. She'd been awake since about one o'clock that morning. Between the exhaustion and stress of the situation, something had to give.

"Sit here, Ellie," Tillie kindly offered, indicating the chair next to her. Elaine laughed again, taking the seat next to Tillie. Tillie patted Elaine's shoulder, smiling as she said, "She'll be okay. She's just really tired."

Ty started to back out of the kitchen as he said, "I'll get Annie and make sure she stays out of the glass."

"I'll get a broom," Jake volunteered.

As Tillie gently patted Elaine's shoulder, wondering when her stressed-out sister-in-law would stop her maniacal giggling, she happened to glance into the backyard. A familiar man stood at the end of the deck.

"Ben?" she whispered.

"Who?" an officer replied, following Tillie's gaze. As soon as their eyes met, Ben turned and ran. Several officers charged through the deck door and into the backyard after him.

"No!" Tillie yelled, trying to get to her feet. "Leave him alone! He works for my husband!"

The telephone rang, and since Jake happened to be right next to it, he answered, "Hansens'."

"Jake, it's Dad. Is everything okay over there?"

"No," Jake answered in an incredulous tone. "Some guy just tried to grab Tillie, but they beat the daylights out of him." Jake glanced at the young man on the floor, still stunned from the blow to his head.

"They? Is Angel there? Can I talk to her?"

"Sure." Jake handed Tillie the phone. "It's Dad."

"Angel, what's going on?" Noah breathed, feeling tears of relief build in his eyes.

"Wow, Noah," Tillie whispered as she watched several officers wrestle Ben Simmons to the ground. "This guy was here…actually, he's still here. We sorta knocked him out —" Tillie was momentarily interrupted when Elaine laughed out loud again, and she smiled. "Ellie got him with the biscotti. I think I'm gonna give her a Darvocet. She's *really* stressed."

"Sal *called* me," Noah said. "I'm almost home. I'll be there in just a couple of minutes."

"He *called* you?"

"It's a long story. I'll talk to you about it when we get there," Noah answered. He took a deep breath as the tears crept from the corners of his eyes. "I love you, Angel."

"I love you, Noah."

Chapter 20

Noah and Marquette took the front porch steps two at a time, sprinting into the house. They nearly knocked over a police officer standing just inside of the door as they raced to the kitchen to find their family. Several police officers were in the kitchen with all of the children, and Tillie and Elaine. Tillie's knee was packed in ice again, but she didn't look as upset as Noah thought she should be. Elaine was seated next to her, and Jake was calmly pouring them coffee.

"Hey, Dad," he said, grinning when he saw his father.

Elaine softly giggled and Tillie smiled at Noah. Annie was on her lap, wide-eyed with curiosity, munching on an animal cracker.

She reached for her father. "Papa."

Noah took his little daughter into his arms as he knelt beside Tillie's chair. "I was so scared," he said. "I thought he had you for sure."

"Can we ask you some questions about that, Mr. Hansen?" a police officer asked.

Noah scowled, standing up to face the officer. "Actually, yes," he replied. "And I'm gonna have a few questions for you and the troops. How did he get past everybody? Weren't you guys payin' attention?"

Annie clung tightly to her father's neck, mimicking his scowl.

Marquette put a friendly hand upon Noah's shoulder and said, "Let us sort the thing out before we tear them to pieces, Noah."

"This is *crazy*," Noah stormed on, as if he hadn't heard Marquette's gentle protest. "I had faith in you people that everyone would be safe, or I wouldn't have left."

"Mr. Hansen, we're very sorry," the officer apologized.

"Noah, Ben is here," Tillie interrupted, reaching for his hand.

Noah looked down at Tillie with a confused expression. "Ben?"

She nodded. "They've got him cuffed out back. Noah, it looks like there were two of them and Ben knocked one out and tied him up. Ben was on the deck when the other one was with me. He would have stopped him when we tried to leave —"

"Except that Mom and Aunt Ellie got him first," A.J. said with a grin.

"And he's busted up real bad," Ty added. "Tillie wailed on him with her cane."

"His arm was broken and he might have a concussion," Laura nervously chirped. "They had to take him to the hospital."

"Where is Mr. Simmons?" Marquette inquired. "And may I speak with him?"

"We've got him out back," the officer answered. He looked curiously at Marquette. "Are you Marquette Caselli?"

Marquette raised both of his eyebrows, smiling proudly as he answered, "In the flesh. May I see Mr. Simmons?"

"Sure," the officer answered. "He's with a United States Marshal, but I'm sure he'll let you talk to him."

"Very well then," Marquette said with a deep breath. He bent to kiss his sister. "I am glad you are safe." He looked at Noah and asked, "Would you care to join me? Perhaps there are a few things we can sort out with Ben."

Noah placed Annie back into her mother's lap, gave Tillie another soft kiss on her lips and smiled into her eyes. "I'll be right back," he said.

"I'm not going anywhere," Tillie replied.

"And she *means* it," Elaine chortled.

Noah managed a quiet laugh at the two of them, and he and Marquette left through the deck door.

A United States Marshal had detained the man Noah knew only as Ben Simmons. His hands were cuffed behind his back, and he was sitting in a lawn chair. His head hung when he saw Noah. He would not look at his face. "Forgive me, Noah," he pleaded. "I failed you and your family this day."

"Not from what I heard," Noah replied.

"Okay, who are *you*?" The Marshal questioned Noah and Marquette with a stern expression.

"Marquette Caselli," he answered. "This is my brother, Noah Hansen. I must be allowed to question this man as he is part of an ongoing investigation. May I?"

"Certainly," the Marshal answered.

"Does he have to be cuffed?" Noah asked as he reached for a nearby lawn chair, placing it beside Antonio Ponerello. He seated himself and attempted to look into his face.

"He's an illegal alien," the Marshal answered. "He's gotta be cuffed."

"I have already told them my true identity," Antonio confessed. He slowly lifted his head, bringing his eyes to Noah's.

"Why?" Noah asked. "Why didn't you tell me who you were all those years ago when I first hired you?"

Antonio swallowed and answered, "I had taken a vow to protect you and your family from my uncle. Had I revealed my identity, you would have lived in fear and my vow would have been for naught."

"And you are Antonio Ponerello?" Marquette questioned.

"I am," he answered.

Marquette took a deep breath, let it out and smiled. "I have searched the ends of the earth for you and now here you are before me. I have so many questions for you. First of all, do you have any idea where Salvatore has taken my brother?"

"I do not," Antonio answered. "He knows the area very well and they could be anywhere."

"And you guys faked Della's death?" Noah questioned. "Did Carrie know her mother was still alive?"

"Yes," Antonio answered. "The money you found missing shortly before her death was used to keep Della at Colonial Manor and pay for a place for the rest of us to live." He took a breath, continuing, "So many times I wanted to tell you the truth. The mysterious circumstances surrounding Carrie's death weighed heavy upon your heart, and we ached for you. She was with all of us that day in Custer, the day of her accident. She truly loved you, and we were happy for her. She wanted to tell you Della was still alive, but our father forbade it. We just could not risk Salvatore finding us again. He thought he left Della for dead, and we took the opportunity to hide. You see, Salvatore had tracked us down at that time and attempted to kill Della in order that a threat would force my father to turn over something he took many years ago. When we lived in Florida, Salvatore found us and wanted my father to share in the wealth of a diamond theft. My father was terrified we would be exposed and so he stole the diamonds himself and concealed them in the handle of his dagger."

"So have you guys been here the whole time?" Noah questioned.

Antonio nodded. "We watched your little boys grow into fine men and we longed to hold them in our arms."

"How old were you when you left *Sicilia?*" Marquette asked.

"I was six years of age."

"Do you know why you left?" Marquette asked.

"My father wanted nothing more to do with the family. My mother was murdered and he feared for my life as well. We fled in the middle of the night, and have not been back since."

"What do you know of Schneider Rauwolf?" Marquette questioned.

"The Wolf worked for my father for many years."

"In what capacity?"

"He was an expert at forging documents and tracking down people," Antonio answered. "He had friends in your government that were willing to give him information for a price. That is the way we kept track of Salvatore and managed to stay out of his sight for so long."

"When did he find you again?" Marquette asked.

"In 1993, when Ben Stahlheim's plane crashed," he answered with a heavy sign. "There were so many stories in the news at that time, Salvatore not only learned that Matilde Martin was your sibling, but that Noah Hansen had once been married to Carrie Miller, a girl he believed to have died of a drug overdose. There was a particular news story at the time reporting that Carrie's mother, Della Nelson, predeceased Carrie Miller. He supposed Carrie's husband would have information about the family, and started to watch Noah. He spent a considerable amount of time in *Italia* in order to completely investigate the Casellis so that he might get close to Noah. The whole world knew Noah Hansen had struck up an unusual friendship with the famous Marquette Caselli, though only my family and I knew how. When Noah and Angel finally married, we could not believe our misfortune. During that time, Salvatore stumbled upon the large amount of property Marquette still owns in *Chianti*, and the adjacent Andreotti property. He was determined to get revenge for his father, and decided to assume the identity of the deceased Luigi Andreotti. His plan was twofold: first to destroy the Casellis, and then to recover his hidden treasure. I discovered that Salvatore had returned to Rapid City at that time. I fed him fraudulent information for nearly two years, and then Della was diagnosed with Lupus. We had no money left. I then began to bargain with Salvatore. I asked him for money, and he asked me for information. I continued to give him small doses of what I thought to be whimsical knowledge. However, when the senator decided to christen his new yacht, and somebody wrote a story about it in the *Rapid City Journal*, Salvatore decided the time to strike was right. He went to New York, pretending to be Luigi in order to establish contact with Noah."

"How did he learn the diamonds were with the dagger?" Marquette questioned.

"He does not know for sure," Antonio answered. "He only assumes, and I have done everything I can to sway his opinion."

Marquette thoughtfully scratched his chin, asking, "Why did Rauwolf kill my associate, John Peters?"

"It was an accident." Antonio shook his head with remorse. "We thought he was sent by the rest of the family in *Sicilia*. My father only intended to frighten Mr. Peters. However, The Wolf had a taste for blood that night and he could not be stopped. My father and Carrie tried to get him to the hospital, but he died along the way." He sadly sighed, "Poor Carrie. She never got over it, and we did not think she would ever be sober again."

Marquette frowned pensively, rubbing his temples with his forefingers. He took a deep breath and bit his lip as he looked at Antonio. "And you were only six years old when you were taken from *Sicilia?*" he questioned.

Antonio nodded.

Marquette continued, "Well, then, I might have an idea for you."

*****

After Marquette finished questioning the accomplice Antonio had subdued in the backyard, Joe Patterson and Deputy Jon Danielson arrived on the scene. The three of them questioned Tillie and Elaine, and reviewed the letter that had been left with them. The letter was addressed to Noah, instructing him, *without the aid of authorities*, to deliver *Il Dagger Del Dinastia* to the Tilford, South Dakota exit. At the Tilford exit, Noah would find a 1978 Dodge pickup, parked along the side of the ditch. Noah was to put the dagger in the glove compartment, and leave the area immediately. The writer of the letter, who identified himself as Salvatore, said there would be further instructions once the dagger was in his possession.

According to the information extracted from Tillie's would-be captors, they were to leave her in her vehicle securely bound, at the intersection of U.S. 385 and State 87, in Wind Cave National Park. The destination was nearly seventy-five miles south of Rapid City, while the Tilford Exit was only ten miles north.

"Chances are," Jon opined, "he plans on grabbing the knife and getting out of the area."

Marquette took a deep breath and slowly let the air out. "And he probably does not intend to reveal to us where he has stashed my brother and the mayor."

"We could send Josie Calloway to Wind Cave in Mrs. Hansen's car," Joe suggested. "She's been an officer on the force for many years. She's got the same coloring as Mrs. Hansen, and we could throw a curly wig on her."

"Maybe put a couple guys in the car with her so that it looks like they all got away," Jon suggested.

Marquette raised his eyebrows. "But how do we get someone to the Tilford exit to protect Noah?"

Joe shook his head as he thought. "That's gonna be tough."

"How 'bout a delivery truck?" Jon asked. "I can get a cargo unit from UPS and put a bunch of agents inside. What's up at Tilford? Gas station or anything? Some place where a guy could get a pop and a candy bar on break?"

"The Tilford exit is only an exit," Noah answered. "There's *nothing* up there."

Marquette bit his lower lip. "Noah's pickup is equipped with a very large tool-box. How many men can we fit inside?"

"In the tool-box?" Noah questioned with surprise. "Maybe if I empty out all of my tools, we can get *one guy* in there, but it's not gonna be that safe. It's sealed for rainy weather and stuff like that."

"I'll go," Joe offered. "I bet we can rig up something for fresh air."

"Sounds good to me," Jon said decidedly. "Now let's get this show on the road before Sal figures out that something's up." He raised his eyebrow and looked around. "By the way, has anybody heard from my partner?"

Everyone shook their heads.

Jon sighed. "Well, I hope she's okay."

*****

Jason and Alyssa had been on their hands and knees for nearly an hour when Jason's arm cramped and he fell flat on his face. Alyssa helped him into a sitting position.

"Here," she said, handing him another Advil. "Why don't you let me check your wound." He nodded and she gingerly removed the heavily soiled bandages from his shoulder. "This is really bad," she murmured, carefully changing the dressing with the extra gauze she'd tied in a bag at her hip. His wound was bleeding more now, and his fair complexion had drastically paled. "Do you have any feeling in your fingers?"

Jason swallowed hard as he wiggled his fingers. "I got all kinds of feeling in my fingers. They hurt like crazy."

Alyssa taped the fresh gauze into place as she said, "There. That oughta hold you for another hour or so."

"Thanks Deputy. By the way, whatever got you into martial arts?"

Alyssa looked at Jason, raising one, mysterious black eyebrow as she answered, "I picked up a stalker my second year at Harvard." She packed the extra gauze into her bag as she explained, "At first, I didn't think anything of it, but then one night he came over to my apartment. Naturally, I didn't want to let him in. He totally lost it and smashed in my door with a fire extinguisher. I frantically dialed 9-1-1. Thankfully, Angelo happened to come home and he beat the daylights out of the guy before the cops even got there." She chuckled. "They didn't know who to arrest, so they arrested them both until they got it figured out. Shortly after that happened, a girl in my political science class invited me to attend some of her Tae Kwon Do classes. She had already chosen her major and was going to be a U.S. Marshal and thought maybe she'd need something of martial arts in her future. I went along and got hooked on the stuff."

"Interesting," Jason commented with a soft furrow between his brows. "Is that what made you decide to become a Marshal?"

"Maybe a little, but, I've always really loved my Uncle Marquette's stories and the way he and Tara travel the world over. I think that's probably what made me decide."

Jason nodded. "Well, why don't you help me back on my knees and let's see if we can get a little further."

Alyssa grabbed his good shoulder, helping him maneuver into the position he wanted. "You sure you're gonna be okay?" she asked.

"Why, I'm right as the mail," Jason said, mimicking a Southern accent.

Alyssa smiled, shaking her head. "*Tombstone.* I loved that movie. That was Doc Holliday's line."

"Yep. He was my great, great, great grandfather you know," Jason bragged.

Alyssa nodded. "I saw that in your record, but history was my minor. Doc Holliday didn't have any children."

"Oh, but he did," Jason argued with a smile. "My great, great, great grandmother was a young nun by the name of Mary. She named her illegitimate baby Henry Holliday, after the man she would later write about as the only person in the world she loved more than God. Henry Holliday was my great, great grandfather. He married and had several sons, the oldest of which he named Jason Henry Holliday, and he's my great grandfather. His one-hundredth birthday is coming up here in October, and that's what my mom was flying to Valdosta for. He named his eldest son Jason Henry, Jr., who is my grandfather. Jason Henry, Jr., had a daughter, my mother, whom he named Jacqueline Mary, and she named me Jason Henry Holliday Patterson."

His story was wonderful, but Alyssa was skeptical. "Do you have genealogy records to prove that?"

"Yes, ma'am," Jason answered. "And we have the old love letters from Mary to Doc, and from Doc to Mary."

"Why didn't he marry her?"

"'Cause he had to run off with the Earp brothers and catch those nasty, ole cowboys."

"Oh, yeah, that's right."

"Now, come on," Jason coaxed, attempting to crawl along. "Let's get this show on the road and see if we can't find our parents."

"How much farther do you think we're gonna have to go?" Alyssa questioned as she crawled along behind him.

"Probably a couple more hours. By the way, whatever happened to your Tae Kwon Do buddy?"

"She's my boss."

*****

Officer Calloway put on a curly, dark wig, blue jeans and a pink blouse. Two younger-looking officers, along with Officer Calloway, got into Tillie and Noah's blue Suburban and headed for Wind Cave National Park.

In the meantime, Noah emptied the toolbox in the back of his pickup and drilled air holes in the side. The police department provided Noah and Joe with a two-way radio each so they could communicate with one another if need be. Deputy Danielson had secured a cargo truck from UPS, and his team planned to fake a stall out on the highway intersecting with Noah's destination.

Joe Patterson wasn't a small man, and Noah wondered how in the world he would ever survive the trip to the Tilford exit. But Noah knew in his heart if it were Tillie in Mrs. Patterson's position, he would attempt anything to get her back. Making the requested delivery to the Tilford exit was the least Noah could do.

"Are you sure everything will be okay?" Tillie asked nervously as she watched her husband prepare.

"I think so, Angel," Noah assured.

"I'm not comfortable with this at all. What if something happens?"

Noah put his arms around her and said, "Nothing's gonna happen, Angel." He whispered in her ear, "And what about poor ole Joe? He misses his wife so much it's killing him. If we have the chance to somehow figure out where Sal put her, and your brother, then it's all worth it. I'm gonna be fine." He mischievously smiled and winked. "Besides, I'm not even afraid."

"Well, *I'm* afraid."

"Okay, Hansen," a voice interrupted, and Noah and Tillie turned to see another officer approaching them. He had with him the box that held Sal's knife, now loaded with fake diamonds, and a flak jacket. "You'd better put this on."

Noah nodded as he took the jacket from the officer. "I haven't seen one of these since I was in Vietnam."

"Then you're in for a surprise," the officer answered, helping Noah into the jacket. "These days they're a lot lighter in weight."

"Okay, we're ready to move over here," Deputy Danielson said. "Patterson's getting his jacket on and we're getting him a canteen of water. The team in the cargo truck is just on their way, and they're gonna make sure they stall on the highway just before the exit. Hopefully, we won't look too suspicious —" Danielson was suddenly interrupted when Noah's cell phone rang. He raised an eyebrow. "I bet that's our little buddy. When you answer, you tell him you got the note and you're on your way."

Noah swallowed, took a deep breath and answered his phone, "Hansen."

"Hello my friend." Sal laughed. "By now you must know that I have your precious Angel."

"I got your note," Noah said gruffly. "I'm on my way."

"Goodness," Sal replied with mock surprise. "That did not take you very long. Now, as soon as you make the delivery, you must leave the area *immediately*. I will return your brother, the mayor and your Angel to you after that."

"Where can we find them?"

"I will call with more details," Sal answered, and he turned off his phone.

Noah looked at Jon and said, "He thinks he's got Angel."

"Well then we're just gonna help him keep believing that."

"As soon as he learns he does not, he will undoubtedly rage against Vincenzo and the mayor," Marquette commented, walking toward them. He smiled into Noah's eyes and kissed each of his cheeks. "May God go with you, my brother." He looked around at the small task force assembled in the driveway of Angel's Place. "We must move out as quickly as possible. The Ponerellos are quite rageful when they are deceived. Sal must be captured before he can be permitted to hurt my brother or Lieutenant Patterson's wife." He took a breath and looked at Deputy Danielson. "And I guess I shall go along as well."

"Where will you ride, Marquette?" Tillie questioned.

"On the floor in the back seat," he answered. "There will be plenty of room for me back there, and I do not believe Sal will see me." Marquette smiled and raised a brow. "I must be there when my oldest foe is finally apprehended."

Deputy Danielson took an uneasy breath. "Do you have a weapon?" he asked.

"I do."

Danielson nodded.

Another hour had passed and Jason and Alyssa were reaching the end of the ditch.

"That's the end of our cover," Jason groaned, leaning back against the berm. "We're gonna have to cross the road to get into the other ditch...and I need another Advil...and maybe a Rolaid."

Alyssa's stomach was twisted into knots. He was pale again and his dressing was wet with fresh blood. He'd taken so much Advil by now that he was sick. "You shouldn't take any more for awhile," she said.

"Just get me another one," he insisted. "And let's get this wet dressing off so we can put on a fresh one."

Alyssa groaned, fishing out another Advil. "You'll be of no use to me if you wind up passing out," she said. She reached for the wet bandages, adding, "I don't have any more Rolaids." She cringed when she saw his wound. The trickle of blood that had started more than two hours ago was increasing. The gash appeared to have opened even more than from when she'd checked it the last time — and this fresh dressing would be what they had left of their supplies. "Jason, you're in big trouble here," she told him. "You've lost a lot a color in your face —"

"I've got two candy bars in my jacket," he interrupted. "And if you're really nice, I'll let you have one."

"You can have them," she muttered, finishing the new dressing. She peered out of the ditch at their surroundings. After a brief scan of the area, she reported, "Okay, we're past that old barn where the drug operation was set up. I think there's a small house about a mile west of that." She looked at him and asked, "Where's that map?" Jason reached around to his back pocket. Alyssa unfolded it for him, asking, "About where do you think we are?"

Jason pointed and said, "We're right about here...just west of Mud Butte."

"Then this gravel is this unmarked road that runs north and south," Alyssa said. "If we continue north, we're gonna run into the Moreau River, and we'll hit that little house along the way. Do you think you can make it?"

"I do," Jason answered with confidence.

They rose to their feet, looked around them in all directions, and ran for the ditch on the other side.

*****

"How are you Detective?" Marquette questioned, speaking into the two-way radio from his crouched position in Noah's backseat.

"Doin' okay," Joe answered.

"Does he got enough air in there?" Noah asked.

"Noah wonders if you have enough air," Marquette relayed.

"I feel fine. How much further?"

"Just a couple of minutes," Noah answered. "We're almost there."

"Noah says we are almost there," Marquette answered.

Noah's cell phone rang, and he took a startled breath. "It's probably him."

"Just be calm," Marquette coaxed. "Answer and see what he wants."

"Hansen."

"You fools!" Sal raged. "You thought you could fool me! Continue with your delivery, but know that just for your trickery, I shall kill Caselli's brother!" The line went dead.

"Sal?" Noah said into the phone. "Are you there, Sal?"

"What did he say, Noah?" Marquette questioned.

"He said that for our trickery, he's going to kill Vincenzo."

"He knows we still have Angel," Marquette pronounced, sitting up in the backseat of the pickup. "Pull over, Noah. We might as well get Joe out of the back and head back to Rapid City."

"He says I'm supposed to make the delivery anyway," Noah said, heading for the shoulder of the interstate.

"We will not make the delivery without the verification that both hostages are alive," Marquette said with confidence. "He will not jeopardize the lives of the hostages if he thinks we are not willing to turn over the dagger."

Chapter 21

Laura closed Jake and A.J.'s bedroom door and looked at her brother and stepbrothers. They had listened to the adults talking in the kitchen until Tillie sent them to their rooms. Obviously, there was something else happening that the "children" weren't supposed to know about.

"Does anybody have a South Dakota map?" she asked.

"Right here, Laura," Jake answered, pulling a map from between the books on his shelf.

"I've got an idea." She opened the map, laying it on Jake and A.J.'s desktop. She took a deep breath as she studied the map. "Okay, they found something just west of Mud Butte yesterday, and Noah was headed for the Tilford exit today with a mysterious box. Of course, we all know that the mysterious box is actually the dagger full of diamonds." She dramatically raised her eyebrow, adding, "Even though nobody said the diamonds are in the knife, we know this to be true."

Ty frowned. "And how do we know that for sure, Laura?"

"Because we're smart," she replied, tucking some of her black curls behind an earlobe. "Now listen to me, guys, we heard Deputy Danielson say, *Ponerello is threatening the hostages.* Obviously, Sal knows he doesn't really have Mom, so he must have threatened Uncle Vincenzo or the mayor. However, we must assume he can't realistically threaten anyone, unless he's very, very close to them."

"So what are you saying, Laura?" A.J. questioned.

Laura looked at the map, pointing as she said, "He wanted Noah at the Tilford exit, diamonds in hand, and yet he's nowhere in sight as of the last update. My guess is he's somewhere extremely convenient so he can easily get back and forth between Tilford and the hostages. I think he's up over here someplace."

"And that would put Uncle Vincenzo and the mayor up there as well," Ty finished.

"Exactly," Laura agreed. "And think about it, guys, he's gotta get at least as close as Sturgis to get his cell phone to work, because we know for a fact that Noah's cell phone *never* works in the Northern Hills. He can't get a signal once he gets past Sturgis." Laura paused and looked at her cohorts. "And we positively *know for sure* that he's using a cell phone because the U.S. Marshals' tracing equipment didn't work."

"So Sal probably left Sturgis, or someplace even closer, at the time that he called Dad," Jake summarized.

"Yes," Laura agreed. "And look at this." She pointed to a highway on the map as she said, "Straight north of Sturgis is Highway 79, and it links up with 212 at Newell."

"Which runs directly into Mud Butte," A.J. excitedly finished.

"And there's also a gravel road parallel to that route," Ty added. "If he wanted to hide, he could take the gravel all the way to Mud Butte."

"I think he's got 'em up there," Laura said, folding the map. "Let's go tell Uncle Marquette."

A.J.'s face was aghast. "We can't do that, Laura!" he exclaimed.

"Why not?" she questioned. "They have to get to Uncle Vincenzo and the mayor before Sal kills them. They can take a helicopter or something."

"But that's a big area," Jake said with a skeptical frown.

"Well, I'm going downstairs," Laura said with determination. And with that, she headed out of their room. The boys followed reluctantly.

In the kitchen, Tillie and Elaine made another pot of coffee, Annie sat in her high chair with some crackers and cheese, and Noah, Marquette and Deputy Danielson sat at the kitchen table deep in discussion.

"What do you need, kids?" Tillie asked when she saw them in the kitchen doorway.

"Laura's got some sort of an idea," Jake offered with a dry smile.

Noah rolled his eyes. "Can it wait? We're really busy."

"It's about the case," Laura offered bravely, spreading her map out on the kitchen table. "I think I know where Ponerello has Uncle Vincenzo and Mayor Patterson."

"She's done some eavesdropping," Jake said with the same dry smile.

Laura frowned at her stepbrother and muttered, "Be quiet, Jake. This is important."

"How much eavesdropping have you done, Laura?" Marquette inquired.

"Just a little," she replied. She took a breath, but before she could speak, Ty interrupted.

"I think it's at least worth a listen," he said. "I know I'm convinced."

Marquette slowly nodded as he said, "Well then, I suppose at this dreadful juncture, it cannot hurt to at least listen to what you have to say."

Laura pointed to a blue dot on the map near Mud Butte as she said, "I think they're up here somewhere."

Marquette shook his head. "No, Laura, they cannot be there. The area has been searched extensively by chopper and Ponerello is nowhere to be found."

Laura took a nervous breath, continuing, "He *has* to be there. We know that he's calling from a cell phone, and we know that Noah was on his way to Tilford. Ponerello's gonna stay close to the hostages so that he can reasonably threaten them if he needs to. And look at these roads..." she pointed to the highway and the gravel road that she and the boys had just discussed. "There are a million ways he could hide up here and you guys would never see him. He probably knows the area better than we do."

Deputy Danielson took a deep breath, frowning as he said, "From what I saw of the area, there's absolutely no cover, only cornfields and a couple of sheds —"

"He would see us coming from miles away," Marquette interrupted. "He has given himself plenty of time to find cover of some sort by setting himself up in such an open area."

Laura quickly continued, "Plus, we know that he's using a cell phone, and Noah's cell never works once he passes Sturgis. Ponerello would have had to come in as far as Sturgis in order to make that untraceable call."

Marquette slowly nodded in agreement. "How long has it been since he made that last call?"

"Almost ninety minutes," Danielson answered.

"How soon before your men can move?" Marquette questioned.

"I have a Black Hawk waiting at Camp Rapid," Deputy Danielson responded, dialing his cell phone. "We can put some of our men in with the National Guardsmen. I've got Marshals in Sturgis I can send up both of these roads and see what happens."

"So, you're gonna try this?" Laura nervously asked.

Marquette looked at his young niece and smiled. "It certainly cannot hurt," he said. He scratched his chin and frowned. "Perhaps we should have thought of this avenue before."

"We're definitely going to have to talk about that eavesdropping," Tillie announced from the other side of the kitchen.

Jake laughed nervously and shook his head. "Whatever you do, don't talk about anything that you don't want us to know," he said. "The dining room vents directly into Laura's room and we can hear everything.

"Shut up, Jake!" Laura whispered, giving him a soft shove with her elbow.

Noah frowned with a small smile. "I guess I'll have to fix that."

Jason sat down hard, looking at Alyssa as he breathed, "We're outa cover."

Alyssa sighed and sat down across from him. "I'm thirsty." She fumbled with the binoculars around her neck, taking a look outside of the ditch to see what surrounded them next. It was nothing but bare, open area around them. However, in the not too far off, but closer to the river, was an old, dilapidated shed. She could just make out the outline of a brick foundation nearby, as if a house had been there in years passed.

"What time is it?" Jason asked

"Three-thirty. And I can see some kind of a shed about one hundred yards from here. The road goes almost directly past it, but we don't have any cover. There's no ditch left." She turned to look back at him, noticing the dressing on his wound was blood-soaked again. He was bleeding more now than he was only an hour ago and they didn't have any more gauze.

Jason looked back into Alyssa's concerned expression, noticing the smudges of dirt on her pretty face. She was still a striking woman, even in this horrendous situation. Her dark eyes were so black and shiny, and her face glowed like nothing he'd ever seen in his life...He shook his head, looking away from her as he thought, *what in the world was that all about? Am I delirious from loss of blood?* He peered out of the ditch and said, "Let me see those binocs." Alyssa handed him her binoculars and he took a look for himself. "I see the shed. And I think there's a window in the door." He handed the small binoculars back to Alyssa so she could have another look.

"I think you're right."

"But there's no cover," Jason pointed out. "So if we get caught going up to the shed, he's gonna kill us, and then he'll finish off our folks."

Alyssa took a thoughtful breath, setting down the binoculars as she said, "If our parents aren't in there, and we expose ourselves needlessly —"

"We're not gonna expose ourselves needlessly," he interrupted. "What about Emmanuel? Don'tcha think He's been with us all day?"

Alyssa's eyes opened wide with surprise. "I thought you didn't believe in that stuff," she asked.

"Well, *something* kept me from passing out all day long. Besides, I've been rolling it around in my mind for a couple of years now."

"Rolling around what?"

"You know, the salvation message. I want to ask Jesus to forgive me for my sins."

Alyssa's eyes were so surprised at that moment it made Jason laugh out loud.

"Come on, Deputy," he laughed. "Help me pray, and then let's find our folks."

Alyssa let out the breath she didn't realize she was holding and slowly nodded her head. She reached for Jason's hand and smiled as she said, "Pray with me, Detective." Jason closed his hand around Alyssa's and she began, "Father, we are so afraid at this moment. Help us to make only good decisions and guide us to our parents. Give Jason strength for the rest of our journey, and send your angels to minister to us. Be with my mother as she struggles for life, and be strong for my brother if something should happen to her while I'm away. Jesus is our fortress, and even if we should perish on this mission, we know that we'll be with Him soon...In Your Name, I plead for strength and success. Amen."

Jason increased his grip on Alyssa's hand and smiled into her eyes as he said, "I've never prayed before in my life, so don't laugh."

"I won't," Alyssa promised.

Jason took a breath and quietly prayed, "Father, forgive me for I know I've been a sinner. I believe everything about Your Son, Jesus, and I know He's with us now. And I'm not trying to bargain with you, Lord, but if we get out of this mess, I'll do my best to tell my parents about You. Amen."

Alyssa smiled at Jason. It wasn't the most eloquent prayer she'd ever heard, but short, sweet and to the point. It was enough to get him saved, and for that she was grateful.

Jason grinned. "Okay, now we gotta think of a way to get from here to that shed. What do you say we just run for it?"

Alyssa raised one eyebrow. "Do you think you're up for that?" she asked.

"I can do it."

"If Ponerello sees us, he'll kill us."

"But if we make it to the shed, we can use it for cover," Jason reasoned. "The river is only about fifteen or twenty feet from there. We can hide there if we have to." He attempted to get to his feet, stumbling.

Alyssa reached for him and they teetered at the end of the ditch. "Are you sure you can make it?" she questioned again.

"Positive." Jason took her hand into his good one. "Now, how fast can you run?"

"Pretty fast," Alyssa replied dryly, after all, she was six feet tall. She looked through the binoculars down the road and reported, "Nobody's on the road. We'll be okay if we hurry." She hung the binoculars around her neck and looked at Jason. "I'm ready as I'll ever be."

"Okay, let's go." Jason tightened his grip on her hand.

They stepped out of the ditch, sprinting for the shed as quickly as their legs would carry them. Alyssa's heart pounded in her ears as she wondered how Jason's wound would hold up under the extra pressure.

Jason felt his pulse in his arm as he ran toward the shed, and for a brief moment he thought he might faint. However, in less than a minute they'd reached the shed. They flattened themselves against the side, taking heavy breaths.

"Are you okay?" Alyssa whispered, noticing the whiteness of his face and the trembling in his hand.

"I think I'm good. Let's have a look in that window."

Automatically, they let go of each other's hands, drawing their weapons as they approached the door with the window. Jason leaned toward the window and shook his head. "There's something over the glass. I can't see inside."

"Ponerello could be in there," Alyssa whispered.

Jason shook his head. "There are no vehicles around here and no one's on the road. He's not in there, Deputy."

Alyssa swallowed and said, "Okay, try the door then."

Jason reached for the knob and groaned. "It's locked. The stupid door is locked."

"I think I can kick it in," Alyssa said.

"But what if our parents are on the other side and we hurt one or both of them?"

"It's better than *shooting* off the lock," Alyssa pointed out.

Jason nodded and Alyssa touched the surface of the door. She backed up a few feet and gave the door a hard kick with one of her long legs. It didn't budge.

"Do it again," Jason coaxed.

Alyssa backed up again, giving the door another, very hard kick. The lock broke and the door swung open to reveal two people tightly bound in chairs.

"Jason?" his mother asked with astonished eyes.

"Alyssa?" Vincenzo squinted in the light shining through the door.

"Papa!" Alyssa exclaimed with a smile, rushing to her father as she holstered her gun. She put her arms around his neck, giving each of his cheeks a kiss. "Boy it's great to see you!" She noticed that his face was warm and dry. They were probably dehydrated by now. She took out a small jackknife, and cut away his ropes.

"How is your Ma`ma?" Vincenzo asked.

"We left the hospital about eight hours ago," Alyssa answered. "She was still alive —"

"I knew it!" Vincenzo laughed out loud. "She still lives! I knew I would feel her go!"

"We've gotta get you guys out of here fast," Jason breathed, cutting away at his mother's ropes. "We don't know where Ponerello is and there's no cover out here except for a ditch about one hundred yards away."

"Jason, what happened to your arm?" Jacqueline asked as she stared with horror at the bloody rag hanging on Jason's wound.

"It's just a little flesh wound," Jason assured with a smile. "Forget about it. Are the two of you up to a real, quick jaunt across the prairie?"

"Ready as I will ever be," Vincenzo answered, getting to his feet as he gave the skin on his wrists a good rub. "I will say one thing for the old derelict, he can certainly tie a knot. We could not escape no matter how hard we tried."

"How did you ever find us?" Jacqueline asked as Jason helped her to her feet.

"Emmanuel," Jason answered, and his mother gave him a curious look.

"I said the same," Vincenzo tittered with confidence. "I told Jacq that Emmanuel would lead you to us and she said that she would —"

"Papa, I love you, but we gotta get outa here," Alyssa said.

"Come on," Jason coaxed them toward the door. "We have to run all of the way to the ditch, and then drop to your knees. It's the only cover we're gonna have."

"Does he have any weapons?" Alyssa asked.

"I saw a knife in his sleeve," Jacqueline answered.

"There's something coming down the road," Jason whispered. "I see dust, but I don't see a vehicle yet."

"Papa, you have to help Jason to the field. Can you do it?" Alyssa asked.

"I can," Vincenzo answered.

"Good, then let's go." Alyssa grabbed a tight hold of Mayor Patterson's hand and led her in a sprint across the openness. Vincenzo took a tight hold of Jason's good arm, sprinting behind them.

It went brown before Jason's eyes, and he stumbled.

"Come along, my friend," Vincenzo encouraged, helping the young detective to his feet. "The car is closer."

Alyssa and the mayor dove into the ditch, but before Jason and Vincenzo could reach them, the car on the road, came to an abrupt stop. Obviously, they'd been seen.

Vincenzo and Jason reached the edge of the ditch and dove in beside Alyssa and Jacqueline.

"Stay on your knees!" Jason instructed as they began to crawl frantically into the tall grass. Jason's mother started to whimper, but she crawled behind Alyssa as fast as she could.

"He can't find us in here," Alyssa said, hoping it was true.

Suddenly there was automatic weapon fire behind them, and something that sounded like hail.

Jason looked at Vincenzo and groaned, "Bullets."

The weapon fired again, and Vincenzo yelled, "Keep going! He is just trying to get us to stop! He cannot see us!"

Jacqueline fell suddenly, and Alyssa reached for her. To her complete horror, the mayor's forearm was bleeding profusely. She'd been hit.

"Mom!" Jason shouted when he saw what had happened, lunging for his mother.

"It's not too bad," Jacqueline grimaced. "I think it's only a flesh wound."

Alyssa rolled her eyes, took Jacqueline's wounded arm and strung it over her shoulder as she said, "I'll help you. Papa, stay with Jason." They started to crawl again, and another shower of bullets hit the weeds around them. Jason fell on his face.

Vincenzo turned Jason over, and his mother screamed. He'd been hit twice: once in his right side, and once in his right thigh. The wound in his thigh gushed.

Vincenzo ripped off his shirt, tore it quickly and tied a long piece around the wound as Jason cried out in pain.

Alyssa left Jacqueline and went to Jason and her father. "Can you get up, Detective?" she asked.

"I don't think so."

"Shhh," Vincenzo whispered. It was eerily quiet all around them. For some reason the firing had stopped.

"He's listening for us," Jacqueline whispered.

Alyssa nodded, and they heard footsteps coming through the weeds. He was following the trail they'd undoubtedly left behind them.

Before any of them could think of another escape route, Salvatore Ponerello appeared above them, aiming his Russian Kalishnacov into where they were huddled.

"Well, hello there," he said with a coy smile. "I seem to have done some significant damage."

"You're goin' to hell, Ponerello," Jason said.

Salvatore laughed and said, "Okay, enough jokes. Which one of you shall I kill first?"

"I'm extremely accurate," Alyssa threatened in a deep voice. "You won't get any of us before I get you first."

Vincenzo swallowed, looking from his daughter to Salvatore.

"Now, dearest Deputy Caselli," Salvatore said, another coy smile curling around his lips. "All that I want is my treasure. Perhaps we could make some kind of a deal."

Alyssa reached for her gun, but Jason touched her hand. "Now wait a minute, maybe we *can* work a little something out," he rasped.

"The half-dead man speaks," Salvatore mocked.

"Listen, Sal," Jason said with a smile, his half-lidded blue eyes twinkling with a plan. "Is it okay if I call ya Sal?" Unseen by Salvatore, Jason reached inside of Alyssa's jacket for her gun. His arm was well concealed and he was sure he could get her weapon out before Salvatore even knew what was happening.

"Mr. Ponerello will suffice," Salvatore answered. "Now what kind of a deal are we talking about?"

Jason fought off the urge to fall asleep, swallowing hard as he answered, "Well, if you could just let me confer with my partner, maybe I can get her to agree to a few things." Jason paused and looked questioningly at Salvatore. "Okay?"

Salvatore scowled, shaking his head as he replied, "No conferences."

Jason suddenly groaned as if he were in pain, which he was, and Alyssa looked down into his eyes.

"Have you ever played beer ball?" he whispered, mischief in his expression.

Alyssa shook her head, thinking, *he's near death now...he'll ramble for a little while. I can make his last moments a little easier by humoring him.* "What's beer ball, Jason?" she whispered.

Jason swallowed and answered, "It's just a friendly, little game of softball, except you have to down a beer every time you get on base." He paused to laugh, but he coughed instead. "And the trick is to convince the other team that you're just too far gone to make it back to home plate." His delirious eyes twinkled and he winked. "I *really like* you a lot, Alyssa."

With those final words, Jason reached for her gun, pulled it out above her shoulder, and fired at Salvatore with his good arm. Salvatore's gun flew from his hand, and he reached for the knife at his wrist. Jason fired again, and Salvatore fell backwards into the ditch behind him. Jason's arm dropped to the ground beside him and he whispered, "Secure the prisoner, Deputy." And then he closed his eyes.

Alyssa's ears were ringing from the close-range shot. She hadn't heard Jason's last directive, but she grabbed her weapon from his hand, charging to the place where Salvatore had fallen. There was a puddle of blood covering his chest, running in little streams onto the ground around him. His eyes were open, staring vacantly into the sky. His open hand revealed the knife he'd been about to throw. She reached for the vein in his neck. *Nothing.* Jason had delivered a perfect shot to the heart and Salvatore was gone.

"He's dead," she announced.

"Jason!" Jacqueline yelled, hovering over her unconscious son, her own blood dripping down on him. "Jason!"

Alyssa came back to them, crouching beside Jason, reaching for his neck. "He's got a pulse," she said, "But I don't know how we're gonna get him outa here."

"Salvatore's car," Vincenzo said, getting to his feet. The sound of a helicopter was heard above them, and Vincenzo smiled. "Or a helicopter." He frantically waved at the military vessel above them.

"Praise God," Alyssa breathed with relief. "I wonder how they found us."

Over a loud speaker from the helicopter, Jacqueline heard her husband's voice say, "Put down your weapons and come into the road."

"They can't see us," Alyssa advised.

"Well, we can't leave Jason," his mother protested.

Alyssa nodded. "I'll stay with Jason. You and Papa go into the road with your hands up." Jacqueline looked skeptical, but Alyssa assured her, "It'll be okay. Besides, I'm gonna bet that my Uncle Marquette is on that chopper and he'll explain everything."

Vincenzo took a very reluctant Jacqueline onto the road, and they put their hands into the air. The helicopter commenced its landing. At the same time, a cloud of dust on the gravel was approaching in the distance. Several National Guardsmen were the first to exit the helicopter with their weapons drawn.

"Gentlemen, please," Vincenzo said with a polite smile. "There is a police officer down in the ditch. He is hurt very bad."

A Guardsman nodded, rushing into the ditch, while others frisked Vincenzo and Jacqueline.

Joe Patterson and a team of police officers were the next to exit the helicopter. Joe ran to his wife. Marquette and Deputy Danielson were close behind.

"Okay, these are the hostages," Danielson informed. "Who's in the ditch?"

"Jason's hurt," Jacqueline cried.

"Alyssa's with him," Vincenzo added. "They saved us."

"Jason killed Ponerello," Jacqueline said. "He's in the ditch with them."

The National Guardsmen went into the field, while two men with a board and a black bag sprinted in after them. They found Jason and Alyssa immediately.

"He's in bad shape," Alyssa said in a quiet voice. "He's been losing blood since early this morning from the wound in his right shoulder. The wounds to his side and thigh are new. I think the wound in his thigh is near an artery."

"I think so too," the medic agreed. "Let's get him on this board and fly him back to Rapid."

"What about Sturgis?" Alyssa questioned.

"They can't take care of something like this, ma'am," the medic answered. "Besides, we can be at Rapid Regional in about thirty minutes. The trauma unit will be ready."

They stabilized Jason the best they could under the circumstances, and he was loaded into the helicopter. U.S. Marshals gave up their seats so his parents, along with Vincenzo and Alyssa could ride.

As the helicopter left the ground, heading for Rapid City, Vincenzo looked at his brother and smiled. "How did you find us, my brother?" he asked.

Marquette laughed and replied, "Laura sent us."

The helicopter landed behind Rapid City Regional Hospital shortly before four-thirty that afternoon. An ambulance took Jason and his mother to the trauma center, while a police car sped Alyssa and her father, along with Marquette, to the hospital's entrance.

As Marquette led them to Kate's room, he nervously explained, "I have not had the chance to call everyone so they will undoubtedly be surprised when we arrive."

As they ran through the waiting area, Marquette noticed it was empty and he wondered where everyone was. In a matter of minutes, they were in Kate's doorway. Guiseppi was in the corner, asleep in a chair, snoring loudly, while Angelo sat on the edge of his mother's bed, holding her hand. Kate was still sleeping soundly. Her dark complexion was a ghastly yellow.

"My Lovely Kate," Vincenzo gasped under his breath.

Angelo looked up in surprise at the sudden commotion in the doorway. "Papa?" he exclaimed in a whisper, wondering if he had fallen asleep and was only dreaming that his father was there? He looked hard at the muddy, haggard figure, dressed in a blue U.S. Marshal's t-shirt, standing beside someone that resembled his sister, Alyssa. "Alyssa?" he breathed.

"My son," Vincenzo replied, seeing the confusion in Angelo's exhausted eyes. He stretched out his arms as he went to his son, embracing him where he sat. "How is Ma`ma?" he asked.

Angelo looked into his father's eyes, but could not reply. Vincenzo saw the tears and worry. He let go of his son and went to Kate. He tenderly touched the bruises on her pretty jaw, and the bandage covering her injury. He lovingly kissed each of her cheeks, whispering, "My Lovely Kate." Being very careful not to disturb the many tubes and wires attached to Kate, Vincenzo lay down beside her. Settling his head on the pillow next to hers, he began to sing softly in Italian, *"Amilo Tenero..."* ("Love Me, Tender...")

Angelo and Alyssa held each other, crying as they listened to their father sing. It was Ma`ma's favorite song in the whole world, and she loved it most when Vincenzo sang it in Italian. They'd been told the story thousands of times, about when their parents went on their first date, in 1956. It was the theme song to the Elvis Presley movie, *Love Me Tender*.

Guiseppi must have heard the soft singing through his loud snoring and he awakened. He saw the dirty man in bed with his daughter-in-law and whispered, "Could it be? Is that my Vincenzo?"

Alyssa and Angelo nodded, and Marquette went to his father. "I thought you would nap at the hotel with Gabriella and Michael," he said. "Where is Petrice?"

"Ma`ma is still sleeping," Guiseppi answered, "Petrice and Michael went to fetch Sam and Becky-Lynn from the airport. Gabriella will stay with her grandmother until she is rested." He frowned into Marquette's eyes, explaining, "We are *old,* you know, and require just a little rest."

Marquette smiled. "Yes, Papa, I know."

"Where on earth did you find them?" Guiseppi questioned.

"Our tiny Laura found them, Papa," Marquette answered with a sad smile. "And we must pray. Our young detective friend may have given his life for this. He is in the trauma center as we speak."

Guiseppi got to his feet, nodding his head. "Have you called the rest of our family?" he asked.

"I was hoping perhaps you could give me a hand," Marquette replied.

"It would be my pleasure," Guiseppi answered. He shuffled to where Vincenzo lay beside his wife. He put his hand on Vincenzo's shoulder, gave him a soft kiss on the cheek, and then he and Marquette left the room.

Petrice and Michael were on their way down the hall with Sam and Becky-Lynn.

"We got here as quickly as we could. How's Kate?" Sam asked.

Guiseppi took Sam's hand into his own, looking into his eyes as he answered, "She is not doing so well, Sam. The doctor says we must prepare ourselves."

Becky-Lynn took a quiet breath, gripping Sam's other hand as she said, "Can we be with her?"

"They are allowing only immediate family with her," Guiseppi answered. "Vincenzo has crawled into the bed with her and I fear he may be thrown out as soon as he is discovered."

"So he's been found?" Sam questioned with surprise.

"You have found Vincenzo?" Petrice asked.

"Yes," Marquette answered. "It is a very long story, however, both hostages were found alive. The mayor and her son are both being treated in the trauma center as we speak, and her son, the detective, is in very bad shape." His black eyes shined with tears. "I saw men in Vietnam injured far worse and survive, so I have hope, as I have hope for Lovely Kate."

"How about Ponerello?" Michael questioned.

"He is dead," Marquette answered. "Detective Patterson killed him."

"Marquette and I are about to call Angel and tell them to come to the hospital so that we may all pray together," Guiseppi said. "He looked at his grandson. "Michael, perhaps you could drive me to the hotel where Nonna is resting so that I may tell her in person the good news of our son."

"And while we are getting everyone together, I will find Pastor Hansen and his wonderfully redheaded wife," Petrice suggested with a tired smile. "When I left for the airport, they had gone to the chapel to pray. Perhaps they can help us get some saints together so that we might offer prayers for Kate and Detective Patterson."

Chapter 22

Joe and Jacqueline Patterson sat next to each other in the small waiting room just down the hall from where their son was having surgery. The wound in Jacqueline's forearm had been stitched and wrapped. Someone from the police department had brought her a clean jogging suit and she'd changed her clothes. Several police officers and detectives stood around the small room with the Pattersons, but no one spoke. Jason was not unlike his fellow officers — they wouldn't have thought twice about giving their lives so others might be saved. It was a sobering reality they *all* faced.

Petrice and Marquette found the waiting room and went to the Pattersons, kneeling before them.

"How are things going for your son?" Marquette asked.

"We haven't gotten an update in a while," Joe answered. "He's lost a lot of blood and some of his intestines. His femur was nicked, and I think they're pretty worried about that. That's all they've given us. How's your sister-in-law doing?"

"The same," Petrice answered. "Pastor Hansen and his wife have contacted their church and it seems a great deal of them have come to the small chapel here at the hospital to pray with us. We are all praying for your son and for our sister-in-law and we wanted you to know about that."

"Thank you, Senator," Jacqueline replied with a tired smile. "We appreciate it."

"Of course," Petrice said. "If you need anything at all, please let us know. Marquette and I will be by from time to time to check on you." He sighed heavily. "They will not allow us to see our dearest sister at this time and our father has appointed Marquette and I messengers of sorts."

Joe smiled as he listened to Petrice's comments. The dignified, senior senator was nearly sixty years old, yet still followed the orders of his father. That was really something.

Tillie hobbled up the hall of the hospital as quickly as she could, leaning heavily on her cane. Noah was beside her, helping her along, while Ty followed with Annie in his arms. Jake, A.J., Laura and Ellie brought up the rear. They were greeted with smiles and embraces from Guiseppi and Rosa, and Gabriella and Michael in the special waiting room just down the hall from the Intensive Care Unit. Gabriella and Michael reached for their mother.

"What a day for you, Ma`ma," Gabriella whispered into her mother's ear as she held her. "You are *so* awesome!"

"Thanks, Gabby," Elaine said, smiling into her daughter's eyes. "I can't wait to tell you guys all about it."

"Way to go, Ma`ma," Michael congratulated, kissing her cheek.

Elaine smiled at her son. "Where's Papa?" she asked.

"Grandpa sent him and Uncle Marquette to check on the detective," Michael answered. He leaned close to his mother, whispering, "He's not doin' so good, Ma`ma. Pastor Hansen has about half of the church down by the chapel and they're trying to pray him and Kate through this."

"How *is* Kate?" Elaine asked.

Gabriella and Michael both shrugged.

"The same," Gabriella answered. "Uncle Vincenzo stays in there with her, but Angelo and Alyssa have been coming out to give us updates every now and then."

Alyssa and Angelo appeared at the end of the hall, coming to where their family was gathered near the waiting room. They were tired, and distraught. Alyssa was still dressed in the dirty jeans and bloody t-shirt she'd worn since the morning of the day before. Her pretty face was stained with tears and her sparkling, black eyes were dim with grief.

Tillie gently reached for Alyssa. "How is she?" she asked.

"The same, Auntie. Papa's still in there with her, and the nurses told him to get out of the bed but he won't."

"He keeps singing her that song," Angelo whispered, his dark eyes shining with tears. "I hope he'll be okay."

"My sons are strong," Guiseppi said.

Alyssa swallowed with a nod. "How's Detective Patterson?" she asked.

"We do not know yet," Guiseppi answered. "Petrice and Marquette have gone to check."

Alyssa nodded and half-smiled at Laura. "Hey, kiddo, I heard you're the one that sent the cops after us. Good work."

Laura shyly smiled, looking the other way, but Guiseppi reached for her chin and said, "We are so proud of you, Laura."

Jake rolled his eyes and whispered to A.J., "Jeez. It was *my* map and she's gonna get all the credit."

"Hey, Alyssa," Michael said with a curious expression, "how'd you guys get the idea to take off for Mud Butte anyway?"

"It was all Jason's idea," Alyssa answered. "He had the thought that Sal would stay in the same place. At first I thought he was crazy, but once we got into it, I had a gut feeling we were gonna find our folks."

"He's a really nice guy," Gabriella said.

Alyssa nodded. "He really is," she agreed, and suddenly frowned. "Hey have any of you ever played beer ball?" Everyone looked confused, *except for Noah.*

Tillie smiled and shook her head.

Michael frowned and nervously bite his lip, while Gabriella giggled, giving him an elbow.

Elaine frowned at her son, asking, "What's beer ball, Michael?"

Michael shrugged and replied, "Beats me, Ma'ma."

Noah smiled and shook his head. "Come on, Michael, the truth will set you free."

As Michael searched his brain for some sort of a benign explanation, his father and Marquette appeared in the waiting room. Michael sighed with relief.

"Ellie!" Petrice exclaimed, taking his wife in his arms, holding her close. "How are you after your experience?"

"I feel like I can handle almost anything," she answered, "How's the detective?"

"They do not know yet," Petrice answered. "However, the mayor has been patched up. They will not require her to stay in the hospital, but she will be here until her son is out of danger."

"And how is Kate?" Marquette inquired.

"The same," Angelo answered with a heavy sigh. "Her vitals are still erratic, but at least she's breathing on her own."

"Josh is praying down in the chapel with a whole bunch of people from the church," Noah said.

"Can we bring you some food or coffee?" Tillie asked her niece and nephew.

"Sure," Angelo answered, and Alyssa nodded.

"We'll get some sandwiches from the cafeteria and bring 'em up," Ty offered. "That way you won't have to leave."

"Thanks, Ty," Alyssa said. "I haven't eaten since yesterday."

*****

The doctor who'd updated the Pattersons during their son's surgery appeared in the doorway of the waiting room. He smiled as he took a deep breath, sitting down across from them. "We're done, and I think he's gonna be okay," he announced.

Joe put his arm around Jacqueline and she took an excited breath as tears of relief fell from her eyes.

"He spoke a little after we brought him out of the anesthesia and removed the respirator," the doctor went on. "There was a fair amount of damage done to his lower intestine, but I think we got everything repaired. His colon was still completely intact, so that helped a lot. He almost lost a kidney, but my partner was able to save it. He's gonna have a lot of abdominal and back pain, but I've already ordered something for that. His femur was nicked, as you know, but I think with a little bit of rehab he'll do okay. We couldn't do much for the injury to his shoulder. It'll heal pretty ugly, but as long as there's no infection it'll continue to close and that'll be that." The doctor chuckled and shook his head. "He's one tough kid."

"Yes he is," Joe agreed with a proud smile.

"And he learned everything he knows from his father," Jacqueline added.

Joe laughed nervously. "When can we see him?" he asked.

"We gotta watch his vitals for a little bit here," the doctor answered. "We'll take him to ICU when we're sure he's stable, and then you can be with him."

The Pattersons smiled with relief. Even though neither one of them said, they both were thinking, *perhaps Emmanuel did watch over us today.*

*****

Ty, A.J. and Jake went to the cafeteria for sandwiches, bringing them back to the small waiting room just down the hall from Kate. It was nearly the supper hour, and everyone was hungry. They also picked up some cartons of milk and a few bottles of soda. The kind nurses in the ICU ward kept the coffee makers going.

Tara called to let everyone know she would arrive in Rapid City after ten o'clock p.m. that evening. She was surprised at all that had transpired since her last conversation with Marquette, promising to pray for Kate and the young detective during the rest of her journey.

Annie had had a big day for a child her age, and fell asleep in her father's arms shortly after she'd downed an entire sandwich.

"We are old and cannot take much more excitement," Guiseppi groaned to Noah. "Perhaps you and Angel should take my Rosa and me home with your Annie so we may all rest. The hospital does not allow us to be with Kate anyway."

Noah looked at Tillie. "Are you comfortable with that, Angel?" he asked. "Do you wanna take your folks and the baby home?"

Tillie nodded. "I guess so."

"We can stay, Mom," A.J. quickly offered.

"Yeah," Michael chimed in. "I've been up late before. We'll stay for Alyssa and Angelo and you guys take Nonna and Grandpa home." He looked at his parents. "And you and Ma`ma could really use some rest too. You guys and Uncle Marquette should go over to the hotel at a decent time tonight and get some sleep."

Marquette sighed. "Deputy Danielson and Detective Nichols will be meeting me here shortly. There are still a few loose ends we must tie up."

At that moment, footsteps approached and the Pattersons were in the doorway of their waiting room. Everyone got to their feet, reaching for them with outstretched arms.

Tillie embraced Jacqueline with a smile. "It's so good to see you again, Jacq," she said. "How's Jason?"

Jacqueline hadn't talked to Tillie, aside from an art show or two, since her first husband filed for divorce, so she was surprised at Tillie's display of affection. *How can these people be so sweet and caring and not even know us?* she thought. "He's gonna be okay," she answered with a teary smile. "They're bringing him up here to ICU, and then they'll let us see him. How's your sister-in-law?"

"The same," Tillie answered, "Her kids and my brother are in there with her, but there hasn't been much of a change."

"Hi, Jacq." Noah stretched out his hand to greet her. He hadn't seen her at all since the divorce episode. "How ya been?"

"Fine." Jacqueline smiled into his dancing, blue eyes, spontaneously thanking God that Noah had finally gotten his Angel. *Where did that come from?* she thought. *I don't believe in that sort of thing. Do I?*

*****

Marquette met with Deputy Danielson and Detective Nichols in a separate office at the hospital, along with the county coroner's assistant, Todd Yearwood, and a man Detective Nichols introduced as Detective McPhearson.

"The dentals you left with us this afternoon identified John Peter's body," Todd informed. "Our office has contacted his wife and they are making arrangements to have him brought back to Baltimore for a proper burial."

Marquette sadly nodded. "He had a passion for his work and I have missed him terribly these years."

Detective Nichols looked at Marquette and said, "And I thought you might like to know...we pulled Della's death certificate. You're never gonna believe who signed the thing." Marquette looked at the detective, and Nichols replied, "Roy Schneider, M.D."

"And the funeral director's sworn statement was also signed by Roy Schneider," McPhearson added. "His signature in both places was notarized by Ben Simmons."

"So I'm gonna have even more questions for Antonio," Deputy Danielson said with a frown. "Chances are, Mario will give himself up if he knows we have his son." He raised his eyebrow. "And I think I've got a good deal worked out for the two of them. We just gotta get 'em to talk."

Marquette took a thoughtful breath. "Well, perhaps we should go out to the ranch and have a visit with Mario. We shall inform him we have his son and then we shall see what happens after that."

"Agreed," Deputy Danielson replied.

With the help of Detectives McPhearson and Nichols, Deputy Danielson put together a small team including Rapid City police officers and United States Marshals. They drove out to Rapid Valley Quarter Horse Ranch without sirens and lights, and parked in the small yard in front of the house. Several officers stepped from their vehicles with their weapons drawn, while Marquette and Deputy Danielson waited in the lead car. They wore flak jackets, *just in case*, but it did nothing to calm their nerves.

"It is unlikely she will admit her father's presence here," Marquette opined as he looked at the house. The sun had set over the Black Hills, and it was very dark. Lights were on in what appeared to be the living room, but no porch light greeted them.

"Maybe she'll give him up," Jon suggested.

"Perhaps," Marquette admitted, and he looked at Jon. "This is probably the pinnacle of my career. You cannot imagine what I am feeling at this moment." He nervously bit his lip. "I wish my Tara was here to share this with me." He took a deep breath. "Are you ready my friend?"

Jon nodded grimly, clicked on his radio and said, "Okay, guys, we're going up to the door."

"Copy," came a male voice from Jon's radio.

"Let's go," Jon said, opening his car door and stepping into the yard. Marquette followed, and they made their way up the steps and to the front door. Jon loudly knocked and took a few steps back.

Charise watched quietly from the dark kitchen window. Della sat nearby in her wheelchair. "Who is it, dear?" she asked.

"The cops," Charise whispered.

She allowed a long moment of silence, and Jon's loud knock was heard again. Charise's heart thumped inside of her chest as she wondered what to do. Antonio hadn't returned that afternoon.

"Ms. Nelson, we know you're in there," Jon barked from the other side of the door, and Charise took a panicked breath.

"You better let him in, dear," Della coaxed. "He's an awfully nice man."

Charise's eyes filled with tears as she made her way to the door. God only knew what news waited on the other side. Did they have Antonio? Was he dead, or on his way back to Sicily by now? With a shaky hand, she unlocked the door and opened it. She held her breath when she saw Marquette Caselli standing on the front porch. At first she thought she might be hallucinating. She staggered from the surprise and Deputy Danielson reached for her arm in an attempt to keep her from falling onto the porch.

"You okay, Ms. Nelson?" he quickly asked.

Charise shook her head and softly whimpered, "What are you doing here now? Antonio is gone and I don't know where he is."

Jon felt pity for the young woman. She'd hidden from everyone most of her life, and it was all coming apart now. "We've got Antonio in custody," he said.

Charise drew in a sharp breath and sobs erupted from her very soul. "No!" she cried. She covered her face with her hands, shaking her head. "What are we gonna do now?"

"Ms. Nelson," Marquette said. "We do have a measure of good news for you. Your uncle, Salvatore Ponerello, died this afternoon."

Charise looked at Marquette with disbelief, asking, "Are you sure? He fooled you once before."

Marquette smiled through his embarrassment. "I saw the body for myself this time," he said. "I can confirm he is definitely dead."

"What of your brother and his wife, and the mayor?" Charise whispered.

"Our Kate is still very near death," Marquette answered. "However, we have safely recovered my brother and the mayor."

Jon took a hesitant breath, asking, "Ms. Nelson, we really need to talk to your father. Can you please help us?"

"What do you need Papa for now?" Charise cried. "He's a good man and Sal's dead. What can Papa possibly do for you now?"

"He can tie up some loose ends," Marquette replied.

"I am here," came a voice from just behind Charise, and she jumped with surprise. "Let me talk to them, Charise."

From just behind the door stepped a very old man. His hair and his brows were as white as snow against his dark skin, and his face and forehead were deeply furrowed with wrinkles. He leaned on a cane, gently nudging his daughter out of the way. He looked into Marquette's eyes and smiled. "Mr. Caselli, I am Mario Ponerello."

Marquette was without words for a moment, feeling his heart beat as when he was a young man. He'd obsessed over this man and his family since 1955. For the better part of the past thirty years, he'd searched the ends of the earth for him. Now there he stood, and Marquette had not one word to offer. He felt agony for the young woman with him. To be separated from her father would be difficult, but perhaps it would only be for a short time.

Marquette offered his hand and said, "Mr. Ponerello, this is an honor."

Mario took Marquette's hand and replied, "Likewise, Mr. Caselli. You have lived your legend in a most honorable way."

"Thank you, sir," Marquette replied.

Mario's old, black eyes glinted with tears. "Let me say goodbye to my wife —" he began.

"No, Papa!" Charise cried, reaching for her father's hand.

Mario tenderly touched the tears on his daughter's cheek, smiling into her eyes as he said, "Many sins have I, Charise, and God now asks me to atone for them. Let me do what I must and perhaps save my son."

*****

Alyssa padded along on the cold, tile floor in her stocking feet. She was exhausted, but Jason had sent his mother to find her. She left her sleeping cousins in the waiting room, following Jacqueline down the hall of the Intensive Care Unit.

A dim light was on above his bed and a nurse checked his blood pressure and heart rate. A conglomeration of tubes and wires were strung from Jason to different boxes and poles around his bed, the steady rhythm of a heart monitor hummed above him.

The nurse beside him looked up when she saw Alyssa in the doorway, frowning as she said, "Family only."

Alyssa swallowed hard, producing her badge with a shaky hand.

Jason coughed and said in a gravely voice, "Listen, Nurse Lady, I'm in a lot of trouble. You'd better let me see the deputy."

Jacqueline *almost* laughed, but forced it away so as not to make a spectacle of the situation.

"Okay, detective, but only for a few minutes," the nurse replied, and hustled out of the room.

Jacqueline sighed with relief, and slipped quietly down the hall for a cup of coffee with her husband.

Alyssa came to Jason's bedside.

"How's your mom?" he asked, reaching for her hand.

"Not too good," she answered around the lump in her throat, feeling Jason's weak hand close around her own. "I think the doctor is pretty worried."

"I think she's gonna be okay," Jason said with a quiet confidence that surprised Alyssa. "God's making everything right and that's gonna include your mom."

Alyssa swallowed away her tears. "Making all *what* right?" she whispered.

Jason grimaced slightly and Alyssa saw him push a small button he held in his hand. "It's for pain," he explained. "I've got my own morphine pump. No wonder druggies don't wanna give up this stuff." He started to laugh, but grimaced again, forcing himself to be serious. "What I'm trying to say, Deputy, is that God's making everything right...your Uncle Marquette was supposed to catch the Ponerellos in 1975, but everything got screwed up. If he would have caught 'em in '75, then Mario could have ratted out Sal, won himself and his son citizenship in America, and lived happily ever after. Your Aunt Tillie and Noah have already sacrificed 20 years of what should have been their life together — God's not gonna turn around and ask you to sacrifice your mother for this. Remember, Alyssa, Jesus died for our sins, so nobody ever has to die for someone else's sin again."

"But what if it was just her time?" Alyssa whispered, tears running down her pretty cheeks. "And who are we to know the mind of God? Maybe it was supposed to happen like this."

"I just don't think so," Jason replied. "I've been in this business a long time and I've seen some pretty strange things, but nothing ever convinced me to believe in salvation until you and your family came along. You guys are awesome."

Alyssa felt a measure of relief at his words, but her mother was still in such desperate shape. And Jason didn't really know what he was talking about...*did he?* After all, he was just a *new* Christian — just a babe in the Lord. Alyssa caught her breath as the words *faith of a child* echoed somewhere in the back of her mind. She smiled into Jason's eyes. "I think she's gonna be okay, too," she admitted.

Jason nodded, looking into Alyssa's dark eyes with a smile as he said, "You're a great gal, Deputy Caselli."

"Thanks. And you're a great guy, Detective Patterson."

Jason smiled and seemed as if he were about to say something more, but his eyes closed and he fell fast asleep.

Alyssa smiled into his sleeping expression, wondering what was happening. What was this she felt within her every time she looked at this wonderfully rough man who'd risked his very life to save them that afternoon? He was certainly a little ragged around the edges, but definitely a knight at heart.

Dr. Stattler paused in the doorway of Kate's room. Most of the Casellis had finally gone home, but rumor had it that the chapel was still packed with prayer warriors from some church across town. The tall young man who'd stayed faithfully with his mother since early that morning was sleeping peacefully in a chair in the corner of the room. The dirt-covered man who'd crawled into the bed with Dr. Stattler's patient earlier that afternoon was still there, sleeping next to her.

"He's filthy," the nurse whispered to Dr. Stattler. "I've asked him to leave about a hundred times but he won't even answer me."

"It's okay, Amy," Dr. Stattler replied. In his entire life he'd never seen such devotion. He swallowed away the lump in his throat. "He's really not hurting anything. Let him be with her and don't make a fuss. She's not gonna make it through the night."

Tara sprinted down the gangway and into the waiting arms of her husband. He held her tightly, kissing her passionately on her lips.

"It is so good to see you again, my love," he whispered, holding her close. "I have so many things to tell you."

"How is Kate?" Tara asked.

"She is the same, but I believe she will be better soon. God is making all things right this day." Marquette took a tired breath and smiled with satisfaction. "My Tara, Mario Ponerello is in custody."

Tara drew in an excited breath. "Did you see him? Have you spoken with him?"

"Yes," Marquette excitedly breathed. "I was there for the arrest. It was the most amazing moment of my life and I wished only for you to be there."

Tara playfully frowned. "He was always *your* obsession, Marquette. I was merely along for the adventure." She gave him another soft kiss on his lips and smiled into his handsome eyes. "And what a wonderful adventure it has been."

Noah sat Tillie down on their bed. Her knee was so swollen by now she couldn't navigate the steps when they had returned home. Noah put a pillow beneath her leg and carefully packed the bag of ice around the joint. "There," he said. "We'd better keep it elevated tonight."

"Thanks, Noah." Tillie sighed as she lay back in the bed. "Do you think the kids will be okay at the hospital all night long?"

"Yep. We got a great bunch of kids."

"Yeah, we do," Tillie agreed. "Even the little one wasn't so ornery today."

"It was probably all of the excitement." Noah took a seat on the bed to remove his boots. "Say, do you think your niece sorta likes that detective."

"Jacq's boy?"

"That's the one." Noah dropped a boot to the floor.

"Maybe."

"She said he accepted the Lord this afternoon before he was shot," Noah said. "She got to pray with him."

"Really?"

"That's what she told me." Noah removed his other boot and started to unbutton his shirt.

Tillie sadly sighed, "I'm so worried about Kate. I've known her for all of my life. Kate's always been here. Some of the best memories of my childhood were spent with Kate and Vincenzo. They took me everywhere when I was little." She swallowed away the emotion in her throat and whispered, "He has always loved her so much. I sometimes wonder if they've ever even had a fight."

Noah lay down next to his wife and took her into his arms. "I think she's gonna be okay, Angel," he said. "We just have to trust in the Lord that He's making *all* things right now."

Tillie nodded as the tears rolled from her eyes.

"I remember being afraid of God's next move for a long time," he went on. "And then finally realizing He doesn't let things go. Whatever gets *off*-track, He'll get back *on*-track. We can't thwart the Will of God. He's got a plan and He'll stick to it. And He's not gonna take Kate just yet...she's not even really met her future son-in-law, let alone all the kids they're gonna have."

Tillie laughed.

Noah smiled. "Kate's gonna make a *great* Nonna. God's not finished with her yet."

Chapter 23

The sun awakened the Black Hills and it was a new day. The heavy drapes were open on Kate's hospital window, early morning sun beams shining on her face. She felt the heat in her dream, but couldn't quite pull herself into consciousness. *What's making me feel so heavy?* she thought.

The loud scuffle of someone delivering the breakfast cart in the hall outside of her room roused her a little more, and she slowly opened her eyes. She squinted against the bright sunlight in the room, wondering where she was. *I don't think I'm in the hotel…this isn't familiar at all.*

She tried to move, but the effort alone nearly put her back to sleep. She could tell that Vincenzo was lying very close to her, crowding her even, his arm resting on her middle. *But where on earth are we? Was I dreaming, or has Vincenzo been singing "Love Me Tender" in Italian?* She felt the stubble of his unshaven face against her cheek and she tried to turn her head in his direction. Nothing. She couldn't move. The sharp pain in her neck stilled her as that place in her throat took a painful breath. Only air passed from her lips as she whispered, "Vincenzo."

Vincenzo stirred beside her. "Is that you, my love?" he whispered, propping himself up to look into her eyes. "Good morning, my love," he said with a smile, and Kate saw his tears spill onto his cheeks. He gently touched the side of her face and ran his fingers through her hair. He softly kissed her lips. "It is so good to see you."

Kate smiled, trying to reach for his face, but she couldn't lift her arm off of the bed. Her eyes were startled and confused as she whispered, "Something's wrong, Vincenzo."

Vincenzo slowly nodded, more tears spilling out of his eyes as he replied, "You have had a dreadful accident, my love, but you will be fine now." He lovingly kissed her lips. "I love you Kate Martin and I always will." Then he kissed her again and lay back on the pillow next to her.

Alyssa awakened next to her cousin Michael, who'd slept all night in the chair beside her. She glanced around the small waiting room to see that *all* of her cousins, except Annie Laurie, had stayed the entire night as they'd promised. Somehow the hospital staff was able to accommodate most of them on small cots. However, they were short just the one and Michael had volunteered to stay in the chair. All of them were still sleeping soundly, and Alyssa shook her head with a smile. What devotion.

She got off of her cot, creeping out of the small waiting room. She just had to peek in at her mother and see how things were going this morning. She made her way down the hall, pausing by the door, stunned with surprise. Her father sat on the edge of her mother's bed, visiting with the doctor and Alyssa's mother. She took an excited breath, leaping into the room.

"Ma`ma!" she exclaimed, carefully approaching the bedside, reaching for her mother's free hand.

"Hello, Alyssa," Kate whispered with a tired smile. "Papa told me what you did."

Alyssa kissed her mother's cheek and said, "We had the most amazing day. I can't wait to tell you all about it." She rolled her eyes and made a funny face. "I've put in for a *huge* vacation and I'm spending it all on Reata."

"Wonderful," Kate whispered with a smile. "We'll quilt and crochet."

"And make pies!" Alyssa giggled.

"How long will my wife have to stay in this place?" Vincenzo asked the doctor excitedly. He was ready to take her home right now.

"I can't really say at this time," Dr. Stattler answered. "Mrs. Caselli has been through a severe trauma most people don't usually survive, and her blood pressure still isn't that great. She did arrest once."

"Arrest?" Vincenzo asked curiously.

"Her heart stopped during surgery," Dr. Sattler explained, and he looked back at Kate. "I'm really surprised you made it. There's also been some major damage done to the nerves and muscles in your neck, and to your vocal cords. We won't even know how extensive that damage is for a couple of days yet. You're gonna have to stay put for a while."

Vincenzo sighed heavily, "Well, I suppose that we can stay in the Black Hills just a little bit longer."

Dr. Stattler smiled. "That would be best." He turned as if he was about to leave, but took a slow breath and said, "Mr. Caselli, you need to take a shower."

Vincenzo politely smiled at the doctor. "As soon as I have time for that, I will take care of it."

The doctor nodded, leaving them alone in the room. Vincenzo looked at his daughter and suggested, "You need to shower as well, young lady."

"Yes, Papa," Alyssa chuckled. "I promise to do that soon."

*****

Annie was up bright and early. She squirmed out of her tiny bed and hustled to her parents' room at the end of the hall. The door was open a crack, and she barged right in to find them sitting on the edge of their bed, looking at her mother's knee.

"Well, good morning, Annie," Noah said, scooping up his baby daughter.

"'Morning, Papa." She gave him a kiss on the cheek. "How's Ma`ma's knee?"

"It's all better, Annie!" Tillie softly exclaimed, reaching for one of Annie's pudgy hands. "Look!" Tillie's horribly swollen and bruised knee was without discoloration or puffiness. "It doesn't even hurt," Tillie said with surprise, flexing her leg at its joint.

"Praise, God!" Annie squealed, clapping her little hands together.

Noah was surprised at the child's reaction. He wrapped his arms around both her and her mother as he said, "Yes, Annie, praise God." At that moment the telephone rang, and Noah reached behind them to answer it. "Hansens'."

"It's me, Dad," Ty said. "Aunt Kate is awake and she's talking. She's gonna be okay."

Noah took a breath and smiled at Tillie. "Kate's awake, Angel," he said.

"Thank You, God," Tillie breathed.

"Wake everybody up," Ty said with a laugh. "Are Uncle Marquette and Aunt Tara there?"

"They slept in the guest house last night," Noah answered.

"Well, wake 'em up!" Ty exclaimed. "Get Grandpa and Nonna up and tell everybody that Uncle Patty is buying us and whoever stayed over from the church, breakfast in the hospital cafeteria."

"Okay," Noah said, chuckling. "I'll get everybody together."

"Thanks, Dad."

"You bet," Noah replied, and as he was about to hang up he said, "I love you, son."

"I love you, Dad."

Noah hung up, smiling into Tillie's eyes as he said, "Your brother's buying everyone breakfast in the hospital cafeteria."

Tillie laughed. "Well then, we'd better get going, because I'm starved!"

Before they went to the cafeteria, Tillie and Noah, with Annie in his arms, along with Guiseppi and Rosa and Marquette and Tara went to the ICU. Miraculously, they found all of their children, along with their cousins, quietly milling in the hall while they waited for word from Alyssa and Angelo.

"They've been in there *forever*," Jake grumbled to his father. "We *still* haven't seen Uncle Vincenzo, and we don't know if Aunt Kate can have any visitors yet.

Annie climbed out of Noah's arms and into Jake's.

"Well, I've gotta see somebody real quick anyway," Noah said. "I'll be right back." With those words he turned and headed down the hall.

Noah waited for the nurse to leave Jason's room, and then he slipped sneakily through the door. The detective was awake, *barely*, and he managed a small smile for Noah.

"Hey, Hansen."

Noah crouched down beside Jason's bed with a smile. "Now listen to me, kid," he began, "those nurses are gonna throw me out once they find me in here, so I've gotta talk fast. I fell in love with an outa-town girl once, and it took twenty years to straighten the thing out."

"I know." Jason quietly laughed, grimacing at the pain in his middle. He reached for the heavy blanket the nurse had placed above his abdomen, gently pressing it like she'd told him. "Now don't be goin' and gettin' all funny on me, Hansen, I really can't handle it today."

"Okay," Noah said, forcing away his smile. "I'll try to be as serious as I can." He took a piece of paper out of his shirt pocket and laid it on the nightstand next to Jason's bed. "That's Alyssa's phone number and address in Denver, and also the phone number and address of Reata." He raised an eyebrow. "*Millions* of people in America would kill for that information and you just got it for free. Don't lose it."

Jason smiled. "I won't," he promised. "How'd you know?"

"Knights know one another," Noah answered with a mischievous sparkle in his dancing, blue eyes. "I don't know how, but we just know."

"A knight? What are you talking about?" Jason asked.

"Believe it or not it's somebody like me," Noah dryly admitted.

Jason laughed again, holding onto the blanket over his abdomen. "You said you'd be serious."

"I *am* bein' serious," Noah said with a crooked smile. "My wife says that I'm the *perfect* knight. Now, I've never admitted that I believed that to another soul until this very moment."

Jason held tight to the blanket at his middle, trying desperately not to laugh at Noah. "Can you give me another example of a knight, besides yourself?" he chortled with a gasp.

"Marquette Caselli," Noah replied. "He's the *best* one I know."

Jason slowly nodded his head. "Do you think a girl like Alyssa would be interested in a guy like me?" he asked.

"Oh, *definitely*. I think you drive her crazy."

Jason sighed with a contented smile and his half-lidded, tired eyes twinkled with delight. "Okay, Hansen. I'll see what I can do."

"Atta boy." Noah gave Jason's good shoulder a soft pat. "I'll be prayin' for ya."

Noah went back to the waiting room. Sam and Becky-Lynn had joined the family now, and Petrice happily led everyone down the hall.

"Come along!" he waved with one hand, while he held Elaine's hand in the other. "Vincenzo's children can join us when they have been with their parents for a time."

"Hey, where are Uncle Josh and Auntie Mona?" Jake asked as they sauntered along.

"Papa sent Uncle Marquette to fetch them," Gabriella answered with a smile. "And I think he's gonna be in for a big surprise when he sees how many people from the church spent the night in the chapel."

Annie smiled sweetly into Gabriella's eyes, reaching for her cousin.

"Do you want to come to me?" Gabriella asked the baby, and Annie wriggled free of Jake's grasp.

"You be good, Annie," Jake said.

"I will," Annie promised, putting her arms around Gabriella's neck.

Noah smiled as he took Tillie's hand into his own. God had given him the most amazing family and an incredible life. Who could ever ask for anything more?

Joshua and Mona, along with half of the church and Marquette and Tara, were waiting in the cafeteria when everyone else arrived. Guiseppi had quite a laugh when Petrice realized how many people he had to buy breakfast for that morning.

"Do not worry, my son," Guiseppi chided his eldest. "You are a wealthy conservative, and your money pours forth. The only thing I regret is that these folks cannot vote in New York."

Petrice sighed. "Yes, Papa, I regret that as well."

Noah and Tillie, along with their family, were finally seated and had started to eat when Tillie spied a large, old black woman storming into the cafeteria. She frowned terribly at Tillie, waving as she marched over to their table.

"Hi, Maggie," Tillie said, as she and her children and Noah stood to greet one of their dearest friends.

"Hi, Maggie," Noah said. "How'd you know we were here?"

"Good grief, Noah, it's all over the news," Maggie grumbled with a scowl. "Why didn't you call me? I woulda brought some sandwiches or something."

"It all happened so fast," Noah explained with a humble smile. "Can you forgive me?"

"If you buy me breakfast, I'll let the thing go," Maggie growled.

Noah and Tillie's children laughed at the humorous old woman, and Noah slid his own seat out. "Sit here, Maggie. I'll get ya some breakfast."

"Don't mind if I do," Maggie retorted, accepting Noah's seat. Noah hurried away to get her some food and Maggie looked at his family. She raised one eyebrow, demanding, "Give me the low-down on *everything*, and don't spare any of the gruesome details."

*****

That afternoon, Deputy Danielson and his supervisor, Marshal Cameron, questioned Mario and Antonio Ponerello at the Federal Courthouse. Marquette and Tara Caselli were also present so that every detail would be brought to mind. Marshal Cameron offered the Ponerellos their right to attorneys, but they refused.

"Okay, here's the deal we got for ya, boys," Jon said, looking at the humbled Ponerellos across the table from him. "Complete immunity and naturalization if you guys tell us how you got the social security numbers." He took a breath, raising his eyebrow as he looked only at Antonio and said, "You've filed income taxes under the name of Ben Simmons since the late seventies. When and where did you get the numbers and the names? Also, we found some old income tax returns filed under the name of Jack Nelson, last dated for the late sixties, with an address of Miami, Florida."

Antonio and his father looked hesitant, Mario biting his lip as he murmured, "What about the safety of my wife and daughter?"

Marshal Cameron looked surprised. "Your brother is dead —" he began.

"But there were thirty-eight in my family," Mario said. "Presumably they have had children and they will seek us out."

"Mr. Ponerello," Marquette said with a smile, "I personally imprisoned thirty-seven of them in August of 1968. There were no more children born to the wives left behind. The existing children, and there were only eleven, did not live long into their adulthood. Six died in prison, and the other five were killed during criminal acts. The thirty-seven, including your father, passed away in prison. You have nothing to hide from any longer, and it is best that you take this deal placed before you so that you might live a normal life here in America."

"Do you know this for a fact?" Mario questioned.

"It was my obsession," Marquette admitted unashamedly. "I would venture to guess that I know more about your family than you do at this juncture."

Mario took a deep breath and slowly nodded his head. "The Wolf came with us from Germany," he said. "His real name was Dr. Schneider Rauwolf. For a price, he hid my son and me in Berlin in 1964."

"He was an alien?" Jon asked.

"Yes," Mario answered. His eyes became sad as he continued. "I had thought of leaving the family for many years, and always knew I would go once I had the courage and a plan. I met The Wolf in the summer of 1963 on a trip to *Roma* for my father. The Wolf had a reputation, and it was well known he had connections in the American government. He was young and I decided to trust him. Somehow, my brother Salvatore learned of my plan, and in the spring of 1964, he murdered my wife. He then threatened to kill Antonio if I continued to meet with The Wolf, and I pretended to submit. One night, I slipped out of *Ustica* on a boat. We made it to the Messina Strait before sunup, where The Wolf met us. He took us on a larger boat all of the way to Naples, where we got on a plane for Berlin. Once we were there, The Wolf talked of nothing else but coming to America and beginning a new life away from the crime we were both accustomed to. He had all of the connections, and wanted to get out of Germany quickly. What I did not know was that The Wolf had a dreadful temper, and would easily kill when provoked. It took only a matter of months before he obtained the appropriate documents. I became Jack Nelson, Antonio was Tony Nelson, and The Wolf became Dr. Roy Schneider."

"So your citizenship was forged *before* you came to America?" Cameron asked.

Mario shook his head. "We did not come into America as naturalized citizens, we came as people that had been born and raised here. Only our passports were fraudulent. For a price, there were people in New York who found Social Security numbers of citizens that had died, but had fallen through the cracks of your system. They worked with a document expert in Vienna, who was later captured and questioned by Mr. Caselli. Jack Nelson was my age, and his name and number was given to me so that I could pass easily into the country as an American traveler. According to my passport, I had merely visited Germany, but my permanent address was Miami, Florida. That is where we chose to relocate."

"How about Rauwolf? How'd you come up with his name?" Danielson questioned.

"A name could not be found for Rauwolf, and so they made one up," Mario answered. "The same people in New York who forged my passport forged one for Rauwolf as well. They obtained a Social Security number from their network."

"How 'bout Tony Nelson?" Cameron questioned.

"At that time in America, Social Security numbers were not required for children his age. Antonio was only six years old at the time, and traveled as my son."

"When did you become Ben Simmons?" Danielson questioned.

"1978," Antonio answered. "The same network that helped us in 1964, got my name the same way they got the name of Jack Nelson."

"Do you know any of these people, or their names?" Cameron questioned.

Antonio hesitantly nodded, admitting, "I do. Some have passed away, others have moved on, but there is still an intricate network at INS, and within the IRS."

Cameron took an agitated breath, frowning as he said, "Okay, do either of you want a lawyer yet? Because I'm gonna call in a stenographer to take down these names."

Antonio and Mario both shook their heads.

Cameron continued, "That okay with you, Caselli, if I get these names down first and then you can question them?"

"Fine with us," Marquette answered. "I have waited thirty years to question Mr. Ponerello. I believe I can wait a few more minutes."

*****

Once they were finished questioning the Ponerellos, Marquette and Tara and Deputy Danielson went to the hospital to visit with Alyssa. After all of the work she'd done on the investigation, they knew she would want to know how the entire mystery had played itself out.

"I'll bet Noah's glad this whole thing is over with," she said.

"Oh, he is very glad," Marquette assured with a faint smile. "And he wants nothing more than for Antonio to come back to work for him."

"Can that happen?" Alyssa questioned.

"Yes," Jon answered. "We worked out a deal for immunity and naturalization if they fingered the people they know at INS and the IRS. There's gonna be a lot of folks going to jail for a long time."

*****

Noah bought a nice plot at the cemetery on Mountain View Road in Rapid City, and he paid for the casket Ty chose for his father. He ordered a quartz headstone with the man's real name engraved on it: Schneider Rauwolf.

Jake and A.J. and Laura and Heidi used their own money to buy funeral sprays, and had them delivered to the church on South Canyon Road. Tillie's brothers and their children also contributed to the purchase of flowers, and the ladies of the Fellowship Committee at Joshua's church put together a luncheon for after the interment.

Noah purchased himself a black suit and complained about it to no one. He didn't *want* to have to go through the whole drama of burying Ole Roy, but it was the *right* thing to do. He plastered a mournful expression on his face and took his family to the funeral.

It seemed everyone who belonged to the church on South Canyon Road turned out for the funeral that day. They comforted Ty and his family, and expressed their genuine delight and joy to learn that Ty's father had accepted the Savior before his death.

Ty, Jake, A.J., Angelo, Michael and Marquette carried The Wolf to his final resting place. Tillie and their children stood with Noah and Ty as Joshua said the final prayers over the casket in the bright morning sun. Tillie and Laura and Heidi even managed a few tears for the old blackguard. Annie Laurie didn't so much as peep as she stood beside her mother. She held Tillie's hand during the entire service, not fidgeting once to get away.

Maggie May stood behind them in a black veil *and* sunglasses. She bit her lip in order to keep a decent composure, but she wasn't fighting back tears. Ty's "father" had hung over Noah's head for the last twenty years like the devil himself, and now Noah didn't have to worry about it. While everyone made nice and pretended to mourn the old blackguard, Maggie hid her joy, thanking God for finally taking him home. She was happy he'd gone to heaven, of course, but she was more than delighted that Noah didn't have to worry about that stuff anymore.

The interment was over, and Noah quietly thanked God for giving him the strength to get through it, and also for being such a wonderful God He could even save someone like Schneider Rauwolf.

"It was a nice funeral, Dad. Thanks for everything," Ty said with a faint smile as they turned to walk back to the cars.

"No problem." Noah gave his son a soft pat on the shoulder.

"I gotta go thank the pallbearers. I'll see you guys at the church."

"Are Jake and A.J. gonna ride with you then, or what?" Noah asked.

"We're all riding back in the limo," Ty answered.

Noah half-smiled at his son in response, and Ty was off to finish his obligations.

"Hey, we're gonna ride with Uncle Patty and Gabriella," Laura said as she and Heidi backed away from Tillie and Noah. "We'll see you guys at the church."

Tillie nodded at her daughter, watching the two walk away. Annie's little hand tried to wriggle free for the first time that day, but Tillie hung onto it. "Stay with us, Annie," she said. To her surprise, the child obeyed, continuing to walk along with her parents.

It was quiet as they walked along. Tillie took a deep breath as she said, "The church ladies have a nice lunch planned for us. "That'll be…nice."

Noah gave Tillie a dry smile. "*Nice*? Are you nervous or what?"

Tillie almost giggled, replying, "Sort of, I guess. This is awkward." She leaned close to Noah and whispered, "And I think I heard Maggie snickering behind us."

Noah forced himself not to smile. He'd heard it too.

As they continued to walk back to their cars, where a mob of funeral goers awaited them for condolences, Noah spied a vaguely familiar woman. She stood by herself, near the fender of his Suburban, wearing a black dress and dark glasses. *Who is she?* he wondered, knowing that he should know her from somewhere, but he just couldn't place her. She was a small woman, with black hair and a slight build. *Where have I seen her before?*

As they got closer, she stepped toward him, removing her dark glasses. Noah froze in his tracks. He hadn't seen Charise in more than twenty years, and she was just a kid then.

"Hi, Noah," she said.

"Charise?"

She nodded, giving him a hesitant smile.

Noah swallowed hard, glancing at Tillie as he said, "Angel, this is Charise…Carrie's little sister." He looked back at Charise, reaching for her hand. "How ya been?" he asked, and that was all he could think of to say, though a million things went through his mind. For instance, *where's Ben, or Antonio, or whatever his name is? I know he's out of jail by now, so where is he? Why didn't anybody tell me they were still around so the boys could have had some kind of a family when Carrie passed away? Why —?*

"We've been okay," Charise answered, extending her hand to Tillie. "It's nice to finally meet you, Angel."

"Yes," Tillie answered with a warm smile, surprised at Noah's sudden cold demeanor toward this woman. "It's nice to meet you."

"I'm sure you're wondering why I'm here," Charise said.

Noah frowned. "Yeah, I'm wonderin' about quite a few things," he grumbled.

Tillie grasped Noah's hand tightly in her own, giving Charise another warm smile as she said, "I know what you want. We know that your mother is still alive and I bet she'd like to see the boys."

Charise nodded, tears of relief falling from her dark eyes. "Yes," she breathed. "She wants to see all of you." She took a breath and smiled at Tillie. "Ma`ma hasn't been this alert in a very long time and I can hardly deny her."

"You call her Ma`ma?" Tillie quietly gasped.

Charise nodded. "Papa stayed home with her today so that Tony and I could come to the funeral. We've known Rauwolf for a very long time."

"Ben's *here*?" Noah questioned.

Charise swallowed and said, "He's already in the car because he didn't think you'd want to see him anymore."

Noah smiled, shaking his head. "Listen, Charise," he said, "you work out the details with my wife, and I'll get the boys out to see your mom." He took a deep breath and asked, "Where are you parked?"

Charise nervously bit her lip. "What you going to do to him?" she asked.

"I'm gonna tell him that he's gotta get his tail back to work," Noah answered.

Charise nodded with a grin. "Okay," she said, pointing with her index finger. "He's right over there in that black Caprice."

Noah headed in the direction Charise indicated, stealing up behind the black sedan. Antonio was reading the newspaper, unaware that Noah had come around the side of the car. Noah tapped on the window glass, and Antonio jumped with a startle. His eyes were huge when he saw it was Noah. He hesitantly rolled down the window.

"Hey, how's it goin'?" Noah asked.

"Better. Thanks for your testimony," Antonio replied.

"Listen, I can't afford to let you have any more time off so you're gonna have to get back to work here as soon as you can."

Antonio's mouth dropped open with surprise. "What are you talking about, Noah?" he asked.

"Your job. I can hardly keep the place going without you. Either you come back or I'm gonna have to find somebody to replace you."

Antonio was stunned. "You would take me back after all of this?"

Noah shrugged. "Sure. Why not? But what I'm supposed to call you now, 'cause it's gonna be kinda weird at first. Do I call ya Ben, or Antonio or just Tony —"

Antonio laughed. "Please call me Tony," he said.

"Sure thing." Noah smiled curiously. "What do you think Lucy's gonna say?"

Antonio laughed again. "I hope she will yes to a date, because I have nothing to hide anymore," he said, his focus shifting to where he could see Charise and Tillie visiting. "Is that Deputy Danielson with my sister?" he asked.

Noah looked at the tall, blond man smiling into Charise's eyes, noticing that she was smiling back. Tillie looked uncomfortable, but when she saw Noah's gaze, she gave him a sly wink.

Noah laughed and said, "Don't worry, he's a really nice guy."

*****

It had been two weeks since Jason's near-fatal shooting, and Kate's attack in the parking lot of the Plaza Civic Center. Dr. Stattler was releasing Kate from the hospital, but Jason would have a more lengthy stay and rehabilitation. Jason had been rigged with a GI tube from his nose to his stomach. They'd removed the tube just the day before, and started "reintroduction" of food into his system.

"After weeks of starving me practically to death, they throw me one cup of lukewarm gruel," Jason complained. He was propped up in his bed, staring down at the empty dish before him. To make matters worse the nurse had commented that he'd been a "good boy" to finish his lunch.

Alyssa sat in the chair beside his bed, trying to be understanding.

"And if I'm a *good boy*, I get a cup of green Jell-O and a little whipped topping," Jason ranted. "Jeez, I need a steak or something."

Alyssa giggled. He was such a man, and she found him irresistible. "Listen," she said, "I'm going home with my folks, but I promise to come for a visit before they let you out of here. I've already asked my Auntie if I can stay with her and Noah, and she said it would be fine."

Jason rolled his eyes. "Well, can I at least call you on your cell phone?" he asked.

"Yes, but I thought you were told to have it turned off in the hospital."

"Whatever," Jason grumbled. "They want to shut me off from the rest of the world. Some lady came by the other day and asked if I wanted to pay five dollars a day to watch television." He rolled his eyes again. "I guess they think that's the only contact I need. Just set me up with the soaps and I'll be fine."

Alyssa giggled again, and Jason couldn't help but smile. His behavior was terrible and he knew it, yet Alyssa found him humorous. Her dark eyes sparkled when she looked at him, and had she been any lighter he was sure there would be a soft blush upon her cheeks. With a heavy sigh he asked, "So how long are you gonna be on leave?"

"Until after the Labor Day weekend," she answered. "That way I can be home for Reata's 37th Annual Apple Picking Party. Ma`ma's going to need some help this year, and I want to spend some time with them."

"Thirty-seventh annual?" Jason asked.

"Every year since they were married in 1962, Papa and Ma`ma have hosted what they call the Annual Apple Picking Party," Alyssa explained. "There's an enormous orchard on Reata and Papa figured out a long time ago it's worth having everybody in the state come over and pick apples for a few dollars a sack, rather than to pay someone to harvest the apples for him. You pay an entrance fee at the gate and get to take home all the apples you can carry. Grandpa has these two, really old cooks who come down and roast meat sandwiches for everyone. Nonna *always* bakes fresh, homemade buns for the sandwiches, and Ma`ma and I will be baking apple pies. There's this lady, Mrs. Engleson, who used to bake chocolate sheet cakes with my Grandma Martin, but now she bakes them all on her own, and she'll bring like a dozen of them. They're Papa's favorite."

Jason smiled as he watched the pretty lady talk about something she loved. "You must really like it there on Reata," he said.

"I do. And I wish I could spend more time there. But you know, the job takes a lot of my life."

Jason nodded. "I get all of this leave, but my entire summer's shot...just like me."

Alyssa grinned. "Hey, why don't you and your folks come over to Reata for the party? You'll be out of here by then and you'll have a ball."

Jason smiled into her eyes. "I'd love to."

*****

Noah put the Suburban into park and looked at the small, but well-kept farmhouse. A soft breeze touched the Shasta daisies beneath the wooden porch, and stirred the weeping willow in the yard. Beyond there, several horses pranced gracefully in their pasture. He glanced at Tillie, and she took his hand into her own.

"It's gonna be okay," she encouraged with a smile.

Noah swallowed and nervously bit his lip. The intense silence inside of the vehicle told him his boys were nervous as well. He turned around and said, "You guys ready for this?"

Jake frowned. "We already have grandparents. Why do we have to do this?"

"Because your mom would want it this way," Tillie answered gently.

A.J. put his hand on Jake's shoulder. "Come on, Jake," he encouraged. "It's gonna be great. She wants to see ya so bad."

At that moment, Charise and Antonio appeared on the porch, waving with smiles. With heavy sighs, Noah and Tillie and their children got out of the vehicle. Their children ambled toward the steps while Noah gathered Annie out of her car seat. Then he and Tillie followed.

"I'm so glad you came!" Charise exclaimed through tears. She reached for Jake's hand. He politely returned her shake, and then slid his hand carefully away.

"Boys, this is your Aunt Charise, and your Uncle Tony," Noah introduced. He faintly smiled at Antonio. "'Course you already know Tony, you just have to call him something else now."

Everyone nervously chuckled.

Charise reached for Ty and he accepted her hand.

"Hi," he said with a hesitant smile and a shine in his gray eyes.

The expression on his face nearly took Charise's breath away as she realized *he has Carrie's eyes.*

"Well come on inside," Antonio invited. "Charise has made us a wonderful dinner, and your grandmother is very excited to meet you."

They all nodded, following Charise and Antonio into the house.

The kitchen was small, but it smelled *delicious*. Tillie inhaled deeply...*roasted capon*. One of her favorite meals. Just off the kitchen was a dining room, and the table was set perfectly. Another table, to accommodate more people was set in the living room, and that's where they saw the elderly couple waiting.

The old man's hair was as white as snow, and his dark skin deeply furrowed with wrinkles. His white bushy eyebrows nearly covered his eyes, but he wore a smile as he stood by the old woman in the wheelchair.

Her hair was almost as white as his, and her blue eyes twinkled with delight when she saw the visitors. Her lap was covered with a blue afghan, and in her hands she held knitting needles.

Jake and Ty stopped in their tracks, just short of walking up to the pair awaiting them. Near their grandmother was a coffee table filled with snapshots and enlarged photos of Jake and Ty at different ages in their lives. On the wall just beside the old man, was a framed, poster-size photo of Ty in his Post 22 uniform.

Noah saw his sons hesitate, and he placed his daughter into Tillie's arms. With an outstretched hand, he reached for Mario, greeting him with a hearty shake. "Hi, Mario. It's good to see you again."

"And you as well, Noah," Mario replied.

Noah knelt beside Della's wheelchair, taking hold of her hand as he said, "Hello, Della. It's been a long time."

Della's tears fell to her cheeks, but she smiled as she said, "Noah Hansen, you haven't changed a bit. You were always so handsome." Her eyes were alight with curiosity as she looked into Noah's expression. "Did you bring them?"

Tillie tried to swallow her tears away as she watched her husband greeting his old in-laws. They still adored him, and it was plain to see. *How hard it must have been for them to stay away all of these years.*

A.J. gave Jake and Ty both a soft shove toward their grandparents.

Laura noticed the commotion beside her, and she softly scowled at her stepbrothers, whispering, "Be men."

Ty was the first to shake Mario's hand, and then he knelt beside his grandmother as Noah had. Noah stood up beside Tillie, and Jake moved in. He shook Mario's hand, and then he knelt beside Ty. Della took one of each of their hands, smiling at them.

"I'm Ty."

Della saw Carrie's soft expression shining out of his eyes.

"And I'm Jake."

Della smiled and asked, "Will you call me Grandma?"

The boys nodded.

Della sighed with contentment. "I have missed you so much."

Epilogue

September, 1998
Reata, South Dakota

Since September of 1962, the year Vincenzo and Kate were married, they'd hosted Reata's Annual Apple Picking Party. This year was the thirty-seventh time they'd held the event. Preparations were made as usual, even though many things had changed over the years. Rosa, Kate, Alyssa, and Barbara, the ranch foreman's wife, got together the weekend before and baked buns for the roasted meat sandwiches. They made delectable pies for dessert and strained hundreds of lemons for their famous pink lemonade punch. In the past, Kate's mother, Francis Martin, and Diane Engleson had baked the famous chocolate sheet cakes together. However, Grandma Martin had been gone for nearly ten years and Mrs. Engleson continued alone. She was getting on in age as well, nearly as old as Rosa, and so her daughter, Ginger decided to pay her mother a visit that fall in order to help.

Ginger Maxwell was Tillie's best friend, they'd been friends since birth. They'd grown up just a few houses away from one another in the same neighborhood where their parents still resided. They'd gone to the same Sunday school classes, grade school, junior high, and eventually graduated from Sioux Falls Washington on the same day in 1975. Ginger was Tillie's Maid of Honor when Alex and Tillie were wed in 1977. Ginger eloped with Bobby Maxwell in the spring of 1980. They moved to Nevada that year, where they'd lived for the last nineteen years in apparent marital bliss. Ginger and Bobby had seven children.

Guiseppi ordered the restaurant closed, as he had from the beginning, so that everyone could attend the apple picking festivities. The men still had their storytelling contest, and there was a pie contest for the ladies. Top prizes of fifty dollars had been upped in recent years to one hundred dollars, which enticed people from all over the eastern corner of South Dakota to attend. Even people from the close-by western corner of Iowa, and the very northeastern corner of Nebraska, dropped what they were doing to attend the famous Reata Apple Picking Party.

In 1962, the entrance fee onto Reata was fifty cents, and each family could have all of the apples they could carry out of the orchard. Over the years, Vincenzo had raised his price to five dollars per family, and everyone agreed it was still the best deal in the state.

The entire orchard was open, except for the special place beneath some smaller trees on the west end. That place was always roped off and no one was allowed there, for that was where Uncle Angelo and Aunt Penny rested.

When Uncle Angelo was still alive, he and Vincenzo designed a roasting pit from memory identical to the one the Andreottis had in Italy. As in the days past, Old Doria and Georgie used the pit to roast two hogs and a side of beef. But this year, they roasted *three* hogs and *two* sides of beef. They slow-roasted the meat for hours, sliced it thin, and laid it into the fresh buns the ladies had prepared the weekend before.

Each time the special event was held, God provided sun to warm the South Dakota prairie on Reata. Reata's Annual Apple Picking Party had never been canceled because of rain.

In 1998, the grand event took place on the first Sunday in September, during the Labor Day Weekend. Great barrels of water and ice were always set on the property and in the orchard so that no one would suffer from dehydration while picking apples on the hot, late summer day.

Angelo and Michael were mounted on prancing stallions at Reata's entrance gate, directing the large amount of traffic winding its way in and out of the ranch. Vincenzo always designated and mowed a large portion of grassland where the participants could park. That way, cars would not be brought up too close to the main house where the eating, pie contest, and storytelling took place. Petrice collected the money, like he always did, telling the same joke that he had for years: "There is no one better to give your money to than a conservative."

Laura served the chocolate cake that year, standing at attention at one of the tables while people politely filed by for their piece. She smiled at each one and they responded with "thanks" or "great party." Her thick, black curly hair was pulled back in a tight, French braid, to protect her from heat stroke, according to Nonna. Already the heat and humidity had forced tiny curls out of their place in the braid, and soft tendrils stuck to the back of her neck and the sides of her face.

Jake and A.J. served the meat sandwiches this year, as Rosa and Guiseppi had announced their retirement. Old Doria and Georgie coached Ty and Noah as they quickly sliced the meat, placing it into the buns Jake and A.J. handed out to the hungry apple pickers. Old Doria and Georgie had announced their retirement as well, but agreed to "train" the new help before leaving.

Tillie and Ginger sat on a blanket with Annie, Ginger's three-year-old Madeline, and Ginger's newest baby, Libby. Libby was nine months old and just beginning to learn to crawl. Tillie shook her head and smiled asking,

"So are you guys done yet or what? Good grief, Ging, you're forty-one. You can't possibly have any more decent eggs in there."

Ginger giggled. "For sure, we're done this time." She giggled again and rolled her eyes. "Well, at least I *think* we're done." She winked at Tillie. "How 'bout you and Noah?"

Tillie shrugged with a smile as she answered, "You know we don't have babies as easily as you and Bobby do. Annie's probably gonna be it, and we're blessed to have her." She leaned over and whispered, "Noah's gonna be *fifty* when she starts kindergarten."

Ginger grinned. "Is he feeling weird about that?" she asked.

"A little." Tillie let her gaze drift to the man helping their sons serve up Reata's famous sandwiches. She sighed with a wistful smile. "But he's still as handsome as the day I first met him."

"Yeah," Ginger breathed. "What a looker."

Tillie looked at Ginger, raising both of her eyebrows as she asked, "Was that a fun trip or what?"

"It was a trip all right!" Ginger laughed. "Remember how he begged you to go for a ride on his motorcycle?"

"Yep." Tillie giggled. "Remember how worried Sara and Melissa were?"

Ginger laughed. "They were so stupid. Remember how drunk they got?"

Tillie giggled again. "Do you ever hear from those two?"

"Never," Ginger answered. "How 'bout you?"

"Never."

Tillie looked back at Noah, and at just that moment he looked up and caught her glance. She smiled into his eyes, blowing him a kiss from the palm of her hand. He pretended to catch the kiss, giving his cheek a pat.

Ginger guffawed. "What would they say if they saw this?"

Tillie shook her head and laughed.

Alyssa looked around at the hundreds of people buzzing about, remembering the event from her childhood. She and Angelo had always worn miniature Stetsons and moved in and out of the crowd to help the elderly and children. Puppies were usually in the barn about this time of year, and the hog confinement was filled was piglets. When she was very little, she remembered her grandfather carrying her into the hog confinement, and she'd hung on for dear life. *If you upset the sow, she might bite*, he said.

Her parents were seated at a picnic table beneath the shade of one of Reata's largest trees. Kate's injury had healed as much as it was going to, and it had left her with no voice. The scar where she'd been cut was still wide and purple, but Vincenzo didn't seem to notice. He hovered about her, like he always had, taking the extra moments to look dreamily into her eyes. He *loved* her, and that had been the best part of Alyssa's life.

Jason and Marquette, along with a very animated Tara, carried on what appeared to be quite a discussion just a short distance away. Jason and his parents had arrived at Reata, via Senator Caselli's Learjet. The gracious Senator loaded up his own family in New York, and then flew to Rapid City where he picked up the Pattersons. They landed in Vermillion early that morning, and Noah had driven over to the small airport to pick them up. After two more surgeries on his intestines, Jason had finally been released from the hospital in August. He was as thin as a rail, but Rosa assured everyone that some pasta was all the boy needed. Alyssa had made several weekend trips to Rapid City to visit him in the hospital, and their friendship grew into something she couldn't do without. His knowledge of the Lord grew in leaps and bounds that summer, and Alyssa was amazed every time he opened his mouth. He shared the Word with his parents, and he was certain his father had started to soften to the idea. Jason was convinced if his father gave in, his mother would soon follow.

Alyssa saw Gabriella and her grandparents paging through a folder of papers, while Elaine paged through another. Elaine had said that her daughter was writing the Casellis a very special story. They all sat together on a blanket in the shade of a hayrack, and occasionally Elaine would dab at the corner of her eye with a tissue. Guiseppi must have been pleased, because he kissed his granddaughter and smiled into her eyes with approval.

Angelo had announced his promotion into the Pentagon. It would be a good step for him in his career as a professional soldier, but Alyssa knew Papa was not pleased. Everyone was aware that Vincenzo wanted Angelo to come home to Reata, get married and have lots of babies. Perhaps he would someday, if the right girl should come along.

Jason, Marquette and Tara strolled over to where Alyssa watched the goings-on of the ranch. Jason automatically reached for her hand, asking, "Hey, what are you doing over here?"

Alyssa sighed, "Just looking around and remembering."

Marquette inhaled deeply, looking around the ranch. "I do love it here," he said. "There are so many wonderful memories."

Tara smiled at Alyssa and said, "Dearest Alyssa, we have a thought to bounce off you."

Alyssa raised one brow. "Oh?" she asked. "What's that?"

"My Tara and I are retiring," Marquette stated. "We wish you and Jason to take over our business."

Jason's eyes gleamed with excitement, while Alyssa's mouth fell open in surprise.

"I have a job," Alyssa whispered.

Marquette laughed. "You can quit your job. You are not blood-bound to that."

Alyssa's mouth fell open again, and Tara patted her tall niece's shoulder. "Alyssa, your uncle and I have prayed and prayed about this and we are most assured that you and Jason are the ones intended to work our business. We have a liaison that takes care of everything. You need not even worry about contacts. She makes all travel arrangements, money exchanges, accommodations and fee collection."

"We are quite aware you wish to spend more time with your family," Marquette added. "As does Jason. This job, as you know, perfectly suits both of you. You are young, in reasonably good condition, and have the ingenuity that it takes. So what do you say?"

Alyssa took a deep breath, considering their offer. It was something she'd always envied about her Uncle Marquette, and now he was handing it to her on a silver platter. She felt Jason softly squeeze her hand, and she looked into his wonderful blue eyes. The idea of working full time with Jason was hard to resist, however it would be inappropriate at this time. Certainly, they'd developed a deep friendship, but she wanted more. She could see Jason as her husband, but he hadn't said anything about their future together. She shook her head and murmured, "I just can't swing it right now."

"Listen, Marquette," Jason said, "let me talk to Alyssa for a second alone, and we'll come right back. Okay?"

"Of course," Marquette replied. "Take all the time you need."

"Thanks." Jason smiled at Alyssa, gently tugging on her hand. "I haven't seen the orchard yet. What do ya say we go for a short walk?"

"Sure," Alyssa replied, and they ambled toward the orchard.

Jason inhaled deeply as they walked along. "It's sure nice here," he said. "What a great place to grow up."

"I love it," Alyssa admitted. "The best part of my life has been here."

Apple pickers were still here and there in the orchard, and Jason tried to steer them into a spot that wasn't so populated. They were alone when he stopped beneath a tree and looked into her eyes. "I know why you won't accept Marquette's offer," he began. "But I've already ironed out most of the details."

"Oh really?" Alyssa questioned with half of a smile.

"Yes, really. Alyssa, I talked to your folks this morning and they've given me permission to ask you a certain question."

Alyssa's heart nearly stopped and she softly gasped.

Jason laughed and looked into her eyes. "Alyssa, will you marry me? We can have the wedding right here on Reata if you want to, and go anywhere for our honeymoon. Your dad says you gotta say yes, or the deal's off, so what do you think? I love you and I think I'll make a pretty good husband."

Alyssa smiled into his eyes, and for a second she glanced away from him. At the edge of the orchard stood her parents, and Papa gave her a thumbs-up sign. She looked at her feet and laughed, and then she looked back into Jason's eyes. "I do love you, Jason, and I think you'll make a great husband. I want to be married."

Jason sighed with relief and fished the small diamond out of his shirt pocket. He reached for her left hand and quickly slipped it on. He gave her hand a soft kiss, and then he looked into her eyes, "I thank my God everyday for having met you, Alyssa Caselli." He took her into his arms, and kissed her lips....

To be continued....

A Special Message for the Reader

"...Ty told me he prayed with Roy when he was up to see him last night...I guess the old blackguard took Jesus for his Savior, so he's in with the rest of us now."

What a difficult, and seemingly *unfair*, truth Noah faced that morning. The man who'd fathered Noah's eldest, and once sought the baby's death, now stood in the presence of a forgiving Savior. Despite the fact that Rauwolf had broken each and every one of the Ten Commandments, he was extended the same grace each believer receives when we come with a sincere heart of repentance and leave our sins at the cross of a mighty Savior.

Jesus gives a most compelling account at Matthew 20:1-16, wherein the owner of a vineyard hires workers in the morning, afternoon, and toward the end of the day... "So when those came who were hired first, they expected to receive more. But each one of them also received a denarius. When they received, they began to grumble against the landowner. 'These men who were hired last worked only one hour,' they said, 'and you have made them equal to us who have borne the burden of the work and the heat of the day.'

"But he answered one of them, 'Friend, I am not being unfair to you. Didn't you agree to work for a denarious? Take your pay and go. I want to give the man who was hired last the same as I gave you. Don't I have the right to do what I want with my own money? Or are you envious because I am generous?'

"So the last will be first, and the first will be last."

There will be those who enter the Kingdom of Heaven at the last minute, *just like Rauwolf*, and they will be afforded the same grace that those of us who entered many years before received. We must not be jealous or resentful of our Master's gift, for it is His to give.

Noah bought a nice plot at the cemetery on Mountain View Road in Rapid City, and he paid for the casket Ty chose for his father. He ordered a quartz headstone with the man's real name engraved on it: Schneider Rauwolf.

It seemed everyone who belonged to the church on South Canyon Road turned out for the funeral that day. They comforted Ty and his family, and expressed their genuine delight and joy to learn that Ty's father had accepted the Savior before his death.

That, my beloved friends, is where those of us who have served the Lord for many years, must consistently dwell. We have no option other than to rejoice and delight in every sinner's salvation, whether it happened 50 years ago — or 50 seconds ago! "In the same way, I tell you, there is rejoicing in the presence of the angels of God over one sinner who repents." Luke 15:10.

Beloved, if you are reading this and you think it's too late to make it into the Kingdom of Heaven, or you think you've done too many bad things to be forgiven by a holy God, consider Jesus' words: "...there will be more rejoicing in heaven over one sinner who repents than over ninety-nine righteous persons who do not need to repent." Luke 15:7

Tell Him you're sorry and ask for forgiveness. You have nothing to lose and Eternity to gain!

*Please comment on our website **www.PretenderBook.com** or our Facebook page: **The Pretender: A Blackguard in Disguise**, if you accepted the Lord or recommitted your life to Jesus while reading this series. We would love to hear from you!

Ta`Mara

Other Books in The
Caselli Family Series:

Book I
The Pretender: A Blackguard in Disguise

Book II
Pit of Ambition

Book III
A Blackguard's Redemption

Book IV
The Gift: The Story of Annie Laurie

Book V
The Truth: Salvatore's Revenge

Book VI
A Place Too Far From Grace

For future release date information, check out
www.PretenderBook.com

SPECIAL SNEAK-PEEK PREVIEW

BOOK VI
A PLACE TOO FAR FROM GRACE

Deir ez-Zor, Syria
September, 2001

Alyssa's head was pounding and her mouth was dry. She felt hard metal beneath her. It took a few moments to realize that she was gagged and tied to a chair. When her vision cleared, she saw Jason gagged and tied to a chair just a short distance away. He raised an eyebrow as she looked at him. She nodded in reply.

They were in a small room with shelves of what appeared to be detergents and bleach, and it sort of smelled like a laundromat. The floor was cracked white vinyl, and the walls were dirty plaster. A television with an old VCR underneath it was on a table in front of them.

The door opened and in walked three North Korean men, dressed in Syrian clothing. They were heavily armed with grenades, automatic weapons, and ammunition. Someone slammed the door behind them.

"Sleeping beauty has awakened," one of them said in very broken English. He roughly untied Alyssa's gag, and another man untied Jason's.

"Hi, honey," Jason greeted with a crooked smile. "You must remember Mr. Lin?"

Alyssa narrowed her eyes as she studied the man next to her. "Where are we?" she asked.

"We have taken you to North Korea — " Lin began.

"Liar, liar, pants on fire," Jason retorted, frowning at Lin. "I was awake for the whole thing." He looked at Alyssa and said with a smile, "Don't worry, honey, we're still in Deir ez-Zor. They shoved us in the back of a laundromat.

The guard next to Jason slapped him hard, and a little blood trickled out of his nose.

"You speak too much," Lin growled.

Jason smiled at his captors.

Alyssa groaned and rolled her eyes. "What do you want, Lin?"

Another guard near the door went to the television and turned it on.

"It is time now to watch the destruction of your country — then we will tell you what we want," Lin answered.

Alyssa and Jason sighed, turning their eyes to the television before them. The guard put a video into the VCR, and a taped news program began. First there was what appeared to be a burning tower at the World Trade Center, and as they watched, a plane crashed into the other tower. The next scene showed the flaming ruins of the Pentagon, and then flashed back to the World Trade Center as the first tower collapsed.

Jason rolled his eyes again and smirked, "Do you really expect us to believe that drivel? Do you know what *drivel* means? How good is your vocabulary anyway? 'Cuz it sounds pretty bad to me. Whose dumpster did you pull that third-rate piece of garbage out of anyway?"

Jason was struck across the face.

"Silence! There is more!" Lin shouted. "We will bring it to you later, and then we will discuss our demands. Use this time together to discuss what you could give us to buy your freedom, though you no longer have a country to go home to."

Jason humphed. "Well, we're gonna need some steaks while we wait. I assume you're familiar with the Geneva Convention rules with regard to the care and upkeep of prisoners of war."

It was Alyssa's turn to roll her eyes. They'd been in a few similar situations, and Jason always provoked his captors. He said that it kept his attitude right. She was afraid that it would eventually get them killed.

"We are not at war," Lin replied. "Therefore, we do not have to obey the Geneva Convention."

Jason guffawed. "Gotcha! If those pictures you just showed us are real, then, buddy, we're at war."

Lin scowled at Jason, striking him across the face again. "You are a crazy person!" He shook his head, motioned to his cohorts, and they left the room with a loud slam of the door.

Alyssa looked at her beaten and bedraggled husband. She squinted, examining the place where his tooth should have been. "You've lost another tooth."

Jason shook his head. "No…it's the same one I lost in Venezuela last year."

"But you had a bridge put in."

"Broke it off a day or so ago…I have no idea what happened."

Alyssa sighed, giving the television a glance as she said, "Do you think any of that is true?"

Jason shrugged. "Could be. If it is, we're in a lot more trouble now than we were a couple of days ago."

"What do you suppose Lin wants?"

Jason shrugged again. "I 'spose how much we know about the reactor. Then he's probably going to kill us."

"Figures."

Jason chuckled. "Poor devil doesn't know what he's gotten himself into."